Grumpy ROMANCE
NIA ARTHURS

COPYRIGHT

This is a work of fiction. Similarities to real people, places or events are entirely coincidental.

GRUMPY ROMANCE
Copyright © 2021 Nia Arthurs
Written by Nia Arthurs
Edited by Jalulu Editing
Cover Design by GetCovers

CHAPTER 1
THE ERUPTION

KENYA

I KNOW something's off when I walk into my apartment.

Our apartment.

Mine and Drake's.

The air smells stale, like none of the windows have been opened all weekend. The clock's broken too. The hands are exactly on twelve fifteen.

I feel like I'm frozen in time.

It's creepy.

I tighten my fingers on the sparkly yellow suitcase rattling behind me. The luggage doesn't exactly scream 'ambitious pencil pusher crawling up the corporate ladder', but the long and pretentious title applies to me. Even if no one acknowledges it.

It's seven o'clock on Monday morning and I just returned from my first business trip.

The woman who was *supposed* to attend the workshop caught chickenpox.

Sad for her.

Wonderful for me.

Somehow, I got an amazing opportunity to prove myself as a competent, knowledgeable member of the team.

And I aced it.

My reward? Aches and pains from being cramped in economy next to a bodybuilder and his chatty manager. And a generous offer to come into work one hour later than usual.

Hurrah.

I shuffle deeper into the apartment.

My feet protest.

The past forty-eight hours, I've been marching up and down a well-lit conference room, speaking to Belle's Beauty sales reps about my top ten secrets for customer acquisition.

It's not like I'm an expert, but I do have experience. I've worked a variety of sales positions since high school. From what I've learned, people just want to feel seen. Heard. Valued. It's not that complicated.

Sure, there are a few pretentious customers who complain over nothing and ruin it for everybody. And those customers suck. But for the most part, people are good. I genuinely believe that.

I let the yellow suitcase bang to the ground.

The broken clock keeps staring at me.

It feels like a bad omen.

I pretend it's not there and pad to the bedroom, falling into the twin mattress. My hand automatically slides to Drake's side of the bed. It's cold.

Eyebrows wrinkling, I sniff.

The sheets still smell like my favorite detergent.

Weird.

Drake has a particular cologne that gets on everything. I had to change to a different laundry method to get that fresh scent I like.

Did he not sleep in our bed all weekend? I crawl out of the bed and stare at the rumpled blanket like it's an alien species. At that moment, my screen lights up with a call from my step-mom.

I pick it up. "Hey, Felice."

"Sweetheart, you're up. Perfect." Felice's voice is as breezy and whimsical as her personality. "Could you do me a huge favor and go check on your sister? She hasn't been answering any of my calls this weekend. I'm worried."

I jerk my attention away from the bed, my body on high alert. "Is she okay? Did she relapse? What did the doctors say?"

"Oh, it's nothing like that," Felice says.

I let out a sigh of relief.

"Her last check up was good. No sign of the cancer coming back. As long as she keeps going in routinely, we'll be fine."

"That's good," I mutter, but my heart is still beating fast. I suck in a deep breath. Sasha's okay. Everything's okay. Everything's *great*.

"When you visit, can you pick up strawberries from the farmer's market? The ones she likes?"

"Uh…" I stare with bleary eyes at the grey clouds and drizzling rain.

"And make sure you get the grapes too. Get seedless, alright? It's better for her digestion."

A familiar rebellion rises inside me, but I tamp it down.

This is about my sister. Not about me.

I paste a tired smile on my face, although Felice can't see. "Of course."

"I'm worried she won't eat well now that she's got her own place."

"Sasha's not going to starve herself."

"I'm still anxious. I hate that she moved four hours away. The only thing that makes me sleep at night is that she's living close to you."

"Don't worry. I'll keep an eye on her."

"You're such a good sister, Kenya. In fact, people think you two are blood-related, you know. I tell them you and Sasha might as well be."

My chuckle is short but genuine. I met Sasha when she was thirteen and I was fifteen. My dad married her mom and we moved in together. She used to follow me around everywhere. It was kind of adorable.

"How are things with you and Drake?" Felice asks.

I drag myself to the closet and pull out a thick jacket along with a cute red dress. It's a bit over-done for work, but I haven't seen Drake all weekend.

We've exchanged a couple texts and one phone call, but it only made me miss him more. I want his jaw to drop when we meet up later. That's the only acceptable expression.

"We're good. He's super excited about a promotion at work." Thank God. I barely saw him at home when he was competing for that position.

"When are you two getting married?" Felice asks, a teasing edge to her tone.

Anticipation makes my heart slam against my ribs. I try to keep it out of my voice. "Oh, we're not in a rush."

"Sweetheart, what's the hold-up? You and Drake have been together for what? Three years now?"

"Yeah. We met my second year of college." It was like something out of a movie. The dashing basketball jock. The shy, Lit major. A romance no one saw coming. Hallmark will call to make a movie about our love story, I'm sure.

"See? That's more than enough time to put a ring on it."

I sit on the edge of the bed and pull out my adorable ankle-high boots. "When we're both ready, it'll happen."

"Alright, I know a brush-off when I hear one."

I laugh.

"Give Sasha a kiss for me, sweetheart. And tell her to answer the damn phone when I call."

"I will, Felice."

The line goes dead.

My plans of getting a few hours of extra sleep derailed, I shower and dress for the day. As I hop out of my steaming bathroom, the odd *something's not right* feeling passes through me again.

I freeze.

Walk back.

Stare at the tiny sink where Drake and I keep our toothbrushes.

His favorite face care products are gone. That man moisturizes like he's allergic to dry skin. I've never seen him run out.

My heart flip flops.

I notice his toothbrush is still there. So are his prized signed basketball jerseys. He wouldn't leave without taking those.

Calling Drake's phone leads me to voicemail.

The uneasy feeling doubles.

Something's weird about today.

The bed dips as I sink into the edge of it. I haul the ankle boots on, grab my purse from the closet and stalk past the mirror.

My harried reflection reveals a dark-skinned woman with a deep crease between her eyebrows, a flared nose, and frizzy black hair. I threw my coils into a bun because I don't have the time or the patience to wash it.

Whenever my hair gets attention, it's a twelve-hour affair. There's deep conditioning. Sectioning. Shampoo. Conditioner. Detangling. The styling part is another six hours. Whoever said natural hair was easier than relaxed hair owes me an apology.

Once outside, I take a deep breath and smile at the earthy scent of rain. The clouds are grey and the sky is angry, but it doesn't scare me. The city is getting a much needed rinse-down.

All is well.

As I walk to the bus stop, I tell myself I'm being ridiculous.

A broken clock is a broken clock.

And maybe Drake ran out of his favorite products. That explains why they're missing from the counter.

I'm exhausted and overthinking everything.

Drake's been an amazing boyfriend.

And I'm an amazing employee.

I should be celebrating. I *know* I impressed the higher-ups with my sales performance or they wouldn't have invited me to HQ. After only a few months fetching coffee and feeling like I was dating the printer, they tapped me into the business meeting.

That means I'm being noticed.

Is that a coincidence?

No way.

Not even close.

When I worked in the department store, I stole the crown of 'Employee of the Month' three times straight. I know how to draw people in. Now that I'm a temp at Belle's Beauty HQ, I've been using every opportunity to prove I'm a hard worker.

Yeah, my Lit degree is gathering dust while I head in a completely new direction, but student loans don't really care if I'm following my dreams. I love food too much to be a starving artist.

What's important is that I'm no longer traipsing from one temp gig to another. It looks like I'm on the road to a permanent position.

Good things—no, *great* things are going to happen for me.

I catch the bus to the farmer's market and absorb the cacophony of activity. Baskets of fresh fruits delight the eyes. Flowers, paintings and old antiques are everywhere. Customers haggle over prices. Crowds jostle for warm coffee.

I'm in serious need of java, but I get the strawberries and grapes first. It doesn't take me long to make the purchase and I reward myself with a cup.

I slurp loudly and ignorantly. An old man gives me a dirty look, but I forgive him because he's probably not gotten his coffee yet and even I hate people before that first sip.

The coffee keeps me company while I catch a bus to Sasha's apartment.

So far, the rain still hasn't let up.

Not a problem.

My umbrella's handy right here.

When I finally stumble into Sasha's building, I'm wide awake thanks to the mad dash from the bus stop to her front door.

Shaking my umbrella to rid some of the water, I twist it tightly and lock it.

It makes a click when it hits the floor and I smile. Using the umbrella as a cane and channeling my inner gangster, I swagger to Sasha's front door and tap my knuckles against it.

No response.

"Hey, Sash! You home?"

From inside, I hear a faint groaning sound.

Panic overtakes me. Is Sasha hurt? Did she faint and hit her head against the tub? Do I need to call an ambulance? What if her cancer came back?

Dropping the act, I shove my hand into my giant purse and search for the spare keys Felicia slipped me when Sasha moved to the city.

My fingers shake and the keys jangle noisily, protesting my lack of coordination. Why do I always shake like an addict going cold turkey in times of crisis?

With a deep breath, I steady my fingers and stick the key into the lock.

There.

Open.

I desperately crash through Sasha's front door and barrel into the living room. My eyes skate across the overly girly decor—fuzzy pink pillows in a soft purple couch, funky beaded chandelier, fuzzy orange rug.

Sasha fancies herself an Elle Woods aficionado and her apartment reflects that. It's a little outrageous. A little cutesy. Very endearing even if it's hard to understand.

I swivel directions and head toward her bedroom.

Then I smell it.

That…

It's Drake's cologne.

I'd be able to pick it out in a crowd because I'm the one who got him his first set. He loves it and douses it on liberally wherever he goes.

My fingers tighten on the bag of strawberries and grapes. The rustling sound is soft, like the wind rushing through the trees, but the groaning that comes from Sasha's room is loud. And breathy. And way too low to be a sign of pain.

It finally dawns on me.

What I heard outside—the sound that made me barge into my sister's place uninvited—was not an *'I've fallen and I can't get up'* groan. It was something else. Something a lot more… private.

I take a step back, heat burning my face. My sister is an adult, so it shouldn't surprise me that she's getting certain… itches scratched. But I still remember her as the scrawny tween who wanted to be everywhere I was. It's hard to reconcile what I knew of her to that of an adult who can…

She's breathing hard.

Must be nice.

I should go. Maybe I'll call Drake and find out where he is. See if we can meet up to get our own time in. A weekend apart was long enough to go without holding him.

"You like that, baby?"

I freeze.

All of me goes cold.

Every. Single. Part.

Why did that voice sound like my boyfriend of three years?

I swear I have an out of body experience while I desperately try to make sense of everything my brain is throwing at me.

It can't be Drake. Even though it's the very same timbre. The very same growl. The very same husk that he uses when we're loving on each other.

It's not him.

Maybe it's his brother? Maybe it's a close relative? Or an impersonator?

People are into all kinds of crazy things these days. Impersonators aren't the weirdest…

Who am I kidding?

Stretching one foot in front of the other, I approach Sasha's bedroom door like one of those blondes in a horror movie.

The little voice in my head is screaming at me the way I scream at the TV.

What are you doing, you idiot? Don't you dare go into that room. What the hell are you opening the door for? Are you stupid? Do you want to die? See, this is why black people can't be in horror movies. We'd run at the first sign of danger.

But I keep walking.

Turns out, running straight toward death might not be a black or white thing.

It might be a 'person in a horror movie' thing.

Because even though I'm scared of what I might see, I can't stop walking toward the door. Can't stop the curiosity and the dread twining in my veins. Can't stop the pounding in my head that urges me to keep going even if it hurts.

I have to see.

Have to know.

I push the door with my hand.

It opens slowly.

Oh.

Oh, my go—

The bag of fruits falls out of my hand.

Grapes and strawberries roll through the room, scattering like teardrops on the floor.

I gasp, terrified by the sight of my sister on top of my boyfriend. I can't see what body parts are sticking into each other because a blanket is draped over their hips, but I can guess by the way they're moving that they're not exactly praying under there.

"*Yes*," Sasha is bawling. "*Drake…*"

Drake?

Heart pounding at the confirmation, I twitch. The next thing I know, the umbrella is gone from my hand. I see it sailing through the air as if I'm not really connected to my body. As if I'm having some kind of trippy dream.

The umbrella slams Sasha square in the middle of her tan back.

She curses and goes sprawling down on Drake's chest.

He makes a garbled sound of distress as she crashes into him.

The angle must have been painful.

I hope she broke it.

I hope he can never have kids because of it.

"The hell?" Sasha flings her hand and presses it to her back. Her neck twists next and her head whips around.

That's when our gazes collide.

Deafening silence fills the room as she stares at me.

It's funny the way horror crawls over her expression.

If it wasn't my sister and my boyfriend—

If it wasn't *my* life—

It would be almost satisfying to see that split second of *oh damn, I got caught* slip into her eyes.

But it is my boyfriend.

And it is my sister.

In bed.

Together.

'Making the beast with two backs', as Shakespeare would say.

My hands start shaking again.

Hell.

Holy crap.

This can't be happening.

"Kenya!" Sasha gasps, grabbing for the blankets and covering herself. Her long, straight black hair curtains half her face. Big brown eyes, soft and soulful like her Mexican grandmother, dart to the ground.

"Kenya?"

That voice belongs to my boyfriend.

Ex-boyfriend as of now.

Drake pokes his head up from where it had been resting on Sasha's fuchsia-pink pillow. He's sweating a little. I guess he was putting in some work.

His jaw is square. His beard is long, full, and perfectly lined. He's got big brown eyes and a sharp set of cheekbones.

Chocolate perfection.

It hurts.

Damn.

The whites of his eyes threaten to overtake everything else as he stares at me like he wants to climb under a rock.

Pain rattles through my chest.

I can't breathe.

I can't freaking think.

Flight or fight?

The instincts roar inside my head. Should I grab the umbrella and go mad? Should I offer my sister and jerk of an *ex*-boyfriend a lashing they'll never forget?

"Kenya, I can explain," Sasha says, her voice tight.

All at once, I'm too overwhelmed to keep standing there in a room that smells like sweat and lovemaking.

I need out.

I need air.

I pump my arms and try to run, but my heels catch on the shag rug at the foot of the bed, tripping me up. My arms flail. I wobble in an attempt to keep upright, but I step on a grape instead and it upends me further.

I fall hard, landing on my elbows. My bones rattle and a physical pain jangles my fingers all the way up to my shoulder. I come nose to nose with Sasha's lingerie that was, apparently, discarded right along with Drake's boxers.

Tears fill my eyes, but I forbid myself from crying.

"Kenya, are you okay?"

Wow, my sister sounds like she actually cares.

That's ironic, isn't it? Not only that she's concerned about my fall but that she thinks I could be okay right now?

Who in their right mind would be okay in this scenario?

My sister and boyfriend are screwing each other.

And I just fell hard on my face.

I'm freaking *peachy!*

Scrambling to my hands and knees, I push myself up and throw myself at the door.

"Kenya, wait!" I hear cloth rustling and footsteps pattering the ground behind me.

All of a sudden, this *is* a horror movie.

Except there's no guy in a mask with a chainsaw.

There's no clown peeping at me from the sewage pipes.

There's no possessed doll rising from my collection with an evil sneer.

I'm being chased by my naked sister, a white sheet trailing behind her. She doesn't have a knife. Because she already slammed it straight into my heart.

I'm the one bleeding.

I'm the one fighting to survive.

"Kenya, please! Wait a minute!"

I power through the living room without looking back.

There's a picture of our family on the television stand. There's dad, his shorn hair and dark face beaming at the camera. There's Felice, her tan skin, bright brown eyes and warm smile catching all the light. And then there's me and Sasha.

I've got my arms around her. My hair is kinky curly while hers is long and straight. My skin is dark while hers is a sun-kissed tan.

Different. But the same.

Sisters.

Not by blood but by choice.

I charge down the stairs and crash through the exits.

My mouth is open.

Big gulps.

I'm out in the street and people give me funny looks while I race past them. A dark-skinned teenager sees me running and he takes off too, needing no explanation other than that a fellow sister is on the move.

I want to tell him it's okay.

I'm not running from thugs.

I'm running from family.

Isn't that nice?

A glance over my shoulder reveals Sasha has given up the chase.

My phone rings.

It's Walt from work.

"You need to come in now," Walt says without so much as a greeting.

I stare unseeingly at the horizon, the cell phone to my ear.

My arms hurt.

My head.

My heart.

"Do you hear me, Kenya? Someone very important is visiting today and you need to be here to—"

"I understand."

He makes a choked sound and probably wants to scold me, but I don't give him the chance. I hang up on him and drift to the bus stop, my eyes on the ground and my body extremely numb.

The world passes me by and I don't really register a thing. Somehow, I get on a bus and get off on the right stop.

The moment I walk into Belle's Beauty HQ, I wish I'd just gone home. Walt is standing guard at the front desk, his eyes squinting at me like I ran over his dog.

Not a great addition to my day, but it's too late to whirl around and head home. He's caught me.

Walt frowns. "You're late, Kenya."

My nostrils flare. Usually, I wouldn't say a thing. After so many years of working under annoying bosses, I've trained myself to keep my sharp comments at bay. Plus, this job pays much better than when I was working in the store. I'm not in a hurry to lose it.

But the image of my sister and boyfriend together is tattooed behind my eyelids and I'm a little short on patience.

Walt wags a finger in my face. "Do you think you can slack off without repercussions? This isn't a playground! I expect more from you!"

"You're the one who told me I could come in an hour later," I snap.

Walt blinks rapidly, his thick cheeks swelling as he gives me an astonished look.

I glare right back at him.

He turns a bright shade of red. "Check your attitude, young lady. You had our very important guest waiting for an hour and—"

"That's enough, Walt."

My eyes lift to the man stalking around the corner.

My heart trips over itself.

Holy Fitzwilliam Darcy.

It's too horrible a day for a man so *fine* to descend from Mount Olympus.

Over six feet of chiseled muscle strains beneath an Italian suit that probably costs as much as three student loan payments combined.

The sharpness of his chin, divine.

Thick brown hair like a shampoo commercial.

The slashing eyebrows, well-groomed beard, and cut of his cheekbones all whisper he's as dangerous as his *do anything to annoy me and I will end you* scowl insinuates.

What makes me *almost* forget about my awful morning, though, are those eyes.

Sure, they're hazel, but to call them a 'pretty brown' or 'amber' or even 'unique' would be a gross letdown of the English language.

His golden-toned eyes are sunbursts, thrumming with a cold, lashing energy. Still so riveting, it's impossible not to draw close to the fire even though you know it'll burn and probably even kill you.

His gaze sends an instant thrill down my spine and my whole body tightens. My toes curl inside my rain-drenched ankle boots. I feel like I've just been electrocuted.

He… he has to be the new spokesmodel for the company, right? There were talks of expanding the product line into men's care.

"*This* is the sales associate who attended the workshop?" Hercules frowns. His expression lingers on me, making it hard to keep my balance. One eyebrow arches higher than the other as if I'm expected to curtsy or kiss his hand.

Are all men this obnoxious?

I fold my arms over my chest and meet the jerkface's stare head-on. Running out the door with my tail between my legs is only going to happen once today.

Once.

His regard turns even icier.

If I were a little more like myself, I would have glanced down to check if my zipper were open or if I had something on my face. But I'm not in my right mind at the moment.

I'm delirious with hurt and fury.

And he so happens to be the closest and most deserving target.

"It's impolite to stare," I snap.

Walt's eyes widen.

The stranger shifts his feral gaze away from me and locks it on the chubby manager. "*This* is her?"

Walt bobs his head.

Stroking his chin, the cold stranger returns his glare to me and watches with a clenched jaw.

I frown. "Can I help you?"

Walt stares up at the man like he owes the guy money. "Why don't you rest in my office, sir? I'll send Kenya to get you a cup of coffee before we talk."

My jaw drops and an astonished laugh pops out of it.

I'm a doormat.

A freaking doormat.

It must be tattooed on my forehead.

Total Push-over. Can Screw Boyfriend.

Not that I think Mr. Grumpy Pants would *want* my boyfriend. He strikes me as the type who's so self-absorbed he's evolved beyond human dating. I can see him looking into mirrors, sweet-talking an electronic version of himself. The jerk.

Why Walt is working his butt off to please this guy is not my concern. But dragging me into the ridiculous power play in order to stroke an attractive stranger's ego? Yeah, I'm not going to be a part of that.

Walt makes a slight hand gesture, shooing me away.

I fold my arms over my chest. "Fetching coffee is not in my job description."

Walt's eyes widen. "Kenya."

"You're going beyond your boundaries, Walt. And I'm not going to take it."

His jaw drops.

I don't care. "I'm here early even though you gave me an hour off today. And I didn't complain about that," I speak calmly, but I can hear my voice start to climb. "Even though I've been working all weekend and I *deserve* a full day off, I took the crumbs you threw at me and didn't complain."

Shut up, Kenya. The little voice in my head chirps. *You need this job. You have bills to pay. And now that you're breaking up with Drake, you'll need to find somewhere else to live. You might have to pay more rent. It's not the time to act brave.*

But I keep seeing Drake and Sasha in bed and the acid keeps pouring out of my mouth.

"If you're asking me for a favor, I'll consider it, but bossing me around is not going to fly here."

The hot stranger continues with his grumpy stare-down. It's strange. Tucked behind his frigid stare is an undeniable assessment. And it's aimed at me.

I stare into his annoyingly gorgeous face and dig my fingers into my purse. This time, I'm too nervous to hold my ground. Butterflies take flight in my stomach and make it impossible not to feel flustered.

He holds a big hand up and points it directly at me. "How long has she been working here?"

I grit my teeth, annoyed by the fact that he's talking about me when I'm standing right there.

Walt makes a motion with his hands. "She just started about three months ago? Previously, she was working in a store, but she was responsible for so many sales at the product relaunch that we brought her into HQ on probation."

"Hm." The stranger glances at me again. "She's the one who tripled sales? With this attitude?"

I want to slap his face.

Who does this guy think he is? My father?

He should try getting cheated on and betrayed by his sister. Maybe he'll have a smiley disposition and higher BS tolerance.

You need this job, Kenya.

My mouth doesn't seem to be in agreement with my brain. "Do you know how disrespectful you're being right now?"

Hot Grump blinks rapidly. "Me?"

Read my lips, Neanderthal. "If you have any questions, you can direct them to me."

"I have nothing to say to you."

My blood boils.

Of course he's a giant prick.

Of course.

Because today seems like the day where men turn out their skins and show their real, worst selves to me.

At least the rose-colored glasses have been stripped from my eyes.

Walt is capering behind the stranger, shaking his head 'no' and motioning for me to zip my lips.

Really? You want me to cram it shut when this guy who doesn't even know me is being mega disrespectful?

With a snort, I stand my ground. If looks could kill, there would be a mushroom cloud where this rude, pretentious, wickedly handsome jerk is standing.

"K-Kenya, why don't you calm down and come with me?" Walt mumbles.

"I'm not going anywhere with you." I give the jerk a floppy wave. "I'm here to work, so if you'll excuse me…"

"Freeze."

I go still. Not because the stranger's command is that powerful —which it kind of is—but because I can't believe he just said that.

Freeze? As if we're playing cops and robbers and you're the hero who came to save the day? Is this narcissist for real? Does he think he's my boss or something?

Before I can string all the colorful four-letter words in my mind together and fling them at him like an atomic bomb, the stranger stomps closer to me.

"You're going to pack up your things and you're going to HR." His voice is as delicious as his face, but the words…

I meet his eyes and frown. Can he do that? He can't, right?

Confusion descends as I try to figure out what's going on. It's a challenge to keep my wits about me given how close his stupidly gorgeous face is to mine.

My inquiring gaze shifts to Walt.

He swallows and glances down, shaking his head as if I dug my own coffin and he's not going to help me out of it.

"Didn't you hear me?" The stranger growls. The sound is almost barbaric.

I blink, shocked at his tone. It's only a momentary pause. Anger surges forward again. I still have some choice words lined up for him, but before I can push those suckers out, he folds his arms over his chest and his brows plunge together in a pointy V.

You know… I'm starting to think he didn't *descend* from Olympus. He was probably kicked out because of his heartless behavior.

"Who are you to tell me where I can and can't go?" I snap.

He looks astonished again. "How did you get this far being so unlikeable?"

Me? I'm the unlikeable one?

"How dare you," I scowl. "You don't know me. I bet you wouldn't last one day in my shoes. I bet," I give him a once-over, "you've never had to work a day in your life. And with that pretty face, people don't say no to you. Well, I'll be the first. I don't care how important you think you are, I'm not going to bow to you just because you snarl at me."

"Kenya. Stop it. *Stop* it." Walt prances to me and grabs my hand like I'm a red-zone Pit bull jerking on the chain.

"Let me go!"

Walt points to the stranger. "This is Holland Alistair."

"I don't give a—"

"Our boss."

"Boss?" All the fight leaves my body at once.

"He's the owner of Belle's Beauty."

Boss.

Colossal Prick is the owner of the beauty label.

That doesn't make sense. He doesn't look like someone who cares about organic skin care products. Did he inherit this business? Or is Walt playing a joke on me?

"Why didn't you just say that?" I hiss, horrified.

Mr. Alistair turns away from me. "Take her to HR."

"Yes, sir."

I stare at his back as Alistair walks down the hallway. The view from behind is just as good as the front.

Too bad that knowledge is going to cost me.

Alistair's tone remains arrogant as he calls over his shoulder. "Ms. Jones, pack up *all* your things."

I see the full picture in an instant.

And it's not looking pretty.

Pathetic Girl: 0

Massive Jerkface: 1

Walt gives me a *sucks to be you* look.

I return it with a scowl and then point my glare at the brute. If I had my umbrella with me, I would have let it fly at his back. For sure.

What a wonderful day.

My boyfriend betrayed me, my sister stabbed me in the back and now I'm about to lose my job.

I can't go any lower than this.

My eyes slide around the room for something I can throw. It would be satisfying to hit him just once. At least I can get free housing and three meals a day in prison.

"I'm sorry, Kenya," Walt whispers, grabbing my arm.

Sorry? He's sorry? How does that help me now?

"You heard him, you need to pack your things and report to HR."

As Walt ushers me off on the walk of shame, I can't resist tossing a dark look over my shoulder. The prick, Alistair, is turning back too. He's watching me with an assessing look that I can't quite interpret.

He doesn't seem confused or annoyed anymore.

It's more like he's… grudgingly intrigued.

Maybe he's the kind of sadist who gets off on hiding his identity and axing innocent employees when they don't recognize him.

The most annoying part of this whole thing is, even after his insufferable behavior, he's still gorgeous. Or maybe I'm just delirious from all the horrible things that have happened today.

I need to go home and lie down. Wait, I don't have a home to lie down in because I'm moving out of Drake's apartment.

My steps are heavy when I follow Walt to HR.

I will *not* allow Mr. Giant Ego or Drake or even my sister to keep me down.

I'm going to show them all that I'm stronger than they ever thought I was.

And no amount of betrayal or icy hazel eyes will stop me.

CHAPTER 2
THE HELLCAT

HOLLAND

Her bun tilts at an awkward angle from the force of her head whip. She massages her wrist as Walt drags her to HR.

My eyes fasten on the way she cradles her arm. Is she injured?

A flash of regret strikes me, but I get rid of it fast. If she was in pain, she could have spoken up like a mature adult rather than scream and snap like a lunatic. I have no time for tirades and that woman seems to be full of them.

What do you know about working hard? The ignorant ones are always the loudest. I guarantee I've sacrificed more in my life than she could ever know. She's welcome to keep her narrow-minded opinions, of course. I'm not going to correct her.

I lift my phone and glance at the employee sheet that was sent to my email.

Kenya Jones.

Three time Employee of the Month.

Darwin Department Store's star saleswoman.

How could someone like *her* cause such a stir in the company? I can't imagine she would convince many customers to choose Belle's Beauty products with such rough mannerisms.

Yet, the facts speak for themselves. I've received incredible feedback about her performance at the workshop. Words like 'sunny disposition' and 'contagious charisma' were thrown around by the managers.

I wonder if they've all been hit in the head.

Or perhaps they're suffering from mass hysteria.

The other conclusion is, of course, that something about *me* brings out the tigress in this woman.

A valid theory.

And it's not one-sided.

Something inside me responded to her sharp glares and her even sharper tongue. It was raw, carnal and completely uncontrollable.

Frightening, really.

It's been a while since a woman has made me feel anything.

Not since Claire…

But that's different.

She's nothing like Claire. Not at all.

And yet an electric current swam through my veins when Kenya Jones shot her verbal poisoned darts at me.

Even now, there's no hiding my interest.

There's something about that woman.

Unfortunately.

My steps slow.

My eyes return to her even when I tell them to move away. I notice the way she turns and watches me too. Deep, onyx-eyes. They glitter with flames. A line digs into her brown forehead. And her lips—full, kissable, and a shade of purple-brown—twist into a hard scowl.

She knows who I am.

The boss.

Not someone to be trifled with.

And she's still snarling.

Have I just encountered a hellcat?

I frown at her, wondering if I should keep her or toss her.

"*Screw you,*" she mouths.

My eyes widen.

She turns her head away and I find I cannot do the same. Why am I so fixated on her?

Could it be the way her red dress hugs her petite body, highlighting curves that beg for my touch? Could it be the way the top stretches across her generous cleavage or the skirt that flares around her hips?

I can tell she's got a plump backside. I imagine cupping her tightly. I have a feeling she would be soft beneath my palm.

A sinful thought.

An even more wicked image.

I brush it away.

She's messing with my head. Or my several years of celibacy have finally caught up to me.

Perhaps I should return Kayla's calls and plant myself in Make It Marriage's chair again. Perhaps not. I doubt the matchmaker would care to find me a friends-with-benefits relationship. She is annoyingly devoted to her mission.

Make It Marriage. 'Marriage'. It's in the name, Holland. I can hear her even now.

I glance at Miss Jones's employee sheet again and try to stay focused. She's smiling prettily in her headshot. It's an expression I didn't know her face was capable of. Especially after what transpired between us.

Shame that I'm just as attracted to her scowling face as I am to her smiling one. That doesn't bode well for our professional cooperation. I'll need to keep her scowling. At least then she won't get too soft on me and tempt me with things I can't have.

"That went well." The dry voice belongs to Ezekiel, my executive assistant. I like to think of him as the Alfred to my Batman, if I could be so bold.

He's got a dry wit, an impassive face, and he's always one step ahead on delivering what I need. I figure that's enough to overlook the fact that he doesn't have the British accent.

Ezekiel approaches from the conference room. His wrinkled hands are filled with a stack of heavy binders.

I move swiftly over to him and scowl. "There's no need to personally deliver the files when we can have them sent over."

"Some things are better done yourself." He shoos me away when I try to snag the binders from him. Ezekiel takes great pride in his work. He's been known to snap at me when I doubt his abilities.

I slip a hand into my pocket and glance at the empty hallway.

Walt and Miss Jones have disappeared.

Ezekiel's low voice echoes behind me. "She doesn't take to you."

"The feeling is mutual." Sort of. I take to her body. If that counts.

"Should I tell them there's a change of plans?" Ezekiel arches a bushy grey eyebrow. His chin is as pointy as his nose which protrudes noticeably and is a little crooked thanks to a fight he's never told me about.

"Change of plans?" I frown.

He blinks steadily at me as if I should know. As if he doesn't have the energy or the inclination to spell it out.

"Why would I change the plans?"

"She's uncontrollable."

I cock my head to the side. "But I like that."

"She has no respect for authority."

"I like that too."

Ezekiel glowers at me. "She's beautiful."

"That has nothing to do with her capabilities."

"You've noticed."

Who wouldn't notice? "There will be no change of plans."

Ezekiel studies me. He may be many things—intelligent, quick on his feet, inflexible and so tightly wound I worry he's going to end up in the ER for an aneurysm—but he's loyal and trusts my decisions.

Finally, he dips his chin. "Shall we head back to the car? Our work here is done."

I nod.

He hustles forward, opening the door for me and escorting me to the truck that's waiting downstairs.

On the way to Fine Industries, I open my phone and thumb through Kenya Jones's employee files once more.

A Lit major. I wonder if she was disappointed when the only job she could get after graduation was at a department store. Working as a store clerk seems like a steep departure from her major. Perhaps it was intentional. I don't know.

Ezekiel's phone rings.

He answers brusquely. "Walt. Yes? Yes." His stony eyes meet mine as he turns to look over his shoulder. "She won't be fired?"

"You know the answer."

"Walt's asking."

No he's not. "I won't repeat myself."

Ezekiel sighs like a parent tired of disciplining their child and now content to let them make mistakes without interference. "Continue as we've discussed. Tell HR to clear out the last of any payment owed and then send her to the Fine Building for her next assignment."

Ezekiel listens to something on the other end and his eyes snap to me. He pulls the phone away. "What if she learns the nature of her next assignment and chooses not to stay?"

"Then don't tell her," I say simply, scrolling to another page of the pdf. "I'll convince her myself."

Ezekiel's thin upper lip goes stiff. "Get her to the Fine Building at all costs. Use your discretion."

I toggle to the page that has the mangers' feedback from the workshop. My eyes snag on that 'sunny disposition' line again.

I recall Kenya's snarling face and shudder. *Where?*

First impressions aside, Miss Jones's work speaks for itself. I won't argue with results. And I need her particular skillset.

Social interaction isn't my thing and neither is sales. I'm a data man. And though I delight in being left alone with my computer and my statistics, I understand that there is a need for a human touch in business.

It's why I value what Kenya Jones can bring. Her track record is almost miraculous. Much better than the management team I hired to oversee Belle's Beauty while I focused on my contact-less real estate empire.

Today's decision was not taken lightly. Kenya's name kept appearing on progress reports from one store to the next. It caught my attention at just the right time.

I'm in a bit of a spot. My last assistant cracked under the pressure and left her resignation letter several weeks ago. The expectations I have for Belle's Beauty was more than she could take.

Something tells me that Kenya wouldn't be so fragile. I have a feeling she's exactly what Belle's Beauty is in need of. Someone with spunk, with guts, with a sharp tongue and poisoned darts that shoot out of impossibly plump lips—

No.

Damn.

That mouth is not something I should be thinking of with such eagerness. Not if I'm going to be working as closely with her as I need to.

I keep business and pleasure separate. At all times.

No exceptions.

Kenya's left her mark though. And given the ache down south, it's safe to say I want her.

On my management team. In my bed.

It's hard to say which excites me more.

Troubled, I stare at the passing city and try to find my equilibrium again. One woman can't shake many years of self-restraint. I'm not living for myself anymore. There's something much more important to consider.

It's why I need to become more involved in Belle's Beauty. It's not just a company. It's a legacy. And I hate that none of the management companies know how to make that legacy thrive.

"Ezekiel."

"Yes, sir?"

"Contact Make It Marriage. Make an appointment with Kayla," I say.

Ezekiel gives me his signature blank stare, tugs on the cuffs of his stiff white shirt, and nods.

I inwardly squirm. *Don't worry about why I need Make It Marriage after five years. Just pretend it's a normal task.*

"I'll see that your visit to Make It Marriage remains discreet," Ezekiel says in a dry tone.

The Fine Building rises into view, tall and grand. I built Fine Industries after getting told that contactless real estate was insane and would never catch on. My program was rejected by everyone in the business.

Fast-forward ten years later, and I'm the CEO of the world's leading contactless agency. I've shown that I can take impossible or grandiose ideas and turn them into billions of dollars. Now, the companies that rejected me are the ones begging to work with me.

Ezekiel and I climb out of the car and head into the elevator.

"Your meeting with the spokesmodel is in ten minutes." He pulls out his phone and swipes. "But I've gotten word that she's already waiting in your office."

I scowl. "Who let her into my office?"

The elevator keeps going up.

"Our security team finds it very hard to handle her."

"Fire the guard who let her through. Reprimand Stanley." My head of security should run a tighter ship.

Ezekiel nods. "Yes, sir." He taps furiously on his phone.

I stride into my spacious office with a bird's eye view of the city. Silver, black and red are the main color themes. Or so my interior designer said when I paid her an exorbitant amount of money to prepare this space.

There's a mini bar in the corner and a cabinet filled with top-shelf liquor for when I'm entertaining. The model—Sizzle (yes that's her name)—touches one of her long, pale fingers to my prized whiskey.

I want to smack her hand away, but she would probably have me sued and plastered all over the news for assault. Keeping my peace, I pretend not to notice her and stride to my desk.

Ezekiel follows me. "I'll let you know when Make It—when Kayla is available."

"Thank you," I say.

Sizzle hears us and spins, her heavily Botoxed face straining to smile while none of her cheek muscles are cooperating. "Holland!"

Ezekiel turns to leave.

I call him back. "Let me know when Ms. Jones arrives."

He dips his head.

Sizzle sashays toward me after Ezekiel closes the door. She's a tall, slim woman. Her green dress drips with elegance. She's got an Old Hollywood flair that's hard to fake and even harder to hold on to.

Sizzle's waning popularity made her almost obsolete but, for my purposes, she's well worth her hefty endorsement check. Fine Industries isn't looking to serve young adults who praise the latest social media stars. Our data has ruled that the younger generation are, increasingly, living at home to avoid the rising cost of home ownership.

Folks in their mid-thirties to upper fifties, the demographic who remember Sizzle from her glory days, are exactly the right targets. I want those who would otherwise avoid technology to see Sizzle's face and believe that ours is a product worth trusting.

Our calculations have worked out brilliantly. Sizzle tripled our initial investment and I've already signed her on for a second campaign.

She slows her walk as if she's a bride dragging a heavy train. Her hips shift back and forth in a slow, deliberate sway. I wonder if she'll do a pageant bow or perhaps wave to an audience of invisible fans.

"It's been too long since we've seen each other, Holland." She stops right at my desk and I'm grateful there's a barrier between us or she would have been up in my face. "How have you been?"

"Busy. As usual." I flip open a document and scan it intently. It's easier to pretend she's not there than allow my annoyance to take control. Female feelings are *so* fragile. And right now, Sizzle is a product I need to handle with kid gloves.

"I heard your company was featured in *Forbes*. I was so excited when I saw the articles online."

"Hm."

She giggles. "You don't seem excited."

"Only because I control my emotions more strictly than others."

She laughs again and it sounds like nails against a chalk board.

"We should get a drink to celebrate." She rounds the desk and leans into my personal space. Her breath smells like coffee and something a little acidic.

I put my hand on her shoulder and ease her back. "Perhaps another time."

"Oh come on now." She places a hand on my chest. "A gentleman shouldn't turn down a lady who asks him out."

"You're mistaken." My eyes harden. "I'm no gentleman."

She shudders like I licked her ear. "Oh, I love it when you talk gruffly, Holland."

This woman is delusional.

I shoot to my feet and walk to the file cabinets.

Somehow, she doesn't notice I'm running from her. Perhaps too many years of cameras flashing in her eyes has given her a brain injury? Or maybe choosing to be polite is ruining my ability to convey my distaste.

"I'm so lonely these days." She slips her dress sleeve down her shoulder, revealing creamy white skin. Walking closer to me, she whispers, "I could use a friend."

"Hard to believe you would be in need of company."

"You'd be surprised at how dense men can be. Especially when a woman is flashing all the right signals." She follows me like a shadow. "What would you suggest in a matter like that, Holland? How does a woman get a man to notice her?"

Since she's following me, I lead her to the door. "A good question. Perhaps you should ask someone who has more time and interest. Ezekiel, maybe?" I open the door and gesture to it. "I need to get back to work."

Her seductive smile drips into a frown. "You're always working, Holland. When do you have time for fun?"

I gesture to the door, out of patience. If she asks me any more foolish questions, I'm going to snap at her and then I'm going to be down a very lucrative spokesmodel. No need to ruin a good thing with my own impatience.

I'm grateful when she finally takes the hint.

"Fine. I can see that you're in a funk. Why don't I come back another time?"

Please don't. "We have a meeting in ten minutes."

"Yes, but I'm not in the mood now." She pouts.

"Fine. We'll reschedule."

"Perhaps at a more private venue?" she purrs.

"No, you'll be meeting with my PR team from now on. We have no reason to meet in private."

Sizzle scowls.

I motion to the exit again. She rolls her eyes and stomps through the door. At least she leaves without further comment.

Grateful for the silence, I return to my desk and look through the latest data pull. I let a team handle day-to-day tasks, but I like to keep my finger on the pulse in case there are cracks in the code. Life is a flux of new variables constantly throwing a wrench in the algorithm. Data is no different.

I comb over the numbers with precision. I'm known for being unbending, rigid and demanding of all technicians. 'Impossible standards' is the feedback. But a high salary and great benefits means a low turnover rate. There are always enough hands on the wheel, even if I rarely take mine away.

Control.

I don't have an easy time letting go of it.

It's why Fine Industries has a reputation for excellence. And it's also why I feel more and more drained every day.

When this latest data update is pushed through, I'll raise the pay for each of the technicians and license the program to other companies. A royalty deal is something I've been fighting against, but I can't do everything on my own.

To grow this company to the next level, I need to learn to give up just a little more control.

* * *

By mid-day, Kenya Jones still hasn't reported to my office. I take a sip of my tepid coffee and scowl at the door. I'm in a state of limbo and it's starting to annoy me.

I press the button on my telephone. "Ezekiel."

"Yes, sir."

"Any word from Walt?"

"No, sir."

"Call him and get back to me. Tell him Ms. Jones needs to be in my office in the next hour or he might need to reconsider his position."

"Yes, sir."

I push the coffee away, move to the bar and pour myself a glass of whiskey to take the edge off. The view of the city is breathtaking. Enough to get my mind off the restlessness.

Cars speed down the highway. I see another algorithm. A million strings of code heading toward their destination in a desperate pull to get more. More money. More time. More things.

I have all the money I could ever want, but I still feel like them. Like I'm on a treadmill with no breaks.

When I hear a soft knock on my door, I expect Ezekiel.

Sorry to barge in. It's a voice that does not belong to my executive assistant.

I turn slowly. There's a limited amount of people permitted entrance to my office. Kayla Humes is one of those people.

She prances into the room and shuts the door. Her straight ponytail swings like a pendulum. Back and forth. Back and forth. As precise and cutthroat as she is.

Kayla's about five years younger, but I admire her achievements as if she's my senior. Her matchmaking business is one that completely baffles me. I would never expect her matchmaking strategy to be relevant in this day and age. Apps and data-driven matches are the way of the future, but Kayla's proven that there is still a need—no, a *demand*—for human involvement in the process.

I'm one of her success stories. She and the Make It Marriage crew set me up with my wife and then rallied around me after she… after my life went to hell.

Kayla habitually checks in on me, though we haven't spoken since the last time I brushed her off.

"Are you okay?" Her voice is light and musical. I'd assume she was a fresh college graduate if I didn't know she has two kids and a decade-long, blissful marriage to Brendon Humes, a good friend of mine.

I smile slightly because I know why she's here.

She stares at the grin and freezes. "That's it. I'm calling an ambulance. There's no way you're okay."

"Kayla, sit down." I gesture to the sofa.

She doesn't take her worried eyes off me. "When Ezekiel called, I thought the worst."

"Aren't you relieved then?"

"Is it terminal?"

"I'm not sick."

"You're not admitting it?"

"I'm not sick," I say again. "I called because I need your professional help."

A heavy sigh rolls out of her slim body. She blinks as if my words just aren't computing. "What happened? Blunt trauma to the head?"

"You're not being very professional."

"If this was about being professional, I wouldn't have driven over here like someone escaping from prison."

"Nice visual."

"I need a backstory."

"Do you?" I say lightly.

"Nothing you do is random, Holland. You plan out what suit you're going to wear a week in advance."

I get a little red. "It's not that bad."

"Venus, Tierra, Amina and I would disagree."

"You and the other matchmakers are nosy."

"Concerned."

"Overbearing."

She narrows her eyes. "We have been lightly suggesting—"

"You mean outright insisting?"

Her eyes sharpen on me. "Lovingly nudging."

"Same thing." I wave away the argument.

"The point is, we've been trying to get you back in the Make It Marriage database for *years*. And you always said no. It was a hard no. A never in a million years no. I thought for sure you wouldn't change your mind."

"I'm ready now."

"Why?"

"Does it matter?"

"Yes, it matters."

"I think it's time."

Her eyes light up.

"But you're not going to like the next part," I say.

She wilts into the chair. "Let me sit down."

"I don't want a marriage."

Kayla's the only woman I know who can look at you like you're an idiot without it feeling insulting. "I see I'm wasting my time."

"Make an exception."

"Don't start barking at me." She lifts a finger. "You know I don't play those games."

I laugh because she sounds like my grandmother and I keep having to remind myself that she's younger than me. "I'm willing to pay double."

"You could give me half your estate and that wouldn't change my answer."

"Are you sure about that? Half my estate is a considerable sum. Nothing to sneeze at."

"Don't brag. It's unsexy. And also, I have my own gorgeous billionaire. I don't need your scraps."

I roll my eyes.

"Let's get back to the point." She crosses one leg over the other and bounces her heels. "Make It Marriage is not an escort service. It's not a friends-with-benefits service. And you wouldn't need my help with that anyway." She scans me, her nose scrunching. "I'm sure you have plenty of opportunities."

"Is that a compliment?"

"That is an objective opinion based on my many years as a matchmaker."

I cut her some slack. "You know I have more to consider." My eyes slide to a photograph on the desk. My only one.

The ice around my stone-cold heart melts at just the sight of her.

Belle.

My reason for living.

Her long brown hair is dancing in the breeze and her gap-toothed grin beams at the camera. She's got her mother's smile, but her eyes, nose and lips are all from my side of the family.

"So rather than find a woman who can be a mother to Belle, you're going to find one you can sneak in through the back door when Belle's asleep?"

"My daughter has no understanding of adult matters."

"Belle isn't stupid."

"I know that. She's the smartest four year old I've ever met."

That's no exaggeration. Belle already has a sharp sense of self. Her favorite activity is gathering all her teddy bears for tea and conversation. "She's a prodigy."

"Holland."

"Kayla." I mimic her dry tone.

Before Kayla can lash into me, Ezekiel knocks on the door. He waits a moment before poking his head in.

"I just got off the phone with Walt."

Kayla arches both eyebrows *who's he?*

"No one you need to know." I motion for Ezekiel to continue.

He steps fully into the room and closes the door. "I have bad news."

I stiffen. "Where is she?"

"Gone."

"What do you mean 'gone'? A human being can't disappear into thin air."

"Miss Jones stalked out of HR when Walt wasn't looking. She took her box of personal items and left. Security cameras show her exiting the premises and…" He reddens.

"What?"

"She knocked over one of the ferns on her way out. Just… kicked it down."

I can't help it.

I laugh.

Ezekiel's eyes nearly pop out of his head.

Kayla shoots to the edge of her seat. "Explain that." She points at me and gives Ezekiel a worried look. "Explain this."

"I don't know if I'm at liberty."

"Now I'm even more curious. Holland, who's the fern killer and why are you laughing?"

"Ezekiel." I motion for him to explain.

"Her name is Kenya Jones and she is Alistair's new assistant."

"A second one?"

"Only for Belle's Beauty."

"She destroyed private property and you're hiring her to lead Claire's company?"

I shake my head. "Not lead. She'll assist."

Ezekiel exchanges a look with Kayla. "Miss Jones and Alistair had a verbal spar today."

"She had the guts to put you in your place?"

"I was instructed to screw myself."

Ezekiel pulls his lips in.

Kayla snorts. "I don't know whether to be impressed or scared."

"That is *exactly* why I want her on the team."

"Not just on the team. You're putting her at the helm of Belle's Beauty."

"I'm the one at the helm. She'll only assist."

"You leave a lot of tasks to Ezekiel's care. It'll be the same with her."

"Not this time." I lift a hand. "I've been disappointed with the management companies. Which is my fault. I wanted to be hands-off with Belle's Beauty because I don't have the time to handle it. I should have known it was better to do things myself. Now that I'm more involved, I want someone who can meet my high standards."

"And this girl, who clearly has an anger management problem, is the solution?" Kayla sounds unconvinced. "I don't understand."

"She's more than capable."

"It doesn't matter how good her resume is, an attitude like that is tough to work with."

"Her resume is not that impressive either," Ezekiel mutters.

I slant him a *who's side are you on* look. "She's got a good track record."

"And not an MBA in sight."

I frown at him. "I didn't expect you of all people to be so stuffy."

"You're the one who created the rules. The only applications you've ever considered are those with awards and degrees from top universities."

Kayla lowers her voice. "Does she have something on you, Holland?"

"She has practical skills and the ability to triple sales in any store she's placed in. I want her to clone herself. That's all."

"He's adamant," Ezekiel confirms. As if Kayla can't already hear it in my voice.

"You fought with her." Kayla rubs her chin.

"We had a difference of opinion," I correct her.

"And right after that, you call me and reestablish a link with Make It Marriage…"

I don't like the conclusions she's jumping to. Even if they're right. "Miss Jones's pedigree is a little lacking, but I believe her work experience can make up for it. I've tried employing someone with more knowledge than on-the-job experience. It drove Belle's Beauty into the ground. We're near obscurity. Not to mention our dwindling sales. This woman is a breath of fresh air." I grab the binder with Kenya Jones's evaluations and flip it open.

Kayla ignores it. "You're attracted to her."

"I'll see myself out for this part." Ezekiel backs away.

"Don't run, Ezekiel. I'll need you to confirm that I'm not the crazy one here."

"That's exactly why I must leave," he says dryly. "Would you like coffee brought in, Kayla?"

"I'm good. Thanks. I'm about to tear into him and I think I'll be full after."

Ezekiel nods *very well*. He shuffles out of the room and closes the door softly behind him.

"You realize you just threatened me?" I arch both eyebrows at Kayla.

"Why did you promote a sales clerk to head manager of Belle's Beauty?"

"She's different."

Kayla presses her lips together. "I'm insulted you thought that was the answer I was looking for."

"It's the only answer you'll get."

She folds her arms over her chest.

I mimic the position. Ms. Fern Smasher may not be the conventional choice for this position, but I know my instincts. I trust them. They've gotten me this far, and I believe what my gut is telling me about Kenya Jones.

Other parts of my body have things to say too, but I'll learn to ignore them.

Kayla picks up her purse. "I'm denying your request to rejoin Make It Marriage."

"But I asked so nicely."

"You're running from whatever that girl is making you feel and we're not a distraction from that. You can find your own means of coping." She yanks her purse over her shoulder. "But if she ever wants a consultation, you can let her know that Make It Marriage will be happy to provide our services. On the house."

My good mood evaporates and my smile flattens.

"Don't threaten me, Kayla."

"The fact that you consider my words a threat tells me way more than you'd like, Holland."

I stare her down.

She smiles prettily. "I'm glad you're finally moving on, but it'll end in disaster if you can't be honest with yourself."

I am honest with myself. Kenya Jones will be working closely with me because she has the skills to do so. Anything beyond that is off-limits.

CHAPTER 3
HOUSE OF GLASS

KENYA

I BLOW my nose loudly and toss it into the Mount Everest-sized tissue mound. I'm hunkered in my best friend's couch, throwing germs all over her sofa and sobbing into her pillows.

Sunny flops into the couch beside me and drops a new box of tissues on the coffee table. She eyes the growing Mount Everest and sucks in a deep breath. I can practically *hear* her rationalizing her germphobic urges away.

"My head is killing me," I whine, looping my arm around hers and burrowing my head into her shoulder.

She pats my hair that has gone full Simba from *The Lion King*. "Keep crying all you want."

I hug her arm tighter. "I don't think I have a drop of water left."

"Finally. If you cried any more, the couch would start floating."

"You're not funny."

"I wasn't trying to be. I was genuinely wondering if you were hooked up to a water hose. This is the fifth box of tissues you've run through."

"I'll pay you back." It hits me that I'm broke and I start sobbing again. "Oh, wait. I can't."

"Why not?"

"I got fired today."

Her eyes widen. "You got axed the same day you found Drake..."

I sob pathetically.

She raises a fist and yells at the ceiling. "Whoever's in charge of what's going on down here, can you give my friend some slack? You don't have to be so cruel!"

I bawl hard.

She rubs my back. "What are you going to do?"

"I have to get my stuff out of his place, first of all. And then... I don't know."

"You can stay here as long as you need."

"Thanks." I sniff. "I don't even want to think about job hunting right now."

"That's fine. Plenty more to think about."

"Like what?"

She taps her chin. "What you're going to do about your relationship."

I reach for another tissue and blow my nose.

"Has Drake tried to reach out at all?"

"No, he hasn't. But Sasha's been calling." My phone is full of messages from her.

I'm sorry.

We need to talk.

Why are you being like this?

Let me explain.

Answer your phone!

It's tough seeing her name on my screen. Tough seeing her picture pop up, all smiley and cute, when she calls.

Tears spill from my eyes and I wipe them away with the back of my hand. "I can't believe Sasha would betray me like this. I'm hurt about Drake, but it's not the same. He can go jump off a cliff for all I care. I don't want to be dating a cheater anyway. But Sasha is my sister. She's my family. How could she do this to me? How could she tear my heart out like this?"

"Because she's spoiled and entitled." Sunny growls.

I'm not surprised she'd jump on the 'Bash My Little Sister' train. Sunny has never been a fan of Sasha.

"Please don't start," I beg.

"Start what? I'm only speaking the truth."

I curl into a ball on the other end of the couch and push my throbbing head deep into a pillow. "This isn't my life. Tell me this is just a nightmare."

"Sorry. Can't do that."

I tilt my head back and open my mouth to wail when Sunny sticks a Twinkie into my face. The sweetness gushes through my mouth and temporarily makes the dark shadows glitter with light.

"I'm not trying to knock on sick people, alright?" Sunny says, her thick eyebrows pulling together. "But Sasha is a little brat."

I frown at my best friend. Sunny has strong Mayan genes and it's super apparent when she's angry. The red undertones beneath her brown skin get stronger, and her eyes glitter like ancient jewels.

Her folks migrated from Belize and I thought it was cool that she was a real Mayan descendent. Sunny embraced it too, dressing up in cultural clothes at every special event. She'd always get a ton of attention. Heck, even when she's *out* of her traditional Mayan dress she makes heads turn. Her features are striking and exotic. She's got thin lips and a regal grace in every movement of her body.

Sunny flings her long, black hair over her shoulder. It's shiny and glitters like a waterfall. "Sasha's been getting everything she wants since the moment she got diagnosed."

"Whoa, whoa. Sasha's entire world exploded when she found out she was sick."

"See? You're taking up for her."

"These are two separate matters," I yell back.

"No, it's all connected. This crappy behavior went unchecked for years. That's the reason she thought it'd be cool to screw your boyfriend."

I wince. "She went through a lot back then."

"What about everything *you* went through when she was sick?"

"I didn't have a hundred rounds of chemo."

"No, you just had to give up all your extra classes—"

"That wasn't her fault," I say.

"Yes it was."

"It wasn't like she could control being sick."

Sunny glares at me.

I scowl right back. "My parents' lives stopped too. They had to take out a bunch of loans to afford the medical bills. There was no money to spend on me."

"That's bull. They could have been more supportive. They could have remembered you were just a kid yourself. But what did they do? They guilt tripped you into giving up the things you liked and forced you to get a part-time job instead."

"It was my idea."

"What happened when you wanted to stop?" Sunny arches an eyebrow.

I glance away.

"Your parents didn't let you," she reminds me. "And it caused a big fight. You told them you weren't able to focus on school, but did they care that you couldn't juggle everything? No. They *expected* you to be the strong one. On top of that, you had to give them all your money and take care of Sasha on your downtime too. It didn't matter if you had something you wanted for yourself. You couldn't have it because Sasha needed it more."

I close my eyes. "You're focusing on the bad parts."

"There were good parts?" She throws her hands up.

"I remember sitting with Sasha in her hospital room, learning how to crochet. We knitted hats for the kids going through chemotherapy. I remember sleeping next to her when she was scared. I remember talking to her for hours before surgery."

"And now your boyfriend is the one sleeping next to her and talking to her for hours," Sunny points out.

I frown. "Stop it."

"Stop what?"

"It's hard enough to process on my own."

"I'm trying to get you to open your eyes before you talk to her. She's going to guilt trip you like she always does."

"Sunny…"

"I kept quiet because it's your private business, but I'm angry on your behalf. You're my best friend. And if it were anyone else, you wouldn't try so hard to make them into a good person."

"But it's not just anyone else. Sasha's my sister."

Sunny pops out of the sofa. "Which is exactly why she should never have done this! The very thought should have made her want to puke. I'm your friend and the suggestion that I could ever get with your boyfriend behind your back gives me the hives."

"Maybe there's a reason."

"Damn!"

I glance up in fright.

"You always do this. You always take up for her when she does shady things."

"Because…"

"Because you remember her when she was sick. Well, she's not sick anymore. She hasn't been for almost seven years. You gotta start letting her take responsibility for her actions."

I groan loudly. "I don't want to think about this anymore."

"Fine." Sunny huffs. "Come to bed."

"I'll stay up a little longer."

"Suit yourself." Sunny stalks out of the living room. I hear her slap the water faucet in the bathroom. The water gushes out loudly. She starts brushing her teeth and I wonder if she'll have any enamel left after this. I can hear those bristles rubbing like sandpaper.

Curling my arms around my legs, I bring my knees to my chest.

My phone sits next to my foot.

It's turned off.

The device has been exploding with messages. Most of the calls were from Sasha, but there were a few from Walt.

It feels like this day has been going on for hours. I just want to close my eyes and erase the past twenty-four hours from existence.

Are there any fairytale godmothers out there for me? Now would be a really good time to show up.

Rather than a glowing, ethereal creature, my best friend pokes her head out of her bedroom door and mumbles, "Come to bed, Kenya."

"I thought you were mad." I turn slightly to face her.

"I'm not mad. I just want the best for you and I hate seeing people treat you poorly." She tilts her head toward the room. "But we can argue about it tomorrow. For tonight, let's just forget everything."

My smile wobbles, but I offer it to her with as much gratitude as I can and follow her into the room.

Sunny sleeps on her side of the bed while I sleep on mine. She tosses and turns more than a toddler with a stomachache, so I end up on the floor with a blanket under me, huddling into a fetal position for warmth until morning.

When sunlight tiptoes into the room, I open my eyes and find that my vision is blurry. My head pounds like the seven dwarves found a new cave to explore.

"Morning." Sunny looks down from her perch on the bed.

"Morning."

"Ugh." She points to my face. "Girl, what is... did you slam into a wall last night?"

"It's that bad?"

She makes a *yes it is* face and rolls to her other side. Grabbing the handheld mirror she keeps on her nightstand, she offers it to me.

I stare at my reflection in horror. My hair expands all around me like someone filled it with helium and it's trying to run away. The thought of detangling those curls crushes my soul.

My eyes are puffy and the left one is red-rimmed. My face is swollen too. It looks like I went on a serious bender last night and I came back with the kind of tale you can never tell anyone.

I shove the mirror back into Sunny's hands and burrow under the comforter. "That's it. I'm never going out into polite society again. I'm going to stay right here under this comforter and become a professional snail."

"I don't think you can change species, Kenya."

"There are professional mermaids," I snap. "Don't tell me what I can and can't do."

Sunny grabs the top of my soft, protective shell. "Don't be ridiculous. You can't stay under there forever."

I resist her, fighting to keep a grip on the blanket.

"Come on. Get dressed and put on makeup. We're going out to eat."

"Don't you have work?" I squeak.

"I can grab breakfast."

The blanket explodes off me as I sit up and grab Sunny for a hug. She owns a freelance interior design business and rarely takes time off. Since she's a one-man band, every gig helps build her portfolio. She's always hustling to find work, so I know it's a sacrifice to take the morning off.

"You're the best."

"Yeah, yeah. I know. Now hurry up and make yourself presentable. I'm starving."

I inch back and give her a puppy dog face. "Until I get back on my feet, I can't go anywhere expensive. Where exactly are we going?"

"The usual place. Don't worry. I'll handle it."

I give her another hug.

She pushes me off. "Your breath stinks."

I blow a breathy kiss in her direction because I'm annoying like that and scamper out of the bed with a smile…

Until I remember everything that happened yesterday.

I cry in the shower and try to brush away the evidence when I emerge.

If Sunny knows I was bawling my eyes out while wasting her hot water, she doesn't give any indication.

We set out for a Caribbean brunch place next to her apartment.

It's a gorgeous day for a walk and the sunshine falling on my face energizes me. The world doesn't seem so bleak anymore.

I mean, it's still pretty dark.

But at least I don't have to think too hard about it.

There are barely any clouds in the sky, allowing a pure, unbroken blue. Trees arch their faces toward the sun, trying to soak in as much warmth as they can before winter. The weather is balmy today, so both Sunny and I are in light jackets.

We settle into our spot at Jamaican Patties, a tiny building with zero curb appeal and the best fry jacks I've ever tasted. Apart from the ones Sunny's mom makes, of course.

Sunny pulls her mojito close and takes a sip. "Has Sasha called you since morning?"

"I don't know." I flash my cell phone at her. " I haven't turned on my phone."

"Bold."

"It's not like I have to worry about my boss calling me," I say glumly, wrapping my fingers around my orange juice. I have a feeling I'll start bawling if I consume an ounce of alcohol, so I've chosen to play it safe.

Sunny slips one of the golden-brown fry jacks into my plate. "I'm sorry you lost your job."

"Compared to all the horrible things that happened yesterday, it's not the worst."

"You're right. Way to look on the *sunny* side." She wiggles her eyebrows and grins. "Huh?"

"That was horrible."

"Made you smile though."

We share a laugh.

I shift my attention to the delicious spread. Apart from the basket of fluffy fry jacks, there are side dishes like steaming-hot beans, shredded cheese and grilled chicken.

I wonder if I have any spare doggy bags in my purse. I have to start thinking about how I'm going to pay for groceries because skipping meals isn't my style. This breakfast can serve as lunch too. The chicken topping can go on salads and sandwiches. And maybe I can hide some fry jacks away for tomorrow's breakfast.

"Why are you staring?" Sunny asks.

I shake my head. "Just trying to get used to the new normal."

"It must be weird. Yesterday, you had a boyfriend and a job. And now..." She sighs so hard her straw turns in a circle.

"Thanks for the reminder."

She winces. "Sorry."

I munch on a fry jack. "Oh, I didn't tell you everything that happened yesterday."

"There's more?" Her eyes bug. "Sheesh, I should have bought a lottery ticket. What was yesterday's date?"

I lean my elbow on the table. "Right after I saw... you know." A picture of my sister and Drake flashes in my head. My heart pains me like someone plucked the strings, but I forge on. "I got a call from Walt to go into work. When I got there, this jerk was, like, *lurking* in the hallway..."

"Like a pervert?"

"He's too hot to be a pervert."

Her eyes snap to mine and she grins. "Oh? He was hot?"

"Not the point." I glance away because I cannot deny that Holland Alistair was fire-alarm levels of smoking. "This guy, he acted all mystified by me. He kept saying *'you're* the one who tripled sales?' Like he couldn't believe I was capable of such a thing."

"The prick."

"Right?"

"You think it was a race-thing?"

I scrunch my nose.

"Or maybe it's just women in general." She scowls. "You should blast him online. Get him cancelled."

"I bet there's a forum that already exists online. He strikes me as someone who's awful to everyone. Not just black people. Or women."

She relaxes into her chair. "A jerk who believes in equality. That's fair."

I choke out a laugh. "Anyway, he acted all rude and condescending with me, so I said some things I probably wouldn't have if I wasn't so upset about..."

"Yeah."

"And the next thing I know, this guy tells me to pack my things and report to HR."

Sunny slams her hand on the table and gasps. "No."

"Turns out, he's some guy named Holland Alistair and he owns Belle's Beauty."

"Wait. *That* Holland Alistair?"

"How many people in this world go by 'Holland'?"

She shakes her head, her shiny hair tumbling around her cheeks. "Girl, give me a second. Let me look this up." Sunny pulls out her phone like a spy genius on a mission. Thumbs clamoring away, she mumbles, "I've heard that name on the news before."

"On the news? Is he like... a criminal?"

Mr. Alistair didn't strike me as a crook. But what if he is? What if he comes after me because of what I said to him? And what I did to his fern?

"Not a criminal. A billionaire." She turns the phone over to me and there's a stuffy picture of Holland Alistair scowling into a camera.

He looks just as gorgeous in this still photo as he did in person, and it is so unfair the way my heart skips a beat.

"He's a data analyst genius or something. There was a whole write up about how he was revolutionizing the real estate game."

"So he has a reason to act as arrogant as he does?"

"Hey," she holds out a dark hand, "that's no reason to be a prick to people. He should know better."

I nod.

"What exactly did you tell him?"

"I don't even remember. I just said he was disrespectful. Something like that."

"Wow." She flops back into her chair and barks out a laugh. "You told off a billionaire to his face? Way to go, girl."

"I also knocked over his fern." My voice wobbles. "I kicked it a few times."

Sunny stops for a moment. Then she throws her head back and guffaws. "That's *amazing*! Was it a real fern?"

"I thought it was fake until glass shattered and dirt went flying everywhere." I cringe inside. I haven't done anything that childish in years.

"That's… I'm speechless."

I rub the back of my neck. "You don't think that fern was expensive, do you?"

"Don't worry. A man that rich won't track you down because you kicked over his fern. He has too many important things to do." She leans forward. "Did it make you feel any better?"

"Kind of," I admit. "At the time, all I could think about was how unfair he was. I did amazing at that weekend workshop, but I ended up losing my job. All because I didn't know he was the boss."

"Would you have cared if you'd known?"

"Probably not." I slap the table. "He was *so rude*, Sunny. He talked about me as if I wasn't even there. And he acted so entitled."

"He kind of *is* entitled. He's a gazillionaire."

"He's human, isn't he? And so am I. Who cares that he has a lot of money and I'm broke?"

"Don't get defensive. I'm on your side."

I pull her phone closer and stare at the articles about Mr. Alistair. One in particular catches my eye.

Tech Mogul Loses Wife In Tragic Accident
Stunned, I click on the article.

Sunny finishes off her mojito and waves at a waiter to refill it. She notices my expression and frowns. "What's with that face?"

"It says here that Holland Alistair lost his wife four years ago." My eyes scan the page in rapid fire. I've been devouring books since I was four, so I tend to read at a faster pace. "It says Belle's Beauty is his late wife's company."

"That's so sad."

The nerves in my stomach tighten. "I mean… it still doesn't excuse him for being a major jerk, but it does humanize him a little."

"It's horrible, but you can't forget what he did yesterday." She wags a finger. "See, that's your weakness. You keep letting tragic backstories fool you into thinking evil people are good."

I rub my temples. "Can you not start?"

"Fine. Fine." She raises both arms. "But your sister is—"

"Here." I breathe in shock.

"What? No, it's a five-letter word and it starts with b."

"No, I mean she's *here*." My eyes lock on Sasha. She's wearing a sharp white blouse and a little pleated skirt that swishes around her long legs. Ankle boots, similar to the kind I wore yesterday, adorn her feet.

Heads swivel in her direction as she passes by. She doesn't pay the men any attention as she searches the tables. When her gaze collides with mine, I get a sick feeling in my stomach.

Sunny charges to her feet. "Oh hell *nah*. What is she doing in my territory?"

"I don't want to talk to her right now," I croak, unable to keep my food down. "Sunny, can you—"

"I'm on it, sweetie. You get out of here."

It's pathetic that I have to run from my own sister, but all the ugly, churning feelings in my gut tell me I'm not ready to have this conversation. The wound is too fresh and the pain is too thick.

Charging through the restaurant, I head to the back door and crash into the alley. From there, I take off in a random direction, eager to put space between me and the woman who stabbed me in the back.

When my feet start hurting, I look for the nearest seat I can find. A bus stop isn't that far away, and I take refuge under the shade. Two teenagers are nearby, school bags, a trombone and a guitar at their feet. They're holding hands and whispering sweetly to each other.

I remember when I had a love like that. I was a little older than them, in college, but I was feeling all those gushy, heart-pounding thrills for the first time.

I want to tap the girl on the shoulder and warn her that this romance won't feel like a fairytale for long. Just wait until she catches her boyfriend *tromboning* into her sister.

But I keep my mouth shut and reach for my phone. Sunny will want to know where I am, and I'll need an update on whether it's safe to return to her apartment. If Sasha knew to find me at the restaurant, that means she knows I'm with Sunny.

My phone powers on with a loud chirp. I wait for it to go through the loading process and then tap my message icon.

I'm stunned when I see the latest message.

It's from an unknown number.

Good morning, Ms. Jones. You've been chosen for a position at Fine Industries. Kindly come in for an interview at your earliest convenience.

I scrunch my nose. Everything about that job offer screams 'scam', but an opportunity is an opportunity.

Settling into the bench while the teenagers whisper about how much they love each other, I google 'Fine Industries' and nearly fall out of my seat when I spot the name of the CEO.

"Holland Alistair?" My eyes whip up to the busy highway. That doesn't make any sense. Why would Holland Alistair offer me a job?

Unless this is a trap.

Does he want to lure me to his office so the cops can get me? I imagine a group of cops—who, strangely, all have handlebar mustaches—crouched beneath Alistair's desk.

At that moment, my phone rings.

It's Sunny.

Feeling paranoid, I glance left and right before whispering, "Sunny, Holland Alistair just gave me a job offer."

"What?"

"Holland Alistair…"

"What? I can't hear you?"

"The hot prick from yesterday wants me to work for him!"

The teenagers both go silent.

Heat burns my cheeks and I lower my voice, "This is a trap, right?"

"I don't think so." Sunny sounds breathless. "He's outrageously rich, right? And all the articles talk about how strict he is with his time. Someone like that wouldn't waste his precious hours trying to trick you into seeing him."

"So you think it's a legitimate offer?"

"You did say they were stunned by how you'd tripled sales. And you did a smashing job at the weekend workshop. It makes sense that Alistair would be interested in meeting the person everyone was raving about."

I wince. "And I snapped at him."

"You didn't ruin your chances. They still reached out."

"Don't you think that would be shameless of me, though? I did knock over his fern."

"It's not like you're going to work for *him*. Do you know how often regular employees see the owner of a company that size? Like never. The probability of you running into him is zero."

"I don't think that's how probabilities work," I mumble.

"It's not like you have any other job offers."

"True."

"And we can't keep sharing a bedroom forever."

I pout. "Why not?"

"Because you're sleeping on the floor, for one thing! And also, one day, I *am* going to get myself a boyfriend."

"When? You barely leave the house."

"Not the point. I've been trying my luck on those dating apps. One day, I'm going to swipe right on a guy who *doesn't* think a great pick up line is 'do you want to see my Wiener?'"

I burst out laughing. "They do not."

"It's never the dog, Kenya. They never have a dog."

My smile grows. "You really think it's a good idea to work for his real estate company? Isn't that kind of… brazen?"

"You might as well be brazen for once, girl. Everyone else in your life has no problem doing that."

My cell phone vibrates and, as if summoned, I get an incoming call from Sasha. I reject the call before putting the cell back to my ear. "This is either going to be the best thing I've ever done or—"

"No 'or'. It's time for you to catch a break and this just might be Fate balancing the scales."

"Maybe."

"Thank God you did your makeup before you left. Head straight to that interview and don't think about anything else."

I pause. "Did you… say anything to Sasha?"

"Girl, didn't you hear me? Secure the bag first and then worry about your back-stabbing sister later."

"Sunny."

"I'm not going to apologize. A spade is a spade."

"I'm hanging up now."

"Good luck on your interview."

Suddenly nervous, I spy on Holland Alistair's biography again. Hitting the back arrow, I return to the images tab. My phone screen fills with pictures of Alistair's arrogant, rigid, impossibly beautiful face. Those firm eyebrows look like thunderstorms waiting to send lightning bolts in my direction.

What does the angry god of Mount Olympus want with me?

It still feels a little too dangerous to stomp into his territory, but a job at Fine Industries would be a serious notch on my resume.

And Sunny's right. I *was* getting attention from the higher ups before I was brutally kicked out of my place.

The only problem is… this offer didn't come from Belle's Beauty. It came from Fine Industries. I know nothing about data or real estate. Where would I even fit in a company like that?

Does it matter? A job offer dropped into your lap. Are you going to take it or not?

I get on the bus and head to Fine Industries. Going for an interview beats unemployment, running from my sister and hiding under Sunny's comforter all day.

Hopefully, I don't run into Alistair. He might have his own tragic backstory, but I still find him to be arrogant and insufferable. If going through a tragedy gave everyone a free pass, we would live in a totally uncivilized society.

And if this *is* some twisted way of getting revenge on me, then I won't hold anything back. I've been slammed to the ground more than once. If Alistair dangles hope in front of me only to pull it back, I'm going to aim for something a lot more painful than his fern.

* * *

Everyone at Fine Industries wears business casual like it's a magazine shoot. Three-piece suits. Pencil skirts. Shiny shoes. Sensible heels. I shouldn't have listened to Sunny when she told me to come down here in my T-shirt and jeans. This is absolutely inappropriate for an interview.

I turn to leave when I hear a voice call my name.

"Miss Jones?" A security officer barrels toward me. "*Miss Jones?*"

Oh sweet Lord. I knew it! This is a trap!

My heart leaves my chest and runs out the door before I can catch up. Eyes widening, I make a mad dash for the exits.

As a unit, the security guards spring into action. One slides in front of the door like he's rushing into home base. Three more sprint toward me, forming a circle to lock me in.

The commotion causes a stir in the crowd. Curious eyes swerve my way. *Look at that hooligan with the big curly hair and plain T-shirt. Look at her all unprofessional. The fern killer. Plant murderer!*

I suck in air like it's going out of style. "I can explain," I babble, wondering if we get internet reception in jail. I'm on the last level of *Candy Crush* and I can't afford to let all that effort go to waste. "I didn't know the fern was real."

The security guard approaches me like I'm a rabid dog and he's afraid I'll bite. "We've been instructed to take you upstairs."

I make one last attempt at escape, but the security guards easily block my way. Damn. They make sexy getaways look so much easier in *Charlie's Angels.*

The burly guard grabs my arm. "Upstairs, ma'am."

I swipe at him. "Let me go."

"Ma'am!"

So asking nicely isn't going to work?

Fine.

"I'm not afraid of the *popo!*" I channel my inner Madea, picturing myself as a six-foot cross-dressing man in a granny dress and sand sacks for breasts. Hauling my body around, I shriek, "I ain't afraid! So let me go!"

The men gawk at me like I'm an alien beamed down from the mothership. I notice cell phone cameras zooming in my direction and stop abruptly, hiding my face behind my current warden's back.

If yesterday was the worst day of my life, then today is gunning for that trophy. I wonder what I did to deserve this madness. Should I just step into on-coming traffic and take my chances with the afterlife?

"This way ma'am," the burly guard says, indicating the elevators. He sounds genuinely concerned for me.

Like a troubled inmate assigned extra security, I'm briskly

escorted to the lift. The guards stay hot on my tail, but I'm not going to run. I'm too humiliated to bother.

This is that jerk's fault.

Holland Alistair.

He *knew* I'd come. He prepped his security team to welcome me.

I wrench my hand free and turn on the guard inside the elevator. "This is a violation of my rights."

He arches an eyebrow and grunts as if he doesn't talk English.

Silence fills the tiny space.

Seconds later, the elevator chirps.

We've arrived at the top floor.

The doors open to a wall of giant windows and a view of the city that makes my eyes water. A man unfolds himself from a chair at the front desk and stares me down. He's built like a Gucci model, so tall and muscular he could probably punch his way through the walls if he ever goes full Hulk.

My heart slams against my ribs, wanting a second try at escape. I whirl around, intending to act on it, but the burly security guard looks at me with a frown.

I force myself to turn around and face the dominating Holland Alistair.

CHAPTER 4
OUT OF SORTS

HOLLAND

Kenya Jones is completely out of her element, but it doesn't stop the glint of defiance that lights her eyes when she sees me. It's visceral. Her distaste. And it shouldn't excite me as much as it does.

She looks smaller today. Probably because her mouth is closed rather than open in a tirade of self-important judgements. Her T-shirt and jeans is an odd choice for an interview. Perhaps she has no intentions of taking the job.

Unacceptable.

I want her.

So I must have her.

It's very simple.

"What you just did is illegal," Kenya huffs, stabbing a dark brown finger at me.

I look past the fuming woman to Stanley, the giant in charge of my security team. "Thank you. You may leave."

He dips his head and steps into the elevator alone. As the doors close, a small smile stretches over his face. His amusement is either a testament to Kenya's spunk or relief at the break in his daily monotony.

Given the struggle she put up in the lobby, all of which I spied on the security feed that was sent to my phone, I can understand why Stanley finds this woman entertaining. Her increasingly undignified behavior is, somehow, more intriguing than off-putting.

Ezekiel hustles past me. "Miss Jones, you're here. I apologize for the reception in the lobby."

She stabs me with a look that's full of murderous intentions, completely ignoring Ezekiel.

I glare right back.

"The security team was instructed to escort you upstairs at all costs."

Kenya scowls. "*His* idea, I assume."

There is no mistaking the 'him' to whom she's referring.

I nod, quite proud of myself. If not for my quick thinking, she would have slipped through my fingers like a ghost.

Walt's been trying to contact Kenya Jones since yesterday. He even stopped by her apartment to see her and was told that she didn't live there anymore. The message was delivered by a man who, in Walt's words, 'looked like he'd been sucker punched in the gut'.

I don't know where Kenya's been hiding. I'm just glad she waltzed right into my trap. Now that she's here, I won't let her leave without getting what I want.

Her face darkens. "You're not above the law, Alistair."

"Neither are you, Miss Jones." I keep my tone stiff. "Should we discuss compensation for the property you damaged yesterday?"

Her eyes widen.

Some of the steel crawls out of her spine.

Ezekiel gives me an inquiring look before gesturing to the elevator. "Ms. Jones, why don't we head down to the HR department, so we can log you into our system?"

"I appreciate the fact that you're *asking* this time." Her voice is heated and, again, I get the sense that barb is aimed at me. "But I haven't yet decided to take the job."

My irritation spikes. I have a packed schedule, but I'm choosing to be here for this interview because getting Belle's Beauty back on the right track is more important than anything else.

"What are your objections to the position?" I growl.

Ezekiel casts me another warning look as if begging me not to speak, but I don't take his silent advice.

Kenya Jones folds her arms over her chest and engages in a stare-off with me. "You. You are my biggest objection."

That mouth of hers. Damn. There are so many better things those luscious lips could be used for. I imagine her lying flat on my desk, her legs bent over the edge and her skirt scrunched around her ankles. Her mouth would be open and gasping my name—

No. What the hell are you trying to do?

My inappropriate thoughts annoy me further. I have never struggled with an attraction like this before. And never for an employee at the office. The whole thing reeks of a scandal I want no part of.

My eyes swerve to Ezekiel, whose increasingly reddening face tells me this interview is heading south. Fast. And it's mostly my fault.

I motion to him. "As soon as Miss Jones is made aware of her new responsibilities, send her to the PR meeting. Preferably within the hour. You can set up her company email and any other miscellaneous introductions when she returns."

"Excuse me?" Kenya scoffs.

"Also, get her into more appropriate work attire." My eyes slide down her body. I can't help it. She's too beautiful for me not to notice. "She's representing me and Belle's Beauty now. We can't have her looking like… *this*."

"That's it! I'm going to jail today." She takes big, angry steps toward me.

Ezekiel slides into her path. "Miss Jones, I assure you that Alistair is very sincere."

"Sincere?" Furious brown eyes cut through me. "The tone you're using is more appropriate for a dog you're training, Alistair. Not a human being that you're seeking assistance from."

"Seeking assistance?" My words end with a stunned breath.

"You had me kidnapped by your hired thugs and whisked me to your ivory tower." She gestures to the office lobby. "And now you're growling at me like *you* weren't the one who came crawling into my inbox, asking me to take this position."

Ezekiel hides his laughter behind his hand.

My own amusement clashes with my irritation. It's a fight that has no clear winner.

I stare at Miss Jones intently. That snarky, porcupine-inspired act was acceptable when she didn't understand who I was and what I expect, but she's not carrying that attitude over into our cooperation.

"I don't care what you think about me or the offer you received. The moment you step through those doors," I point to the elevator, "you are not to question me. You are not to taunt me. You are not to argue or flash those angry brown eyes at me." My long-legged stride closes the distance between us. "And most of all, you keep that sass to yourself until I give you permission to let it loose. Understand?"

Her face becomes a mottled shade of brown and red. I want to enjoy it, but I truly don't have the time. Stepping back and out of her personal space, I gesture to Ezekiel who hurries forward.

"Explain the compensation before Ms. Jones can gather her thoughts."

He turns to her. "The starting salary is—"

"Do you have any idea what a narcissist you are?" Kenya launches forward, her tennis shoes stomping over the tiles.

My body gets caught in a sudden heat wave as she stops right in front of me. Tilting her head back, she pokes a dark finger in my jacket and spits, "I don't want to work with someone as demanding, condescending, egotistical—"

"One hundred and fifty thousand dollars!" Ezekiel blurts.

Kenya Jones goes very still.

"Starting salary," Ezekiel recites calmly. "It also comes with impressive insurance coverage and a stock option after a certain number of years."

"How many?"

"Negotiable."

Kenya's eyes widen. "All for doing what exactly?"

I step back and watch her contemplate the offer.

"Your working title will be second executive assistant, but if you can do with the other stores what you've done at Darwin's, you'll be in charge of revitalizing Belle's Beauty sales campaigns. In this regard, you'll be working directly under Mr. Alistair." Ezekiel motions to me.

Kenya bites down on her bottom lip and glares in my direction. "Don't you have your own company? Why are you personally involved in Belle's Beauty?"

"I've already made myself clear, Miss Jones. Your job is not to ask questions. Only to get the work done."

Her face turns thunderous. "You know what? I don't care how sweet the money is. I can't do this."

Incredible.

She'll really walk away from a deal this good?

"I thought you were an intelligent woman." My words echo over the lobby. I can't help the taunting that enters my tone. "How often does a job with a six-figure salary just drop in your lap? You've had, what? Five different entry positions in your career? Given your qualifications, I'm being beyond generous."

Her back stiffens and she whirls around. I see the muscles in her jaw tense as she clenches her mouth.

"You don't like me. Fine. But I know you need a job."

"Only because *you* got me fired."

"Semantics."

"Is it?"

"You're missing the big picture. Will you let someone you despise keep you from an opportunity of a lifetime?"

"Don't manipulate me."

"I'm stating the facts."

"You're being a shark. But I guess, from what all the articles said about you, I should have expected that."

My curiosity rises. "You looked into me?"

"You looked into me," she snaps back.

Fair.

"What did you learn?" The tabloids have been mixed in their reviews of me. No one knows what to make of my business strategy. I don't follow the crowd because I tend to swim upstream. The more challenging a project is, the better for me.

I don't subscribe to mind games either. Rubbing elbows with other suits in the name of networking is the worst part of my schedule. My work speaks for itself. If I need to rely on connections to get ahead, I haven't done my job properly.

"You're a perfectionist. You expect everything to go your way or you throw your technicians out. You're unreasonable with your demands and unruly with your displeasure, but you compensate well."

"That's all?"

"Your technicians tap into their hidden potential because you push them past their preconceived limits." She glares at me as if she believes that part is made up. "You make the impossible come true."

I tap my fingers against my wrist.

Kenya takes a deep breath as if she's trying to suck all the air out of the room and then she lets it out in a gush. "Tell me the starting salary again?"

Ezekiel rattles off the benefits of the position.

As he speaks, Kenya turns and gives me an assessing look. She's weighing me. Analyzing the golden opportunity against the threat of seeing me everyday.

Her stubbornness was admirable yesterday, but I don't have the patience to deal with it now. She is in *my* territory and I've given more than enough attention to her temper tantrum.

"My last assistant left and I'm in need of someone to fill the position. Now, are you going to take it or not?"

"Why did she leave?"

"I ask the questions."

Her pink tongue darts out to wet her lips, and I have to turn around to hide the flush running up my neck. She's like catnip. I need to find a way to build up a tolerance against this woman.

"All you read about me is right. I will push you and I will expect the impossible. I compensate well because I know it can be torturous." Spinning around when I have a handle on myself, I look down at her. "Are you up for the challenge or not?"

"Last question."

Ezekiel shuffles from one foot to the next.

My impatience jumps out of me. "No."

"Why me?" She frowns at Ezekiel. "You were both there yesterday. You saw what happened between us. You even know about the fern."

"May he rest in peace."

Her eyes narrow on me. "We don't get along."

"An apt way to put it."

"You turn me into the kind of person who picks a fight with greenery. And I make you... well... you were already this way, I suppose. So why do you want to work with me? Why give me a chance when you *know* I've only ever had entry-level positions?"

I tilt my chin up and look past her. "Ezekiel, take her now before I lose my patience."

Her eyebrows slant together. "Hey!"

"This way, Miss Jones." Ezekiel clasps her arm.

"I'll be at the data bridge," I say.

Ezekiel nods.

"Get your hands *off* me. I can go by myself."

I smile as I walk away from the spitfire who is now officially my employee and officially off-limits. We'll see if she can handle all the plans I have for her. And I'll see if I can keep my hands to myself.

* * *

FIFTEEN MINUTES LATER, I'm seated comfortably in my rugged SUV that's suitable for city and off-road travel. Steam rises from a hot cup of coffee nestled within plush cupholders.

I rest my elbow on the center console as I thumb through the data pulls for the latest update. I've been on-site at the data bridge more often lately because of the changes we're trying to push through.

The software keeps bugging and it's faster to handle them on-site than send instructions.

The data bridge is home to all of Fine Industry's servers. The servers are the brain of the company and, just like when Belle was a baby and I couldn't take my eyes off her for fear that something would happen, the servers are like my children.

We're pushing them as hard as they can go, and I prefer to keep a close eye on their performance in case we need to dial back.

The coffee goes down warm and smooth. The leather seat is melted butter beneath me.

I try not to pay attention to the world speeding outside the window. Although I've gotten much better at being on the road, the queasy feeling in my stomach hits me at random moments.

PTSD, my brother-in-law said.

Unwanted weakness is what I prefer to call it.

I hate that I can't seem to get over this hurdle. It's hard for me to even touch the wheel of a car anymore, which makes late night grocery runs or pharmacy dashes difficult.

Bernard glances at me from the rearview mirror.

I frown at my tablet. "I'd be grateful if you could keep your eyes on the road."

"You okay, boss?"

I sigh. Bernard has been my driver for the past three years. He's always on call and never fails to show up at the most inconvenient hours to shuffle Belle and I where we need to go.

His unique ability to peek into my personal life, unfortunately, gives Bernard the impression that I'm someone to be pitied. He never says it outright but then, he knows I'd have his head if he did.

As usual, I'm brusque with him. "I'm fine."

He knows better than to push me any further.

Another reason why Bernard's managed to stick around for so long. He knows when to be nosy and when to back off.

"Thanks for the coffee," I say grudgingly, swiping my hand across the screen.

"No problem."

My phone lights up with an alert from my home security system. At first, I don't understand what the notification is for. Until frightening words start scrolling on-screen.

Smoke has been detected. Please evacuate now.

I set the coffee away so fast it sloshes over the cup and burns my hand. "Ah!"

"Mr. Alistair!" Bernard's eyes find mine in the rearview mirror.

I snatch my phone. Dialing my nanny's number, I wait on pins and needles for her to pick up. The line rings and rings, but there's no response.

I check my watch and curse. Belle's playdate isn't until three. She's still at home right now. What if the smoke knocked out her nanny? What if my daughter is coughing and crying out for me?

I imagine her crawling on the floor, covered in soot and scars. I see her coughing. Crying. Calling out for her daddy.

No, not again. I can't live through this nightmare again.

I keep calling the nanny.

My heart is about to climb out of my throat and flop on the backseat.

No response.

Curses fly rapid-fire out of my mouth.

"Mr. Alistair?"

"Bernard, take me home *now!*"

"Yes, sir!"

The car engine roars, and the wheels scream as he steps on the gas. We lurch through mid-morning traffic. Panic crawls over my back and tries to latch on, but I focus on what I should do next.

The alarm system should have alerted the police and the fire department. Even if it hasn't, the building super would have seen the smoke and called the authorities.

I focus on calling the nanny until my thumb cramps.

"Come on, come on." I grit my teeth and desperately hit the 'call' button again. "Answer, Mrs. Hansley."

Finally, there's a click.

I lean forward and yell, "Mrs. Hansley, where's Belle? Have you two left the apartment yet? What's going on?"

"Alistair?"

"Is Belle alright?"

"Of course. And did you say we left the apartment? Why would we leave?"

Bernard throws the vehicle into a parking spot in front of our building. I kick the door open. My shoes hit the ground in staccato beats as I run with all my might.

There aren't any crowds milling outside, nor are there flames licking at the windows in the penthouse. I notice the lack of fire trucks and the absence of chaos and curiosity that normally follows any kind of disaster.

"There was no fire," Hansley says.

My steps slow and I breathe out heavily. I'm sweating so hard that the phone slips from my ear. "But my alarm system sent an alert…"

"Oh that?" She cackles breathily. "Belle and I were making brownies and had a minor accident when we were melting the chocolate. The towel caught on the edge of the flames and it burned—"

"Is Belle alright?" I blurt.

"She's fine. The towel was nowhere near her, though it did cause a lot of smoke. I heard the alarm go off, but I threw open some windows and it went quiet again. I didn't know it would alert you."

Of course it alerts me. My daughter is the most important person in my life. If anything happens to her, I won't be able to forgive myself.

"I'm relieved," I say slowly, wilting in the elevator. "But I'll be there soon."

"You don't have to come. I have everything under control."

"It's too late." I step into my house and glance around. "I'm already here."

"Daddy!" A girlish squeal explodes from behind the couch. I look that way and see Belle making a beeline for me.

My heart shudders with relief. She launches her little arms around me, burying her tiny nose in my neck. Her hair flies all over the place, whipping my skin like tiny mosquito bites. She smells like baby powder and chocolate.

I crush her to me, squeezing my eyes shut as wave after wave of relief overwhelms me. The thought that I could have lost her, even if it was a false alarm, shakes me to my core.

"Daddy, you're squeezing." She groans and wiggles out of my arms.

"Sorry, baby." I ease my grip, but I don't let her go. Tilting my head down, I stare into her bright brown eyes. She's wearing a frilly, pink princess dress with a sparkly top and an itchy pink tutu for the skirt.

Her face is smeared with chocolate and there's a chunk in her hair.

I wipe it off with my fingers. "What were you doing?"

"Chocolate!" Belle boasts.

I lift my head, meeting Mrs. Hansley's eyes. The older woman was Claire's nanny growing up. When discussing childcare, Claire and I both agreed that no one else was suitable for the position. It's an excellent choice. Mrs. Hansley treats Belle like her own granddaughter and delights in spending time with her. She's been an absolute lifesaver.

"Did you run here, Alistair?" Her voice crackles with affection. "You're sweating."

"You weren't answering the phone." My tone is dark and it's a very obvious scolding.

Her chuckle dries up.

I stare her down, waiting for an explanation.

"I'm sorry. I was focused on opening the windows and getting the smoke out. I didn't have my phone next to me."

"From now on, you need to answer the moment I call," I say forcefully.

She bites down on her bottom lip and her eyes drop to the ground.

I realize I'm being harsh and soften my tone. "I was worried for your safety. And for Belle's."

"I'm okay, daddy." Belle presses her palms to my face.

I turn my head slightly and kiss her small fingers. "Are you behaving well, Isabella?"

She nods.

I kiss her pudgy cheek and then set her down.

Mrs. Hansley approaches me with slow, hesitant steps. "I really am sorry. Nothing like that has ever happened before. I didn't mean to scare you."

"I know." My eyes slide away from hers. I hate the pity entering her watery blue gaze. Hate the way it makes me feel so small and helpless. I try so hard to pretend that I'm okay. That I'm untouchable. It's hard to pretend nothing has changed in my life when everyone treats me like I'm fragile.

It's insulting.

"Daddy, come here." Belle tugs on my ring finger. Her palms are so small that she can barely wrap her full hands around mine.

I give her a warm squeeze and follow her to the playroom. It's a little-girl wonderland, complete with a toy-sized kitchen, a mini grocery store filled with plastic cans, cereal containers and grocery baskets and a parking lot for Belle's Mercedes Benz and Lexus electric vehicles.

Belle pushes me into a seat around a child-sized table and produces a magic wand from somewhere in her toy chest.

"Boo!" She touches the wand to my nose.

I stretch my arms high and try my best at a high pitched voice. "Boo!"

She shrieks with glee.

I smile at her adorable face, my heart rearranging in my chest. I didn't know I could love another person without ever meeting them, but I've been obsessed with Belle since the day I found out she was coming into the world.

Even before I heard her first heartbeat or felt her kick her mother's stomach, I knew she would be the best thing that ever happened to me.

The moment I first held her in my arms, all my gut instincts proved right. She's put her stamp on my heart and she hasn't returned ownership.

"Daddy, drink tea." She hands me a tea cup.

I hold it the way you're supposed to, with one finger sticking out in the air like royalty. "Wow! This is delicious!" I make a big show of slurping down the invisible beverage, much to my daughter's amusement. "Can I have more please?"

The Oliver Twist impression is lost on my four-year old, but she laughs uproariously because she loves me. Or maybe it's because a mere fart sound can tickle my daughter's fancy.

Belle giggles and pours me some more, watching me drink the air with delighted brown eyes that sparkle in the sunshine.

I stare at her, still trying to convince myself that she's okay. When I rushed over thinking she was in danger, I truly couldn't breathe. Now, seeing her smile and play, I'm just starting to take a proper breath.

There's a knock on the door.

Mrs. Hansley pokes her head in and gives me a tentative smile.

"We haven't put the brownies in the oven yet. I was just about to do that before you arrived."

"Chocolate!" Belle takes off for the kitchen.

"I'm so sorry we interrupted your day, Alistair."

"It's okay. I'm just glad no one was harmed."

"Would you like Belle to say goodbye before you head to the office? I'm afraid once she gets her hands on those brownies, she won't be able to focus on anything else."

"I'm not ready to say goodbye yet."

"No?" Her bushy eyebrows jump forward.

I rise from the miniature chair. "I'll stay with her for a few hours."

Her eyes widen. "Alistair, if you have somewhere to be—"

"Nowhere more important than where I am right now." If I'd lost Belle today, the company, the data bridge, the licensing play—none of it would have mattered. Not a single dollar.

I've already lost my wife. I would never forgive myself if I lost the child Claire left behind.

* * *

"Grab Mr. Ducky," I tell Belle, swirling my hand through the warm bath water. "It's time to dry off now."

"No," she cries out, splashing her pudgy arms in the bathtub.

I bite down my impatience and keep my tone light. "Belle, bath time is over. It's time to dry off and change now."

"No!" She yells the word louder at me as if I didn't understand the first time.

I'm crouched over the bathtub, my long-sleeved shirt rolled up to my elbows and my back bent at an uncomfortable angle. I'm too tall for this particular daddy duty, but when I came back home from the data bridge, I told Mrs. Hansley I could handle the nighttime routine.

She looked at me like she doubted my skills, which only made me more determined to see Belle clean and fresh before her bedtime. How hard could it be?

The answer?

Very hard.

Extremely difficult.

My daughter is a stubborn little thing.

"Belle…"

"Splashy! Splashy!"

"Young lady, you need to…" A wave of sudsy bath water crashes into my face. I taste the gentle tang of Belle's organic soaps on my tongue and resist the annoyance slowly building inside me.

It doesn't help that my daughter finds her water attack extremely funny and is laughing her head off.

I wipe my face dry with my palm and give her a warning look.

The laughter dries in her throat. Her big brown eyes fill with tears and her bottom lip starts trembling.

Immediately, I surge toward her and pat her back. "It's okay, Belle. Daddy isn't angry."

But it's too late.

My daughter tilts her head back, opens her mouth and starts bawling.

Moments like these, I struggle not to feel utterly defeated. I never thought this would be my life. Never thought I'd be stumbling through single parent-hood while building my own company and trying to keep Belle's Beauty alive. Claire and I were supposed to build that company together. We were supposed to raise our child together.

The fact that she's not here is your fault.

I sit in the puddle created from my daughter's exuberant bath-time play, while her sobs shatter my eardrums. Gently, I take her out of the bathtub and wrap her in a towel.

"It's okay, Belle," I whisper. "It's okay. Daddy's not mad at you. He's not." I bounce her up and down. My voice cracks with the weight of my self-loathing. "I'm sorry. Daddy didn't mean to scare you."

She only settles down after I give her some warm milk and read three bedtime stories. I've already made an idiot of myself once tonight, so I find plenty of patience and humor her until her eyes get heavy and she sinks into her pillow.

Easing away from her bed, I watch my daughter sleep for a moment. Her brown hair feathers her cheek. Her thick eyelashes—she got that from Claire—curl softly. She's wearing princess-themed pajamas with unicorns and rainbows printed all over it.

My little sunshine.

I don't know what I'd do without her.

Easing out of her room, I head to my office. Though it's my daughter's bedtime, I have a lot of work to catch up on thanks to my impulsive decision to stay at home with Belle.

My first call is to Ezekiel.

"How did she do?" I ask, reaching for the latest numbers from the data pull.

"Who?"

"Miss Jones." I settle my glasses on my nose.

"The managers at the department store were not too welcoming. I think they find it unpleasant that someone who used to work under them is now telling them what to do."

"Miss Jones was never promoted to manager, was she?"

"No. She was always just a clerk. Mostly because of her age, I think. No one wanted to take a chance on her. Until you."

I ignore the not-so-subtle question in that statement. "Anything else to report?"

"No. Miss Jones will visit the store again tomorrow. I don't know what her plan is but—"

"I meant with other matters."

"Oh. Right." He launches into an update on our latest licensing negotiations. The lawyers have already written up the final drafts of the agreement, but I'm having a meeting with them to finalize the details.

"I'll look over those drafts and send you my notes for the meeting."

"Good." Ezekiel lingers over the phone.

I take my glasses off and roughly bark. "Anything else?"

"Your brother-in-law called."

I stiffen. "You told him I was busy?"

"He didn't really want to hear that."

"I'm fine."

"You don't have to tell me."

I scowl into the darkness. "I'll see you tomorrow, Ezekiel."

He hangs up.

I set the cell phone facedown and run my hand briskly over my face. Darrel is my brother-in-law, but he's also a therapist. Our conversations usually lead to him asking me how I'm doing and then not believing me when I tell him I'm okay.

Even if I'm not, I won't discuss it with anyone. Talking about feelings and pulling out bad memories to analyze them is not my idea of a good time. I prefer my coping method. Which is to pretend, as much as I can, that everything is back to normal.

At least then, I don't have to face those demons until I'm good and ready.

* * *

I WORK until three a.m. but, when I drag myself to sleep, there's no peace. The darkness I've been running from during the day creeps out of the shadows and crawls all over me.

In my dream, I see Claire frowning at me in the hotel room.

"Baby, you've been working all day. It's one in the morning. You can't drive right now. You're exhausted."

"I can handle it, baby."

I see everything clearly, as if it's happening all over again.

My heart beats faster.

I reach out, trying to get the Dream Me's attention. Trying to warn him. *Listen to her, you idiot!*

"Honey, I have a meeting at six o'clock sharp. It's very important. I can't miss it."

She pushes out her bottom lip. "We can stay here and then catch a plane back."

"I'd rather hurry. Just in case. You never know what could happen with those planes and delays…"

"But Holland—"

"Claire."

No.

Don't do it.

Don't leave.

"You have nothing to worry about." My hands wrap around Claire's arms. "I'll play your favorite audiobook on the way. The romance one with the pirate and the girl who dresses up as his medic."

"Deal." She laughs and walks out behind me.

Sweat rolls down my face. I try to run out of the room, but I'm stuck. Stuck listening to their footsteps get softer and softer. Stuck wishing I could call them back and keep Claire alive for one more day.

Sorrow falls on my chest. It cuts off my ability to breathe.

I'm trapped.

Running to the door, I bang my fist against it, but it won't budge.

"You. You are my biggest objection."

My eyes widen as the door bursts open and Kenya stands on the other side, her chin high in the air. She scoffs and turns abruptly. Hips swaying, she sashays down the hotel corridor.

I stumble behind her, hardly believing my eyes.

At that moment, I wake up.

Darkness presses around me.

I'm in my bedroom.

Damp sheets. Sweat-stained pillows. Filmy curtains.

My breathing is loud and erratic.

I sit up groggily, trying to make sense of the nightmare. It's one I've had many times since the accident. But it's never changed. Not once.

Until tonight.

What the hell is Kenya Jones doing in my dream?

I scrape my palm against my bristly cheek, not sure what to make of it. My new employee has an effect on me in real life. I'm aware of that. She's blaring temptation. Soft brown skin. Coily hair. Mocha eyes. A body so dangerously curvy she's a man's walking fantasy. I'm into her. I want to touch her, taste her. No doubt about it.

But this is different.

She's not only messing with my head when I'm awake. She can slam the brakes on my nightmares.

And that is giving Kenya Jones far more power than I'm comfortable with.

CHAPTER 5
THE PUSH-OVER

KENYA

I GIVE squinty eyes to the laptop, staring at all the numbers and trying to make sense of it.

None of the formulas compute.

I moan pathetically.

It's one thing to act tough in front of the Grump That Stole Happiness. He's a raging egomaniac with a gorgeous face and rippling muscles. I'm biologically programmed to *want* him as much as I wish to knock him down a peg or two.

But it's another thing entirely to get thrown off the deep-end on my first day.

Yesterday doesn't count. It was basically running from a shouting match with Holland Alistair to a Siberian cold-shoulder with the store managers.

What a day, right?

After another cry session in Sunny's couch last night, I'm back for Round Two.

Oh man.

I hope today is better than yesterday.

Fine Industries is bustling this morning. Harried employees are tucked into cubicles, focused on their tasks. No one's been particularly friendly. Most of them don't know why I'm here since I'm technically working for Belle's Beauty.

They don't know that Alistair wants me under his watchful eyes. Eyes that cut through me like a butcher knife when we happened to bump into each other this morning.

I returned the scowl in full before remembering that I'm to 'check my sass at the door'. Or something to that effect. His condescending words tend to get translated into much harsher language in my head.

The prick.

He better not ask me to make his coffee because I *for sure* am spitting in it.

But back to the numbers.

I stare at the computer screen, my head throbbing while I try to make sense of all the columns and tabs. I'm not a stranger to a spreadsheet. I know *why* I'm staring at these numbers.

But I don't know *what* they mean.

There's a reason I chose Literature as my college major. My right brain is probably oversized because it gets the most exercise. My left brain—the one that's supposed to be analytical and information driven—is probably the size of an expired gumdrop.

I sigh heavily and slump over the Fine Industries assigned computer. It's the most expensive model out right now. I don't want to know how much it cost to have one sitting on everybody's desk.

My phone pings with a message.

Sasha: Please call me, Kenya.
Sasha: I'm sorry.
Sasha: I need to talk to you.

I ignore those like I have all the others, but my sister is relentless. I put the phone on silent and concentrate on the numbers. Maybe if I stare and stare, they'll eventually make sense.

In the corner of my eye, I notice a sudden flurry of activity. At first, it's just background noise. Pieces of paper stuffed into organizer bins. Chips and cookie crumbs brushed off white desks. Trash in garbage cans. Picture frames arranged. Crocs exchanged for dress shoes and heels.

I lift my head, wondering why everyone is bustling around like an unspoken game of musical chairs.

Am I missing something?

When I see McGrump himself turning the bend, I finally understand.

My heart jumps out of my chest and I haul my chair close to the table. Staring at the computer with narrowed eyes, I type nonsense into the spreadsheet.

"Mr. Alistair."

"Good morning."

"Morning, sir."

Greetings pop out in tandem. Every eye follows Alistair's trek through the office. He doesn't respond to anyone, clearly on a mission.

I pity the employee on the receiving end of that skewer gaze.

Please walk past me. Please. Please.

My prayers go unanswered because the gorgeous prick stops in front of my desk and gives me a look so dark I might as well dig a hole and bury myself in it.

Fingers freezing on the keyboard, I swallow hard and turn my chair to look up at him. He's sans-entourage today. Usually, Ezekiel would be on his tail, ready to smooth all the ruffled feathers Alistair leaves in his wake.

Did he ax his own right-hand man?

I shake the thought from my head. Alistair wouldn't be that stupid. Who in their right mind would work with him if he got rid of Ezekiel?

Dark shadows pull through the room when Alistair looms over my desk. Lightning charges out of his stunning hazel eyes. They're more green than brown right now, swimming emerald seas with a little too much mud.

Everyone is watching me. I can feel my pulse thrumming all

the way down in my toes. It's pretty obvious that being singled out by the world's grumpiest boss is not a good thing.

"My office. Now."

My eyes dart away from his. Maybe if I pretend I didn't hear, he'll go away?

"*Now*, Miss Jones."

I wince. Who does he think he's talking to?

"Can I help you, Mr. Alistair?" I gesture to the desk, silently indicating that I'm not moving.

The room goes silent.

I hear someone whimpering on my behalf.

Fear trips down my spine, but I force my chin up and pretend that I'm not sweating out seventy percent of the water in my body.

Alistair's back stiffens. He turns slowly, his jaw clenching. "Did I not make myself clear yesterday?"

Which part of yesterday's conversation is he referring to? The part where he said *'when you walk through that door, leave your opinions, your thoughts, and your dignity behind'*? Because I'm definitely not subscribing to that advice.

"Walking out here to collect you is already a waste of my time." His voice remains even, but his tone is like flames against my back.

I hate him.

I hate him with every breath in my body.

"You should have called…" I tip my cell phone up. To my surprise, there are missed calls from an unknown number.

His, I presume.

Okay. My bad.

I meet his stare head-on because something deep inside won't allow me to cower to this man.

"I'll be sure to check my company email more often." I lift my phone. "But I had no understanding that I was expected to run when you called."

His eyebrows fall into thick, black lines and I know I messed up. Royally.

"Miss Jones, don't make me repeat myself." He turns and marches down the hallway.

I rise slowly. My limbs are as heavy as lead.

I've only been called to the principal's office once in my life. Because of my part-time job, I was late to school, missed assignments and did poorly on tests. When my homeroom teacher announced that the principal wanted to see me, it shocked the class and made my pride shrivel up and die.

Everyone knew me as the good girl.

I don't get called out.

Not unless it's for an accolade.

My steps are hesitant. Shuffling behind Holland Alistair is way, *way* worse than my high school trek to the principal's office.

My co-workers are reluctant spectators. They offer looks of pity mixed with silent sighs. *They're* not the sacrificial lamb today and they're happy about it. Where's the solidarity?

My fingers slip over my phone as sweat makes my hands clammy. I have three missed calls from Alistair's number. Each try must have sent my boss flying over the edge.

Damage control, Kenya.

I make my case as soon as we're in his office. Locking the door behind me, I fly toward his desk. "I can explain."

He takes a seat and looks at me through stony, hazel eyes. "Open the door."

"What?"

He points to the entrance. "The door."

My lips tighten in annoyance. I will *never* get used to that condescending tone of his. Stomping over to the door, I wrench it open. *Happy?*

He points to the chair. No good morning. No 'how's your day going?' Nothing.

It's not like I expect him to make small talk, but pointing at the chair like I'm a dog who moves on his command is not going to work.

I remain standing. "What would you like to discuss?"

He doesn't press me to sit. Instead, he opens a binder and flips through it. I watch him, hating myself for noticing how good he looks with glasses on. They perch on the edge of his straight nose, softening his otherwise deadly charisma.

He's wearing a simple button-down with the sleeves rolled up at the cuffs. They expose his strong forearms and the thick veins running down to giant hands.

It really, *really* sucks that he's so gorgeous.

I can't even hate him in peace.

"Did you receive the files on the Yazmite location?"

"Yes, I did." I clasp my hands together.

He glances up impatiently as if he expects more.

"I'm still getting acquainted with the numbers."

"Still getting acquainted?" He flings his glasses off his nose carelessly. I wince on the spectacle's behalf. He could probably afford to buy a million of those, but he should still treat his eyewear with care.

"Yesterday was about getting the lay of the land. I wanted a feel of the way they do things."

He accepts the answer with a gruff nod. "What was your assessment?"

"I found that the managers were…" I think of their scowling faces when I walked in, "less than cooperative, so I don't have any concrete thoughts. Since it was my first time meeting with them, I observed their system and made some notes."

"And?"

"I'd like to have a proper conversation with them before I implement any changes. That's why, today, I plan to hold a meeting with them."

For the first time, the evil laser beam screaming from his eyes softens. "A meeting? To discuss what?"

"What they think the problems are."

"We have our own reports," he points out.

"I saw that."

"And?"

"And what?"

His eyes narrow again. "The reports have all the information you need to know. I don't require further investigation. I need solutions."

"The answers sent in to corporate are often prettied up by management. They don't want you to know how bad things are in case you blame them for the issues. That lack of trust is what makes those reports undependable. How can I solve something based on only half the truth?"

"You're overthinking this. The bottom line is they're not making money."

"Yes, and you as the owner, are focused on that. But while making money is the end goal for the company, it's just a byproduct for the employees."

"And how do you plan to fix that?"

"I don't know yet." I can't keep the annoyance from my tone.

His lips disappear into his mouth.

My fingers are about to snap from how hard I'm clutching my fists. It's clear that we rub each other the wrong way, but he's still my boss. I agreed to be here and I want to do a good job.

I've been working since I was in high school and I haven't taken a single break since. I might not have the education, but I have more than enough experience.

"You hired me for your own reasons," I watch him carefully and he doesn't even blink, "but the moment you handed the reins over to someone like me, it must mean that you're willing to try something new."

He stares at me, processing everything I'm saying.

"I know the management companies you hired have approached the problem from a different perspective. They obviously didn't do a good job or you wouldn't be taking such desperate measures. Although I believe in data as much as everyone else, I think talking to the managers firsthand will give me a better understanding of what the real problem is."

"I want a report written by the end of the day."

"Fine."

"I also want a proposal backed by data as well as a written assessment of future growth projections."

"I have a meeting today."

"I'm aware," he says coldly.

Frustration bubbles in my gut. Does he expect me to skip lunch and work until midnight?

"Is there a problem, Miss Jones?" He shoots me a pointed look.

I'm really starting to believe he hired me just to exact his revenge. My tongue burns with the need to tell him off, but he's spared by a knock at the door.

Ezekiel eases the door open and nods at me.

"You're back," Alistair says, picking up a document and inspecting it.

Ezekiel sets a stack of folders on the desk. "These are the original patent documentation as requested. Our lawyers sent the cease and desist letter to the address we discussed."

"Thank you." Alistair points in my direction without glancing up. "See her out."

"I can walk on my own," I snap.

His head whips up. "You tend to do exactly what you want, Miss Jones. I can never predict when you'll follow directions."

I'm going to punch his face.

One day.

Maybe soon.

My hand will take control and it'll ram right into his perfect jaw.

Ezekiel turns to me. "Miss Jones, do you need any assistance setting up your computer? You went straight to the store yesterday, and I didn't have a chance to get you familiar with the system."

My scowl eases. "Do you have time now? I would really appreciate it."

"Let's go." He gestures to the door.

Eager to escape Holland Alistair's presence, I stomp out of his lux office. For all the fancy amenities in there, he might as well be in a dark dungeon with the skulls and bones of his victims littered everywhere. It would suit him better.

Ezekiel gives me a warm smile. "He's not as gruff as he seems."

I stare at the executive assistant, wondering if the old man has been turned. Maybe his brain is sitting in Alistair's evil lair right now, bouncing around in a jar of brain juice.

"Tell me the truth. Did he hire me just to punish me for what happened at Belle's Beauty?" My hands slam against my hips. "It's so obvious he has it out for me."

"Alistair is not that petty." Ezekiel gestures to his desk. It's a nice piece of furniture that's set up just outside of the Grump's office. "You can have a seat."

I fall into the soft chair. "You're right. 'Petty' is too tame a word for what he is. Monster is probably better suited." I realize what I've said and freeze. It's probably not a good idea to go badmouthing the boss to the only co-worker who bothers to speak to me.

Thankfully, Ezekiel chuckles. Which tells me he has a much better sense of humor than his employer.

"He's demanding. That's undeniable. I understand why it can get frustrating for anyone who isn't used to his style of leadership."

"There's a 'but' coming, isn't there?" I groan.

Ezekiel's straight-laced expression shifts to a softer one. "He's juggling two very big companies and he doesn't want to see either of them fail. It's why he walks around with that hard exterior. He has no time to coddle anyone. One mistake and all the plates he's spinning will crash. All the people who depend on his company will suffer. It's a lot to put on a thirty-two year old's shoulders."

"He can quit."

"'Quit' is not in his vocabulary. Once he puts his mind to something, he'll tear himself apart trying to get it done."

"He'll tear us apart too," I mumble.

Ezekiel laughs again. "He might."

"I'm surprised he has anyone who'd take up for him when he's not around," I say.

"Don't let the snapping and growling fool you. Alistair is feeling a lot of pressure right now. It was a hard decision to keep Belle's Beauty open after…"

My eyes seek his out when he snaps his mouth shut. "After what?"

"Nothing." He opens his laptop and swivels it to face me. "The important thing is that he believes in you and your abilities."

"Didn't we establish that I'm here as punishment?"

"Everything Alistair does is calculated for the good of the company. Nothing matters to him more than seeing Belle's Beauty thrive."

"Is that why no management company wants to work with him?" The reports I've been thumbing through told the frustrations of each management team. There were at least five different logos on the binders. And I haven't gotten through all the files yet.

"Yes, he's been through a lot of management companies, but it's only because he has high expectations and they couldn't meet them. I assure you, if you take the time to catch his vision, he'd have no choice but to acknowledge you."

I fold my arms over my chest, picking apart everything Ezekiel said. One approval from the guy who works closest to Alistair is not enough to change my mind about his wicked ways.

"It's alright if you don't believe me. In fact, I admire that. I think you have exactly what it takes to turn things around."

"You do?" I lean forward. After being torn down by Alistair, any drop of encouragement is like a bottle of water to a dying man.

"Professionalism is his weapon. It takes a special kind of person to rattle him. You do." Ezekiel taps something on his computer and brings up the spreadsheets that were giving me a headache out in my cubicle. "Those management companies didn't stick around long enough because they couldn't work with him. The constant stops and starts is why Belle's Beauty hasn't been able to grow. If you can stick it out, you'll be leagues ahead of them."

"That's if I can make it. It's my second day and I've already gotten on his bad side." I sigh loudly. "Although it feels like he *only* has bad sides."

"Mr. Alistair is fair, and he rewards good work. I've never met an employer who's as generous as he is. If you do well, he'll respect you. It's really that simple."

I think about the load of work he assigned me. "It feels like he's purposely trying to keep me from doing well."

"Then fight back. That spunk of yours comes from somewhere, doesn't it?"

I lift my head. "Beat him at his own game?"

"No one else could do it. They ran when it got tough. You didn't. From the moment you met him, you were fighting. That's why you're here." He tips his chin at me. "So what are you going to do about it?"

It feels like a pep talk from a boxing coach. I'm on the mat, bleeding all over my body, but the adrenaline rush is enough to push me back into the ring.

Ezekiel pats my shoulder warmly. Holland Alistair has someone willing to paint him in nicer colors. I don't see myself doing that. Ever. But I want that elusive prize of his respect. Not because I'm in need of his approval but because I want him to eat his words. I want to show him he was wrong to toy with me.

My personal life is going to hell and everything I touch keeps spiraling out of my control. I might not be able to face my sister, and I still haven't gotten my things out of Drake's apartment, but I can take the bull by the horns at work.

It's going to cost me a few rounds with the dragon, but I'm ready.

Let's get the Yazmite store back in order.

* * *

I TAKE the bus to the high-end shopping center, my notebook filled with scribbles from Ezekiel's crash course in business management.

He knows how to break things down in a digestible manner and I plan to go home and study everything I learned today until it becomes second nature.

Just because I've graduated, it doesn't mean I've stopped studying.

"Excuse me. Sorry." I weave through the crowds hustling into the mall.

This late in the afternoon, the shopping center is filled with office workers looking to grab a quick bite before heading back to work.

I haul my purse higher on my shoulder and take the escalator to Belle's Beauty.

According to the files Ezekiel provided this morning, the Yazmite location is the oldest in the company. There are only three locations completely dedicated to Belle's Beauty products.

The other stores sell products on contract. The problem with that strategy is Belle's Beauty has to compete with a hundred other skin care lines.

Competing for shelf space can be ruthless. Belle's Beauty isn't a household name yet and paying for premier space isn't just about money. Those spots are reserved for bigger brands that can draw a crowd.

Since I'm more acquainted with *that* type of consignment-based production, it gives me an interesting perspective on the Yazmite store's downward spiral.

Surely, if Belle's Beauty is selling well in general makeup stores, an entire space dedicated to the company products should be doing better, right?

At least, that's what Holland Alistair expects.

I step into the store and one of the clerks walks up to me. "Hello there. Welcome to Belle's Beauty. Can I help you?"

"Yeah, um…" I stare at her, unable to place her face. I stopped by yesterday and met everyone, but I didn't see her. "I'm sorry. Were you working yesterday? I don't recognize you."

Her big brown eyes get wide. "Oh, I was hired yesterday."

"You were hired *yesterday*?"

She nods.

My eyebrows pull together. There was no discussion about firing anyone when I visited. "Did someone quit?"

"Uh…" She glances around as if she's not sure she should be discussing this with a customer.

"Oh, I'm Kenya Jones. I'm the executive assistant in charge of Belle's Beauty." I don't have a business card, so I just show her my company ID.

Her eyes get wide. "You're in charge?"

"I work directly for Mr. Alistair." My smile is awkward. "I look young, right?"

"No, it's just… they said the new assistant was some airhead who's probably sleeping with the boss—" She gasps and slaps a hand over her mouth. "I'm so sorry."

My eyes shift around the store as I try to hide my smile. It's nice to know what the managers really think of me. An airhead, huh? I guess that's a compliment. Most people look at me and assume I'm a nerd.

Which I am.

A proud one.

But that part about screwing Alistair? If only she knew how much Holland Alistair loathes me. She wouldn't jump to such ridiculous conclusions. That man would rather run me over with a truck than invite me to his bed.

Not that I want to be in his bed anyway.

Okay, maybe I wouldn't mind seeing him shirtless because *come on*, that would be glorious, but Holland Alistair topless is as far as I'll go!

"Miss Jones." One of the managers hustles toward me. She's a big-boned woman with fair skin, black hair tied into a bun and bright red lips. "I didn't expect you back so soon."

"I said we were having a meeting today."

"Well, you see. We're a little busy right now."

I glance around at the empty store. There are throngs of people downstairs. Shoppers are also passing up and down in front of the location, but none of them have stopped in Belle's Beauty.

She gives me a condescending smile. "I'm afraid we'll have to reschedule."

"No, we're not."

Her eyes widen. She didn't expect me to be firm. Understandable. I don't present myself as coldly as Holland Alistair does.

I nod to the new clerk but keep my eyes on the manager. "What happened after I left yesterday?"

"I don't know what you're talking about," she says sourly.

"That's fine. I can jog your memory if need be. We'll have our managers meeting in the lounge."

"Why?"

"Why the lounge or why the meeting?"

"Why the meeting?"

I stop and turn around. "Because I asked you. Nicely."

She stares me down.

I glare right back. Sure, she might be older than me, but it doesn't matter. Holland Alistair is breathing down my neck and I have something to prove. That means I'm on business from day one.

I wait for her to back down first.

She does, her gaze squirreling away from mine. "We'll be there."

I nod.

After settling my things in the lounge, I notice the door opening and all the employees walking in.

My eyes widen. "I didn't ask to meet with the clerks. Only the management."

"They need to hear whatever you have to say too," the head manager snaps at me.

I frown, trying not to let my annoyance show. They're employees. Just like me. It's not that I'm better than them. In fact, they're probably more knowledgeable about this space than me, but we need to at least respect each other before any progress can be made.

"I only asked for the management team," I repeat myself clearly, in case she didn't understand the first time.

"And I believe that it's imperative for the rest of them to be here as well."

My fuse gets a little shorter. I stare her down. "I know that I look small and smiley, but please don't misinterpret that as a weakness. I know when to be sweet and when to flip the switch." Keeping my tone light, I tilt my head. "Please don't let me bring that other side out this early on in our cooperation. I'd really like to keep things pleasant."

She stands her ground, glaring at me without moving an inch.

"If you insist on being stubborn, I can make a call to HQ right now." I lift my phone like a robber announcing he has a bomb. "And you can take up any complaints with Mr. Alistair himself."

I'm sweating beneath Sunny's yellow jacket. She lent me the piece since I don't have any clothes fancy enough to fit in at Fine Industries.

The manager licks her lips and stares at the phone. I'm afraid she'll call my bluff, but she doesn't. Shoulders slumped, she gestures for the clerks to return outside.

I let out a giant breath, my heart still hammering my ribs. "Please sit down."

The sound of chairs scraping the tiles is all that breaks the silence. I pull my fingers beneath the table and squeeze my hands together.

"First, I'd like to know why an employee left yesterday," I say.

The head manager stares straight ahead with an expression of pure annoyance on her face. "She wasn't a good worker anyway."

"I don't understand. All the clerks seemed to be in high spirits when I introduced myself yesterday."

"That's because you're basically one of them," someone mumbles.

I hold my tongue and pretend not to hear.

The head manager leans back and throws an arm over her chair. Getting more and more comfortable, she motions to me. "It's hard for kids these days to understand the value of hard work. They just want to play on their phones and lazy around." Her eyes slide over my body. "Or they want to sleep their way to the top."

The other two managers murmur their agreement.

I ignore the dig because it's pointless gossip. "Let's say the kids are lazy. What are *you* doing when those workers are on the phone?"

Her eyes widen, but it only lasts a second. She glances away as if my words mean nothing.

I drum my fingers on the table. "You all know the store is doing poorly. It's why I'm here." My eyes dart to the other managers. "In your opinion, what is the biggest problem?"

"The new hires."

"What about them?"

"They never stay long enough to make a difference."

I bob my head. "I did notice the turnover rate was high."

"It's 'cause nobody wants to work anymore. Kids these days are too privileged. Too many participation trophies. It's softened them."

I don't buy it. Clerks at this store keep leaving. It can't be because *all* of them are lazy and irresponsible. When I was working, I met my share of disinterested co-workers, but it was mostly because the manager didn't care either.

"Okay. The new hires," I say, going along with them. "What other problems are you facing?"

The head manager folds her arms over her chest. "Aren't they paying *you* to tell us what's wrong?"

"No." There's a little more heat in my voice because she's getting on my nerves. "I want *you* to figure it out."

"Me?"

"Yes. You gave me one reason." I gesture with my hands. "Every single person who walks through those doors and applies for a position is lazy. The clerks are the biggest problem. Fine. What else?"

They exchange looks.

Good.

I want them to hear my sarcasm.

One of the other managers pipes up. "We don't have a proper system in place."

The other managers glare at her.

She shrugs. "It's true."

"That's good. A sales system. What do you think you should do to improve that?"

They go quiet.

I let the silence stretch. The head manager is pouting, but it's the kind of petulance I want to see. They're not idiots. It's plain to them that they can't throw blame at the entry level workers and skate off into the sunset.

Pressing them, I insist. "What's wrong with the sales system?"

"I don't think we're doing anything wrong."

I try not to roll my eyes. Maybe that was acceptable to the management teams that came before me. A bunch of business snobs might be more eager to jump on the 'blame the little guy' train. But since I am still technically a little guy, I'm not drunk on arrogance.

I've been in many positions where the *management* was the lazy, irresponsible party. Even if they weren't, if we had a good manager, the store thrived. With a bad manager, no matter how good the employees were, things always fell apart.

I rise from the table and walk as I speak. "'*The wife is the mirror of the husband*'. I read that in a book somewhere."

They look at me like I'm crazy.

I keep going anyway. "This doesn't just apply to marriages but to all kinds of relationships. The connection between a manager and the employees is like a mirror. And what the workers are reflecting is telling me they'd rather be anywhere in the world than with you."

Huffs of outrage pop around the table, but no one speaks.

"While you might be getting a steady paycheck, the part-time workers are not. They don't *have* to stay here. They didn't sign a contract." I pull my hands behind my back. "But you need them. *We* need them. They're an important part of the conversation and they need to have a voice."

"So why aren't they here?" The head manager glares at me. "When I tried to bring them in, you kicked them out!"

"Because I'm not the one who needs to collaborate with them."

She goes quiet.

"You said you don't have a proper system, so make one." I press my palms against the table and lean over. "Come together with your staff, put forward your best tactics and implement them."

She rolls her eyes. "Fine."

"Great. We're on the same page. I'd like you to have that meeting today and then implement the changes. Evaluate those tactics in the next three days and send me a report."

"What do you mean send you a report?"

I ignore her outburst. "I've seen the files from the previous management companies. Things have gotten bad because communication is breaking down right at this critical point." I gesture to the managers. "Another problem is that sales tactics get handed down from the sales team, but they don't always fit. One line on a sheet of paper sometimes can't be translated in real life." I know. I've seen some random crap thrown at me while I was a clerk. Those initiatives were clearly the work of pencil pushers trying to look relevant with no idea how grass-roots sales works. "The reports are to evaluate whether those tactics are effective. It's also to have a proper record so we can track their value over time."

The managers squirm in their seats.

"One more thing." I straighten. "We only tackled two problems today, but I'm sure you can find some more. I'm willing to listen to whatever other issues you have and I'm also willing to work with you to find a solution." I glance at each of them. "I have your back."

Someone huffs. "Yeah right."

"We're all working together for the same goal. We're on the same team. And the better you do, the better I do."

The head manager still looks annoyed, but the other two seem a bit more encouraged. I don't know if it's their first time dealing with a sales manager like me, but at least they're not protesting.

I check my watch and nod. "That's it."

"That's it?" The head manager raises an eyebrow.

"Yes." I smile. "Oh, I do have one more thing. I've really gotten into this online series about leadership and vision. I'll make a group chat and send you a link. Study it and send me some ideas for the store based on the lessons."

"You're giving us homework?" The head manager bursts out laughing.

I don't join in.

Neither do the other two.

"What exactly are you being paid to do?" I ask calmly.

She scowls at me. "To manage this store."

"Which means what?" I tilt my head. "Barking orders at people?"

Her eyes shift away.

"You're being paid more than those store clerks, not because you're better than them but because you're supposed to be thinking differently than them." I point to my temple. "You're *leading* this place. Now, I don't know all the answers, but that's why we study. To learn."

She purses her lips, visibly annoyed.

As silence washes over the room, my phone buzzes with a call.

It's Felice.

I quickly pick up my purse because I've done more than enough for one morning. If I push the managers any more, it'll be too much.

Stepping briskly out of the store, I place the phone to my ear. "Hey, Felice."

"Why aren't you picking up your sister's calls?" she shrieks.

My eyes widen. I pull the phone away from my face and stare at it in shock. Is she for real right now?

"Felice, I don't know what Sasha told you but—"

"She's crying every night, Kenya. You're breaking her heart."

My steps slow. "What about what she did to break mine?"

"Meet up with her. Let her explain. You can't keep avoiding her. It's not good for her health."

That guilt-tipped arrow lands right where it's supposed to.

"I'll think about it," I say.

And then I hang up.

CHAPTER 6
GREAT TEMPTATION

HOLLAND

EZEKIEL slams the coffee mug next to my files and looks down with a disapproving frown. His chin firm, he hovers around the desk, not saying anything.

My fingers slow on the keyboard. "Your eyes are boring into my skull."

"My apologies."

"Spit it out."

"Are you sleeping well?" He clasps his hands behind his back and stares through the window like he's contemplating the wonders of life.

The view outside is gorgeous. It's a balmy day. The sky is a limitless blue. The sun is bright. The clouds are wispy.

It's nice.

But it's not worth that much scrutiny.

"Why are you asking?"

"Your brother-in-law called."

Damn. "Tell him I'm busy."

"He's insisting."

I'm not surprised. Darrel is Claire's older brother and, just like she did, he believes it is his personal responsibility to fix all that's broken inside me.

"You can't keep avoiding him."

"I'll try as hard as I can."

Ezekiel sighs.

I expect him to leave, but he doesn't.

Dropping my pen on the table, I massage my wrist. "What?"

He grunts. "Nothing."

"It's clear something's on your mind. Get it out so I can focus."

He frowns at me. "On her first day, you assigned our worst-performing store. Was that a tactical decision?"

It doesn't take a genius to figure out he's referring to Kenya Jones.

"You have a problem with that?"

"No." He spits out the word like he just sucked on a lemon slice. "I'm trying to figure out what you're thinking."

"She tripled sales at the Darwin location with nothing but her charisma and wit. I hired her to invigorate our sales quota. She has more tools at her disposal now. It's not a reach."

"That's bull. You're throwing her off the deep end."

"It's a strategy."

"Effective." He scoffs.

"You're not usually this sarcastic."

"I'm still unsure of your intentions."

"You doubt me?"

"Not to your face."

My eyes narrow. Kenya Jones is rubbing off on the old man. Now Ezekiel is starting to make smart comments too.

"Do you want her to prove herself or do you want her to fail?"

My fingers drum the table. Unlike other employees, Ezekiel doesn't flinch in the face of my ire. He's grown numb to my growling, but there are times I wish it was more effective. Like right now.

"She thinks you're punishing her."

"When has it ever mattered what an employee thinks about my conduct?" I grumble.

"You're the one who hired her despite the fact that she has no formal training or experience. Expecting her to outperform the professional management companies on her first try is—"

"I have high expectations of everyone. No matter who they are."

"A more official orientation would have been helpful. Half the workers in this building don't know what she's doing here."

I return my attention to my laptop. I can't believe he interrupted me for a topic like this. "Should I have gathered the welcoming committee and thrown a party?"

"Of course not. If we threw welcoming parties every time you changed your staff, we'd go bankrupt."

"That was then. I'm more involved in the details now."

"Exactly why I feel I must speak up. You're harder on her than you were on the professionals."

I glare at him. "Are you intentionally trying to get on my nerves or is there a point to this?"

"It's her second day."

"I'm aware." He has no idea how much. I'm in-tune to everything about Miss Jones. My traitorous brain has decided there is something about *her* that I must have. I can't seem to get her out of my head, which is unendingly irritating.

She's stubborn. Aggressive. Beautiful.

Her dramatic entrance in my dreams is already a concern.

I've never had a change in my recurring nightmare. It's always the same. Claire smiling. Me walking out the door. Blood on my hands.

My own personal hell.

Yet, last night, Kenya barged into my subconscious mind just like she barges into everything.

Because of her, I fell to a new low.

For the first time in my adult life, I stalked someone.

It turns out Miss Jones is very open about her private life. Her social media accounts are public and she has a plethora of photos showing her and her boyfriend.

The moment I saw the shots of him, I wanted to smash something.

Even now, I'm still annoyed.

She's taken.

Damn it.

I shouldn't be thinking about her at all, but now I *know* I can't let her get to me. She belongs to someone else, and I don't believe in breaking up relationships to get what I want. Even a brute like me has lines he won't cross.

I grit my teeth and twirl my pen around my fingertips. I thought I was making progress, but Ezekiel's concerns have exposed the truth. Despite my best intentions, Miss Jones is still in my head.

This is a problem.

She is a problem.

I'm beginning to wonder if it's worth the hassle of keeping her around. "What are you really asking?"

"I need to know if I should begin looking for another management company."

"You think she's that weak?"

"I think the odds are stacked against her."

Keeping my expression contained so Ezekiel won't catch wind of my turbulent thoughts, I slip my glasses off my nose and set them aside. "You're right. I ignored her lack of credentials when I handed her this position. That means Miss Jones has more to prove than any other employee. I've given her a big job, but the *real* task of managing all of Belle's Beauty stores is a much larger one. I need to test her now before we waste time on someone who can't handle the pressure."

"Is that all?" His eyes fasten on me. "You're just preparing her for a bigger job?"

My gaze moves away from his.

"She's naive but goodhearted. I don't want to see her spirit broken."

I frown. "You're getting soft in your old age, Ezekiel."

"And you're getting colder." He picks up a stack of binders from the table and starts to leave.

I call him back. "I'm not expecting Miss Jones to return until late this evening, but let me know when she arrives."

He nods and leaves.

Opening a spreadsheet in the Belle's Beauty files, I glance over the numbers and frown when I notice the records only go back to the last two years.

My fault.

The management company I hired functioned independently for too long. I didn't even read their reports. It was easier to block them out while I adjusted to life without Claire. In those first few months, I couldn't even look at the Belle's Beauty logo, much less steer the company.

My lack of involvement shows. Claire's company is failing and that is on my head. I will do everything to bring it back to the glory she envisioned.

Starting with the details.

I need those files. We can get a better picture of profit trends if we have all the information, and I want to make sure we're not repeating tactics that have failed.

I'm about to forward the spreadsheet, along with my concerns, to Ezekiel when he knocks on the door.

My eyebrows hike. "Yes?"

"Miss Jones is back, sir."

"So soon?"

"Yes, sir."

I wrap my fingers around the coffee mug and take a sip. It's still hot. It hasn't been that long since Ezekiel brought it to me and it hasn't been that long since Miss Jones left for the meeting at the Yazmite location.

What could she have accomplished in so little time?

GRUMPY ROMANCE

I lean back and stare at the artwork on my wall. It's of a ship crashing into a giant wave. Weary and stalwart, it forges ahead despite the storm. I would hope it's synonymous with my journey.

"Do you want me to call her in?"

I shake my head.

A small chirp fills the room. It's my email alerting me to a new message.

To: Holland Alistair
From: Kenya Jones
Subject: Yazmite Project Update

Mr. Alistair,

First, I'm incredibly grateful for the opportunity to jump right into work. Your decision to assign me the most difficult store reveals your thoughts about me. Please be assured. I'm happy to rise to the challenge.

A smile climbs on my face as I read. Each word is polite and yet I can hear her tone in my head, slathering every sentence in sarcasm and a sly, underlining defiance. Even her use of superlatives reeks of attitude.

Second, kindly review the report I attached for your consideration. The initiative is underway and the managers will be sending a summary every three days for me to review. When I receive that information, I will organize it and forward it to you.

Interesting strategy. Engaging the managers is a tactic I would have used myself.

As you requested, I've also attached a spreadsheet with our growth projections. I leaned heavily on the calculations made by the previous management, but I increased the margins because I like a challenge.

I laugh out loud.

I've also requested a budget for the cost of in-store promotions and sample bottles. In the coming weeks, we will be organizing an event for the store.

If you have any concerns, please hesitate to contact me.

REGARDS,
Kenya Jones
Belle's Beauty Team

I READ and reread the last line of her email again. Every other word in the message was carefully chosen.

Please hesitate to call me?

It could be a mistake, but why do I get the feeling that it was intentionally left there?

Intrigued, I click on the report that's attached and read through it. It's far more literary and engaging than I expected. I can see Kenya Jones's Lit degree poking its head out of her prose.

My cheeks hurt from smiling. I have to stop to gather my thoughts before continuing to read.

Rather than a staid and to-the-point summary, her language is colorful. I find myself racing through the report like a story, and then I realize I don't remember any of the pertinent information.

Rubbing my face to rid it of the grin, I pick up my phone and call Ezekiel. "Send Miss Jones to my office."

Two minutes later, Miss Jones knocks on my door. Sunshine follows her in. In fact, she's wrapped in it. The mustard jacket is exquisite on her dark brown skin. Dazzling.

Her hair is pulled back, much like it was the day she beat my fern to death. The only difference is that, today, she has a thick ponytail with tight curls falling to her collar.

Her face is composed, but her eyes give her away. I can read them like JavaScript and I like that. It's boring when everyone's too careful around me.

She walks into the room with gumption. Her expressive brown eyes fall on me and stay there. A challenge.

I don't meet her stare. I'm too busy gawking at her. Same as I did when I saw her earlier this morning.

She's wearing a skirt that looks like it was painted on. The dark fabric hugs her legs and stretches as she walks, drawing the eye to her generous backside.

My chest rearranges as I imagine drawing a line down the seam of her skirt and teasing the skin beneath the fabric.

I pull my hands under the desk and form tight fists. These are *not* thoughts I should be having about my new assistant.

Especially this one.

The one in my dreams.

The one with a boyfriend.

I set my face into a severe scowl. I'm aware that I'm staring too hard at Kenya, but shifting this expression will give my thoughts away. And I can't have my new employee sniffing out how much I want to touch her.

Her gaze peels away from mine as I frown harder. It's a small capitulation, but it tilts control back in my corner. Where it belongs.

I shake my head. "Why aren't you at the Yazmite location?"

"I've finished what I had to do with them."

"In so short a time?" Disapproval rings in my voice.

"That store doesn't need more than a couple hours to straighten out."

Her confidence attacks my composure. My eyebrow jumps before I rearrange my expression into a blank slate.

She's being cocky. The Yazmite location is like a bucket with a giant hole. Money drops into that store, never to be seen again.

The management companies I hired had a similar arrogance. Some months, their tactics seemed promising, but their sales would eventually decline. There is no way Kenya Jones could have solved those problems in a couple hours.

"Didn't you read my report?" Her tone is scolding.

"I read it." I fold my fingers together. "And that's another problem."

"What do you mean?"

"Your report was too…" I gesture with my hands. "Flowery."

"Flowery?"

"Say what you need to say quickly. Without all the fancy language. You're not writing a book report."

Her brown lips pull in and I can tell she's imagining my demise. Perhaps she's thinking of bumping my chair into the window and having it crack, while I plummet to my death. Or maybe its something a little more personal? A pen to the throat.

I train my lips not to smile. Keeping my voice harsh, I lecture her. "It's clear you've never written a proper report before, but you don't get any points for how creative you can be. I don't want to see anything like that nonsense again. Understood?"

Her lips disappear inside her mouth while her nostrils double in size.

I arch an eyebrow.

She delivers a tight, "Yes."

"Good. Now regarding the store, whether you manage them from the office or on-site, I expect results. If anything goes wrong, I will hold *you* responsible."

She jerks her chin down.

"The fact that you returned early is a failure in my eyes. A store in such a dire state needs micromanagement—"

"That's where we disagree."

I gesture for her to continue.

"It's crippling to micromanage every store in the franchise. If you want a handicapped staff and a manager stretched thin, we can do that. But I believe we can work smarter rather than harder."

I lean back in my chair and place my hands over my stomach. Her resolve is surprising. I find my admiration jumping a couple notches.

"You have store managers for a reason. Either you have competent people in those leadership positions or not. I'm giving them a chance to prove their competence or improve it if that's the need."

"Even so, you're being hasty." She starts to open her mouth and I lift a hand to stall her protest. "But I'll wait for data to back up my suspicions before I make my conclusions."

"How benevolent of you," she mutters.

I hear it clearly, but I don't address it. "Since you're in need of something to do," I slide the stack of files on my desk toward her, "I have another task."

She stares at it. "What is that?"

"These are physical files related to Belle's Beauty. Ezekiel will give you a key to the file room where you'll find the rest of the documents."

Her eyebrows sink together as she tries to figure out what I'm asking her to do.

I tap the stack of files. "Record-keeping was not a priority in the early days of Belle's Beauty and that's a problem that *you* are going to rectify."

She stabs a dark finger at her chest. "Me?"

"The Belle's Beauty files are a mess. There are loose sheets, receipts, reports, and other things I can't remember. I want them all digitized by midnight..."

Her jaw drops. "Midnight? You just said there were *years* worth of files."

"You didn't let me finish."

"Oh." She lets out a breath.

"By midnight next week Friday."

Her eyes widen. "In ten days?"

"Do you have a problem?"

She sucks in a deep breath and shakes her head. "No."

I wave her out.

She turns stiffly and marches to the door.

My eyes catch on my mug. Perhaps I'm a little wicked when I grab it and say, "Oh, before you leave," I shake the cup, "I'd like some coffee."

Flames shoot to life in her eyes, but she bites her tongue.

Sure, I may be pushing it too far. Not just with the coffee but with the deadline for her task. There's no way she can get it done in time.

Then again, she just might surprise me. Humans break their own personal records when they're pushed to the brink. Applying pressure can unearth a diamond.

If Kenya Jones has the guts she showed me that day at Belle's Beauty HQ, then she'll rise to the challenge.

Or she'll break.

And I'll be free of her distracting presence around the office.

She snaps the cup from me. In a sickly-sweet voice, she croons, "No problem, Mr. Alistair."

When she's gone, I call Ezekiel to take the files off my desk and move them to the storage room. He doesn't say anything about my actions, but I know he's displeased.

Too bad.

I'm having a great time.

Kenya returns to my office with a steaming cup of coffee on a tray.

"Here you go, Mr. Alistair," she says, her eyes betraying how much she detests me.

I nod to the desk. "There."

She sets it down lightly, tilts the cup so the handle is facing just so, and steps back. The forced smile remains on her face, but one glance at her fingers show them gripping the tray like she wants to break it over my head, karate style.

"Ezekiel will show you to the storage room now."

"Okay." She nods and moves backward.

When she's gone, I pull the coffee to my nose and sniff. The scent is strong. Steam rises from the hot black liquid. I prefer my coffee sweetened until it's a shell of its former self, but I feel no need to tell her that.

There's no way I'm drinking this coffee.

Oddly satisfied, I dive into my work and only emerge when Ezekiel brings a tray from the canteen and forces me to eat a bite.

The day gets hotter and hotter as I swing between meetings for Fine Industries and Belle's Beauty. Now that I've taken on the work of the management companies, there's a lot to catch up on.

Hours later, I slide my hands through my hair and check the time. My eyes widen when I see the clock glaring at me. A glance at the window confirms the sun has gone down.

My eyes are bleary and I cover my mouth as a yawn pops my jaw. Stepping away from the desk to stretch my legs, I call Mrs. Hansley.

She picks up my video call and points the phone at Belle.

"Daddy!" Belle shrieks, waving green and red-stained fingers.

I smile. "Were you painting, Belle?"

"Mm-hm." She bobs her head. "I paint for you!"

"I'm excited to see it. Can you show me?"

"Not yet."

"Ah." I grin broadly.

Mrs. Hansley rubs Belle's hair. "Another late night, Alistair?"

"I don't think I'll be there in time to tuck her in."

"I'll take care of it." She pulls Belle close and kisses her cheek. "What do you think, Belle? Should we make mac and cheese for dinner?"

My daughter grins from ear to ear. "Yeah!"

I laugh softly. Belle's meals are catered everyday, but she'd eat five bowls of mac and cheese a week rather than indulge in her perfectly balanced meals.

"Daddy will be home late tonight," I tell her, holding the phone away from me. "But I'll come in and kiss you goodnight as soon as I get back."

"Okay. Bye, daddy."

"Bye." My heart melts as I watch her wiggle her fingers.

It kills me that I can't spend more time with her, but Claire wanted our daughter to have Belle's Beauty as her birthright. My lack of attention has been squandering the legacy she wanted to leave behind.

This frenzy won't last forever. For a short spurt, I'll reroute all my energy into reviving the business. When I'm through, Belle will reap the benefits for generations to come.

* * *

Hoping to move my body around, I open the door and head outside. The office is quiet and the hallway is dark.

Most of my employees have gone home.

I knock on the edge of Ezekiel's desk, smiling when he lifts his head and rubs his fists over his eyes.

"You can go home now."

"I leave when you do."

"I'm not leaving any time soon. I have to go over the latest data pull."

My *real* job starts after hours. Since so much of my day is dedicated to Belle's Beauty, I have to catch up on Fine Industries at night.

Ezekiel gives me a concerned look. "Managing the two companies is stretching you thin. When will you have time to sleep if you keep this up?"

"Who needs sleep?" I grin.

He shakes his head. "What about your daughter?"

"I asked Mrs. Hansley to stay over. She'll tuck her in tonight."

Ezekiel yawns loudly.

I nod to the exits. "Go on. If I need anything from you, I'll make a note of it."

"Alright." Ezekiel rises unsteadily and his watery eyes drop to my mug. "Did you want me to get you some coffee before you go?"

"It's alright. I'll drink water instead."

"I can get it for you." He reaches for the cup.

I haul it behind my back. "It's fine. I got it."

Ezekiel scowls, but he gives in and starts gathering his things. "By the way, your brother-in-law said to call and make an appointment tomorrow or he'll stop in for a visit."

"I can have him thrown out before he sets foot in the building."

"But you won't."

"No, I won't." Darrel might have changed career paths and taken on the mantle of neuropsychologist, but he's still wealthy and influential. I won't burn those bridges because he's turned into a nosy do-gooder.

I rub my chin. Between Kayla from Make It Marriage and my brother-in-law, I'm surrounded by people who tell me I have a problem.

Which I don't.

I'm perfectly fine as long as everything goes my way. That's a healthy life philosophy, isn't it?

Ezekiel dips his chin. "I'll see you tomorrow, sir."

I lift a hand in goodbye and head in the other direction. There's no way I can survive the night on water, so I plan to fix my own coffee.

Usually, I prefer Ezekiel's brew but, tonight, I'm willing to make an exception. My hours have gotten longer since I've taken over Belle's Beauty, and Ezekiel isn't getting any younger. I don't want to drag him down the path of over-exhaustion with me. One of us has to be clear-headed and sane.

Halfway to the kitchen, I hear what sounds like a parrot squawking in anger.

My steps halt and my curiosity spikes.

What was that?

I inch through the darkness.

My inspection leads me to the storage room.

The door is open slightly and a square of light falls on the carpet. A shadow dances on the floor.

"Baaabee! Baabee! Baabbee! No! I love youuuu! Don't gooo!"

My nose scrunches and I press my palm to the door, easing it open. To my surprise, I find Kenya sitting on the floor. Her heels are kicked off to the side and her skirt is bunched around her thighs, exposing creamy brown legs.

Boxes are mounted like giant walls around her, reminding me of the pillow fort Belle and I built when she was sick and bored at home.

A pair of headphones tucked into her ears, Kenya tosses her head back and forth and sings—if I can call that atrocious sound *singing*—in a muttered voice.

I cringe and step into the room. Her back is to me, so she's still unaware of my entrance.

"Uh, uh, yeah." Kenya grunts and dances wildly. She's seated and only her upper body is in motion, but I'm impressed by her rhythm.

The song must have shifted to her favorite part because she lifts her hands to her chest and starts pumping. Her back arches and she swings her head in a circle, grooving to the song with a surprising amount of passion.

I cover my mouth with a fist to muffle my laughter, but the sound alerts her to my presence.

She goes still. "Who's there?"

I say nothing.

She twists around in slow motion. The moment her eyes catch on me, she jumps so fast the documents spill from her hand and slide across the floor.

"Mr. Alistair." She vibrates like one of those cartoon cats after being electrocuted.

"Sorry. I didn't mean to scare you."

"What are you doing here?"

"Working." I nod to her. "Why are you still here?"

"I'm working too."

"Why?"

"What do you mean 'why'? *You* should know better than anyone."

I arch an eyebrow.

She glances away. "Sorry. Sarcasm pops out of me when I'm

tired."

"I won't hold it against you." She does look tired. Her hair's frizzier than it was when we spoke this morning and her lipstick has completely rubbed off.

Even exhaustion can't hide how attractive she is. Bare of makeup, her face is even more gorgeous.

Regret pricks me when I see her mouth open in a yawn. Perhaps I took things a little too far by making her work on this project alone. It's a three-man job and I hadn't accounted for all the heavy boxes she'd need to drag around.

"I'm just finishing up." Kenya gestures to the files.

I blink in shock. "Finishing up?"

"Mm-hm."

"Impossible." There is no way she's gone through all of these boxes.

Kenya climbs to her feet and winces when she straightens to her full height. Bending down to massage her leg, she explains, "I was going to stop at the end of the workday, but I was so deep into it by then that I couldn't."

I'm still trying to figure out if she's joking with me.

She keeps chatting. "Have you ever dreaded tackling a huge mess but, halfway into it, you kind of get this drive to finish cleaning until it's all gone? That's what happened to me. I knew if I pushed, I could get it all done before I go home."

I check my watch. It's late. "How can you be finished already?"

"I had help."

"Ezekiel?" Strange. I didn't see him leave his desk.

She points to a laptop on the ground. I didn't notice it before because it was hidden behind a stack of boxes. The laptop is hooked to her phone by a long, white wire.

"You used your laptop?"

"Oh, it's not just the laptop." She laughs and I can't believe how stunning she looks with a smile on her face. "I got a text-to-speech program."

"But what about the printed spreadsheets? Those tables need to be filled in manually."

"Right. I went looking and I found this software called Hoola Lens. You basically snap a picture of anything, words, tables, music notes. Whatever. And it'll rewrite it exactly in the digital format you choose. So the tables are in a spreadsheet with one snap of my phone."

"It's accurate?"

"Yes. I mean, it's technology, so it's not going to be perfect. After I take the photo, I go over the report to double-check the information. It's tedious, but it's much faster than typing it all out by hand. As *someone* wanted me to do."

Heat flushes my cheeks. The dig lands and I don't have a defense.

She tiptoes over the files to get back to her laptop. Somehow, seeing her bare feet feels intimate. Like a dance that's just for me. And I have to remind myself that I'm her boss. And she has a boyfriend. And she also hates me.

"I didn't know you were into tech."

"I'm not. I just believe we can work smarter, not harder. There's always a solution if you're willing to look."

Did she really come up with these solutions by herself? I can't believe it.

She screws her lips. "Your shock is starting to feel insulting. Did you think I was stupid because I don't have an MBA?"

"I don't think you're stupid."

"You think the worst of me, Mr. Alistair. But that's okay. It just makes me want to work harder." She pulls one of her shoes closer to her and slips her foot into it.

I want to walk over there and smack her hand away from the heels. I want to run my hand over her thigh and ask her to wrap her legs around my neck. I want to reward her for her brilliance by teasing her until she moans.

Off-limits, Alistair.

I swallow hard. Time to back away slowly. "Let me know when you're ready to leave. My driver will take you home."

"That's not necessary."

"It's late. You'll be safer with him than trying to catch a taxi." I frown. "Let me know when you're done."

My tone is gruff but it's only because I feel myself getting soft for this woman. Her ingenuity is as much of a turn on as that curvy body and sexy mouth.

I want to take a bite out of her, and I'm getting dangerously close to giving into the impulse.

Turning swiftly, I charge back to my office. Some part of me, a part I thought had shriveled up and died when I buried my wife, is sparking to life again.

Fighting my attraction isn't going to work.

I need something to get Kenya Jones off my mind.

And I need it yesterday.

CHAPTER 7
IT'S RAININ' BOOKS

KENYA

I WAVE my hand to dispel the dust cloud that rises when I set the last of the documents away.

The file room looks like it was ransacked. Boxes are stacked on top of each other. Documents pile up in towers. Papers are held down by clips, staplers and anything heavy enough to get the job done.

A yawn threatens to crack my jaw. I cover my mouth with the crook of my elbow, looking over the room that was my office for the day.

It's a drab, grey space with splashes of cream and white to break up the monotony. Too bad those colors are still shades off the old 'boring' block.

Honestly, this place is sad. If Alistair the Grump banishes me to the file room more often, I'm going to have to do something about those walls. Maybe paint them a candy color. Cherry red. Sunburst orange. Maybe a light brown like his eyes…

Not thinking about that.

My phone rings.

I smile tiredly when I see Sunny's number.

"Hey, babe."

"Why aren't you home yet?" Her words are muffled by a yawn. "I fell asleep on the couch waiting for you and you're still not back."

"I'm heading out now," I say, stomping my legs to increase the blood flow.

"How are you going to get back? Do you need me to drive over?"

"No. Stay there. I'll catch a taxi."

"Are you sure? I don't mind picking you up."

"It's okay. Besides, you have a meeting early tomorrow morning."

"So? You're more important than a meeting."

I smile. She's talking like that because she's delirious with sleep. Being a freelancer means every paycheck—big or small—is the difference between eating out or begging on the streets. Sunny doesn't have the wiggle room to turn down a job.

"Thanks, but I'm good."

"Fine. Text me the license plate of your taxi. I'll wait up for you."

I blow kissy noises into the phone.

"Yeah, yeah." She hangs up.

I limp to my purse and haul it away from a paper stack that so badly wants to be The Leaning Tower of Pisa. If I had an ounce of energy left, I'd put these back in their boxes.

But I don't have the strength.

My hands are cramping. My eyes are bleary.

Everything kind of sucks right now, but in a good, *I did the impossible* kind of way. Seeing Holland Alistair looking mildly impressed was worth giving up my beauty sleep.

Take that, you gorgeous prick.

The ants crawling up my legs slowly disappear. I'm starting to feel the adrenaline rush of a job well done, but it's not like I can run a marathon right now. I'll definitely crash into bed the moment I get to Sunny's apartment.

I poke my head out of the file room, glancing left and right. The hallway is empty and dark. The entire office feels like a ghost town.

Creepy.

One step on the tiles sounds like a gunshot. *Click. Click. Click.* My heels are too noisy. I slip them off so I can tiptoe through the corridor.

It's not hard to channel my inner Scooby Doo. As long as I don't encounter the monster in the dark.

Alistair offered me a ride home, but I don't want to be in the same car with the boss. My brain-mouth filter gets disconnected whenever I'm tired, and I can't risk saying what I *really* think about him.

My first time mouthing off to Alistair got me a job.

The second time, I might lose my position. No way am I letting that happen. I just organized three years worth of Belle's Beauty files. I want to stick around to get paid properly for my efforts.

Taking a left, I check that the coast is clear before ninja-walking to the lobby.

So far so good.

Ezekiel's desk is empty. Poor thing. Alistair must have held him hostage way longer than is decent. I feel sorry for him. What did he do to deserve a boss-hole like this?

I notice Alistair's office lights are off and breathe a little easier. He's gone. Maybe he forgot about his offer to take me home. Or maybe he's playing another one of his dirty tricks.

I ball my fingers into fists and pretend to throw a punch at his door. "You think you're all that just because you're rich?" My words are a harsh whisper. "I don't care how loaded you are. Don't talk to me like you own me, you giant flying cockroach. And next time, get your own coffee."

"Giant flying cockroach?"

"Ah!" I jump so high I'm surprised my head doesn't crack the ceiling.

Holland Alistair unfolds himself from the shadows. His suit

jacket is neatly slung over his left arm. His white shirt is wrinkled, one button undone and the tie loose.

He looks scrumptiously disheveled.

I want to run my hands through his messy hair. And then grab on and slam his head into a concrete block.

My mouth goes dry. "What are you doing here?"

"I would let it slide if it were a regular cockroach." He straightens to his full height and strides toward me.

I step back instinctively. It's like my body knows that, in this situation, Alistair's the hunter and I am most definitely the prey.

Back away slowly, Kenya.

"To compare me to the despicable flying strain…" He shakes his head. "I'm very offended."

I cough slightly. "I wasn't talking about you." My eyes dart to the side. "I was talking about someone else."

"Someone like who?" He tilts his head. Moonlight falls against his perfect jaw and gets shredded to bits, exploding in silver fractures all over the ground.

"No one you know." My gaze hits the ceiling. My back hits the wall.

Holland Alistair bends down so his face is near to mine. "The car is waiting downstairs. I was just coming to get you."

"Oh. I was just coming to find you."

"I see." His eyes drop to the shoes that I'm clutching to my chest like a religious amulet.

"Uh…" I chuckle nervously and drop the heels on the ground. They clomp to the tiles, rolling a bit before stopping against his fancy shoes.

Alistair studies my pumps for a moment. Then he drops into a crouch and tucks his fingers into the back of them.

I swallow hard. "Mr. Alistair—"

"Here." He sets my shoes neatly in front of me.

I blink rapidly, not sure if this is another one of his tricks. Why is he being so nice tonight? He was an absolute jerkwad about my report (which was awesome by the way) and he threw dirt on my management strategy. Not to mention he locked me in the file room to manage the impossible.

Which I did.

But that's beside the point.

I lift one leg and awkwardly shove it into my heels. The task requires more physical agility than I have. Arms wobbling, I do a little twist-inspired, one-legged dance to remain upright.

Alistair's warm fingers snap around my wrist. He confidently drives my hand down on his shoulder. "Hold on to me."

I put on my shoes in stunned silence. When I'm finished, I yank my hand back. "Thanks."

He nods, rises and strides away without another word.

I follow him, wondering what his deal is. The Alistair I know would just as soon push me to the ground than help me.

My eyes slide to his face as we ride the elevator. He's staring straight ahead as if trying to forget I'm there.

Weird.

We step out of the building and I'm hit with a strong breeze. The pavement is wet and I wonder if it was raining while I was locked in the file room.

"Mr. Alistair." A man with warm brown eyes and a greying beard scrambles to open the back door of a shiny SUV.

Alistair nods at him and gets in.

I stop.

The driver smiles at me. "Ma'am?"

"I'm good."

Alistair peers at me with his icy, hazel eyes. "Get in, Kenya."

The words, the tone—everything about it annoys me. I hiss through my teeth. "I don't want to put you out."

"Get in the car," Alistair says dryly, "or don't bother coming to work tomorrow."

Unreasonable flophead.

"You're threatening me with my job?"

The driver covers his laughter by pretending to cough.

Alistair picks up his phone and scrolls casually. "Your choice."

He *is* a flying cockroach. The ones with the wings—they act invincible. Like no one can touch them just because they can take flight.

Little does Alistair know, I *never* let a cockroach live once I find out it can fly. The moment they're airborne, it's a war. And only one person is allowed to walk out alive. Guess who's never lost a battle?

The driver gets ahold of himself and gives me a reassuring nod. "Ma'am?"

Pursing my lips, I dive into the car.

The driver slams the door shut.

I inch as far away from Alistair as possible.

The car is cold. I stare out the window at the city, rubbing my hands briskly over my arms. A jacket gets tossed into my lap. I glance up in surprise and see that Alistair is still staring at his phone.

My eyes narrow.

He sets the phone down and meets my glare with a calm expression. "Where do you live?"

I rattle the address.

"Bernard," Alistair says without acknowledging me, "take Miss Jones home first."

"Yes, sir."

I tremble as the car's temperature turns to Arctic-levels. What is wrong with this guy? Is he a cold-blooded reptile? There's no need to travel in an ice box.

My eyes drop to his jacket. Even sworn enemies cuddle together to preserve warmth in a time of crisis. Besides, this expensive piece of cloth didn't do me any harm. I can't reject it just because it serves an arrogant master.

Pulling the jacket close, I dip my hands into the sleeves and shroud it around myself. The fabric swallows me up. It smells like Alistair. Spicy and expensive.

While the car settles into silence, my phone rings.

I pick up. "Hey, babe."

Sunny's voice charges into my ear. "Have you left the office yet?"

If Alistair hears my conversation, he gives no visual clues. He's sitting with his arms crossed over his chest and his eyes closed.

"I'm on my way," I reply quietly.

"Why didn't you text me the license plate number?"

"I got a ride with someone else."

"Someone like who?"

"My boss," I whisper. "I'll be home soon."

"But—"

I hang up on Sunny before she can say anything incriminating. The language I use to describe Alistair at home is… colorful. With the car as quiet as it is and Sunny's voice as loud as it is, anything she says will be broadcasted in high definition.

Alistair shifts in his seat. "Someone must be worried about you."

"Uh, yeah." I tap my phone against my palm, surprised that he's making conversation.

He shifts again. "Boyfriend, right?"

Boyfriend? More like backstabbing scum of the earth.

Which reminds me. All my things are still at Drake's place. Sunny offered to get them for me, but I'm afraid she'll go full Leatherface with a chainsaw. Sure, I would love to see her shred Drake's couch, take a bat to his TV and set fire to his clothes, but we can't afford to buy those things back. And I definitely can't afford to bail her out of jail right now.

There's no way I'm letting her loose in there.

I shake my head. "No, no boyfriend."

"Oh." Alistair tilts his head back.

It might be a trick of the light but I think I see his lips flicker up in a smile. The expression disappears quickly.

Grey clouds release a gentle rain. The windows fog up and I smile. Pressing my finger to the surface, I draw a circle and poke two eyes. When it's time to draw the smile, I glance over at Alistair.

He's watching me intently.

Turning back, I abandon my usual smiley face for two horns and fangs. There. That's more suitable for the car Alistair drives.

His mouth does that quick flicker again. "Nice drawing."

"It's inspired by someone I know."

"No one in this car, I assume."

"Oh definitely not."

He turns his head away, but I can see him smiling in the reflection of the glass.

When the car slows in front of Sunny's apartment, it's still raining. Alistair rummages for something underneath the driver's seat and hands it to me.

It's an umbrella.

"Don't get sick," he says. I'm almost touched… until he growls, "It was your decision to stay late tonight. I expect you to show up at work on time tomorrow even if you have to carry a tissue box."

My pulse soaring, I roughly haul his jacket off and slam it back into the chair. "Keep your stupid umbrella," I mumble.

When I start to launch out, Alistair stops me. Taking my hand, he forces the umbrella into my palm. His eyes are dark and intense.

With a huff, I grab the umbrella, open it and stomp into Sunny's apartment. The rain falls in torrents, matching the storm in my own heart.

Holland Alistair is an insufferable, inhumane, raving lunatic.

And I'm sure now that he only hired me so he could make my life a living hell.

* * *

I STAY FAR AWAY from Alistair at work the next day and, thankfully, he's off doing something for Fine Industries. I'm spared the sight of his gorgeous, scowling face for a few hours.

But just because the cat's away, doesn't mean little mice—like me—can play. Alistair left a long list of tasks for me to complete by day's end.

All of which I have to cram in between my meeting with the Belle's Beauty store managers. *And* I have to keep pestering the marketing team about approvals for an in-store promotion.

Lunch is a tuna sandwich shoved into my mouth while I pore over sales reports and make summaries of skin-care market trends per the instructions bursting out of my inbox.

I'm in a horrible mood when my phone rings.

It gets even worse when Drake's voice echoes over the line. "Kenya."

My mouth tightens.

He hesitates. Calls my name again. "Kenya?"

Oh. So this is what betrayal sounds like. Deep and velvety.

His breath shudders over the line. "I know you're there."

"I am." My voice wavers. I can't help it.

Heartbreak feels like a thousand sharp arrows digging into the skin. It smells like mustard and soggy bread. It sounds like a voice that used to whisper promises of forever.

I'm assaulted by sweet memories. Drake wrapping me in his arms at our first concert together. Drake clutching my chin as we kiss on the library stairs. Drake inviting me to move in with him.

"What do you want?" I snarl.

"I have your things," he says. "I packed it up for you."

"I didn't ask you to touch my things, Drake. I asked you what time you'd be gone so I could take my stuff."

"Kenya."

"What time will you be gone? I don't want to see you."

The silence stretches like a yawning chasm.

Is there guilt buried in that darkness? Regret? I don't know what I did to deserve this. What signs did I miss? How could I have been such a bad judge of character?

I thought I had high standards. I thought I'd chosen a man who'd love me. Only me. I didn't know I was falling for a rat who couldn't wait to get inside my little sister.

"Kenya, I—"

"Make sure you're not there when I pick up my stuff today, Drake. Or I swear, I won't be responsible for what I do to you." I hang up before he can say a word.

Turns out, Drake chose death.

Because he's there when I stop by the apartment. I smell him the moment I step inside the place I once called home.

The living room is a bright space with vivid swaths of color—blues and pinks—along with swirling abstract art we picked up at bargain stores.

The furniture is earth-toned. Plain. Simple. To balance the zaniness of the color scheme and the little knickknacks I placed on every surface. They're tiny mementos. Photographs. Snapshots of our happiest moments.

Now a mockery of our love.

I made this place into my refuge because *Drake* was my refuge. Now, it feels like an empty shell. Still vibrant. Still youthful. And yet… so hollow.

Drake says nothing when I walk in. He looks at me with sad brown eyes and I don't bother trying to interpret his expression. Coward. He doesn't speak to me. Not that I would listen to a word from his lying mouth anyway.

I drag moving boxes from the bedroom to the hallway outside the apartment. They're the hardest steps of my life. Pain. Anger. Regret. They churn through me. Take turns ripping my heart out.

I know these wounds will need time to heal.

And I know that it's not only fury that I feel. I'm disappointed in myself. Disappointed I made the mistake of believing someone would love me forever.

Sorrow.

Pity.

Not for me. For my sister. She chose someone who's so, obviously, good at lies.

I bend down to pick up the last box. It's heavier than the rest.

They're my favorite books. I have a thousand more on my e-reader, but there's just something about turning those pages…

My knees buckle and Drake is there.

"Let me help you."

"I've got it."

He slides his arms under the box. Our fingers touch briefly and it annoys me that there's still a spark. My body still remembers curling into him on a cold night. Pressing my lips to his in the rain. Wrapping my legs around his waist as he pushes me deeper into the mattress.

Tears prick the back of my eyes. It feels like a part of me is dying. My youth. My naïveté. The part of me that still believed in fairytales.

I yank the box away from him. "I said I've got it!"

Drake holds on anyway.

A loud *rip* echoes through the room. Books cascade out of the bottom of the box, thudding to the ground. The covers open, crushing the pages and forming irreversible creases.

Horror balloons in my chest. I treasure these tomes. I've never even bookmarked a page by bending the ear. The scattered books are worse than shattered glass. Crushed pages are a death sentence. These books won't ever close properly.

"Kenya, I'm sorry."

"Get back!" I snap at him. Dropping to my knees, I gather the books to me like precious children. Smoothing out as many of the pages as I can, I huddle them close and storm to the living room.

Thankfully, I have another empty box left. I deposit the books into it and drag it through the open door.

Drake follows me wordlessly, looking on like someone cut his tongue. I'm glad for his silence. I think I might go crazy if he dares to open his mouth.

I drag the box down the hallway and to the stairs. They thump down every step, but none of them fall out again.

I'm almost to the truck I borrowed from Sunny when I hear someone calling my name.

It's not Drake's voice.

My fingers tighten on the box.

It's Sasha.

"Kenya." Sasha jogs toward me. She's wearing a pair of shorts and a flowery blouse. Her hair flows around her shoulders in dark brown waves. Sunshine follows her like a spotlight as she darts toward me.

My chaotic emotions swing back and forth. In one breath, I'm worried about her overexerting herself and, in the next, I wish she'd trip over a rock and crack her skull open.

Running away isn't going to work this time.

Fine.

We'll talk.

I abandon my box of books and turn to face her. She crashes to a halt, spitting stones and dried twigs. The run caused a flush to spread across her face. It adds a rosy dew to her glossy, tan skin.

"Kenya." Her voice is subdued. "You're here."

Yes, I'm here.

But she obviously knew that already.

Did Drake tell her I would be picking up my things? Did he text her right after I arrived? Was he hovering around me, not because he felt sorry and actually wanted to help me, but because he was waiting until she got here?

"What do you want?" I ask coldly.

Sasha's bulging eyes remind me of when we were younger, and she'd run to me after doing something wrong.

"Kenny! Kenny! I need your help."

I would always be there to take the rap with her. To defend her. To be whatever she needed me to be. Because she's my little sister. One of my people. Under my protection. I go to bat for anyone I consider mine.

It's sad that she didn't consider me at all.

"Please," she steps forward, "can we talk?"

I jerk my chin at the park across the street.

She follows me, walking in silence.

The neighborhood is alive and filled with young families. I used to lie in Drake's lap and envision the family we would have. Two boys and one girl. Overprotective older brothers with his beautiful chocolate skin and impressive height. Basketball players. Both of them. Or only one. Just to carry on their father's legacy.

Why can't the girl be the basketball player? I used to say. And Drake would kiss my forehead and tell me that would be awesome. That he'd love if our daughter was the one who could shoot hoops.

My heart gets so heavy I have to drag it behind me as we walk. Every step pushes me deeper and deeper into the hurt.

I know I can get over Drake.

It won't be easy. It probably won't be fun. But I can.

The part that gouges me is Sasha's involvement.

Why would she do this to me? Why?

"You must hate me right now," Sasha says.

I don't correct her.

We step over the little cement bridge that leads into the park. Bubble-gum pink benches. Sprawling basketball court. Charming hopscotch sidewalks.

The sun is bright, but the trees are plenty. Branches, heavy with leaves, dance in the wind, luring us to sit beneath the shade.

I sit at a bench far away from the kids on the playground. Their cheerful laughter feels a world away from my heartless reality. Drake and I will never bring our kids here. I don't want any more reasons to cry.

"Kenya, I know what I did was *awful*, but Drake and I love each other."

My heart shudders.

This isn't what I want to hear. She's just pushing the knife in further.

"I want to explain," Sasha says. "I want to—"

"Don't bother." My jaw is set. I don't look at her.

"But I can't let our relationship fall apart like this."

I want to laugh like a lunatic. I want to throw my head back and cackle at the sky like someone completely unhinged. She's concerned about our relationship? Where was all this anxiety about our sisterhood when she was bawling my boyfriend's name and clawing at his naked back?

This was a mistake.

I jump to my feet. "I thought I was ready for this conversation, but I'm not."

"Kenya," Sasha digs her fingers into her purse and stares at her lap, "please hear me out."

"If you need a listening ear, call your mother."

Sasha hops to her feet. "Kenya, I can't lose you."

Silence fills the gulf of pain and betrayal between us. It grows until it presses into my skin and makes me feel oily and battered.

"You hurt me, Sasha."

She sobs. "I know."

"But mixed inside that hurt is genuine worry for you." I nod to Drake's apartment that's still visible through the tree line. "I don't want that punk to hurt you the way he hurt me."

"He won't," she mumbles, tears bubbling in her eyes.

Of course she's taking up for him. At least I know they weren't screwing just to pass the time. Sasha's in love with him. And Drake? I don't know if he's in love with her. I don't know about anything anymore.

"I need you, Kenya," Sasha whispers.

"And I need time."

She covers her mouth with a fist. Mascara runs down her face and paints black lines on her cheeks.

I walk away.

"I love you, Kenya," Sasha says to my back.

The words send a chill down my spine. Is this love? Is this agony deserving of that word? Drake looked into my eyes and told me he loved me before I left for the workshop last weekend. And now, Sasha is throwing that word around too.

If this is what love is—if this pain and betrayal is what it has in store for me—then I want no part in it.

CHAPTER 8
GOOD COFFEE

HOLLAND

"Does Miss Jones seem... alright to you?"

Ezekiel stops in his tracks and stares at me as if my head has been replaced with a giant lizard.

I stare calmly at my laptop, my glasses perched on the edge of my nose and my fingers clacking away at the keyboard.

Multi-tasking is not in my skillset. I'm typing studiously, but the words appearing on-screen are not of the English language. Perhaps to aliens in some far-off galaxy, I'm penning the most riveting prose but…

"Excuse me?"

"She fetched my coffee without a retort."

"And?"

"Without a word, Ezekiel."

"Wouldn't you call that… *progress*, sir?"

"Progress?"

"Miss Jones is acclimating to her position as your second assistant. Why are we discussing the matter like it's a problem?"

"You're right." I shake my head. "Forget I said anything."

Ezekiel gives me a long look. "Anything else, sir?"

I wave him out.

As soon as the door shuts behind him, I yank my hands away from my laptop and pick up the mug of coffee Kenya delivered to my office.

Perhaps I'm overthinking it, but I'm quite certain her temperament was off today. She didn't snap at me. Didn't glare. Didn't scowl.

Despite adding more to her workload thanks to a potential partnership with a famous subscription company, she hasn't made a peep.

Her emails in reply to my task list were succinct. No superlatives in sight. No hint of underlying sarcasm.

It's unlike her.

I rub the back of my neck, trying to figure out what the problem might be. Her ex-boyfriend, perhaps? Or is it something else?

What are you thinking, Holland? Why do you care about her private affairs?

I rip my glasses from my face and throw it on the desk. I've got back-to-back meetings. I'm juggling two extremely demanding companies. My head feels like it's about to snap in half. I don't have time to worry about my second assistant and her sudden mood swing.

Ezekiel knocks on the door. "Mr. Alistair, you have a visitor."

"No need to announce me so vaguely, Ezekiel." Darrel's voice barrels through the door that's open a crack. "He'll see me whether he's busy or not."

I sigh heavily as my brother-in-law appears. "You made good on your threat."

"Only because you were rude enough to not return my calls." Darrel strides into my office and takes a seat in the chair across from my desk. He's tall and broad with thick black hair and green eyes, so much like Claire's.

Darrel is four years older than me. Though he's never been in the military, he comes from a long line of servicemen. Hints of his upbringing are everywhere. Shoulders ramrod straight. Back more rigid than a metal pipe.

His eyes flash with annoyance. "You can't keep avoiding your sessions."

"If I knew you'd harass me for years to come, I wouldn't have agreed to see you in the first place."

"Free therapy is one of the many benefits of joining our family."

"Is it a benefit?" I run a hand down my face. "It feels more like a prison sentence."

"That sarcasm. Is it new? I don't remember you being that witty."

I glare at him.

He glares right back.

I give up first. "Aren't you supposed to ask how I'm feeling?"

"Sometimes. And sometimes, I take the liberty of giving you a swift kick up the backside."

"I'll have your license revoked."

"I'd like to see you try."

We stop for another glaring session.

A knock on the door cuts it short.

Kenya steps in. Her eyes are downcast and her fingers are folded in front of her. She's wearing a simple white button-down and a short pencil skirt. Her hair is pulled back in a bun and her lips are set in a thin line.

"Oh." She stops short when she sees Darrel. It's the first spark of life I've seen in her eyes since she came to work. "I didn't know you had a guest."

Darrel gives her a gruff nod, but there's something beneath it too. A hint of interest.

I don't like it.

"Where's Ezekiel?" I bark.

"I'm not sure." She hooks a thumb over her shoulder. "He's not at his desk."

He must be getting tea for Darrel. The traitor. He knows I won't be able to kick my brother-in-law out and he's preparing for us to have a long conversation.

"Miss Jones," Darrel swings his arm over the back of the chair and twists his body so he's facing her, "I don't believe we've met."

"And you have no reason to," I growl.

Darrel ignores me. "Are you new here?"

"Yes." Her eyes dart to me. "I'm Mr. Alistair's second assistant."

Darrel swings his head around. "You need a *second* assistant?"

"She's only assisting with Belle's Beauty."

"I see."

I hate when he says that.

"What do you need, Miss Jones?"

"Your approval for the Belle's Beauty in-store promotion. The PR team is waiting for your signature."

"I haven't had a chance to look over the proposal yet."

Her lips tighten. A sure sign of her displeasure. "Fine. I'll wait until you have the time."

Is that a hint of annoyance I hear? I'm relieved to see the steel back in her eyes, but I'm equally frustrated to have it aimed at me.

This woman drives me insane.

"You may go, Miss Jones."

With a sober nod, she backs out of the room and slams the door shut.

I frown.

Darrel gives me another probing look. "Who is she?"

"No one."

"Why did you hire another assistant?"

"Because I needed assistance."

"Obviously."

"She has a good track record. I made the call."

"Then why do you look so guilty?"

"You're seeing things."

"Am I?"

"Why are we discussing this right now?"

"There's more. I can feel it." He squints at me. "You trust her with Claire's business."

I stop and let out a deep breath. "You're psychoanalyzing me."

"We're having a conversation."

"I'm fine."

"I didn't ask."

"You want to."

"I don't ask questions I already know the answer to."

"This isn't your practice, Darrel."

"I hate meeting patients there anyway. Meeting you on your own turf is better. It forces you to confront things you wouldn't have."

"Screw you."

He sinks into his chair, unconcerned. "The human mind is complex, which is why I never tire of studying it. I don't know your mind, Holland. But I know two things for sure. You're not fine. And you don't look at Miss Jones as if she's only your assistant."

I want to punch the smugness right off his face.

"Are you still having nightmares?"

"No."

"Liar."

I frown at him. "Therapists are supposed to be soft and gentle."

"I didn't know you had a Masters degree in psychotherapy, Alistair."

"I'm busy."

"And avoiding my question." He rises and brushes his shirt down. "If you won't talk, I'll have to seek out Miss Jones and ask her a few questions on my own. Make sure you're not bullying her from a position of authority."

"I'm not a bully."

"Have you read the online articles?"

"How about you pay less attention to the tabloids and more to patients who need your actual help?"

"The people who need the most help are typically the ones who won't ask for it." He gestures to me. "If you can't sleep, you can drop by for a prescription. It won't stop the nightmares though. It's only a temporary solution."

"Darrel."

He stops in the doorway.

I glance aside. "Come over for dinner this weekend. Belle misses you."

"I will." A flash of emotion passes through his stoic face. And then it's gone. Without another word, Darrel leaves my office.

Ezekiel walks in with a tray and two mugs on top of it. "You chased him off so quickly?"

I scowl. "Tell Miss Jones I need to see her."

"Alright." He turns around.

"Leave the coffee."

"Both of them?"

"Yes."

Ezekiel gives me a quizzical look, sets the tray on the coffee table and shuffles away.

I fold my hands beneath my chin and wait. Darrel doesn't know how to crack a smile, much less a joke. The moment he hinted about talking to Kenya, I knew it was a warning.

I'm going to do all I can to prevent that. I don't need my brother-in-law of all people, sniffing out the conflicted feelings Miss Jones brings out in me.

"Mr. Alistair." Kenya steps into the room.

I point to a chair.

She folds herself into it and stares at me with sorrowful brown eyes. It bothers me. The lack of warmth. The lack of sunshine. She was a walking flame. Anyone could see it. Feel it. But now, it seems like someone smothered it out.

I nudge the coffee toward her. "The Yazmite project is doing well."

"It's only a three-day burst in sales. I wouldn't get excited yet."

I tilt my head. *Why so dour, Miss Jones?*

"Is that all?"

"No." I point my pen at her. "I'd like you to accompany me to the Baby Box meeting."

"Really?"

"Yes." I lift my coffee mug and inhale. The fragrance is rich. Decadent. Ezekiel always gives Darrel the good stuff.

"This is our first cooperation with a company outside our demographic. Have you heard of Baby Box?"

"No."

"They're akin to high-level curators for the wealthy. A monthly subscription box with the best products. Their focus is on safe and environmentally-friendly brands. They target customers who don't care about price. And Belle's Beauty fits that bill."

She nods.

"It's a multi-million dollar contract."

Her eyes bug.

"But the money is just a bonus. A partnership with Baby Box would be a huge boost to our brand. We'll be able to establish a presence in a growing market. It's a demographic we haven't had much luck breaking into. We need to stick the landing here."

"They haven't yet decided to go with our brand?" She leans forward.

I note the way she says 'our' brand. It makes my chest tighten in a strange way. "No, we're still in the negotiation phase. The PR team will be meeting with them next week. We're preparing a presentation that *must* guarantee a deal."

"What do you need from me?" Her nose scrunches.

I study her. "What do you think?"

"Am I the errand girl? Do I get coffee for everyone? Buy your food? Go back to dating the printer?"

"Excuse me?"

"Nothing."

"First, I need you to drink that."

Her brown eyes drop to the coffee. "Why?"

I arch both eyebrows.

She sighs, picks up the coffee and drinks. "Happy?"

"I'll need you to liaison with the PR team while they're working on the presentation. You'll attend all the meetings and send me a summary of the pitch. I have the final say, but their input is invaluable. For you personally," I tent my fingers, "I'd like information on the Baby Box brand. I want to know what makes them tick."

Her fingers tighten around the coffee cup. "I can do that." She takes another sip. Her eyes flutter closed and her mouth eases into a soft smile. "That's good."

Her smile is a little ray of sunshine poking through the clouds. It's not quite the beam of light that I've seen her use when she's leaving the office, but it's better than before.

Her eyes open and her gaze catches mine. "I think it's a really good move to partner with Baby Box." She squints into her cup. "And this is good coffee."

"Is it?"

"It's amazing." She takes a more exuberant sip. "My goodness. What is in this?"

"Ezekiel won't tell me. He says it's better if I don't know."

"My eyes are watering right now." She drinks again and moans.

The sound of her low groan immediately fills my head with dirty images. Miss Jones in my bed. Her curls spilling over my white pillowcases. Her heels pressing into the back of my neck as I—

No. That wildly inappropriate fantasy is unacceptable.

And out of place.

She's enjoying her coffee. And I'm not a perverted boss.

Shifting my thoughts to tamer territory, I watch her enjoy the drink. Something that simple can shift her mood. It's disarming to see her expression brighten and feel my world brighten a bit too.

"That's it." I clear my throat when I'm caught staring. "You can return to work."

She bounces out of her chair. "I'll prioritize the Baby Box reports."

I nod, watching her leave.

Miss Jones stops at the door. Suddenly, she whirls around and snatches the coffee off the desk. "I'll take this."

I will not laugh.

Dammit.

She won't make me laugh.

The chuckle bursts out anyway. I sip the rest of my coffee with a smile on my face.

* * *

The meeting with Baby Box is held at their building. I'm impressed by the mother-and-child sculptures in the lobby. It's obvious that they take their branding seriously.

We enter the conference room early. I'm quick to tug my laptop out of the bag. Kenya bustles behind me, hooking up the presentation to the projector and setting out marketing materials at each spot around the table.

I have to say, she's very efficient.

Before Kenya Jones, I couldn't imagine finding an assistant as capable as Ezekiel. The last time I tried to hire someone, she sent a confidential document to the wrong address and caused a frenzy. After raising a stink, she quit without bothering to clean up her mess.

Kenya Jones is surprising me with her tenacity. I haven't been easy on her, but she's flown past all the challenges.

It should have been a stretch to completely organize all the company files in a week. Somehow, she managed to get it done in one day. For the first time in… I don't know… maybe since Claire was alive, Belle's Beauty is fully organized. Every scrap of information is tagged and digitized in a search-friendly database.

It's like standing in a well-maintained library. And Kenya Jones is the smoking hot librarian every guy secretly wants a piece of.

As beautiful as she is, confining her to her looks would be a mistake. She's proven to be capable at her job. And she's been a huge relief from carrying Belle's Beauty on my own.

"Mr. Alistair." Kenya hands me a bottle of water. "Do you want to drink this before it starts?"

"Thank you." I accept the bottle from her.

She gives me a fist pump. "You got this."

I dip my chin, grateful for the encouragement. One of the reasons I handed Belle's Beauty off to management companies is because making pitches and groveling for partnership deals is not my thing.

I hate begging. And I hate relying on other people to get me where I need to go. However, in an industry as cutthroat as this one, going it alone is just not an option.

The door opens and the Baby Box reps walk in. There are three in total, but the man I need to impress is in the middle. Stephen Sutherburg.

He's a short man with a balding head, a red nose, and thick sideburns that must have been in style several decades ago.

Kenya withdraws and joins the other team members in the chairs against the wall. My eyes follow her. The dress she's wearing today is more her style. It's bright red and hugs her body a little too tightly for the office. The jacket is the only thing keeping her outfit appropriate.

Damn. Her curves are a distraction.

I so badly want to find out if she's as soft as she looks.

Her head swivels to me and she catches me staring. Her face gives her thoughts away, revealing amusement and confusion all in one eyebrow quirk.

Setting my lips into a thin line, I focus on Sutherburg instead of my assistant. The man is much older than I'd expected. His team is comprised of older men too. I'm surprised there isn't a single woman in his entourage. For a company that sells mother and baby products, I'd expected to see someone representing the target group.

But then, it's not like I can judge. Belle's Beauty targets middle aged, health-conscious women and I might be conscious of my health, but I'm definitely not a woman.

Sutherburg glances across the table. His eyes find mine and he dips his chin.

I return the gesture. "Mr. Sutherburg. It's good to see you."

"Mr. Alistair, I'm looking forward to this pitch. Belle's Beauty has a reputation for purity in both its product formulation and manufacturing. We've heard great things."

"I look forward to proving why we earned that reputation."

He smiles and motions to his team. "Let's begin."

Kenya trots to the laptop and presses a button. The presentation blasts onto the pull-down screen.

"First, I'd like to share my appreciation for this opportunity. We'd be honored to work with a brand as customer-oriented as Baby Box." The words slip off my tongue like the cod liver oil my mother forced me to take as a child.

See it through, Alistair.

"I'm a data man. As you know, Fine Industries was built on the belief that data is just as reliable as human intuition. Maybe even more so because there's less room for error." Chuckles break out. I hadn't intended that line to be funny. "Let's begin with data, and then I'll explain why Belle's Beauty and Baby Box are the perfect combination."

Sutherburg's team scribbles notes while I talk, but it feels more like a method of distraction than a sign of interest. Sutherburg doesn't move an inch from his chair. His expression remains the same throughout my presentation, not giving anything away.

"In conclusion," I point to the last slide, "Baby Box and Belle's Beauty is a match made in heaven."

The lights flip on.

No one moves.

"It sounds... interesting," Sutherburg says.

I study his wizened features. It's hard to interpret that. Is 'interesting' a good sign or have I just tanked this pitch?

He rubs his eyes like Belle does when I wake her up too early.

Not a good sign then.

I've been around computers for most of my life. Input a code, it's either going to spit out the results or it won't. There's no in-between. No shades of grey.

Humans aren't so easily computable. I can't tell if Sutherburg is just processing or if he's truly disengaged.

Another beat passes.

Alarm bells ring in my head.

I scramble to save what feels like waning interest. "Thanks to the data, we're seeing more and more shifts in cultural norms and expectations. Each generation brings its own unique mark on parenting. Data shows that this generation is having kids later in life."

Sutherburg looks down and paws at something on his shirt.

"Gone are the days when mothers collectively pushed self care aside in favor of raising a family. Culturally, women are determined to have it all. They want to look beautiful *while* running behind their toddlers. Why should they give up on themselves when they've done the work of bringing a human being into the world?"

Sutherburg yawns.

Dammit. Is it my delivery? Is it the data?

Why is there silence? Why aren't there questions?

I need bodies leaning forward. I need eyes sparkling with intrigue.

I glance at my PR team. They're squirming in their chairs. Someone is going to have to write a hell of a report explaining where we went wrong.

"What do you think?" I try to jar an opinion loose. "This is a flexible concept. We're willing to work with you to focus on the angle that serves Baby Box best."

Sutherburg stands and buttons his jacket. The smile on his face reminds me of when Belle has constipation.

His team rises as well.

"Thank you for your time, Mr. Alistair." The person who

speaks is one of the assistants at the end of the table. "We appreciate you coming down here and we'll be in touch if we have any further questions."

Damn it.

I don't need an algorithm to tell me I have a snowball's chance in hell of landing this deal. But throwing my hands up at the first road block is not how I roll. If I'd stopped every time someone slammed a door in my face, Fine Industries would never exist.

Hell, Belle would never exist. Claire wouldn't give me the time of day the first few times I tried to talk to her.

I know I can shift the tide if they tell me where we've gone wrong in the pitch.

My PR team starts murmuring among themselves.

Kenya looks frantic.

I swerve to face Sutherburg who's moving toward the door. "Mr. Sutherburg."

He stops.

"Baby Box has been an established brand for over ten years, but Belle's Beauty has only been established for six. We'd love to hear your thoughts before you go."

"My thoughts?" He returns to his seat.

I hear my PR team breathe a collective sigh of relief. Sutherburg might be humoring me, but at least he's not on the move anymore.

He leans back in his chair and squints at the projections. "Mr. Alistair, I'm aware of your background in tech and I can see that you've applied it to your presentation. Your pitch was very… technical. Filled with data. And I felt bored to death."

It's a dagger to the chest.

"Bored to death?" I mumble.

The PR team is deathly quiet. If we miss this opportunity because of a lackluster pitch, I'm going to take responsibility. As I should. But I'm also going to expect the PR team to take responsibility as well.

"Unfortunately, and I'm being as kind as I can here," Sutherburg sighs, "it's heartless. There's no life here. No sense of connection with the audience. I know it's all about money and data, Mr. Alistair, but the client won't know that. We have to approach it from an angle that puts them first."

My expression remains flat, but I'm cringing hard inside. The data inputs were my addition to the presentation. I thought it was a sure-fire way to convince Baby Box of a collaboration. People can deny feelings, but they can't deny facts. Hard numbers are the only truth that stand.

Sutherburg studies me like he's waiting for me to get on my knees and plead for another chance. I'm not going to do that.

My pitch was trash.

Fine.

I'll take the criticism like a man, but I draw the line at groveling. There has to be another solution. I just need a bit more time to come up with one.

Inhaling a deep breath, I tap my fingers against my pants. Desperation makes people stupid. Panicking would be like throwing gas on a dumpster fire. I need a Plan B and I need it now.

My brain is whirring, fighting to prevent an almost certain rejection from Baby Box, when I hear a chair scraping against the tiles. A soft voice that shouldn't be anywhere near this pitch filters through the room.

"I think you're wrong," Kenya says.

A collective gasp emerges from the PR team.

Sutherburg tilts his head, his eyes glittering with intrigue.

"Belle's Beauty, as a concept and a company, is the very opposite of heartless."

My gaze drills into Kenya. I subtly shake my head to knock her off this path that leads straight off a cliff. Unfortunately, my assistant is not even looking at me. She stands tall and confident. As if she has a right to speak up.

Has she gone insane? Even the PR team knows it's best to shut their mouth when the ship is going down. Why is a second assistant committing mutiny and interfering in a pitch this important?

Sutherburg's eyes drill a hole into Kenya. His lips arch up. "Go ahead, young lady." He presses his elbows on the table and leans forward.

He's going to eat her up and spit out her bones. But at least he's interested. It's the distraction I needed, even if it isn't the one I want.

"Mr. Sutherburg," I smoothly make the introductions as if we'd planned it, "this is Kenya Jones, the newest addition to the Belle's Beauty team."

I give Kenya a hard look. This meeting is already heading south fast. If she speeds up our descent into disaster…

Kenya folds her hands in front of her. "Belle's beauty was founded by a woman who believed in family over everything."

The world turns blurry.

My eyes widen and I whip my head around.

She's not going there.

Hell no.

She's not talking about Claire.

"What if we included her story in the promo material? What if we, at Belle's Beauty, opened our hearts just like all the beautiful, deserving mothers open those boxes?"

I grit my teeth so hard I hear something crack.

"We can print the Belle's Beauty origin story on the flap. Not only will it boost awareness of the people behind the company, but it'll also touch the hearts of all the Baby Box customers. Bring the company from a nameless corporation to a woman they'd meet on the street. A friend. A mother."

"Mother?" Sutherburg rubs his bristly chin. His eyes swerve to me, dancing with excitement. "Didn't you and Claire have a daughter, Alistair?"

My heart slams against my ribs.

Anger burns a path straight up my spine and to the back of my neck.

"Daughter?" Kenya whispers, her eyes widening. She slants me a look of surprise.

GRUMPY ROMANCE

Oh? So she didn't know? She threw my family into a damn business deal without thinking this through?

Sutherburg bobs his head slowly. Excitement. Approval. Interest burns behind eyes that were otherwise indifferent for most of the presentation.

I put a stop to it before the train can run off the tracks any faster. "My daughter," I growl, "is not a commercial. Her details are not public knowledge and that is by choice. I don't want anything about her broadcasted."

Sutherburg jabs his finger at me. "Are you sure about that?"

"Dead sure," I snarl. And I dare anyone—even the outspoken Miss Jones—to try me on that.

The light dims from Sutherburg's eyes. "I see."

He and his PR team gather their things and rise, slowly marching toward the door without further comment.

"We don't have to use real pictures," Kenya blurts.

I slant her a blistering look. *Shut up.*

She either doesn't see or doesn't want to. What the hell is she trying to prove here?

"We can hire a model. Someone who'll be the face of the collaboration. But we can still use real stories. Not only about Belle's Beauty's origin but about the many brave mothers who slowly learned to choose themselves again after a kid consumed their world. It'll be more unique. Every box will have a picture of the same model, but with a different story. We can run a contest. Drive more awareness to the campaign that way. We can even invite people to vote on the stories they'd like to see featured. The winner could get a year's worth of supplies."

By now, I'm seeing red and I'm sure steam is roaring out of my ears. Maybe I've been too soft on Miss Jones. Or maybe I don't speak English. When I hired her, I was sure I stipulated that her job had nothing to do with making presentations.

In meetings like this, she's to be silent as a rock. She's to arrive before everyone, provide the refreshments and the print-outs, and leave after everyone is gone. She is *not* to open her mouth and intervene in things above her pay grade.

Sutherburg remains standing in the doorway for a long beat. While I wrestle with my anger at Kenya, I'm also battling a rising hope that he'll turn around.

But he doesn't.

Lifting a hand in goodbye, he and his posse leave without another word.

When the door slams shut, no one on my team moves. It's almost like they've turned into statues. I can feel the PR team eyeing me, waiting to see what I'll do. How I'll react.

With a deep breath, I turn and face my crew. "We'll discuss this back at the office. For now, get back to Belle's Beauty and continue with your work." My eyes fall on the PR team leader. "I'll need an explanation for this."

"Yes, sir." His voice quivers.

The team leaves amidst frightened murmurs. They're logging what just happened so they can repeat it to the rest of Belle's Beauty. The news will be carried over to Fine Industries by noon. I'd bet money on it.

Kenya plugs out my laptop and slips it into the bag. She moves with slow, lethargic movements. Her eyes are on the ground. Her steps are dragging.

Is she upset because Sutherburg didn't jump on her proposal or does she know what she's in for?

She moves toward the door.

My voice whips through the air, dragging her back. "Miss Jones, I need to speak to you."

She does a sharp turn and returns to the table.

"Sit down."

Her jaw clenches. The fight inside her wants to rebel against the order. At last, she sinks into one of the chairs.

Silence falls in the room, thick and suffocating. The words flying through my head can't be let loose here, inside Baby Box's headquarters. It would be safer to keep my thoughts to myself until we can get back to Belle's Beauty.

But I don't think I'm capable of keeping my temper in check for that long.

Kenya Jones pulls her lips into her mouth. The way she's avoiding my gaze says she's aware of the amount of trouble she's in.

"Mr. Alistair, I—"

I flatten my fists against the table and hiss, "What the hell is wrong with you?"

CHAPTER 9
LIGHT REVENGE

KENYA

I PURSE my lips and stare at my fuming boss. Holland Alistair is standing completely still, yet I can *feel* the fury rising from his skin like heatwaves.

It makes my stomach twist into knots.

It makes me want to defend myself.

"What happened in this room is unacceptable." His fingers grip the back of the chair like he's contemplating whether he should pick it up and throw it at the window. "You're an assistant to the damn assistant!"

I flinch. Nice reminder.

"You forget what you're here for." His voice is so low it rattles the glass cups on the table. "You're not a part of the PR team. You're not in charge of this pitch. And you have no authority to speak out without *my* permission."

I lick my lips in agitation. "Do I need your permission to breathe too?"

"Miss Jones!" He scowls at me.

I keep going because, apparently, I don't treasure my own life.

"I may have spoken out of turn, but I was trying to save the pitch. You saw Sutherburg yawning."

The Baby Box rep looked like he would fall out of his seat if Alistair kept going. It was my first corporate collab and it was painful to watch.

"The PR team had a plan—"

"The PR Team was pandering to your obsession with data and your total disinterest in the human element. You knew that. I warned you there wasn't enough of a relatable draw in the pitch and you shot me down saying the numbers would speak for themselves."

"I'm impressed, Miss Jones." He applauds. I can *hear* the sarcasm in each beat of his hands. "After the crap you pulled, you have the guts to call *me* out? Fan-freaking-tastic!"

His nostrils flare and if he had two horns on his head (at least two *visible* horns), I would have been impaled by them.

"Whether you acknowledge it or not, I *was* trying to help!"

"You didn't, Miss Jones. Not even a little."

"I—"

His voice gets rougher. "Do you have any idea how inappropriate it was for you to speak today? I do not pay you to shout your opinions to my clients. I do not pay you to critique my business choices. I pay you to organize files, write notes and fetch my damn coffee!"

I shoot to my feet because his tone is absolutely unacceptable. Even if he has a problem with what I did today, I'm still a person. At the very minimum, I deserve respect.

I slam a hand against my hip. "*Excuse* me?"

"Don't play offended, Miss Jones. You were brave enough to mouth off in the middle of a meeting and you were brave enough to scold me for ignoring your notes, so you should be brave enough to stand here and take this."

"I threw myself on a grenade that *you* set off." I'm so pissed off that, unlike my boss, I don't keep my tone quiet. "Sutherburg would have walked out long ago and it would have ruined any future collab with Belle's Beauty."

He cocks his head to the side. "You still don't get what you did wrong, do you?"

"I did what I did to help the company and save the pitch. You refuse to see it. Fine. I don't need you to say thanks."

"Thanks?" He blinks as if he's astounded by the word. Or maybe it's the concept. "Miss Jones, you are not a damn hero." He juts a finger at me. "You didn't 'take a hit for the team'. By jumping rank, you spit in the face of the company rules and completely ignored the chain of command. That's not something you can brush off by claiming you did it for the right reasons."

"It was an emergency and I was the only one who responded. You have to—"

"I don't *have* to do anything," he snarls. "If you hadn't tossed the train off the rails, we could have gotten Sutherburg to hear another pitch, but you *had* to jump on an impulse and blow everything up."

"Even if we'd gotten a chance to pitch a brand-new idea, it still would have been rejected by him because your angle is all wrong. You heard Sutherburg. The data isn't what he's looking for."

Alistair's eyes narrow to slits.

My fingers press deeply into the table as I lean over it just like he is. The strain of pushing my weight on my hands makes them cramp, but I don't even care.

My teeth grind together. "I stand by my decision to intervene."

He glares at me.

I glare right back.

"If Sutherburg had agreed to your pitch, we might be having a different conversation right now. But he didn't. And that, Miss Jones, is on you." He lets out a deep breath. "Now that we've discussed the first problem... let's discuss the second."

"If this is about Sutherburg mentioning your daughter—"

"Don't try to shift the blame to Sutherburg. This is about you stepping out of line." A vein in his neck bulges. His voice is pure venom. "How *dare* you throw my family into the ring like our private business is a publicity stunt?"

I swallow hard and slam my lips shut. Suggesting we play up his wife's story didn't feel like an invasion of privacy in the heat of the moment. The information about the founder of Belle's Beauty is online for the entire world to see.

Alistair's wife *did* start Belle's Beauty. This company *is* about her dream to change the lives of women all around the world. I didn't think it would be a problem to dangle that tidbit in front of Sutherburg's nose just to hook him.

But I had no idea Alistair and his wife had a child. No articles exist online about her. At least, none that Sunny found on our initial search into Alistair's background.

My boss seethes in front of me. His eyes burn with flecks of lava and flickers of hellfire. This angry beast is about to level up to a new kind of monster. I can already feel the heat thickening in the room.

"It wasn't intentional." I try to explain myself. "And *Sutherburg* was the one who mentioned your daughter. I had no intentions—"

"I don't give a damn what your intentions were!" he yells. "You had no right to go there without my permission."

I clasp my hands together. "I know. I'm sorry."

"Sorry?" He croaks out a laugh. "You're sorry? I don't think you understand the scope of what you did, Miss Jones. I don't care if it costs this company millions of dollars, you *do not* negotiate with my family."

I flinch. Facing Alistair is like standing in the middle of a fire pit with flaming arrows shooting in all directions. I want to defend myself. I want to tell him that I didn't mean to harm him or his family. That I'm not that kind of person.

But he won't listen.

"That outburst might cost us a multimillion-dollar contract. Be prepared to take responsibility." Eyes narrowing, he steps closer to me. "I won't go easy on you because you're new to this, Miss Jones. Even if you've never stepped foot in a boardroom before, there are some lines you don't cross. And today, you went too far."

My chest is swelling to the point of bursting. I can take everything he dishes out, but I really can't stand looking like a jerk.

"I truly didn't know about your daughter," I blurt.

His face goes cold.

I look into his hazel eyes, waiting for a hint of humanity. There is none. He's an icy, iron monster out to devour me.

The worst part is, I can't fault him for being protective of his family. If anyone came at my people, I wouldn't stop at a scolding. Fists would fly.

"Mess up again and I won't be this kind," Alistair hisses.

Kind? This is his version of kind? Does this man own a dictionary?

Alistair turns away from me and grips a chair as if he needs help to remain standing. Fingers tapping against the cushion, he bites out, "If you know what's good for you, you'll oversee the Yazmite project, take notes and get coffee as quietly as possible. Breathe too hard and I might start regretting my decision."

My heart burns so badly I'm surprised there's no singe marks on my blouse. I messed up. I'm willing to accept that, but his words are like claws scraping against my skin. It feels unfair.

I take pride in everything I do.

It sucks that I tried and failed.

It sucks even more to be called out so harshly for it.

I feel something wet and salty against my lips. Stunned, I flick my tongue out and realize that I'm crying.

Horror sweeps through me.

Turning quickly before Alistair can see that his words drew blood, I murmur, "Understood."

I don't wait for him to dismiss me. That'll be salt in an already gaping wound. Stomping out of the conference room, I throw the door open and let it slam behind me.

The PR team scatters when I walk past them. It's not hard to tell that they were all eavesdropping. *Why am I not surprised?*

Without a backward glance, I stomp to the bathroom and wilt against the door. My heart is trying to climb up my throat. Anger wraps around my skin, pressing down on me like a fur coat in the heat of summer.

I lurch toward the sink and pour water on my face. My makeup washes off. Mascara tracks run down my dark cheeks.

It's okay. I'm okay.

Patting my face dry calms me a bit. When I straighten, I feel a lot more composed.

Deep breaths.

In. Out.

The world hasn't ended.

Sure, I got chewed out by my boss and lost an important account, but at least I didn't get fired. This way, I can write my own resignation letter and fling it in Holland Alistair's face.

I wait in the bathroom for a couple minutes. The PR team should have left by now, right? The last thing I need is to have a conversation with them. Whether it's pity or disdain, I don't have the energy to go another round.

After fifteen minutes, I peer outside the bathroom.

The coast is clear.

Hurrying to the elevator, I hold my breath until the doors open. No one I recognize is around. Score.

When I get to the lobby, I'm surprised to see Bernard standing near the front door. He's hard to miss since he's dressed in a stuffy suit and wearing white gloves.

At the sight of him, every nerve in my body pulls taut. If Bernard is here, that means Alistair is still in the building. What if he's close by?

I glance around desperately, looking for any plants I can hide behind. Too late. Bernard's sharp eyes fall on me and then narrow in recognition. He stalks over, his wide trouser legs flapping with every step.

"Miss Jones," he touches my hand softly. "I was hoping you hadn't left yet."

"What do you mean?"

"I'll take you back to the office."

"Is Alistair looking for me?"

"No." He gestures to the door.

"Uh... I'll catch the subway."

He shakes his head. "I have my instructions."

"From Alistair?"

He nods.

I gulp. What if this is a trap? What if Alistair arranged for Bernard to drop me off in the middle of the desert so I can die of starvation?

Don't be so dramatic, Kenya.

I blink rapidly. "Is Alistair waiting in the car?"

"No, he's not." Bernard motions for me to follow him.

Still not trusting any part of this, I walk cautiously behind the driver. The lobby is crowded. Everyone seems to be in their own world.

I keep a look out for a tall, gorgeous billionaire with eyes like fire, but Alistair doesn't pop out of the throng. He's not there when I walk through the doors. Not there when I get outside. And he's not in the car either.

Finally alone, I relax into the leather seats and close my eyes. The chair is soft. Buttery. I wish I could disappear into the backseat.

It's been a really long time since I've felt this drained.

Bernard clears his throat. "Is something wrong, Miss Jones?"

"Not really," I murmur.

He goes quiet.

"In fact, yeah. Something's wrong." I point to the roof of the car. "This. What's up with this?"

"What are you referring to?"

"Some things went down in the Baby Box meeting today."

"What kind of things?"

"Let's just say Alistair and I didn't end the meeting on a good note. He was pissed."

"Hm." Bernard's expression gives nothing away.

"Why did he arrange my ride back to the office?"

"Didn't you arrive with him?" Bernard arches an eyebrow. I can see it in the rearview mirror.

"Yeah but—"

"Mr. Alistair might be a hard man to please, but he's not unreasonable. He takes responsibility for those under him."

"I'm his responsibility?"

"You're his assistant, aren't you?"

"Second assistant," I say, as if the distance from his line of command is something to be proud of.

"He takes care of his people as much as he demands from them." Bernard smiles warmly at me.

I roll my eyes. "Another Alistair cheerleader?"

"I don't get what you mean."

"Nothing," I murmur, folding my arms over my chest.

"Have I answered your question?"

"Not to a satisfying degree." I sigh heavily. "But I have a feeling you're not going to badmouth Alistair any time soon, so I won't push for more."

"I have no reason to talk ill of him. He's been good to me."

Good? Is there a *good* bone in that man's body?

"He helped me when my wife had cancer."

I drop the attitude. As someone who's been through that experience with someone I love, I feel an instant connection. "Bernard, I had no idea. Is your wife okay?"

"She's great now. She beat it. But beating cancer was easier than paying off our debt. That's when Alistair swooped in. He paid all our medical fees and allowed me to take time off work to care for her."

"Are you sure it wasn't his twin brother?"

Bernard laughs.

I don't. I'm completely serious.

"He may appear gruff, but it's only because he's focused. Whatever he starts, he sees through to the end."

"Look, Bernard, I'm really, *really* happy that your wife's okay."

He nods.

"But you have to understand that the Holland Alistair you're talking about is not the Alistair I've met."

He arches an eyebrow. "Maybe you have met that side of him, and you just can't see it."

I'm not in the mood to sing Holland Alistair's praises, so I return Bernard's smile with a small one of my own and twist slightly away.

The city is a blur of colors. Blue sky. White clouds. Grey buildings. The world seems so big and yet I feel like I could fill it with my hurt and frustration.

The last thing I want to do is go to the office and see Alistair's ridiculously good-looking face. But unless I jump out of this moving vehicle, I don't have a choice.

I'm returning to the lion's den.

* * *

When I get to the office, everyone goes quiet. Their gazes follow me to my cubicle. Whispers burst out like waves behind my back.

In the distance, Alistair stomps down the hallway, Ezekiel hot on his heels. The executive assistant looks frantic. I know that poor man is receiving the backlash from the Baby Box disaster.

My eyes shift to the boss.

Alistair's still angry.

I can tell.

I glare a hole into his beautiful neck. If I aimed my pen just so... would it hit the target?

This man is turning me into a murderer.

I cover my face with my hands, fighting to keep it together. When can I go home? I don't think I can take much more of this awful day.

Just breathe, Kenya.

I straighten and start up my computer. The background on my

screen is Collin Firth because I'm obsessed with *Pride and Prejudice*. There are yellow, pink and blue sticky notes along the bottom of the monitor. Reminders to 'go for it' and 'keep trying'.

"Hey!" Someone kicks the back of my chair.

I lurch forward, my stomach slamming into the desk painfully. "Ow."

The chatter in the room stops.

I whirl around and see a woman in a long blue sweater dress standing behind me. Her eyes are sharp, and her mouth is twisted into a frown.

"Did you really drag Alistair's kid into the Baby Box proposal?"

I turn away from her.

She walks around my chair to face me. "Hey."

"I'm not in the mood, okay?"

"The news is all over the office," she snaps. "You ruined the Baby Box deal."

"Look, if you want to take a dump on me, take a number and get in line. It's not your turn today."

She doesn't move a muscle. "What's your name again?"

"None of your business."

She snarls and glances around. I have my name scrawled all over my notebooks in colorful, flowery handwriting. Her eyes land there. "Kenya."

"Since we're making introductions, why don't you tell me who you are?"

"It's Heather."

Of course it is. I smile tightly. "Heather, you weren't at the meeting, so I'd appreciate if you didn't run around listening to gossip. What I did at Baby Box has nothing to do with you."

"It kind of does," she says in that passive-aggressive, *don't let me call the manager* way. "I heard what you did." She leans down. "And it doesn't sit well with me."

"Is that so?" I doubt she can hear the sarcasm. She's too busy enjoying the sound of her own voice.

"Mr. Alistair doesn't talk about his daughter. Ever. Not to us and definitely not to clients. You need to know your place, errand girl."

Errand girl? I smile. "Thanks, Botox girl. I'll keep that in mind."

Gasps ripple around the room.

Her long, fake eyelashes flutter. "What did you just say to me?"

I glare in her direction. Did she expect me to run crying because she's being nasty? What does she think this is? High school? An hour ago, Holland Alistair chewed me up and spit me out of his mouth. Anything Heather can say is child's play compared to that.

Heather chokes. "You're despicable."

Fine. We won't be friends. If she isn't going to like me, she might as well fear me.

My smile goes flat. "Step back now while I'm asking nicely."

Heather looks annoyed. She leans in so close I can smell what she had for lunch. Tuna. Definitely. "I'll tell you right now; the way we do things around here is different. You don't open your mouth in a team meeting unless someone asks you to. And you don't bring up other people's families unless you have a death wish. Mess with me and I'll show you what happens to people who don't stay in their lane."

"Is that a threat?"

"Just a little advice."

"Thanks for the tip." I rise and step into her personal space. She lumbers back, her triumphant grin dripping into a scared little frown. "But Alistair already ripped my behind for what I did today. So don't worry. You can save your little intimidation act for someone who has the patience." I slam my hand on the cubicle wall near her head. "Mess with *me* again and you'll find out what it means to see your backside from your top lip."

"What?" Her eyebrows scrunch.

"That's a threat. Understand?"

Her eyes narrow.

I pretend to throw a fist at her.

She yelps and jumps back, shielding her face. When she realizes that I was only miming a punch, Heather gets three shades of red. "You're a thug!"

"That's right. I come from a long line of *don't give a damn*. And don't you forget it." I step away from her and fall into my chair, which welcomes me with a loud creak.

The office is deathly silent.

I notice a few phones out and snapping footage of our interaction.

"What are you looking at?" Heather shrieks.

Muffled laughter meets her statement.

Heather huffs and charges out of the office, much to my relief. The other cubicles settle into a semblance of normal. No one talks to me. They seem withdrawn. Waiting. Everyone is tiptoeing around, anticipating an explosion from Alistair.

But it never comes.

"Miss Jones." Ezekiel calls me after lunch.

I notice the executive assistant beckoning. My chair skates back as I jump to my feet. "Do you need something?"

He smiles. "Follow me."

I trail him to the kitchen.

Ezekiel gestures to a table. "Why don't you sit? I'm making coffee for Alistair and he mentioned you enjoyed a good brew."

"*He* told you that? Today?"

"Oh not today." Ezekiel's neck flushes. "He had… different words today."

"I can imagine." I drop my chin into my palm and sigh.

"It's not a big deal," Ezekiel says as he fixes the coffee. "There will be other collaborations."

"It's a huge deal. Alistair sat me down and explained how important Baby Box was." It's one of the reasons I felt desperate when I saw the deal tanking. "Belle's Beauty needed that contract."

Ezekiel pours the black liquid into a smaller cup. "Belle's Beauty isn't hurting for cash."

"Alistair's vision isn't money. It's legacy."

It makes sense now that I know he has a daughter. He's

burning himself to the ground to maintain both Fine Industries and Belle's Beauty. He's trying to build up his wife's company, not for himself but for another generation.

"All problems aside, I think you did a very brave thing." He stirs a spoon around the cup and it makes a light, tinkling sound.

"You're alone in that sentiment."

"He'll never admit it, but Alistair has a hard time connecting with others. It makes it difficult to engage in presentations."

"Are you allowed to say the boss man has flaws?" I ask. "Aren't we all supposed to kiss his ring and talk about how perfect he is?"

Ezekiel laughs. "Perhaps I would use nicer language in front of Alistair, but he knows my thoughts. He knows his own limits as well." The scent of coffee fills the air and loosens the knots in my neck. Ezekiel peers at me. "You were very brave to intervene."

"And you're very brave to be seen fraternizing with me." I glance around in case the Big Bad Boss is stomping up and down the halls.

"I find myself drawn to outcasts."

"Well thanks for confirming that no one likes me here."

He smiles again, but he doesn't deny it.

"I didn't know I was breaking a cardinal company rule. I thought going to a meeting as a team meant playing as a team. I had no idea the boss expects everyone to sit around like mannequins when the ship is sinking." Righteous outrage taints my voice. Until I remember that I screwed up by indirectly mentioning Alistair's daughter. I sink into my chair and play with the hem of my jacket. "I really didn't know Alistair had a child, Ezekiel."

He gets a new cup and pours a second mug. "I heard about the... disagreement you two had after the meeting."

Of course he did. The gossip mill in Fine Industries works harder than I do.

"Honestly, I'm surprised you're still here," Ezekiel adds.

My eyes widen. Does he mean here... in the building.

Or… on this earth?

"I've never heard of anyone speaking to Mr. Alistair like that and remaining in their position."

"I made a mistake. I apologized."

"I'm afraid apologies aren't enough around here."

"No?"

Ezekiel gives me a grim look. "Many have been terminated for far less."

"Well, that's unfair." Does this guy think he's a god?

"Alistair expects perfection from himself as well as everyone else. Which is probably why today's performance put him in such a bad mood. He doesn't tolerate even the slightest mistake."

"That's completely ridiculous. We're not all walking AIs with perfect hair," I grumble.

Though, if I think hard about it, Alistair could pass for a robot. It wouldn't surprise me to find out that there are wires and memory chips behind his gorgeous face.

"My advice is to lay low for a while. And try not to take anything Alistair says to heart. Especially going forward."

"You mean there's more?" After all the yelling he did in the conference room, I thought he'd be tapped out of evil. "I'm sorry. I *am*. I was trying to help. I didn't mean to step out of line."

Ezekiel gives me a concerned look. "Be prepared. It might get worse."

"For how long?"

He clamps his mouth together.

I groan. "Will he punish me forever? He's not that much of a jerk, right?"

The moment the words are out of my mouth, I know the answer. The entire office flits into panic mode when they hear Alistair coming down the hallway. Now that I've incurred his wrath, I'm done for.

"I don't get it. Why doesn't he just ax me?"

"If he was going to fire you, he would have done it on the spot." Ezekiel slides the coffee my way.

I slump over it. The smell is tantalizing, but I don't want my current woes distracting me from the experience. Coffee this good deserves to be indulged.

"Then maybe I should just quit."

"After all your hard work with the Yazmite project, you're not going to see it through?"

I ponder the question. Potential career fulfillment versus subjecting myself to Alistair's revenge? It's a tough one.

"You do good work, Jones."

"Who cares? He hates me. And the feeling is mutual."

"I don't know if it's hate." His shrewd eyes regard me carefully. "You're different. You challenge him."

"I'm his emotional punching bag."

"I've never seen a punching bag that punches back."

I laugh.

"What I'm trying to say, Miss Jones, is don't give up." His smile is warm.

I nod, still not sure what route I should take. "Thanks for the coffee, Ezekiel."

"Not a problem."

I linger in the kitchen because it's quiet, and there are no coworkers whispering about me like our cubicles aren't thinner than sandpaper.

Ezekiel's suggestion that Alistair would have fired anyone else over what happened today makes me think.

If I remember correctly, he never told me why he hired me after the debacle at Belle's Beauty HQ. Today, I royally messed up with Baby Box, but there was no discussion about letting me go either.

Why isn't he firing me?

It can't be because of my prestige or my brain. He has plenty of smart people working for him. I glance at my dress. It's not low cut and it goes all the way down to my knees, but I caught Alistair giving me a once-over as if he appreciated the view.

Is that it? Does he just like me around so he can ogle my body?

Weird. I don't get a pervy vibe from him. He treats his female staff with cold indifference. A scowl is never far from his face and his brutish expressions immediately cut off any flirting or playful behavior.

What could it be?

In the middle of my musing, my phone chirps.

It's an alert from my company email.

To: Kenya Jones
From: Holland Alistair
Subject: Belle's Beauty In-Store Promotion

MISS JONES,

THE IN-STORE PROMOTION for the Yazmite location has been approved. See the checklist of prep work and detailed guidelines attached.

First, create a checklist of necessary samples and promotional materials such as banners and invitations. Cross-check with the PR department and liaison with the graphics department to print the ads in time. Also, compile a list of all the samples available at the warehouse. I want it done by product number. I expect this task completed by midnight tomorrow.

Tomorrow, there will be a meeting with the marketing department regarding this promotion. You'll need to order coffee at six o'clock so it will be ready in time for the meeting. Regarding the coffee order, you'll need to ask the marketing team directly.

For my coffee, I'd like straight dark roast with two cups of cream and enough sugar. No, I can't quantify what 'enough' means. Yes, you'll have to figure it out.

You can get the company credit card from Ezekiel.

Also note that all Belle's Beauty expenses need to be catalogued including the receipts, invoice numbers, and payment stubs.

Do not make any mistakes. Excuses will not be tolerated.

Regards,
Holland Alistair
CEO of Belle's Beauty

• • •

I DEBATE THROWING my phone into the trash. Then maybe I'll find a way to dump Holland Alistair there as well.

What kind of revenge is this? Did I do something that grave? I already explained that I didn't mean to drag his daughter into the pitch. In fact, I took her completely out of the picture by suggesting we hire a model and use real life stories instead.

I tap my fingers against my bottom lip. Is this worth it? Is working with a monster like him worth the amazing salary and benefits?

Frustrated, I start typing out my resignation.

Another email comes in.

To: Kenya Jones
From: Holland Alistair
Subject: Resignation Letters

KINDLY WITHHOLD *from any attempts at resignation or temporary leave.*

Based on your actions at the Baby Box Headquarters, you are liable to be sued for business obstruction and breach of contract as outlined in page four of your employee contract which you signed when you entered the company.

Judgement will be reserved until we receive an official notice about the Baby Box contract. Until then, kindly arrange all the Belle's Beauty order sheets by date and re-upload the accounting spreadsheets for the Yazmite location.

• • •

Regards,
Holland Alistair
CEO of Belle's Beauty

I GLARE across the hallway in the direction of Alistair's office. He's poking me with his bright red pitchfork and I have no choice but to yield.

The jerk.

Maybe he wasn't out to get revenge before, but this isn't just business anymore.

This feels personal.

CHAPTER 10
IN HIS HEAD

HOLLAND

I REACH UP, yanking my collar to loosen a button—or maybe three. My eyes are starting to water. I can't make out the time on the clock, but I think it's saying half past three.

Sleep. I should try to get in a few hours before the meeting tomorrow.

No, not tomorrow.

Today.

Later today.

There's an ache in my back when I stand. I slam my fist against the curve of my spine, trying to massage the knots. Stumbling away from the desk, I plod across the hallway.

A triangle of pink light beckons me to Belle's room. I ease the door open and peek in on my little girl. She's got a princess nightlight plugged into the wall near her bed.

I walk over and kneel next to her mattress. The aches in my body fall away like butter as I stare at her precious face. She's sleeping on her stomach, arms and legs sprawled like she's scaling a wall in her dreams. Her silky black hair falls over her face and I gently slide it away from her eyes.

She stirs and I shush her, rubbing her back until she settles again. When I hear her breathing return to normal, I push away from the bed and stumble to my bedroom.

The air is cold. Still.

I've gotten used to sleeping alone and yet, tonight, I feel the emptiness like a chasm.

Today has been a giant grinder, digging into my shoulders. The mess at Baby Box had me poring over my data, trying to find what I was missing. *The human element?* What the hell is that? Money is the best indicator of success.

I'm too exhausted to think for a second more. My tattered emotions are pulling me thin. Right now, I can barely keep my eyes open.

It takes effort to drag myself to the bathroom and brush my teeth. By the time I fall into bed, I don't need to reach for the sleeping pills. Sleep finds me and drags me into the darkness.

Claire is there again. In my dreams.

A familiar hell.

"Don't drive, Holland. It's late. We should catch a flight tomorrow."

"I can make it."

"Are you sure?"

I watch it play out like a scene from a horror movie. A haunting torture that I can't escape. A lifetime prison sentence.

I sink into the anger and pain. Bathe myself in it. In the regret.

Monsters like me, men who murder their wives, don't deserve peace. They don't deserve love. It's enough that I have Belle. I have to make it up to her. I have to give her everything. All the things.

"Don't drive, Holland. You've barely gotten any sleep."

"I can't miss that meeting."

"You're right."

In my dream, the hotel door opens with a creak.

I startle from my perch in the shadows. Why is the door opening? That didn't happen on the day Claire…

A woman with dark skin and curly hair stomps into my dream. Her eyes are black marbles, glistening with annoyance.

Her mouth is brown. Shades of it. The bottom is darker than the top.

She plants a hand on her hip. With those ridiculously sexy lips, she hisses, *"And so?"*

I stare at her from my perch against the wall. I'm hunkered in the darkness, arms loose at my sides, knees pressed into the cold floor.

There are times when I yell at myself for walking through the door. For dragging Claire with me. For ruining Belle's life.

And there are nights, like tonight, when I collapse into a dark corner of my dream and watch with silent anguish.

The scene of me and Claire goes grey. I blink rapidly as Kenya Jones stomps her way through my memories like she stomps out of my office after an argument.

She has on the dress she was wearing at Baby Box today. The tight red one that clings to her curves. Temptation trapped in fabric. Her small waist brings attention to the curve of her hips. Trim but luscious.

I scramble to my feet. *"Get out."*

"And so?" She glides across the floor, grace in motion.

My eyebrows crash together.

Kenya stops right in front of me. Eyes big and bright, she stares me down. I've conjured her in startling detail, down to the frizz of her wiry brown curls and the slight bump in her flared nose.

I step toward her.

A loud beeping sound jerks me awake. My eyes burst open, and I meet the slow crawl of the dawn. Lingering shadows cling to the corners of my room, fighting to live for a second more while the sun creeps over the horizon.

I press a hand to my chest and notice my heart slamming against my fingertips. It takes me a second to get my bearings.

My breathing remains labored. My chest still burns.

Kenya Jones was in my dream again.

Damn.

I roll to a sitting position, shoulders hunched, on the edge of the bed. My fingers dig into the mattress and I press my feet on top of the cold floor, struggling to root myself to reality.

Yesterday, I almost popped a vein in the Baby Box conference room. I could not believe Miss Jones's defiance. Rather than heartfelt apologies, there was the tilt of her head and the cold set of her lips. There were icy glares and sharp comebacks.

She'd blown a hole in the Belle's Beauty presentation and she didn't have an ounce of remorse.

After everything she'd done, after the way she threw Belle under the bus, firing her would have been the most logical thing to do.

But I didn't.

She's a hard worker and an efficient…

That's not all.

Even so, it's all that matters.

I can handle Kenya Jones in the flesh. All her attitude. All her snarky remarks. That stinger of a tongue that always makes my blood run hot. She's in a box labeled 'do not touch' and I can stuff it away when I put my mind to it.

But seeing her in my subconscious continually is a problem.

A big one.

If she keeps coming back to me in my dreams, I might drive myself crazy.

Confused and groggy, I lumber to the bathroom. When I step into the shower, I hesitate and then go for the cold faucet. Turning it to full blast, I shiver beneath the stream. Water runs into my eyes, down my nose and the column of my neck. I curl my fingers into fists, taking the brunt of it like a man.

What do I do now? See a priest? Hire an exorcist? How do I get my aggravating assistant out of my head?

After stepping out of the shower, I still have no clear direction. What I *do* have is my brother-in-law's number.

I pace my bedroom as sunlight bursts through the windows. For four years, I've resisted asking for help. Opening my head for anyone to inspect was too tall of an order.

Is Kenya Jones going to push me over the edge? Is she the one who'll break me?

I check my watch. Bernard should have picked up Miss Jones by now. If I know her, she's probably steaming. Cursing me to hell and back for forcing her to get up and work this early.

My bare feet skid against the floor. The robe I wrapped around myself sways with each rotation around the room.

Damn it.

I haul my phone and call Darrel.

"Hello?"

"I need to speak to you."

He doesn't balk at the time or scold me for not doing this sooner. "I'll start the tea."

I call Mrs. Hansley, who bustles over in twenty minutes.

"She's still sleeping," I tell her, shrugging into my suit jacket. "I gave her a kiss already but, when she wakes up, let her know that I'll be back late."

Hansley pinches her lips together. "Alright."

I want to get going, but I notice her hesitation and stop. "Is something wrong?" Mrs. Hansley is the closest to Belle. If she's upset, I'm upset.

"Belle has been asking about her mother," she says.

My body runs cold.

My heart drops to my toes.

"I did what you said and told her that her mommy was in heaven, but she kept pressing. I'm not sure if she's noticing the mothers in her play date circle or... I thought you should know."

My pulse goes still for a second. "I'll handle it."

She nods.

As I leave, a massive headache clamps around my head. It squeezes my skull until it threatens to explode.

My greatest fear is Belle finding out what I did to our family. She's too young to understand now, but she'll be old enough someday. I wanted to be the one to explain it to her. I wanted to be the one to admit my sins.

But I don't want that day to be any time soon.

With a giant sigh, I stride down the stairs and into the circular driveway. The car is there, idling. Bernard straightens when he sees me. As usual, he's wearing his pressed black suit and white gloves. I've told him he can change to something cooler, but he always insists on the uniform. Says it's one less decision he has to make in a day.

"Bernard." I nod.

He smiles and opens the door. "You're moving out a little later than usual."

"Miss Jones needed the car."

"I was finished with her an hour ago."

My eyebrows hike. "An hour?"

"Yes. I arrived early to her apartment. You know I prefer to get there twenty minutes before the time, in case of traffic."

I do. It's one of the reasons we've gotten along so well. He does his work impeccably and goes above and beyond. I respect that.

"She was hotfooting it down the sidewalk when I got there. Said she was going to the office to get more work done." He chuckles. "Mind you, Miss Jones left the office at midnight yesterday."

Regret is a cold and distant friend, but it pays me a visit once more. I could have gone easier on her. The workload, this time, is guaranteed to give her stress.

Wicked of me, perhaps.

But flexing my arm to beat her defiance down felt like the right move when I was seething after the Baby Box incident. Now that I'm scrambling to see Darrel because Miss Jones keeps inhabiting my dreams, I wonder who's beating whom.

Grunting, I motion for him to get in the car. "Let's go."

While Bernard speeds through early morning traffic, I review the latest data pulls. Burying my head in algorithms is akin to an addict getting another hit. I can easily get lost in the details, in the story they have to tell.

People often assume that coding is a numbers game. And it is.

But it's also a thrilling ride into another world. Peeling back the curtains of ones and zeroes to the heart of a universe full of possibilities. Sure, those hearts are artificial in nature, but the stories are no less compelling.

Today, I stare at the tablet and feel numb.

The failure at Baby Box.

The licensing play for my technology.

Belle asking about her mother.

Miss Jones ruling over my dreams.

It's all culminating in chaos. A tornado tearing through the tight grip I usually have on control.

Now is not the time to fall apart.

I need to get myself together before my world implodes completely.

* * *

BERNARD SLOWS the car in front of Darrel's farmhouse. The building is surrounded by sprawling oak trees and a wide, picturesque garden.

He's better at growing bank accounts than bluebells, but he's stubborn about that garden. The obsession with growing things started when he suddenly quit investment banking and decided to become a therapist. It's a mysterious change he told no one, not even Claire, the full story about.

"Should I wait?" Bernard asks.

"This won't take long." I climb out of the car.

Darrel opens the front door and nods at me. He's dressed in a simple Henley and khakis. Despite the casual wear, his back is ramrod straight and his lips are stiff. Believe it or not, this is him at his most welcoming.

"Alistair."

"Darrel." I don't know how therapy sessions should be. I've never attended one, even when my family pressed me to go after the funeral.

Asking for help is a cardinal sin. Especially when I deserve all the hell I'm getting.

But Kenya Jones isn't something I can handle myself. As awkward as it may be, I don't trust anyone else with my business. If the wrong person finds out about this, I'll be all over the papers by noon.

"I have the coffee." He points to the kitchen. Although the outside of his farmhouse is rustic, Darrel had the inside gutted and completely redone.

Claire would have gone wild in this kitchen. It's huge and wide with warm wooden cabinets, a long island counter and the latest appliances. There's a kettle smoking on the back burner.

I nod to it. "You tried to cook?"

"A mistake I won't make again." His eyes remain hard, but his lips twitch slightly. "Tea will just have to do."

"I'm okay."

"Drink it. It'll give your hands something to do."

I follow him to the table and sit, but my eyes keep jumping around. Darrel's place is warm and welcoming. The little touches the designer implemented speaks of someone who knows how to turn a bachelor pad into a cozy refuge.

Claire would have... she would have loved everything about it.

"It's your first time, right?"

"Yeah."

"I paid a company. Told them to let the designer do what she wanted with this place." He gestures to the rooms. "They sent someone out who knew what she was doing." He slides the steaming mug over. The scent is minty. I already know that it won't be sweet. "Tell me why you're here, Alistair."

"To enjoy your coffee."

He doesn't laugh.

I didn't really expect him to.

Darrel inhales deeply. "Did you do something to Miss Jones?"

"You heard of the Baby Box meeting?"

He shrugs.

Damn. Gossip really gets around. People outside the company are catching wind of the disaster.

"I don't know what you've heard, but I went easy on her."

"That's unlike you."

"Even if she's insufferable, she's good at her job."

"It sounds like you're trying to convince me."

"Is this the part where you analyze my brain?"

"I'm just listening."

"Maybe this was a bad idea."

"You've come this far, Alistair. Might as well spit it out."

I hate that he sounds so smug about it. "Isn't there a rule that shrinks shouldn't work on their own family members?"

"I'm technically, not a shrink. I'm a neuropsychologist."

I wave away his clarification.

He sets the mug down with a clink. "It's okay to feel an attraction to someone. Claire wouldn't have wanted you to lock yourself away and be miserable."

"You don't know what she would have wanted." My eyes flash. "Because she's not here."

"Alistair—"

"She's in my dreams," I blurt.

He goes still. "Claire?"

"Always. But I wasn't talking about her." My heart slams against my ribs. "Miss Jones."

His eyes widen a bit. "What kind of dreams?" He taps his fingers on the table. "Sexual? Is she naked?"

"Dammit, Darrel. I'm not dreaming of another woman naked while my wife is right there."

"What do you mean 'right there'?"

I blow out a frustrated breath.

Darrel stiffens when it hits him. "The nightmare. Miss Jones is *inside* the nightmare?"

"She bursts into the hotel room. Into that... memory. She gives me attitude and kind of shocks me awake."

Surprise passes over his usually blank face.

"I can't get her out."

"What exactly is she doing in those dreams?"

"The first time, she just appeared. Like a ghost. The second time, she barged through the door right when I was leaving with Claire. She yelled at me."

Darrel stares thoughtfully at the table. "Hm."

"Hm?"

"Has anyone ever entered that nightmare before?"

"Never." I shake my head. "It's only her. Only since I hired her."

He strokes his chin. "This is good."

"Good?" My assistant is parading through my dreams and he thinks it's good.

"Yes." He eases back, one arm resting on the table. "That nightmare has been playing on a loop ever since Claire passed. But it got worse when you decided to tackle Belle's Beauty on your own."

"Worse is an arbitrary word."

"You came to me for sleeping pills." His eyes are sharp.

"That still didn't work," I point out.

"Consider your brain like a mysterious piece of tech. It has pressure sensors that flare when the stress is getting to you. Your mind has been trying to communicate that it's being worn down and mistreated."

"My mind isn't a sentient being."

"It's the control tower. The center of everything that makes up your mind, body and soul. And it's breaking down."

"What about Miss Jones?"

"What about her?"

"She's in my dreams now. She's messing up my head. Should I… fire her?" I hold my breath.

His eyes ram into mine. "Is that what you want?"

I glance away.

"You would have fired her a long time ago if you wanted her out of your life." He drums his fingers against the mug. "But you didn't."

"That's ridiculous."

"You might not want to admit it, Alistair." He arches an eyebrow. "But your brain is giving you away."

"It was just a dream."

"If it was just a dream, you wouldn't be here." His tone is hard.

I think Darrel needs a lesson on the 'human element' too.

"Dreams often play a significant part in exposing what's on our mind at a subconscious level." He lifts a hand. Raises it to the light. "We have the conscious level. The things we do or say regularly come from here." He drops his hand a foot below that. "And we have the subconscious level. That's where the real power is. It's harder to penetrate that domain but, once it does, it's locked in."

"You're saying I have Miss Jones... *trapped* in my subconscious?"

"I believe, this is just a hunch, that you're secretly hoping Miss Jones will save you."

If I wasn't so shocked, I'd probably laugh. "I don't need anyone to save me."

"Your brain seems to think otherwise."

"My brain has been messed up since the funeral. You shouldn't listen to a thing that bastard says."

"Alistair, you *are* that bastard."

I scowl at him.

"Miss Jones keeps showing up in your nightmares. She stops the memory of that night from playing over and over again. She takes the control you don't want to give. She forces you to step away from regret. She's prying your cold, hard fingers off the self-destruct button."

I grit my teeth. "I don't like anything I'm hearing."

"People rarely enjoy hearing the truth but, in the long run, it hurts much less than building a house out of BS."

My phone rings, saving Darrel from a blistering comment.

It's Ezekiel.

"I'm late for a meeting," I say, pocketing the phone without answering it.

My chair scrapes the ground when I rise. The tea remains untouched on the table. I don't have to drink it to know it won't live up to Ezekiel's brew.

"Alistair."

I turn around.

Darrel unfolds his broad, six-foot frame from the table. He stares at me with green eyes. Claire's eyes. It's still hard to look directly at them without thinking of her.

"No one can free you. You're the only one who can get out."

My chest tightens. "I'll try to be there when you visit Belle Friday, but I can't guarantee anything."

"It's fine. Mrs. Hansley basically raised me too. We'll have a good visit."

I hurry out of the farmhouse. Bernard straightens and travels around to open my door. I lurch at the handle and yank it before he can.

My thoughts are whirring. I can't catch them fast enough. Can't make them sit still so I can pore over them. Make sense of them.

Bernard, wisely, doesn't speak to me on the way to the office.

I press my hands into the backseat and focus on breathing. Darrel's pesky analysis can't be right. I'm not pining for Miss Jones. Her appearance in my dreams is not a cry for help from my brain. And Claire, most certainly, wouldn't want her murderer to be happy.

* * *

"You don't look so good," Ezekiel tells me when I charge into my office. "How much sleep did you get last night?"

"Where's my coffee?"

"There." He points to the cup.

I lift the lid. Sniff. Just the right amount of cinnamon and cream. Shoving it toward him, I bark, "You drink it first."

"Excuse me?"

"I'll wait to make sure you don't die and then I'll have it."

Ezekiel's eyes widen. Then he starts laughing.

I glare at him. "What's so funny?"

"Nothing, sir."

My scowl is extra dark because he's lying to me.

Ezekiel sets a new stack of binders on my desk. "Miss Jones returned the company credit card along with the organized invoices and receipts. Would you like me to file them away?"

"No. Let her do it."

"I'll let her know." He clears his throat. "Are you ready for the meeting?"

"Yes."

I shoot out of my chair and swipe the coffee from the edge of my desk.

Spiked or not, I'm in too bad a condition to head into that meeting without a little java. Ezekiel can let the feds know Kenya was responsible for my coffee if I end up crashing to the ground and foaming at the mouth later.

Ezekiel follows me down the hallway.

I stop and arch an eyebrow at him. "What are you doing?"

"I'll attend the marketing meeting with you."

"Why?" My angry eyes dart over the hallway. "Where's Kenya?"

"Attending to matters for the in-store promotion."

"She's not here?"

His eyes dart to the side.

I step toward him. My voice is low and threatening. "It is Miss Jones's responsibility to attend all matters regarding Belle's Beauty. Inform her that if she doesn't show up, she can contact my lawyer to negotiate for the damages regarding the Baby Box pitch."

"Sir?"

"Did I *stutter*, Ezekiel?" I hiss.

His eyebrows fall low over disapproving eyes. "If she upsets you, Alistair, I don't have a problem attending the meeting in her place."

"I need your attention on Fine Industries. There's been another hiccup with the licensing contract."

Ezekiel remains in the hallway, holding his ground.

I step back and rub my temple. "You acting like this makes me wonder if you believe I'm the bad guy."

"Miss Jones entered this company under suspicion. The employees are questioning what she's doing here and what connection she has to you."

"Is that a problem? So she isn't a class favorite. We don't show up to work to make friends."

"Maybe not."

I keep walking. Then I swerve back. "Did she complain to you?"

"Not once. And, as far as I know, Miss Jones has handled all rejection with grace."

His eyes are soft when he speaks about her. It seems Miss Jones has earned Ezekiel's favor. But he did always like the ones with spikes. It's why he puts up with me.

"Well then…"

"Yesterday was different."

I freeze.

"Yesterday," Ezekiel says, "she was outright confronted by one of your admirers."

"My admirers?" I rub my chin. I've trained myself to ignore the physical interest of women in the company. Kenya's the only exception, but it's not because I *want* to notice her. She's derailed my best attempts at keeping my eyes to myself.

"I'm afraid Miss Jones will be further harassed."

"She acts like nothing can harm her. Why are you suddenly concerned?"

"It's a tense time, Alistair."

"And even if there's a damn flying saucer hovering on top of the building, I expect her to show up when she's supposed to and complete her duties as assigned."

His eyes narrow slightly, but he dips his chin. "I'll inform her."

"Ezekiel."

He turns, disapproval in his furrowed brow and the set of his whiskered chin. "Yes, sir?"

"I don't care how much you favor the woman. Don't question me again."

His eyes darken. "Yes, sir."

I enter the meeting room where the Belle's Beauty PR team have gathered. This is an emergency meeting to discuss the failure that was Baby Box and to come up with a Plan B, hence why I've asked them to arrive early. My schedule is so full that I couldn't fit them in at any other point in the day.

Frightened eyes dart to the ground. I take my seat and roll it into position at the head of the table. Heated silence fills the air while I take my time hauling out my laptop.

A moment later, the door opens and Miss Jones marches in. Every nerve in my body tightens at the sight of her. Silky, dark skin drowning in sunshine. Bee-stung lips covered in gloss. Curly hair slicked back in a low ponytail.

I hide my rising desire with a thunderous expression. She meets my glare with a cold look of her own. Refusing to cower, she traipses through the room and yanks out the chair next to me.

Stunned looks get tossed our way. The PR team bore witness to the battle of wills that occurred yesterday. They know it'd be near suicide to sit next to me after making such a mess.

I toss Kenya Jones a dark look. *Do you have a death wish?*

"Can't I sit here?" She answers my glower with a cool expression. "Or is that another company rule?"

It's not that she *can't* sit there, but no one does. The seats to my left and right are usually vacant because no one wants to be within firing distance.

Kenya plunks her notebook and laptop on the table and gets comfortable.

This woman is either crazy or fearless. Either way, she's making it hard to breathe right now.

I ram my fingers together and rest my elbows on the table. "You all know why we're here. Baby Box was a disaster. Before Miss Jones's… untimely interruption, Sutherburg was not biting."

No one speaks up.

Not that I expect them too.

When the ship's going down, no one wants to take responsibility with the captain. I know that it's ultimately my responsibility but, *because* it's my responsibility, I can set things in place so it never happens again.

"We have other deals we can pursue, but that's not the point. Losing the Baby Box pitch jeopardizes our company value. When trying to expand our markets, we need companies jumping on board. Rejection will make the rest of the pack cautious." My eyes slice through Kenya's. "And we don't need any more reasons to look untrustworthy."

Her mouth curls into a frown.

"So," I glance at my team in turn, "what were the holes in yesterday's plan and what can we do to salvage this?"

I listen to the PR team hem and haw their way through the analysis. I give my thoughts, listen to their excuses, and bark out my feedback.

Toward the end of the meeting, I dismiss them all and rub my eyelids. I need a coffee refill.

"Kenya."

"I know." She climbs to her feet and cradles her notebook and laptop. "Milk, cream and 'enough' sugar."

I'd thank her if my head wasn't pounding. Moving listlessly back to my office, I fall into the chair and tilt my head back.

A hard knock on the door alerts me to Kenya's entrance. She plunks a glass of water on the table and tosses an unopened bottle of headache reliever pills.

I stare at the offering. "Where's my coffee?"

"Coffee is only going to make it worse." She folds her arms over her chest and jerks her chin down.

"Didn't I tell you to go about your duties quietly?" I open the bottle and listen to the crack of the breaking seal. Shaking two tablets into my palm, I grunt. "This isn't quietly."

"There are nicer ways to say thanks."

"I didn't say thanks." I knock the pills back and swallow.

She rolls her eyes. "By the way, I had something to say during the meeting, but I didn't want to embarrass you."

My eyebrows hike.

"Why didn't you bring up your delivery as a part of the evaluation?"

I slam the cup on the table. Water sloshes over the rim.

"You don't have to be good at everything, but if you're going to expose what went wrong yesterday, you could have started there."

"My delivery was not the issue. It was the content of the pitch."

"You spoke to Baby Box like you were doing *them* a favor. That might work in some cases, but not when you're trying to convince someone to buy from you."

My eyes narrow to slits. "Did I not make myself clear yesterday?"

"You made yourself very clear." She tilts her chin up. "I stay and take whatever you dish out or you sue me for everything I'm worth."

I wouldn't say it like that, but I'm glad she took it that way.

Kenya holds her ground. "You made yourself clear and I'd like to do that too. I'm here because I want to be. Because it's a good job with the kind of salary and benefits I couldn't dream of receiving, even if I was fifty years old with thirty years of experience."

My impatient stare does not deter her one bit.

She steps toward my desk. "I apologize again for bringing your family into the pitch. That wasn't right and I accept the consequences of that decision." She swipes the cup off the table and yanks the pills too. "But I don't like being threatened and manipulated. I'm not your possession. Keep that in mind the next time you want to force me to do anything."

My eyebrow quirks up. Pushing her into a corner made her even bolder. Her eyes are pure fire. Flames shooting out to rival a bonfire.

If I wasn't so in awe of her guts, I'd ax her on the spot just for *assuming* she can lecture me.

The landline rings.

She turns to go.

I lift a hand. "Wait right there."

Her back stiffens and I can feel her annoyance spreading out like spikes in the room.

I lift the phone from its cradle. "Hello?"

"Mr. Alistair, sir," the receptionist at the lobby screeches, "you have a visitor."

"Who is it?" I bark.

"It's Mr. Sutherburg from Baby Box."

My eyes widen and I speak hoarsely. "Send him upstairs."

CHAPTER 11
SAVE THE DATE

KENYA

He's either going to kill me or fire me. Either way, I'm not keeping my mouth shut.

After talking to Sunny last night and doing some soul searching, I realize what *really* bothers me about Holland Alistair.

He's a jerk. To *me*.

And it shouldn't surprise me since he's basically a jerk to everyone, but it keeps rubbing me raw.

He's gorgeous. Brilliant. Arrogant.

Sure. All the above.

But he keeps treating people like disposable potato sacks. Whenever he's in a room, I feel like I'm a chess piece he can push and prod at will. It was just a hint before because, clearly, he's my boss. Like Heather said, I'm an errand girl. Running after Alistair's every whim is what I'm paid to do.

But it's more than that.

He took away my right to leave his bullying behind.

That really ticks me off.

Even part time jobs allow me to quit on a whim.

I didn't sign my life away when I entered this company. This isn't a kingdom. Alistair isn't my king. I want the freedom to leave if I choose. I don't want to feel trapped, and I hate that I am. That he's the one holding the key.

He hangs up the phone and gives me an astonished look. "Sutherburg is here."

"Really?" My palms start to sweat. "Is that normal?"

He shakes his head.

Weird.

But it's none of my business. If Sutherburg *did* come all the way here to yell at Alistair, I wish him luck. Alistair will slice his head off and pick his bones clean. No one seems to be excluded from his hit list. Not even his business partners.

"I'll continue my work for the in-store promotion," I tell him. Now that I've said my piece, I'm eager to leave.

He nods absently. Then he calls me back. "Wait. Ezekiel is out right now. I'll need you to bring refreshments." His eyes focus on me and sharpen. "Can you handle that?" It's a question, but the fury behind it tells me there's only one right answer.

"Yes."

His stare hardens.

What? Is he upset again? Does he want me to drop into a curtsy when I answer him?

Alistair pulls out his phone and frowns. "Hurry. They'll be here any minute."

If it were anyone else, I wouldn't move until they said 'please'. Just to remind them that we're all humans and that manners haven't gone out of style.

But since it's Alistair and I'll probably be blue in the face before he treats *anyone* like a human being, I decide to let it go.

Hustling through the hallway, I start the coffee brew. I'm halfway through the task when harried footsteps charge toward me.

"Miss Jones!" Our new intern sprints into the room. Her eyes are wide and her red-stained lips are parted. "Miss Jones!"

"What? What's wrong?"

"Mr. Alistair is calling you."

"Me?" My eyes dart to the coffee. "But I just—"

"I'll do that." She extends pale arms and shoos me away from the coffee machine. Her breathing sounds heavy, like she ran all the way here. A glance at her shoes makes me whistle. Mad respect. I'd probably bust my leg open trying to run in those.

"Hurry," she says. "It sounded urgent."

I'm on the move in a blink. What could it be? Did Alistair have an allergic reaction to the headache pills? He's not going to blame me, is he? I intentionally got him a brand-new bottle so he wouldn't say anything stupid about me tampering with the meds.

What if he needs me to give him the Heimlich?

Should I?

Or what, Kenya? You'll leave him to die?

I'm a horrible person.

Skidding past Ezekiel's empty desk, I throw the door open and hustle inside the boss's office. My eyes skate around the room, noting the absence of a fire, flood or chaos.

Instead, I see Mr. Sutherburg. The short man is seated in a wingback chair. From the crimson flush creeping over his ears, he's either excited about something or royally ticked off.

With his protruding stomach, bushy brows and calculating brown eyes, Sutherburg strikes me as a businessman who knows how to turn on the charm or bite you like a snake when the mood hits him.

I let the door click shut behind me.

Alistair grunts. "Sit here, Miss Jones."

My eyes nearly pop out of my face. He's *inviting* me to sit next to him? When I grabbed the chair at his elbow during the meeting with the PR team, I thought I was sitting next to an open fridge. No, worse than that. A meat locker. The kind they use in horror movies to show the serial killer traipsing around next to slabs of beef.

I approach him cautiously. "I didn't get to bring the coffee."

"Oh, we don't have time for coffee," Sutherburg says. His

hands move so animatedly that he might fly out of his seat. The ruddy flush in his ears spreads to his cheeks and neck.

"I see," I murmur, still confused.

Alistair leans close and his intoxicating scent of spice and dry mint washes over me. A thrill goes down my spine.

"He insisted on having you here," Alistair growls close to my ear.

And oh Lord. His voice when it's not barking and grunting at me is pure, decadent chocolate.

The thrum of attraction snakes lower.

I hold myself perfectly still as Alistair draws away from me and straightens his jacket.

Sutherburg gestures to the man sitting next to him. Something about the way he carries himself catches my eye. It's an arrogance. A sign of stature. Of authority.

Alistair has that poise too, except it's muddied by his bad temper and general apathy for anyone with a beating heart. It makes him colder. Clinical. He doesn't strike me as anyone who would finesse his way into a room. He'd just break the door down and, if that didn't work, he'd burn everything to the ground.

This man, though, is calculating. Sly. He has black hair, black eyes, and a thick black moustache. He watches everyone in the room like a hawk. No one needs to tell me he's the one in charge.

"Walsh, this is the young lady I was talking to you about." Sutherburg gestures to me.

My eyes widen. They were talking about me?

"What exactly is this visit about?" Alistair asks, barely managing to sound polite.

Sutherburg yips like an excited puppy. "I couldn't stop thinking about Miss Jones's proposal. It was inspired. Printing real stories on the flaps of all Baby Box packages? It's branding. It's personal. It's out of the box." He chortles, flashing big teeth. "Forgive the pun."

Alistair's face does not give his thoughts away, but his knee does a little jump. I catch it because I'm sitting close to him. And because my nerves are jumping under my skin too.

"You gave the impression that you weren't pleased at the meeting."

"Oh, it wasn't that. I couldn't sign you on immediately because I had to talk to Walsh." He gestures to the sly-faced man. "He's ultimately in charge of big promotions like this. And since the boxes will need to be altered, we'd need his okay. This kind of change involves the production team as well as our PR team."

I lean forward. "So… you *liked* my idea?"

"Loved it." Sutherburg beams. "I thought it was fantastic."

I twist my head around and shoot Alistair a victorious look.

He grunts. "You could have informed us over the phone." His eyes move to Walsh. "Why visit in person?"

"We need to clarify some things."

"What things?"

Walsh's voice is heavy and cultured. "I wanted to read the proposal, but there was none at hand. I was informed that you, Mr. Alistair, had a problem with your wife's story being printed. Given the matter is so sensitive, I came to speak to you personally about it."

I scoot to the edge of my chair. "We'd prefer that none of the stories feature his wife. That's how we came up with the angle of using everyday women."

Walsh's eyes land on me and linger for longer than they need to. An uncontrollable urge to punch the guy rushes inside me. Who does he think he's looking at?

"The problem," Alistair says, his tone hard and scorching, "is the amount of information displayed. I don't have a problem with Claire's story reaching more people. I simply want no mention of our daughter."

Walsh jerks his gaze to Alistair. "That's a difficult request given our boxes are for mothers."

"Nothing is difficult when you're the one calling the shots.

Claire's story might inspire mothers to reconnect with the dreams they gave up when they had their children."

Walsh's lips flicker in a cold smile. "You make a good point, Alistair."

The men hold a staring contest.

An alarm goes off in my head. Pretty soon, they'll jump on the table and start beating their chests.

A knock sounds at the door.

The intern shuffles in.

Glad for a reprieve from the caveman routine, I hop up to help her.

"Let me take this," I say, grabbing the tray.

"Thanks," she whispers, her cheeks flushed.

I watch her scurry out, wondering if it would be more prudent to follow her. When I turn around, I notice Walsh peering at my backside. His eyes lift immediately and he smiles without shame.

My annoyance meter jumps to ten, but I don't let it show. Belle's Beauty has another shot at a partnership with Baby Box. There's no way I'm screwing this up.

There's a time and place for everything. My dad taught me that. Sometimes, I need to don my warrior armor. Sometimes, I put up with perverted old men for the sake of the end goal.

"Mr. Alistair." I hand him his coffee first. Not because he's my boss. It's because Walsh is getting on my nerves, so I need to rebel in some way. "Mr. Sutherburg." I offer the coffee to him next.

"Thank you, Miss Jones."

"And Mr…"

A pale hand dashes out and grabs my wrist before I can get the mug to its rightful place. The hand belongs to Alistair and his grip on me is firm.

I whip my head around, stunned. What is he doing?

Without tearing his eyes off Walsh, Alistair guides me back to the sofa. I almost stumble, but he doesn't give me the time to lose my balance. In a blink, he hauls me down beside him, closer than before, and grabs the coffee from the tray.

"Here." He tosses the cup at Walsh. "Let me."

I'm surprised the cup doesn't spill all over Walsh's expensive suit. The coffee remains in the mug, and the ceramic stops just before skidding to the edge of the table.

Walsh's lips hitch up at the corners. He takes the coffee by the handle and sips it calmly.

Sutherburg clears his throat. "Well, uh, Mr. Alistair, you know that Baby Box has an engaged audience. Our buyers will continue to purchase the products they enjoy. You can think of us like a recommendation system—"

"I'm aware of your company's strengths, Mr. Sutherburg, but there are some things I will not compromise on." His eyes are on Walsh.

I have no idea what's gotten into my boss, but Sutherburg is here, *begging* us to work with him. We can't let this opportunity pass us by. This is my chance to redeem myself and prove I'm an asset to this company.

"Mr. Walsh, you came all this way." I stuff my disgust deep inside and smile prettily at him. "I'm honored that you and Mr. Sutherburg approve of my idea, and I'm excited to see it come to life."

Alistair's eyes bore a hole through my skull. What? Am I not supposed to speak here either? He's the one who told me to attend the meeting.

"No agreements have been made yet," Walsh says, giving Alistair a pointed look.

He glowers in return.

I nudge him in the side. "Mr. Alistair?"

"No."

"No?" Sutherburg nearly falls out of his chair.

"I think what he means to say is that *no one* will keep him from this amazing opportunity." Nervous laughter pours from my lips. "Right?"

Walsh nods at me. "Miss Jones, I think your ability to interpret your boss's real thoughts is spot on."

"Thank you." I clear my throat.

"You're quite talented. It's such a waste to see a young and…" his eyes slide over my body, "generous asset put to waste under Alistair's care."

"Are you poaching my assistant in front of my eyes, Walsh?" Alistair spits.

Walsh rises and buttons his suit. "I've heard what I need to hear and I think a partnership between Belle's Beauty and Baby Box is the right call. If we can hammer out the details, Alistair, I'll send over the contract."

I jump to my feet as well. "Thank you."

Alistair remains seated.

"Here," Walsh approaches me and offers a business card, "call me if you ever get tired of Alistair's frosty mug. I think you'll be very satisfied with my terms."

I throw up in my mouth.

Alistair lurches to his feet, his face stormy. I recognize that look and quickly step in front of him, barring his way so Walsh and Sutherburg can make their exit.

When the door clicks shut, I whirl on him. "Were you trying to sabotage the deal?"

No response.

"Hello?" I wave a hand.

It's like talking to a chiseled, absolutely gorgeous wall.

Suddenly, he raises his hand, palm up.

I stare at him. "What do you want?"

He arches an eyebrow, still looking annoyed.

I let out a deep breath. Who did I offend to have earned a boss like this? Seriously, I'll go back and repent on my knees if I have to.

"What? What?" I wave my arms around in frustration.

Alistair plucks Walsh's business card from me. In two quick snaps of his fingers, the business card is in three pieces. Two more snaps and it's in five.

I blink in shock. "The hell is wrong with you?"

Yes. He's my boss.

And yes, I probably shouldn't yell.

But to hell with propriety. He's the one crossing the line this time.

"Did you plan on taking him up on his offer?"

"That has *nothing* to do with you."

Alistair growls. He's a well-dressed psycho. Hazel eyes violently shout his displeasure. I get lost in the threads of brown and gold. Fury trapped in shifting emerald and mud.

He keeps staring at me without saying a word.

Anger shifts inside my chest, underlined by something else. I feel like I'm drowning in fire and electricity.

My breath turns heavy. "How many times do I have to tell you that. You. Don't. Own. Me."

"And how many times do I have to tell you." He stalks closer until he's in my personal space. "You don't speak in these meetings unless I give you permission to."

"Screw you."

"You care to say that again?" His face is practically on top of mine.

My breath hits the air in quick beats, drumming in time to my racing heart. A tick in his jaw draws my eye there. His face is sharp and dangerous. His mouth is a warning. Thick and full. Promising delight and disaster.

Should I bite them or kiss them?

Awareness singes the air between us. I can't hear my own thoughts over how hard my heart is pounding.

He's your boss, Kenya.

The reminder forces me back a step. Edging away from him to keep my wits about me, I frown. "Walsh is a jerk, but jerks are everywhere."

"He's not just a jerk. He's been a persistent enemy ever since the early days of Fine Industries. His tech company folded. Mine didn't. And even up to now he's had it out for me."

"He'd be stupid to let his personal feud with you get in the way of this deal." I give him a pointed stare. "Besides, this isn't

Fine Industries. This is Belle's Beauty. Partnering with Baby Box is a good move. You said so yourself and I agree." Not that my opinion seems to matter to him. "I know I can convince them not to publish your daughter's information. Let's not beat around the bush or try to act like we don't need them. You know we do."

He turns abruptly and rubs his temples. I wonder if his headache is back. He lumbered into work this morning looking like a microwaved corpse. I don't have to *imagine* how hard this man is working. It's right there on his gorgeous face.

I gave him the headache pills because, if he kicks the bucket, I lose my job.

Also… he doesn't seem to have anyone else taking care of him.

But that's not because I *care* about him.

That's just plain human decency. Something Alistair seems to lack.

"I'll think about it," he says finally.

I brighten and tiptoe in front of him. "Does that mean we're making a deal with Baby Box?"

"It means you'll have double the work. I expect you to get everything done for the Baby Box deal *and* continue with the in-store promotion."

My eyes narrow. "You're punishing me for getting the deal with Baby Box?"

He leans so close that I hold my breath. Lips quirking, he says, "Congratulations, Miss Jones."

My heart flogs my chest.

There's no denying it. Holland Alistair is truly my worst enemy.

* * *

"So he's taking the deal with Baby Box?" Sunny asks me when I drag myself to her apartment and flop into the couch.

"Yup."

"And he expects you to manage the in-store promotion *and* handle the Baby Box stuff?"

"That's right."

"Everything?" Her eyes widen.

I put my head in her lap and sigh. "Everything."

"That's ridiculous!" Her knee flaps around, sending my head flying.

I jerk up. "Can you not?"

"Can *you* not?" Her eyes flash angrily. "You're just gonna let him steamroll over you like that?"

"What other choice do I have?"

"You blast his backside all over the news! He's a billionaire. The tabloids will eat that up."

"He's already threatening me with a lawsuit, and you want to give him fuel to sue me for defamation?"

Her eyes narrow. "I mean… when you put it like that, it sounds stupid."

"I appreciate the thought."

"We can post anonymously."

"Not worth it. He's got an army of lawyers on payroll." I gesture to her couch. "And I'm bunking with my best friend because I don't even have a car to sleep in."

"Hey, even if you *had* a car, I wouldn't let you sleep in it."

I sling an arm over my eyes. "I'm screwed."

"What's his deal anyway? Why is he punishing you for saving the Baby Box deal?"

"He's defending his daughter's honor, I guess," I mumble.

She jerks on my arm, tugging me to sit up. "Your lunatic boss has a kid? Like an evil spawn or an actual human being?"

"She's a human being. A little girl. He protects her like she's his last breath. You should have seen the way he stood up to Walsh. Baby Box was offering us a deal and he was about to turn it down to protect her."

"Whoa." Sunny flops back, her eyes on the ceiling. "I had no idea. There was no mention of Alistair's kid online."

"I know." And given his behavior today, it makes sense why she's out of the spotlight. I don't know any reporters who'd be stupid enough to publish a story about her.

"No wonder he flipped his lid the day you mentioned her in the Baby Box pitch."

"Hey, I didn't mention her."

Sunny waves a hand dismissively.

"But you're right. I felt literal chills go up my spine." I bring a pillow to my face and moan into it. "His attitude is trash, but I can't deny that I shouldn't have brought up his family."

"His wife died a few years ago, right? That means his daughter must be a toddler."

"I don't know. We didn't discuss her."

Sunny blows out a breath. "Man, that's tough." She glances at me. "Can you handle all that work?"

"If I skip my meals and sleep for three hours like he does, maybe."

"Ugh."

I scramble up. "What if I take off in the middle of the night?" My eyes light up with a wild sheen. I grab her wrists. "We could change our names and go live in Belize. Think about it." I lower my voice as I paint the picture. "We can swim in the Caribbean Sea. Lounge on the beach. Sleep in hammocks and listen to the waves crash against the shore."

"I'm not sleeping in a hammock, girl."

"We can rent a nice place then. You have money?"

"I have student loans. Does that count?"

I drop my shoulders. "Do not remind me about my loans."

"Why do I get the feeling that your boss is crazy enough to find us if we run?"

"Probably because you have killer intuition and he would. He'd probably lock me in the file room and have me alphabetize everything."

"How did you get mixed up with someone like him?"

"I have no idea." I bawl into her shoulder.

She pats my hair, pushing through thick curls in order to massage my scalp. "There, there. It's not the end of the world. You can do the impossible."

"I doubt it. He's making *sure* I suffer. He even has me going around to the marketing team, asking for their coffee orders. It's humiliating. If I wanted to fetch people's coffee, I'd work at a coffee shop."

"I could totally see you at a coffee shop," Sunny says, pulling out her phone and scrolling.

"No way. I'd drink all our stock and probably juice myself up so bad I'd fall into cardiac arrest."

"True..." She narrows her eyes. "Yeah, I can see that."

"I wish I'd never met the guy."

"Just take a break and forget about him." Sunny casually taps her phone screen. "This weekend, I'll take you to a nice restaurant... oh damn. She *didn't*."

I propel myself up. "What is it?"

Sunny tries to hide the phone from me, but I snatch it out of her hands.

"Kenya, no!" She moves to grab it back.

I look at the screen and all the blood drains from my face. There's a picture of my sister with her hand out to the camera. The caption reads 'I said yes'. Drake is in the background, on his knees. And on Sasha's finger is a giant diamond ring.

The world rocks under my feet.

"They're... getting married?"

Sunny bites down on her lip.

My blood runs cold. Memories flash before my eyes.

"I'll learn to cook."

"Don't bother, baby. I'll cook for you."

"You spoil me, Drake."

"It's what I love to do."

"How about this? We'll have a rule. You cook. I clean."

"Deal. As long as you throw in an apron that says 'kiss the cook'."

"I can't wait to be your wife."

"One day, baby. One day."

My heart stutters and I don't even register when Sunny pries the phone from my trembling fingers.

She tucks it behind the pillow and grumbles, "What the hell is wrong with her? Does she not have a lick of sense? Is she seriously marrying her sister's ex-boyfriend?"

"Sunny." I swallow hard.

She pounces on my hand and holds it tightly. "Tell me what you want me to do. Even if it means I go to jail tonight, we can get her back. She deserves all the horror you can think of."

"I'm tired. Do you mind if I go to bed early?"

"What?" Her eyes search mine and then her mouth falls into a frown. "Sure. You don't have to ask me."

I rise woodenly and plod away from the living room.

Ice flows through my veins. I know I should feel things. Anger. Pain. Betrayal. Since finding Drake and my sister together, I've run the gamut of those emotions. Dove so deeply into them that I found their roots and inspected those too.

But this…

I'm numb. Too numb to make sense of it all.

Is it jealousy? I don't think so. The burning sensation that comes when I'm envious is absent.

It's not sorrow or even anger.

I stumble to the bathroom and go through the motions of brushing my teeth. My arm feels heavy. The toothbrush feels like a boulder. Everything takes a lot more effort.

I said yes.

Sasha was beaming in the picture. Glowing with love. The smile on Drake's face was large and warm too.

How long have they been together? How is he already proposing? He dragged his feet with me. We were together for so long and all he did was talk about marriage. He never once acted on it. It was just a promise. A carrot dangling on the edge of a stick.

I curl into bed and stare at the darkness surrounding me.

My phone rings.

I don't want to reach for it, but I pluck it from the nightstand where it was charging. My fingers press against the cold shell. It's freezing when I put it to my face.

"Hello?"

"You answered," Sasha says.

My eyes burst open. "I wouldn't have if I knew it was you."

Silence fills the line.

I should hang up, but I keep seeing those words.

I said yes.

It was a gorgeous ring. Something he definitely didn't pick up at a store. It seemed antique. Expensive but with a story behind it. A family heirloom. The one from his grandmother?

His mother told me about it once. His great-grandparents were separated when his great-grandfather went to war. He left the ring with his girlfriend and told her that he'd be back for it.

She kept the ring safe through the cold nights. When his letters stopped coming. And even when she heard that there had been a bomb where his squadron was stationed.

Months later, a man knocked on her door and, when she opened it, he was on his knees in front of her.

It was one of the most romantic stories I'd ever heard.

That ring, his great-grandparents' legendary ring, is on my little sister's finger.

And now her voice is in my ear.

It's the voice that used to wake me up in the mornings, singing songs she'd made up on her guitar. It's the voice that called out for me when she was sick, needing something other than our parents' smothering love to tether her to this world. It's the voice that broke when her body was tired from the chemo.

She's my family.

And she's getting married to my boyfriend.

"Did you see it?" she asks tentatively.

It takes me a while to respond. My eyes are burning, but I tell myself I won't cry again.

"I guess you did," Sasha mumbles. "I was hoping I could talk to you before then, but I didn't have the courage."

"Don't expect me to say congratulations."

"I know we're in a really bad place," Sasha whimpers, "but I'd love if you'd be my maid of honor."

My body jerks in surprise. The phone slips off my face and leans against the pillow.

Did I hear that right? Or is my brain playing tricks on me?

"Kenya, you're my best friend. When I felt like life wasn't worth living, you gave me the strength to hold on." She sniffs. "Remember when we'd lie down in the hospital bed, side-by-side? I told you once that I missed seeing the stars. The windows in my room were small and it felt like I was in prison. You brought a projector for me. You brought the stars to my hospital room."

I lose the battle with sorrow.

A tear drops down my cheek, followed by another.

I'm weary.

Down to my bones.

I don't feel like myself. Normally, the world is sunny and warm. I focus on the bright side of things because that's where I feel the most at peace.

But it's been tougher and tougher to get in touch with that side of my personality. Maybe I'm just growing up. Or maybe my optimism is being smothered by betrayal and pain.

"I don't want to talk right now."

"At least think about it. Please? It won't be the same without you there."

I hang up before she can hear me crying. I hate every single tear that falls from my eye. Hate it with a passion.

The door creaks open and Sunny walks in. The way she moves across the room, I know she heard, and I know she's fuming. But she doesn't rant at how selfish Sasha is. She climbs into bed and wraps her arms around me.

"It's okay to cry, Kenya."

"I'm not crying," I argue.

"You don't have to be Miss Sunshine all the time. No one expects you to keep all that hurt in. No one." She pats my hair and soothes me. "It's okay to cry."

I sob, my heart breaking all over again. It shouldn't feel this fresh every single time. Don't wounds heal eventually? When will mine cake up and dry? When will it stop feeling like my heart is tearing open?

"She asked me..." I breathe hard, "to be her maid of honor."

Sunny's arms tighten around me. "That selfish piece of—"

"I can't do it."

"Of course you can't. She's got a serious problem if she thinks you'd ever say yes to that."

"I don't want to cry anymore." Sitting up, I use the sleeve of my T-shirt to dry my tears. "It's pathetic."

"It's never pathetic to cry. That's you expressing your pain. If you keep that bottled up inside, it'll explode. And that's not healthy." She pats my cheek.

I smile. "What did I do to deserve a friend like you? You're so much more mature than me."

"Mature?" Her eyes flash with something. Shame? Regret? "I wouldn't say that. All I did was make mistakes, but it taught me a few things."

I laugh. "You're kidding, right? What mistakes did you make? Weren't you always Miss Perfect?" My tone is light. "Everyone in school came to you for advice, for help. You were a refuge for the underdog. Weren't you like that even before we met?"

Sunny smiles along, but there's a hidden darkness behind it. "No, I wasn't always like that. There was a period in my life when I was just like Sasha. I thought I could do no wrong, even if I was out of line. That's why what your sister is doing bothers me so much. She's trying to bully you on purpose. You can't give in to her."

I glance away, my heart bleeding all over the floor. Sasha is family. Even if I want to, I've never said 'no' to her before. And I'm not sure I can start now.

CHAPTER 12
THE REWARD

HOLLAND

I TUCK my fingers under Belle's armpits and hike her on top of the counter. She giggles, her sweet, little-girl scent floating over me.

She's still dressed in her footie pajamas. It's a red-and-black striped design that makes her brown eyes sparkle. Her hair flows freely all over her shoulders and her gap-toothed smile makes my world brighter.

"Who's my special pancake helper?" I croon, flipping the spatula because I'm a showman for the people I love.

"Me! Me!" Belle swings her feet.

I rub my nose against hers. "That's right, sweetheart."

Belle bounces. Laughs. Watches me pour the mixture in the pan. The pancake batter sizzles and makes my stomach rumble. I rarely eat breakfast but, for some reason, I'm ravenous this morning.

"Ready to flip it?" I ask Belle.

"Yes!"

"Mind your hands," I say, pulling her into my arms and crouching a little so she can reach the spatula. Her tiny fingers wrap around the handle and tug.

The pancake breaks into three pieces.

Belle laughs. "Daddy, it's ugly."

"No way." I put my hand over hers and turn the pancake over. "This is the most beautiful pancake in the world. Know why?"

"Why?"

"Because my beautiful little girl made it."

She laughs again. Her sweet giggling is melodious. I want to capture this moment and put it in a bottle so it's never lost to time.

"You're silly, daddy."

"Am I?" I pull a funny face, crossing my eyes and sticking out my tongue.

She bursts out laughing.

I give her a kiss on the cheek and squeeze her tight.

These mornings are so rare. Mostly because I'm always on the go. There are a million tasks fighting for my attention and Belle often gets pushed aside.

But today, I couldn't just hop out of bed and go chasing the dollar bills. I have too much on my mind and too many impulses that need to be grounded.

Baby Box wants to do a deal with Belle's Beauty.

I want to tell them no.

Not because of the terms.

Not because of the money.

Not because I'll need to negotiate Belle out of the story feature.

But because Walsh was staring at Kenya Jones like he wanted to peel her clothes off layer-by-layer.

The pervert.

I'm counting it a miracle that I didn't deck the guy. Screw the Baby Box deal. He'd deserve it.

I take care of my employees, and I'd like to think this righteous indignation would burn just as fiercely if it were anyone else. But I don't indulge in lies. Not to other people and not to myself.

Apparently, I'm not as removed from Miss Jones as I'd like to be. And having conflicting interests is dangerous for everyone.

My life revolves around Belle. I'm pulling all-nighters, overseeing two companies, and considering a licensing deal—all for my little girl. I can't let Kenya distract me. As long as I can keep her away from Walsh, there's no need to cancel the Baby Box deal.

"I love you so much," I whisper.

"Daddy, the pancakes," Belle says, completely oblivious to the chaos in my head.

I chuckle, kiss her cheek again and finish making breakfast.

"Something smells wonderful!" Mrs. Hansley chirps, stepping through the front door.

"Morning." I nod.

"Morning!" Belle waves. Her hands are sticky and her cheeks are smeared with syrup.

"We made you pancakes." I tilt the plate toward her.

Mrs. Hansley beams. "Isn't that nice?"

"Belle's going to need a good bath after breakfast." I move over to my daughter and wipe her sticky hands with a napkin. It doesn't work, so I grab the pack of wet wipes.

She dances while I wipe her off, making it difficult to accomplish the task.

"Hold still, Belle," I say firmly.

She keeps dancing.

I'd scold her again, but she's too cute for me to lecture.

Mrs. Hansley grins at me. "She has you wrapped around her little finger, Alistair."

"Undeniably." I finish cleaning Belle and toss the wadded up napkins in the trash.

"What's the occasion?"

"We're striking a deal with a very influential subscription-based service. I work hard so I can celebrate my wins." I nod to Belle. "And this is how I prefer to celebrate."

"Congratulations. Claire would be proud of what you're doing with Belle's Beauty. She had big dreams, that girl."

My heart twists.

Guilt pricks my chest.

Would Claire be bothered to find out I'm having obsessive thoughts about my assistant?

Mrs. Hansley squeezes my shoulders. "She always told me that seeing you happy made her happy. That stuck with me. Nothing mattered more than her family." Mrs. Hansley's eyes travel to Belle. She juts her chin in my daughter's direction. "Has Belle asked about…"

"No." I shake my head. "Not with me. Not yet."

Mrs. Hansley smiles and steps back. "I saw Bernard waiting downstairs. If you're done here, I'll clean up and then take Belle for a bath."

I get ready quickly, kiss Belle on the forehead and head downstairs feeling strangely out-of-sorts. Bernard senses my mood and doesn't talk on the way to the office.

Ezekiel greets me when I step through the doors. His salt-and-pepper hair is, as usual, brushed away from his face and held together with hairspray. His suit is impeccably neat with not a speck of dust in sight. Dark eyes swerve to me and soften.

"Before you ask, I slept well last night. Midnight. A personal best."

"Not bad for you." He sets a cup of coffee in my hand.

I sip. It's sugary perfection.

"The negotiations with Baby Box are underway. I've forwarded your notes to our attorneys. They'll make the amendments to the Baby Box contract once they have your approval."

"Good."

Ezekiel follows me into the elevator.

"Good morning, Mr. Alistair."

"Morning."

"Hi, sir."

I nod at my employees, keeping a straight face.

The elevator closes slowly.

In the distance, I see a woman with dark brown skin and frizzy curls sprinting through the lobby.

My heart jumps in anticipation. Before I've thought it through, I shoot my arm out, blocking the elevator from closing completely.

The silence that falls is visceral.

"Thank you. Thank you." Miss Jones shuffles toward the elevator and then stops abruptly when she sees me.

Her brown eyes widen in shock. They're pretty in the sunlight. Pure onyx. Like dark coffee that no amount of sugar and cream can lighten.

"Mr. Alistair," she says breathlessly. I'm not sure if it's the shock or if it's running crazily across the lobby that's causing the shortness of breath.

Realizing that everyone is staring, I drop my hands and roughly bark, "Get on. Everyone's waiting."

"Sorry." She ducks her head, flashes a sheepish smile at the people in the elevator and then scowls at me. "*Jerk.*"

The word is muffled under her breath, but I hear it clearly.

Ezekiel gives me a curious look.

I ignore him and stare straight ahead as if a vision of my future is embedded in the doors.

The elevator stops.

Employees shuffle past me, glancing curiously at Miss Jones before leaving.

Kenya holds herself stiffly, her shoulders ramrod straight. Her back is to me, but I can still read her annoyance. Jaw clenched. Fists at her sides. Heavy silence.

The elevator stops again.

More people get off.

In the rush, someone bumps into Kenya and she stumbles back. I react instinctually, grabbing her by the arm and settling her on her feet.

She glances at me. Mouth parted. Big brown eyes make it hard for me to breathe. Rather than saying thanks, she shakes me off and steps away.

Off-kilter, I clear my throat. Check my watch. Glance up.

The numbers change slowly.

Someone is tapping their foot on the floor.

Kenya.

She shifts a little, her hip cocking to the side. I assess her body and a thrill hums through my veins. She's in pants today and they're just as sexy as her tight maxi skirts. The blouse is an extravagant number with ruffles and pleats at the neck. It must be new. I've never seen her wear anything like that before.

She's going to distract me all day looking like that.

I dismiss those thoughts and force my gaze forward.

One last stop before our floor.

More employees leave the elevator.

I nod to most of them.

Kenya steps back before the crowd can knock into her, but the move brings her close to me. Her backside brushes the front of my trousers.

Flames dance up my spine.

Damn. She's softer than I imagined.

Her scent fills my nose. I take a big whiff because, apparently, I'm a lunatic when it comes to this woman. The scent trips my wires and makes me lean forward for another subtle inhale.

What is that? It's exquisite. A decadent mixture of soft, feminine fragrances—wild apples, cinnamon, rose.

She glances over her shoulder.

I straighten and work my jaw, my heart flogging my ribs. In a dark voice, I snap, "You have lint on your clothes."

"I do?"

"From now on, you need to take better care of your appearance."

Her eyebrows scrunch together. She picks at her shoulder to find the invisible lint. "I just bought this outfit. How does it have lint already?"

Ezekiel shuffles behind me. I don't bother turning around to face him.

Finally, the elevator arrives at the top floor. I march through the lobby, heading straight for my office. A rhythmic click of heels follows me and so does that amazing scent.

I whirl around. "Can I help you, Miss Jones?"

"Did I ask for help, Mr. Alistair?"

So much attitude. My mind lights up with all the ways I can tame that sharp mouth into submission.

"You're following me."

She scrunches her nose and points to the left. "I'm going to my cubicle."

My chest caves in. "Oh."

She narrows her eyes at me.

"Have the promotional materials gone out yet?"

"Yes. They were posted yesterday. We're working with the production team to produce more samples for the event. It should be ready for next week."

"Next week? The promotion is a month out."

"You can never be too prepared." She waves a hand. "Trust me. Something *has* to go wrong at events like this. It's best to be ready in advance. That way, only little, unforeseen problems can pop up and we can handle them on the fly."

Blood rushes south. The only thing sexier than Kenya Jones in tight pants is Kenya Jones's efficiency and intelligence.

She raises an eyebrow. "Do you need something else?"

I mentally trace the shape of her lips with new appreciation. The determination in her eyes makes something wild and passionate light up in mine.

"No."

She holds my gaze for a second, all glorious defiance. An odd sensation stampedes through my chest. Like something hot and dangerous is being roused from where I'd laid it to rest when I buried my wife.

Her heels click. She steps closer to me.

I lean back. "What?"

"I just realized I haven't gotten a proper thank you yet."

"A thank you?"

"I'm the one who got Baby Box to change their mind. My idea made the man-in-charge drive all the way here just to negotiate with us." She folds her arms over her chest, bringing my attention to her body again. "Where is my thank you?"

I try not to breathe because I don't know what I'll do if I inhale any more of that scent.

She tilts her head. "Well?"

"Your perfume," I bark.

She goes still.

"Is that new too?"

"My perfume?" She sniffs her wrist. "How did you know it was new?"

I whirl around abruptly. "The Baby Box deal isn't through yet. You still have time to mess it up."

"Excuse me?" Her voice roars with indignation.

"You have a lot of work to do, Miss Jones. I suggest you get to it."

"*Flying cockroach,*" she hisses under her breath.

My cheeks break into a smile. I don't bother hiding the chuckle.

Ezekiel follows me into my office and shoves the door. His lips quirk up in a knowing grin.

I lift a finger in his direction. "No comments."

"It's more like a question." He moves toward my desk. "Miss Jones has a point. I don't think her contributions to Belle's Beauty and, by extension, Fine Industries have been properly acknowledged."

I scowl at him. "You're taking up for her again?"

"No, I'm following the rules that *you* set in place. According to company by-laws, any employee with an accumulated achievement such as this one deserves a reward."

"Her reward is that I didn't fire her," I mumble, flipping my laptop lid open. It's connected to my double monitors. Both screens light up when I shake the mouse.

"You're the one who set those initiatives in place, Alistair. If I remember correctly, you wanted to build a business where people were elevated based on their skills, not based on their degrees or social connections."

He's right. "I know my own rules, Ezekiel."

"What arrangements would you like me to make?"

I swing my chair around and face the balmy day. Clouds huff past the window like puppies on a mission. A blue sky stretches over the busy highway. Billboards light up with calls to action, bright enough to rival the sun.

"Would you like me to give you more time to think about it?"

I lift a hand. "Just do the usual."

"What is the usual, sir?"

I spin the chair to face him. He's goading me. "Team dinner. A solo office."

"Is that all?"

I narrow my eyes.

"You very publicly criticized Miss Jones for her impulsiveness during the Baby Box deal. Now, those actions have fostered a relationship between the companies and yet, you've been very silent."

I glare at him. "Just admit it. You'd rather work for Kenya, wouldn't you?"

His smile is serene.

I tent my fingers, tapping them together one by one. Kenya makes my blood pressure spike for all the wrong reasons. I can't afford to go around gallivanting my approval of her. How do I hide my affection if I'm forced to parade it in front of the staff?

"I'll book a nice restaurant. Do you have any preferences?"

"Just find something she likes."

"I'll ask her and forward her responses to you," Ezekiel says.

I stare at him. "Why do I need to know?"

"I have a feeling you'd like to have that information." He dips his head and walks out. "I'll get on that."

Nosy man.

I start my work for the day, focusing completely on the task at hand until my door bursts open. Annoyance is my first response.

The only man allowed to bust into my office is Ezekiel, and he never does anything so uncouth.

I whip my glasses off, mouth open to tear into the interloper. My exasperation vanishes like smoke when I see Miss Jones standing in the doorway, her chest heaving and her eyes glued to mine.

Ezekiel runs up behind her, his expression equally panicked.

I sit straight up, observing them both. "What's wrong?"

"We have a problem." Stomping over to my desk like she owns every inch of the floor, Kenya hovers over me. Her arm brushes against mine when she shoves her phone under my face.

It takes me a second to adjust myself to her nearness.

"Alistair, look at this." She shakes the phone.

I force my attention to the screen. It's a graphic for the Belle's Beauty in-store promotion. Our logo is featured prominently in the center. The date, time and raffle announcement are outlined too.

"I don't see a problem," I murmur, glancing up at her. Sweat beads on her dark skin. Her lips are pinched. Something's wrong.

"Here." She shows me the comment section. The words are too tiny for me to make out without my glasses.

I squint.

"There's confusion about what this date means." She points to the numbers.

11/10

I see the problem before she explains it. My eyes widen. "It could be October eleventh or November tenth."

"People misunderstood the messaging. They think it's today."

"Have you—"

"Yes, I asked the PR team to take the flyers down and amend the—"

"And the—"

"No," she answers before I can finish, "we couldn't get to the popular bloggers we hired. They've already spread the news. The incorrect flyer is going viral."

Ezekiel's phone rings from his desk.

Eyes wide, he waves a hand. "You continue. I'll get that."

"Kenya, contact our social media manager and tell him to send out a boosted post. I don't care how much it costs. We have to clarify to as many customers as possible."

She bobs her head urgently.

Ezekiel's footsteps thump into the room. He skids to a stop, his eyes darting between me and Kenya. "That was the manager at the Yazmite location. They've got a problem."

"A problem?" Kenya pulls her bottom lip into her mouth.

"Customers are pouring in specifically to participate in the promotion."

I tap my fingers against the desk, struggling to remain calm. No solutions can be found by panicking.

Kenya's chest swells and contracts in rapid fashion. "We don't have the samples ready yet. Even if I ask the production team to speed it up, there's no way I can get it done today."

"The store manager is afraid that customers will get rowdy." Ezekiel frowns. "Some of them are already a little too aggressive."

I frown. "They're assaulting our people?"

"No. They're just refusing to leave until they receive what was promised to them. It sounds like it's pandemonium."

Kenya wrings her hands. "If this gets out, Baby Box will drop us like a dead rat. And any other collabs will be ruined."

I rub the bridge of my nose. How could I have let such a small detail pass me by? I should have paid more attention.

Kenya exhales loudly. "I'll go and try to calm the mob."

"No," I snap. "We need to come up with a plan."

"We don't have time for that. You heard the managers. A crowd is overwhelming them. Customers are complaining. We need to take action *now*."

"Taking the *wrong* action now will make things even worse," I bark.

Her eyes light up with fire. "By the time you call an emergency meeting and come up with a proper strategy, Belle's Beauty will be trending online. And not for a good reason."

"Miss Jones!"

"Alistair," Ezekiel steps forward, "she has a point. We need to take action now. If Miss Jones can calm the angry customers and buy us time, it may work. It's the only strategy that makes sense."

My heart burns. I'm not worried about Belle's Beauty getting into hot water with the online trolls. We can bounce back.

But Kenya…

I glance over her short frame. She's small. Fragile, even if she acts like she's ten-feet tall. What if one of the customers get physical? What if she gets hurt?

"I can do it, boss," she says, her jaw tightening. "I know I can."

Ezekiel gives me a pleading look.

A war erupts in my heart. It feels like someone is stuffing old, dirty cotton scraps down my chest.

I glance away and push the words out. "Fine."

"Yes." She pumps a fist.

Ezekiel gives her an approving nod.

I shoot out of my chair and point a finger at her. "Be careful. Don't do anything stupid. And if anyone starts getting aggressive, call the cops at once."

"I will." She meets my eyes and smiles like a ray of sunshine. It's so disarming that I can't even breathe.

With a spray of her thick, curly hair, Kenya turns and hurries out of the room.

The pressure in my chest only gets worse. I press a hand there. "Ezekiel!"

"Yes, sir."

"Call Bernard. Tell him to accompany Miss Jones to the location and follow her inside. I don't want anyone laying a hand on her."

"Yes, sir."

I snap my jacket from the back of the chair and charge out of my office. "I want the marketing team at Belle's Beauty gathered and spitting out solutions in the next five minutes. Anyone with a subpar idea is getting their last paycheck this month."

He nods.

Twenty minutes later, I pace up and down the conference room. This is the second time the marketing team has gathered to taste my wrath in the space of a week.

I have even less patience today than I usually do. Kenya's at the store alone. It's a decision I regret with each passing second. I should have sent a bigger security detail. If the crowd is extremely rowdy, Bernard won't be able to handle it alone.

My eyes dart to my watch.

Twenty-five minutes have passed.

I motion for Ezekiel.

He charges over. "I haven't gotten any word from Miss Jones yet."

"Have you called her?"

"The line rings, but it doesn't pick up."

"What about Bernard?"

Ezekiel shakes his head.

I curse. Kenya's been at the store for too long without word. Sitting here worrying about her is driving me insane.

Ezekiel's eyes search mine. "What do you want to do?"

"Call a cab. I'm heading over there myself."

He nods.

I turn to the marketing team. "Finalize the plan and get the samples from the production team. I want *everyone* at the Yazmite location in an hour. Understand?"

They nod in fright.

My feet slam against the tiles as I stalk out of Belle's Beauty. The taxi takes too long to arrive. I try calling Kenya again, but she still isn't picking up.

Expletives froth on the tip of my tongue. I want to let them loose, but I'm too worried to open my mouth. Why isn't this woman answering her phone? Is she trying to give me a damn heart attack?

Finally, the cab rolls to a stop in front of me. I haul the door open and climb in. Ezekiel takes the front seat.

I keep calling Kenya's number until we arrive at the shopping center. The moment the vehicle slows in the parking lot, I barrel out of my seat and rush into the building.

Ezekiel will take care of the cab fare. The only worry in my mind is Kenya and why she's not answering the blasted phone.

I sprint to the escalator, run up the stairs and dart past people who don't know well enough to get out of my way.

When I near Belle's Beauty, I hear music blasting. A familiar song grates my ears. *"Baaabee! Baabee! Baabbee! No! I love youuuu! Don't gooo!"*

I recognize the tune as the one Kenya was singing the night she organized the Belle's Beauty files. A crowd of customers are pressing into the store, excited smiles on their faces.

What the…?

I inch closer. The music is, surprisingly, quieter inside the store than it was in the mall. Closer. Closer. I'm a head and shoulders taller than the clientele, so I can see through the room. I search desperately for Kenya.

My eyes lock on her in record time. She's smiling and handing a small piece of paper to a customer. Her eyes crinkle to slits and her cheeks bunch up as she accepts the woman's hug.

I stop in my tracks, trying to make sense of what's going on. In my horrific imagination, I saw Kenya getting trampled beneath an angry mob. I saw her dark hand reaching up, begging for someone to save her.

"Are you guys having a good time?" she yells at the crowd, bouncing to her favorite song.

An answering 'whoo!' goes up from the customers.

"Sir?"

I glance to the side and notice Ezekiel standing next to me. His eyes are as wide as dinner plates and take up most of his wrinkled face. He glances around the room in awe.

Sales clerks weave through the crowd, handing out tags and asking customers to line up in order. The managers are huffing and puffing, darting between the counter and the stand where Kenya is jotting things down in a laptop.

Bernard's eyes sweep to mine and he waves.

I lift my fingers, motioning him to me.

He excuses himself from the customer he was speaking to and joins us.

"Mr. Alistair!" he yells to be heard over the music.

"What's going on?" I yell back.

"Miss Jones is having a promotion pre-order party!" He explodes with pride. "Amazing, right?"

Ezekiel and I exchange a stunned look.

Bernard doesn't seem bothered. He rocks his head to the beat. It's my first time seeing my professional driver in such a cheerful mood.

Flabbergasted, I lean closer to him. "What do you mean a promotion pre-order party?"

He extends an arm. "If you look back there behind the counter—" I scowl in the direction he points and notice a clerk with her head huddled close to a monitor—"she's looking at the security feed to identify which customers arrived first." Bernard motions to the employees darting in and out of the crowd. "They're handing out numbered tickets so customers can approach Miss Jones in order."

"Approach her for what?"

"For the promotion pre-order." Because he's shouting, his *didn't you get me the first time* tone is emphasized.

"Should we move closer, sir?" Ezekiel asks.

I nod and follow him to the podium where Kenya is meeting customers one-by-one.

"Next?" Kenya beckons a woman forward, those twinkling eyes exuding so much warmth. Her exuberance is dynamic. Her passion. Her genuine care. It's almost blinding to watch.

The comments from the workshop suddenly make sense. Kenya is the definition of a 'sunny disposition'. Charisma shoots out of her like gamma rays.

"What's your name?" She leans in close to hear and hangs on the customer's every word. "How long have you been using

Belle's Beauty products?" Again, she stops and listens with her entire body. "Whoa. I can tell! You look so good!"

The customer flushes. She's an older woman with greying hair and giant window glasses. Her smile transforms her face and I can tell she appreciates Kenya's compliments.

"Thank you so much for participating in the pre-order promotion. You'll receive a special e-mail to let you know when your sample package is ready. It'll be an exclusive goodie bag just for coming out today."

"I'm so excited," the woman gushes.

Kenya gives her another heart-stopping smile.

At that moment, her eyes lift and meet mine. They glitter in welcome. I feel that odd, tightening sensation return. It rearranges my chest and leaves a Kenya-sized hole in my ribs.

Motioning to one of the managers, Kenya waits for the other woman to take her place and then approaches me.

Her skin is glowing and her smile makes her black eyes dance. Her shirt reminds me of a swan. Long elegant neck. White ruffles. She's moving poetry.

I can't breathe.

"Hey, you're here." Her eyes slide behind me. "And so is the marketing team."

I turn and notice the Belle's Beauty officials looking just as stunned as I did when I first saw the room. They all glance at me, a big question mark in their eyes.

Grabbing Kenya's hand, I haul her away from the noisy store and into the back room. She follows me, stumbling over her feet and shooting me curious looks.

I stop when we're alone. "Are you okay?"

"Why are you asking that?" Twin wrinkles form between her eyebrows.

"You weren't answering your phone," I bite out. "I thought something happened."

"I was busy trying to corral everyone into a semblance of order. Then I had to share my plan with the managers and staff. My phone is…" She glances around. "Somewhere. I left it with my purse."

"You're not hurt, right?"

"No." She looks at me suspiciously.

I exhale, glad to hear that she wasn't harmed trying to get the crowd to calm down.

"Okay…" Uneasily, she edges past me. "I'm not sure why we're having this conversation when it's so busy, but I should get back."

I let her leave.

Once I'm alone, I rub my forehead and try to wrestle my worries back into a corner. Kenya's fine. I saw for myself. She has this well under control. So why do I not want to leave?

Ezekiel finds me in the room. "There you are." He turns his phone and shows me. "Baby Box agreed to share Claire's story *without* mentioning Belle. They're sending the contracts over for us to sign too."

"Really?"

He nods, biting back a smile.

I wilt against the wall and let out a stunned breath. "I thought they'd play hardball. Walsh has no love for me."

"You of all people should know how important it is to separate business from personal matters. Whatever issues Walsh has with you, he knows Belle's Beauty is a good company and Kenya's idea was a good one too."

"She's incredible, isn't she?" Through the crack in the door, I notice Kenya reclaiming her spot on the podium and greeting customers like they're her long-lost friends.

"I think she's one of the best things that ever happened to the company," Ezekiel says.

I'd take it further.

I think Kenya Jones is one of the best things that ever happened to *me*.

CHAPTER 13
STOLEN HEARTS

KENYA

The metal shutters roar as we drag them down. The store fades from sight, barricaded behind a stylish white drape with the Belle's Beauty logo spray-painted on.

"Good work today," the store manager says, squeezing my arm. She looks absolutely exhausted. Her hair sticks out of her bun, her pudgy cheeks are splotchy and dark bags fall beneath her eyes.

I'm sure I look equally zombie-like.

"You too." I croak.

She flashes me a genuine smile. Annoyance flowed both ways when I first took on this job. But today, there's a sense of camaraderie between us.

War can do that to people. Burn the prejudice and assumptions right out of them. Surviving requires working together. And nothing bonds people like shared trauma.

Perhaps I'm exaggerating. The chaos at the Belle's Beauty location today can't compare to *real* soldiers fighting on the frontlines, but it sure felt like a battlefield. A hundred people pressing in at once. Cell phones whirring. Anger singeing the air.

It was anarchy.

I saw the helpless looks from the staff, and I couldn't stand still. My brain threw all kinds of crazy ideas at me. I picked one and jumped right into the fray with the team.

"What you did today was awesome," the manager says. Her brown eyes squint at me. "When I first met you, I thought you were one of those ambitious suits who'd do anything to get ahead."

"Thanks." My voice is scratchy.

She laughs. "I have a lot of respect for you now."

Her words would mean a lot more if I wasn't dead on my feet.

"Get some sleep." The manager points to her throat. "And rest your voice. Sounds like you rubbed your vocal box raw."

I sigh in agreement. I've been talking to customers all day. It's a good thing, really. News of our 'pre-order promotion' spread far and wide. What was *supposed* to be damage control turned into a bigger buzz than anyone had anticipated.

When the last customer left Belle's Beauty, I found that my voice left me too. Now, I'm channeling my inner Ariel from *The Little Mermaid*. Too bad there aren't any forks I can twirl around my hair.

I notice a tall figure prowling in the distance.

It's Alistair. He's wearing a black coat over a white shirt and a pair of grey, fitted trousers. His stride is so powerful that his coat glides with an invisible wind.

My heart starts breakdancing. I'm too tired to pretend that Grump-Vader isn't the most attractive man I've ever seen.

In my mermaid reenactment, would Alistair be the evil sea sorcerer or the handsome prince?

The store manager stops in her tracks, her eyes glued to Alistair. "Is that..."

"Yeah," I croak.

Ezekiel scurries ahead, his warm smile lighting on me.

I nod.

He returns the gesture and approaches the clerks who are standing behind us.

"Mr. Alistair sent tea," Ezekiel says, handing them a cup, "a bonus," he hands envelopes out next, "and an extra, *paid* vacation day that can be scheduled in the upcoming month."

"Yes!" The sales clerks high-five.

I grin, genuinely happy for them. When I used to work part-time jobs, I noticed employers would rather peel their skin off than offer vacation days. One particular hag used to berate me for taking my allotted leave.

My eyes swerve to Alistair in approval.

He staunchly ignores me.

Well then.

"This is for you, Kenya." Ezekiel takes one of my hands and wraps it around the cup. "We heard you lost your voice."

"Did you?" I arch an eyebrow.

Ezekiel steps back and gestures to Alistair. "You all did great work today. We're thankful that you're a part of the Belle's Beauty family and we'd like to assure you that your efforts today have not gone unnoticed."

"T-thank you." The store manager slants a nervous glance in Alistair's direction.

He nods coolly, not saying a word.

What? Is Ezekiel his mouth piece? Will he fall into a coma if he says the word 'thanks' just once?

I roll my eyes and take a sip of the coffee. It burns my tongue.

Even worse, it's not coffee.

"Ah." I cry out.

Before I can blink, Alistair is beside me. "What's wrong?"

"This is tea." I scrunch my nose and accept the handkerchief he offers. "That's disgusting."

His eyebrows pull together in a stormy expression. "What's wrong with tea?"

"It tastes like old dishwater."

Ezekiel snorts.

My eyes dart to him. "I'm serious. I want coffee."

"You're not getting coffee," Alistair snaps. Like I'm a petulant child who doesn't know how to eat his vegetables. "Tea is better for your voice." He points to the cup like a true tea snob. "It's green tea with lemon and honey."

"It's dishwater." I stick out my tongue and try to get the distasteful substance off.

Alistair glowers at me. "I'll be in the car."

Ezekiel looks stunned.

Mr. Big Bad Wolf turns stiffly and stalks away, creating his own storm clouds and lightning.

The store manager shuffles back. "Is he angry?"

"He's always like that." I dismiss Alistair as he stalks out of sight.

The ladies look shocked. And I realize that Alistair's behavior really *is* astonishing to people who haven't been subject to his brand of evil. I've been working with him for so long that I kind of just roll with the punches.

Ezekiel claps to shift the mood. "Thanks again, ladies. Rest well tonight." He raises a hand. "On Friday, you're all invited to the Belle's Beauty celebratory dinner. It'll be a small gathering for the staff to unwind. Nothing fancy. You're welcome to come if you'd like. Mr. Alistair will be paying for food, drinks, everything."

"*Cool!*"

"*Awesome!*"

The clerks look impressed.

I narrow my eyes in suspicion. "Was that your idea?"

"Company policy. We celebrate our wins." He winks. "And thanks to you, we scored a big win with Baby Box."

"They signed?"

He just grins and gestures for me to follow him. I trail Ezekiel to the basement parking lot. Alistair's BMW is idling in front of the door.

Bernard is next to the shiny black car. He straightens when he sees me. Warmth explodes from his smile and I feel a bit of my energy returning.

"Miss Jones." He gives me a subtle thumbs up. "It was an honor to see you in action today."

I wave away his compliment. "Thank you for your help. We were so understaffed that we pushed you out of your comfort zone."

"Seeing what you ladies have to put up with certainly gave me a new appreciation for all you do." He opens the car door for me.

I remain in place.

Ezekiel nudges my side. "You can get in, Kenya."

"Is this... were you waiting for me?"

He nods.

My eyes bug. Why is Alistair taking me home? Does he want to yell at me in the privacy of his own vehicle?

I almost groan aloud. I'm not in the mood to go toe-to-toe with him. My energy's depleted and my social reserves are low. As much as I love being around people, my extrovert batteries have been taxed to the limit. If Alistair starts growling at me, I just might explode.

"Miss Jones." Alistair's hard voice careens out of the car. It lands on me like a missile. "Get in."

I want to argue, but both Bernard and Ezekiel are watching me expectantly. I'm choosing to believe they wouldn't lead me to an Alistair-inspired death. At least, not after the day I've had. No one would be that cruel, right?

With a sigh, I climb into the backseat. Bernard closes the door behind me. When Ezekiel gets in, the car moves off.

I close my eyes, enjoying the quiet.

"Ahem," Alistair mumbles.

I stubbornly keep my eyes closed.

"*Ahem.*"

"What?"

"Rubifier, a brand we're working with, gave me this today."

My eyes burst open and I notice a box with a picture of a giant humidifier sitting in Alistair's lap.

"My arm is getting tired," Alistair grumbles.

I accept the box from him and it nearly falls to the ground. "Why are you giving it to me?"

"I already have one," he says, staring ahead. "It'll be a waste to throw it out."

My eyebrows scrunch together.

His gaze darts away from mine. Pointing down, he mumbles, "I got that too."

"Shoes?" Glee fills me when I see the cheap yellow flip-flops. I eagerly toss the humidifier away.

Alistair catches it with a grunt.

Exuberantly, I kick off my heels and relish the freedom. *Die, you evil shoes!* I was forced to wear my pumps for hours on end while helping out at the store. My feet are throbbing so hard, it's like they have their own heartbeat.

I wiggle my toes, happy to see them free and unconstrained. "Are you working with a shoe brand too?"

Alistair remains silent.

I glance up and notice him staring out the window.

"Fine." I shrug. "Don't tell me."

"Stop talking. It's better for your voice."

"You telling me not to talk makes me want to talk more."

"It's good advice."

"It's *your* advice."

"You'd disobey me to your own detriment?" One side of his lips quirk up. It's a shadow of a smirk. And it's gorgeous on his face.

"Disobedience implies that there's authority. Right now, you're not my boss."

"What am I?"

I yawn. "If I say it out loud, you'll probably fire me."

He looks over my face. His eyes are shadowy hazel pools. "Rest your voice, Miss Jones."

"I'll think about it."

His eyes twinkle with amusement.

Mine start to fall closed. The air conditioner is at the perfect temperature and the road is long and dark.

Silence fills the car.

I'm absolutely drained, and the smooth ride is lulling me to sleep.

No, sleep is for the weak.

I fight to keep my eyes open.

Turns out, I fail that battle. When I open my eyes, the car has stopped moving and my head is tucked against a hard slab. Maybe rock? Maybe granite?

Eyes bleary, I nuzzle closer to the rock, wondering why I chose such an uncomfortable pillow. I thought Alistair was rich. Can't he afford to have more cushion in his car seats?

"Miss Jones," Alistair rumbles, sounding closer than I thought, "you're home."

Horror snaps through me like a crack of lightning. I lurch up, a hand to the corner of my lips as I realize I fell asleep on my evil boss.

Ezekiel and Bernard are up front, sitting as still as mannequins.

Bernard is watching the horizon.

Ezekiel is pretending to be engrossed in his phone.

Both men are acting like they're giving us privacy.

Embarrassed, I scramble away. "I'm so sorry," I tell Alistair, panic sucking the oxygen out of my lungs. "I didn't realize I'd fallen asleep."

His jaw muscles work like they're playing jump rope.

I narrow my eyes at him. My voice rises in accusation. "Why didn't you shove my head off?"

"Let's go." He thrusts the door open, grabs the humidifier and marches out.

I lurch out of the car and stop him on the sidewalk. "Whoa, where do you think you're going?"

"To your place."

My eyes nearly pop out of my face.

"This is heavy." He lifts the box in his arms. His tone is dry. Like *I'm* the annoying one who should see the obvious.

"It's fine." I try to loop my arm around the box to take it from him.

He holds on stubbornly.

"Alistair."

"Jones." He gives me a dark glare.

I try to tug, but Alistair tugs back. And since he's over six feet with the muscles of a bodybuilder, I'm the one who ends up losing my balance.

My body smashes into his, separated only by the box and a few layers of clothing. His eyes bore into mine, weaving a golden spell. Sunshine. He's the darkness, but his eyes are the sun. And he's staring down at me with a gaze so hot I might get sunburn.

Does he know? Is he doing that on purpose? Or is my sleep-deprived mind conjuring things?

"Must everything be a fight with you, Miss Jones?" he growls. But there's an underlying note in it. Something almost like affection.

That can't be right.

He hates me.

I hate him.

It's our boss-employee thing.

I gulp, unable to move away as he leans close. His eyes drop to my lips and my body goes wild in anticipation. It's a frantic energy that whips through me.

My tongue darts out to skate across my bottom lip.

His eyes sharpen. Like a predator.

"You should know that I only become more determined when I meet resistance."

"Oh." The sigh escapes from me, pooling into the space between us. There's a whole box separating my body from his. I have the sudden urge to knock that humidifier to the ground and plaster myself all over him.

But that's not okay.

None of this is okay.

I step back before I can give into the urge.

"Uh…" I touch my neck. My wrist. My purse. My gaze skates across the sidewalk. I point over my shoulder. "This way."

Arguing with him is pointless. The faster I get to Sunny's apartment, the faster Alistair will leave. And take his confusing presence away from me.

We mount the stairs in silence. He follows soberly, observing the damp carpets and narrow hallways.

Sunny's apartment is up ahead.

There's a woman standing in front of it. Tan skin. Straight hair cut to her chin. She's wearing a long, turquoise dress. It's flowery and Bohemian. Exactly Felice's style.

The woman turns and I lurch to a stop. "Felice?"

"Kenya." My step-mother glides toward me. The movement of her skirt reveals the leather sandals on her feet. Despite her earthy style, her toes and fingers have delicate French manicures.

"What are you doing here?" I'm so shocked I can't do anything but stare at her.

"I'm here to talk to you." Her lips are tight. Her brows furrowed. This won't be a pleasant conversation.

"If it's about Sasha—"

"It *is* about Sasha." She frowns.

Her tone. I don't like it at all.

"I came to—" Her eyes dart up and she seems to register Alistair's presence for the first time. "Who is this?"

"No one."

"Holland Alistair, ma'am," he says at the same time.

I frown at him.

"Alistair?" Felice tastes the word on her tongue like it's an expensive gelato. "Where have I heard that before?"

"It doesn't matter." I wave her attention away from him. "You can google it later."

"Google? Oh, yes! You were on the cover of that magazine. One of the tech ones her father likes to read."

Alistair flashes a charming smile.

He. Freaking. *Smiles?* I thought his model of robot didn't come with that feature.

"You must be Miss Jones's sister."

My jaw disconnects from my face and rolls over the floor. He knows how to compliment women? Since when? And why is he being sweet to Felice?

"Sister?" Felice blushes like she just won a million bucks. Fingers dancing over her wrinkled face, she giggles. "Oh, I'm far from Kenya's age."

"I don't believe it." He shakes his head.

Felice laughs, covering her mouth behind her hand like a court lady.

I roll my eyes.

"You remind me of someone I know," Alistair explains. "She's beautiful as well. And quite free-spirited."

"Oh, why thank you."

I step in front of Alistair before he can stroke Felice's ego any harder. "He's my boss and he's not staying long." I pull my hair from my left shoulder to my right. "And honestly, I'm exhausted. So it's nice to see you, but we'll need to find another time to meet."

"How about tomorrow?"

"Tomorrow?"

"Sasha and Drake are having an engagement brunch. It's not the real engagement party yet. Just a small family gathering."

My stomach clenches so violently I dig my fingernails into my pants. Is she inviting me to brunch with Sasha and my disgusting ex-boyfriend? As a *guest?*

"Felice, I'm not interested."

"Why not?" Her face twists into a disapproving scowl.

I bark out a bitter laugh. She must be out of her mind.

Felice lifts her chin. "I know that you and Sasha have your problems right now but—"

"Problems? Yeah, we've got problems, Felice."

"Kenya."

"She slept with my boyfriend behind my back and then, two weeks later, I find out they're getting married!"

Felice's eyes dart to Alistair. She seems extremely bothered that I'm airing our dirty family laundry. I guess telling outsiders the truth is more scandalous than the fact that my sister got naked with my live-in boyfriend.

"Kenya," her voice drops to a hiss, "you know how fragile your sister is. Your inability to be the bigger person is a serious threat to her health and happiness. Now, clearly there were some misunderstandings, but it's nothing we can't work through as a family."

My stomach roils.

I'm seriously going to be sick.

"There was no misunderstanding, Felice. I saw them together with my own eyes. Apparently, Sasha likes being on top."

"Kenya!" The blood drains from her face. She slants another nervous look at Alistair. "You're clearly not ready to have a civil conversation. Perhaps it *would* be better for you to skip brunch. We'll talk again soon." She forces a smile, trying to exude as much dignity as she can. At least, what's left of it. "It was nice meeting you, Mr. Alistair. Hopefully, we can meet again. I know my husband would love to chat with you. He's retired and, in his free time, he likes to pretend that he's a whiz with computers."

"It would be my pleasure," Alistair says in that unusually warm tone.

As Felice runs away, I let the silence settle around me. I'm unsteady on my feet, my head is killing me and now I can't stop thinking about my sister's impending marriage to my ex-boyfriend.

To make matters worse, my boss now knows everything.

I sigh and extend my hand. "Give the box to me."

"No."

"Did I not speak English?"

"You're speaking just fine."

"You've done your duty. You walked me home. What are you sticking around for?"

He says nothing and just studies me.

My lips press together and flames shoot out of my ears. "Why? Why are you so determined to make my life difficult?"

"Kenya."

My heart jumps to my throat. It's the first time I've heard him call my name. Gosh, it's so soft. So loving. It shouldn't sound so tender. It shouldn't make tears crop in my eyes.

I'm exhausted and emotionally overwrought.

He can't see me like this.

This isn't who I am.

Alistair sets the box on the ground. The next thing I know, his powerful arms are around me. I stiffen in shock.

"It's okay," he says, soothing my hair.

It's wrong, but it feels so comforting. I lay my head on his shoulder. My fingers scramble for purchase over his suit and I curl into him before I really know what I'm doing.

"It's okay, Kenya," he says again.

I tilt my face up.

He stares at me, understanding in his eyes.

Is it wrong that I want to hold onto him and forget everything? Felice's visit. My dad's silence. Sasha's expectations. My ex-boyfriend's betrayal.

Yes, it's wrong.

But I want to stay here. In his arms. So badly.

He steps back and I want to reach for him. Find the warmth I'd had in his embrace.

Thankfully, I have enough good sense to keep my hands to myself.

Awkwardness seeps under my skin.

What was that?

I struggle to find an explanation. My boss was just taken over by an alien. He did something that was actually… caring. Which completely goes against his stone-cold, screaming vortex for a soul personality.

"Get some sleep. Don't think about anything else," he whispers.

And I try.

After Sunny and I wrestle the humidifier into the living room and I fall into bed beside my best friend, I do my best to sleep.

But it doesn't happen.

Not because I'm thinking about Sasha or Drake or Felice.

But because I'm imagining my boss's arms wrapping around me. He's laying a hot, scorching kiss on my lips. Without a shirt on. Or pants.

And no matter how much I toss and turn, I can't get those dirty images out of my head.

* * *

I'M IN 'AVOID ALISTAIR' mode for the foreseeable future. It's a task made achievable when he leaves me in the care of the marketing team and gives me free reign with the Belle's Beauty in-store promotion.

I'm not sure if he's avoiding me or if he's finally acknowledging my skills. Either way, I'm glad I don't have to see him.

I've decided to pretend the hug never happened. I only came to that conclusion after hours of hair-pulling. It wouldn't surprise me to find that was his intention all along. To mess with my head. Drive me up a wall with questions.

What did he mean by it? Why did I let myself break in front of him? What if he thinks I'm trying to flirt with him?

That last fear is the one that drives me crazy. Alistair is *hot*. And he knows it. The thought that he'll lump me in with all the other girls who go wild for him makes me sick.

I tap my fingers against my desk and try to calm my rushing thoughts.

"*He's coming.*" Whispers flurry around the room. My co-workers share frantic looks and jump into action. They clean their monitors, sweep away trash and pull their chairs to their desks. Fingers clack against keyboards. Pages flip studiously.

I smell the rising stench of evil.

Alistair is on his way.

I open a new document, trying hard not to hyperventilate. The chances of him bothering me are next to nil. He's left me alone for days.

Please. Please. Please.

A loud set of footsteps pulls me from my prayers. I look up to find none other than the Prince of Boss-holes approaching.

I'm invisible. You can't see me.

"Miss Jones." Alistair stops in front of my desk. His shadow falls over me like a dark cloud.

"Mr. Alistair."

He gestures my way. "Follow me."

Everyone stares at us. Being singled out by Alistair is never a good thing. Ever.

Am I getting fired?

Without another word, Alistair turns and marches down the hallway. I grab my cell phone and stumble after him.

Shooting a frantic glance at Ezekiel, I mouth, *"What's going on?"*

The executive assistant gives me a blank look in return. Wonderful. Whatever this is about, Ezekiel seems to be firmly on Alistair's side.

"This way," Alistair says, pointing down the hallway that leads to his office.

I march behind him and stop when he does. He gives me a hard stare and I realize my dreams have been getting it wrong. Alistair's not capable of gentleness. Maybe my subconscious got the wrong idea because that hug was so tender.

But right now, in real life, I'm getting an emergency refresher course on the *real* Holland Alistair. His gorgeous face is pure arrogance. He's a ruthless ice king. Gorgeous and, at the same time, absolutely lethal.

Ezekiel gestures to a door with a flurry of hand movements. "Miss Jones, welcome to your new office."

"That's funny, Ezekiel." I turn on Alistair. "Look, I don't have time to waste. I'm up to my nose in marketing material for Baby Box. And, thanks to *someone*, I still have a load of organizing to do for Belle's Beauty." I slap a hand on my hip. "Please don't waste my time."

Ezekiel looks stunned.

Alistair narrows his eyes. "No one is trying to waste your time, Miss Jones."

I glare right back at him. Is this really the same man who held me so tightly that night? Whatever. Alistair can keep finding new and unusual ways to torture me. Another day. I really don't have time right now.

"This room is yours," he says, jutting his chin at the office.

Slowly, his words sink in.

Ezekiel produces a name plate from behind his back and slides it into the cradle attached to the door.

My name is printed in gold.

'Kenya Jones. Belle's Beauty sales manager'.

I blink and blink again, sure that sleep deprivation is finally catching up with me. Maybe I'm still in my best friend's couch, my arms sprawled out as I drool into the pillow.

"You're screwing with me," I whisper.

A corner of Alistair's mouth hitches up. He's trying hard to stifle his smile, but it shines through.

"No, we're not," Ezekiel says. "Mr. Alistair was watching you closely over the past few weeks to see how you'd perform. All the challenges he threw your way were tests to prepare you for this position."

My eyes swerve to the office. "No freaking way." I turn and curl a finger at him. "What's the catch?"

"No catch."

"You're not capable of that."

Ezekiel's eyes flicker.

I realize I just said my thoughts out loud. To my boss.

Alistair doesn't look offended though. He seems amused. "Aren't you the one always lecturing me about saying thank you?"

"Something you still haven't done yet."

He leans down. "I thought this gesture would make you a little less prickly."

"If that's what you're going for, you're going to have to try a lot harder."

"How much harder?"

"Until I no longer feel like beating your ferns."

He observes me with a smirk. "Your attitude at work aside, you know how to make sales. And I reward those who push the company forward. This office comes with more responsibilities and a higher pay. Can you handle it?"

"You know I like a challenge."

"I do." His eyes simmer with an unspoken promise.

Ezekiel clears his throat. "Should I give her a tour?"

"Yes." Alistair gestures for us to go ahead. "I'll be on a conference call. It'll last a while." His eyes dart to me. "Do you need a ride to the gathering this evening?"

Flames burn my cheeks. "Uh…"

"Perhaps it would be prudent for me to call Miss Jones a cab instead," Ezekiel says primly.

Alistair gives him a blistering look.

Ezekiel doesn't flinch.

They seem to exchange a silent message before Alistair gives in. "Fine. I'll be in my office."

I watch him keenly as he walks out.

Is it just me or does Alistair look like he's… sulking?

"After you," Ezekiel says, pointing to the door.

I follow him into the office and almost squeal. It's a nice size with a gorgeous view of the city. There are empty bookshelves, a file cabinet and a fern with a bow on it.

I burst out laughing. "No."

"He says it's a real one," Ezekiel informs me. "And that he'll charge you if it dies."

My laughter bounces around the room.

Ezekiel looks pleased.

When I calm down, I turn to him. "Why is he doing this?"

"I can't speak for Alistair," Ezekiel says. "But I've known him for a long time, so I understand him more than he'd like. He's earned a reputation of being cruel because he really doesn't care who you are, who you're connected to or how many degrees are in your pocket. He values one thing only." Ezekiel lifts a gnarled finger. "Results. So far, Miss Jones, your work is impeccable."

"I appreciate that," I murmur.

He opens his mouth. Closes it. Studies me as if he's struggling to say something.

"Go ahead." I motion to him. "I kind of already have a feeling of what you want to discuss."

"I'm sure you do. You're a very intelligent woman." He pauses.

"But?" I smirk. "There's a 'but' coming, right?"

"I'd urge you to be careful. Especially now."

"Careful with what? I haven't done anything untoward, have I?"

"It feels like we're not far away from that."

My cheeks burn. Does he know of the dreams? The ones where I'm crawling over my naked boss?

"I'll be honest, Miss Jones, I have never seen Alistair treat any of his employees the way he treats you. In fact, I haven't seen him this way since his wife…" Ezekiel glances aside. "He's fond of you. And he's making it more obvious now than before."

"Fond of me?" What does 'fond' mean? He's attracted to me? He wants to be with me? He just wants to take me to bed?

"You've earned his respect. That's very impressive." He gestures to my face. "But beating every challenge has taken its toll on you. You drink more cups of coffee a day to keep up. There are bags under your eyes. You look… like you're slowly coming apart."

I frown. Do I look that atrocious? Maybe I should take Sunny up on her offer for facial masks.

"Ezekiel, I wish I could blame that all on Alistair, but there are some personal things going on."

"Even more reason to be careful." He squeezes my shoulder. "I see the potential in you, Miss Jones. You can go far. With an opportunity like this, you can have whatever you set your mind to." His voice drops in warning. "But shooting to the top means that there are more people who want to drag you to the bottom. I'm afraid that Alistair softening toward you, paired with your much-deserved rewards, will cause a problem."

"You think people will assume I'm getting rewarded because he's screwing me. Is that it?"

His face flushes. "I wouldn't use that language."

"It's the language that gets the point across." I lean against the desk, my heart beating fast. "I don't know what you're imagining, but you're with me and Alistair almost everywhere we go. There hasn't been any inappropriate conduct between us."

At least, not outside of my head.

"I know how to draw the line between personal and business. Maybe I am impressing Alistair with my skills, but I assure you that no one can steal his heart because he doesn't have one."

Ezekiel shakes his head slowly. "That's the thing, Miss Jones. He does." A worried look crosses his face. "And I'm afraid it's already in your possession."

CHAPTER 14
FORBIDDEN FRUIT

HOLLAND

Belle's Beauty is running like a well-oiled machine, and all matters regarding the skin care company are sorted by priority so nothing falls through the cracks.

Every email, inquiry or complaint sent to Miss Jones's inbox is returned with a hint of sass and a whole load of solutions. Even when I test her mettle, shooting off email after email in succession like a soldier in a firing squad, she doesn't cower.

I'm even looking forward to her reports. She just can't outrun her Lit major roots. Her word choices are literary, and I enjoy every sentence.

Hell, I even enjoy her sarcasm now. Barbed comments sound—to my ears—like the punchlines of a joke.

Sure, it's a joke at my expense but it's no less entertaining.

It helps that the venomous words are shooting out of a perfect mouth. A body made for pleasure straining beneath long maxi dresses, heavy business jackets, bee-stung lips that demand my attention, curves too dangerous for consumption, and—of course—those riveting onyx eyes.

They've been starring in my dreams every night. Always

bursting in right before I leave the hotel room. Right when the pain usually hits me the hardest.

I wake up torn between guilt and loss. Drowning in my own self-loathing and a building desire that coats my skin in sweat.

I'm losing it.

And it's her fault.

In a handful of weeks, Kenya Jones blasted into my world and left her imprint on everything.

I don't know what's going on with her family but, from the little snippet I heard in the hallway, she's been through struggles of her own. Despite her personal issues, she's been extremely reliable at work with no hint of slowing down.

I don't know if that's a good thing or not.

And the fact that I even give a damn about her mental health and not just her work productivity is a bad sign.

Struggling to focus, I toggle to my email. Ezekiel normally filters my inbox. I don't have the patience to wade through advertising pitches, scammers, new client inquiries, and reporters pushing for interviews that I never accept.

To my surprise, I notice a new message from Miss Jones. There's no denying the way my heart starts beating faster.

I lean forward eagerly. It's my first time receiving an unprompted message from her. Our usual interactions are limited to me asking her to do time-consuming things and her responding with the most polite form of 'screw you' she can muster.

To: Holland Alistair
From: Kenya Jones
Subject: Your Gesture Is Not A Thank You

MR. ALISTAIR,

. . .

The office is *lovely and a surprisingly thoughtful upgrade that, I'm guessing, you had to be convinced to offer. However, that is no substitute for two words of acknowledgement and you know it.*

Perhaps I'm stepping out of bounds and, if I am, you have the documentation to prove it. I'm taking the chance because you seem to be in a giving mood and I'm the kind of woman who likes to push my luck. Life is boring otherwise.

On a separate note, what are the terms of this space? Am I allowed to change it up? Using my own resources of course? My friend Sunny is an interior designer and she would love to add a Fine Industries office to her portfolio.

Kindly let me know if that's agreeable to you. I look forward to your response.

Kenya Jones
Belle's Beauty Sales Manager

I shake my head, laughing at her boldness. So an office all to herself and a pay raise isn't enough for her? She's risking her job just to scold me for not saying 'thanks'?

I don't know whether I should admire her or lecture her.

"What's so funny?"

"Gah!" My head whips up from the computer.

Ezekiel stares at me, his face blank and his eyes boring into mine.

I clear my throat and fiddle with a pen on my desk. "You normally knock."

"I did knock. Several times. I even called out to you. You didn't seem to hear me."

"Oh."

He glances at my computer.

I click off from Kenya's email. "What's the matter?"

"I came to report that Miss Jones is settled into her office."

"Thanks."

He watches me. "You're distracted today."

I am. And that has everything to do with the woman in the office down the hall.

"Did something good happen?" He gestures to the computer.

"I got an email."

He purses his lips. "You smiled because of an email? From whom?"

"No one," I snap.

"It must be Miss Jones then. Since you're so defensive."

Damn him for already knowing the answer.

"Skip to the part where you tell me what you really want to say, Ezekiel. I have a conference call soon."

He nods, his lips in a straight line. "What are your intentions toward Miss Jones?"

I stiffen. The grin slides off my face.

Well, hell.

Ezekiel keeps going to bat for Kenya despite all the barking and growling I've done to get him to back off.

"You know better than I how much she's accomplished in her short time here. This company can't afford to lose her."

"Has she expressed dissatisfaction with the workload?"

"Alistair," Ezekiel's eyes flash, "you pay me to keep your life in order and I have been doing that gladly for many years."

I nod. It's why he gets away with sharing his opinion so much.

He looks me up and down. "Be careful. That's all I want to say."

He's lying. That is *not* all Ezekiel wants to say, but he's always been a man who chooses his battles. He's offering a warning. Friendly or not.

I bristle, something inside me rebelling at the caution. "Miss Jones is a stellar employee. That's undeniable. And you were the one who reminded me that she hadn't gotten her dues. This is all according to the books."

He lifts his chin. His frown says he doesn't believe me.

"I'm not going to do anything stupid. I'm well aware of what she's doing for Belle's Beauty." I lean over the desk. This company is personal. It's for Belle. Ezekiel knows that. "I'm not going to jeopardize our vision for anything."

He studies me for a long moment and then dips his head.

"Is that all?"

"Yes."

I motion to the door.

Ezekiel walks out, closing the door behind him. His warning rings in the room long after he disappears.

* * *

BATHROOM BREAKS ARE A MUST when you consume as much caffeine as I do. Later that day, I'm walking back from the john when I hear Kenya's name whispered in conversation.

"It's so unfair. Alistair gives her an office and she's been here what? A couple weeks? How do you jump from a second assistant to a manager?"

"It's shady," someone responds.

"Disgusting."

"I knew she was that kind of woman from the first day. Do you see those dresses she always wears?"

"Super tight. She's showing everything off."

My steps slow and heated annoyance burns through my veins. A bunch of twittering jealous peasants.

Kenya's dresses have been perfectly modest and always within the scope of appropriate business wear. Her generous curves push the boundaries, but it's not her fault her body is so damn desirable.

"Wasn't she just a store clerk before?"

"People like her make me so ashamed to be a woman. Using her body to climb up the food chain while the rest of us have to work hard."

"Don't feel bad. Some of us have morals. She'll get what's coming to her."

Footsteps alert me to someone's approach. I glance up and notice Kenya walking toward the kitchen.

Her eyes widen when she sees me. "Mr. Ali—"

Loud laughter pours from behind me. The gossipers are leaving the break room, still whispering about Kenya.

For a split second, I consider grabbing her hand and hiding in a storage closet. I consider covering her ears and waiting until the bullets fly past, shielding myself over her so they don't hit her skin.

Instead, I hold my ground. Why should she run? Why should *she* be ashamed for beating the others with her skill and competence?

I fold my arms over my chest and remain right in the middle of the hallway.

The women emerge into the corridor. They go silent and I know they've spotted me and Kenya in the hallway.

"Miss Jones," I let my voice boom, "are you aware that the Yazmite location saw their biggest sales spike in five years?"

"Uh..." She gives me a curious look.

"The customers who attended the pre-order promotion told their friends and family. We saw a surge in product sales and online traffic. The momentum doesn't seem to be slowing down."

"I know. I sent you the report, remember?"

"How did you come up with that idea?"

"Panic and a prayer." She tilts her head. "Why are you asking?"

Turning slowly, I nod at the women. "Ladies."

"Mr. Alistair, were you about to get coffee?" A woman wearing a polka-dot dress nervously licks her lips. "I can make it for you."

"What's your name?"

"Me?" She points at her chest.

I nod.

"Heather." She doesn't seem offended that I don't know her name. Instead, she looks excited. "I work in the admin department."

"Heather." I step slowly toward her. My voice drops to a threatening whisper. "Here at Fine Industries, we value results over everything." I stop, my eyes cold. "*Almost* everything. But see, no matter how much money someone makes for the company, it can't hide the stench of bad character. People like that don't usually stick around for long."

Her eyelashes flutter. "S-sir?"

"It seems you all have too much time on your hands." I step back. A frosty grin flickers over my face as I glance at each of the women. "I'll be sure to let your supervisor know that he's being too easy on you."

They cringe in fear.

I jut my chin at the hallway, and Heather scampers off so fast a plume of smoke trails behind her. The gossiping friends follow suit.

"What was that?" Kenya waves an arm at the disappearing ladies. "Are you so bored you're randomly picking on people now?"

She's the only one who'd dare to talk to me that way and be so unapologetic about it.

With a grunt, I walk past her.

She stalks behind me. "Did you get my email?"

"I received it."

"And?"

I stop and face her. "And what?"

"What's your response?"

"The office is yours. Your friend can do what she likes. As long as it's done during the weekend when no one's work is disturbed."

She smiles wide. There's a small dimple in her chin that I've never noticed before. Unfortunately, now that it's on my radar, I'm probably going to dream about it tonight.

I swallow an annoyed grunt.

"Get back to work, Miss Jones."

"Wait." She stubbornly follows me. "What about the other thing?"

"What about it?" I arch an eyebrow.

She folds her arms over her chest. "Are you allergic to offering gratitude?"

"Let me refresh your memory in case you've forgotten." I point to my chest. "I am your boss." I nod to her. "You are my employee. I say thank you by paying your salary every month. Understood?"

Her lips press tightly together. She's absolutely gorgeous when she's angry. It makes my blood boil beneath my skin. It makes my pants tighten with yearning.

"For someone who prides themselves on being fair, you sure pick and choose who you're nice to."

"Excuse me?"

"Felice." She narrows her eyes. "I didn't know you could be charming, Alistair. What was that nice-guy routine?"

I smirk. It's a backhanded compliment, but it's the closest thing to flattery.

"She really does remind me of someone I know. Someone from Make It Marriage."

"Whatever." She lifts a hand. "Forget I said anything."

As Kenya storms away, I yell at her back. "Did you go to the brunch?"

She stops short.

I slip a hand in my pocket and walk in front of her. The question is inappropriate for work. It's inappropriate *period*. Her private life has nothing to do with me and stepping into that territory is opening doors I need to keep shut.

But it's been gnawing at my mind since I took her home. Felice seemed like a nice enough person. I don't get why she'd push Kenya to support a wedding, a break-up, that obviously still hurts very much.

Her eyes dart to the ground. "No."

"And the wedding?"

"Why do you care?" Her chin lifts. Her eyes collide with mine. "Do you pity me because my family's so messed up? Is my pain entertaining to you?"

She must truly believe I'm a monster.

Annoyed for reasons I don't want to dig into, I clench my jaw. "Think what you will."

She pulls her lips into her mouth. Her nostrils flare.

Then, in a blink, the harsh expression putters out of her eyes. She looks… exhausted. And I don't know if it's the pressure from work or her personal life that's dragging her down but, suddenly, I want to make all her problems go away.

"What's wrong?" I ask, moving close to her.

She lets out a long sigh that seems to go on forever. "Nothing. I'm fine. Everything's great." When she glances up, her eyes betray her anguish. "If you don't need anything else, Mr. Alistair—"

"I don't." I do. I want her in my arms. I want her cradled in my lap. I want my hands framing her face as I kiss her until she spills all the secrets, the spikes, the wounds that she won't let anyone see.

But that's ridiculous.

As Miss Jones trots away from me, I feel stripped bare. Cut to the quick. I told Ezekiel I wouldn't jeopardize my vision for Belle's Beauty, but Kenya is making it harder and harder to stay focused on my goal.

* * *

I'M NOT in the mood to attend the dinner, but I already promised and everyone is expecting me. Since I'll be out late, I take off from work early to spend the evening with Belle.

Alright, maybe a part of the reason I leave work is so I don't run into Kenya. She keeps tugging on my heart when I thought that thing had stopped beating long ago.

A smart man knows when to retreat and, right now, I need to sort myself out before I do something stupid.

Like drag my fingers over her soft brown skin and plant my mouth on hers.

It's a sexual assault case in the making.

And I'm not that kind of man.

"Daddy, I'm not ready to go to sleep," Belle whines, dragging my thoughts away from Kenya.

I run my hand over her hair. "Daddy wants to tuck you in, princess. Can he? Please?"

Belle scrunches her nose.

I laugh. "Okay. How about I read two bedtime stories?"

"Three." She lifts stubby fingers.

My daughter is a natural negotiator. I'm proud. "Deal."

After the stories, Belle's eyelashes get heavy. I press a kiss to her chubby cheeks, my heart stirring.

She's my entire world. I can't wait for the Fine Industries licensing agreement to go through. Now that I've found someone as capable as Kenya to help me with Belle's Beauty, I can finally cut back on those suicidal hours and spend more time with my daughter.

"Daddy," Belle mumbles, half-asleep.

"Yes, princess?"

"When is mommy coming back?"

My heart seizes in my chest. I look down at her in fear. "She's not coming back, Belle."

Her breathing turns heavier.

Silence falls around us while I wrestle with my guilt.

"Daddy," Belle slurs.

"Yes?"

"When will I get a new mommy?"

My jaw drops.

I stare at my daughter as she falls into a deep sleep, her chest rising and falling rhythmically.

A new mommy?

I stumble out of her dark room, leaving the door ajar.

Mrs. Hansley is in the kitchen. She's drying the dinner plates and wiping down the counters. My face pale, I sink into one of the bar stools.

She frowns at me. "Alistair, you don't look too good."

"Belle just asked about her mother."

"What did she want to know?"

"When Claire was coming back. I-I told her she wasn't."

"Is she okay?" Mrs. Hansley winces.

"Yeah, she was..." I let out a stunned breath. "She kind of accepted it."

"Kids are like that sometimes. She doesn't fully grasp the concept of death."

Hell, I'm an adult and I still struggle with that painful reality.

"Is that all?"

I blink once. Twice.

Mrs. Hansley grabs a cloth and dries her hands with it, watching me carefully.

"Belle asked about getting a new mommy."

"Oh." The cloth drops out of Mrs. Hansley's grip. She chuckles and bends down to pick it up. "That's the last thing I expected."

I hop out of the chair, kneel and pick up the cloth for her.

Mrs. Hansley rinses it out at the sink. "Is there any chance that can happen?"

My brain instantly conjures Kenya's face.

I shake my head. "I'm not dating anyone right now."

"But that won't be true forever." She rounds the counter and squeezes my shoulder. "I know you carry your regrets about what happened with Claire, but it's been four years, Alistair. You can't keep blaming yourself—"

"Yes, I can. I made a decision and Claire lost her life for it."

Mrs. Hansley looks stricken. "How much longer are you going to punish yourself?"

I glance at the floor. "I should go. The gathering must have started by now. Everyone is waiting for me."

"Alistair."

I stop halfway to the door.

"You were married to Claire, but I watched her grow up. In some ways I know her better than you." Her voice gets quiet. "She wouldn't like this. She wouldn't want the people she loved to suffer."

No one knows that for sure because Claire isn't here to defend herself.

She's gone.

And I'm the one who killed her.

Clenching my jaw, I step out of the house and catch my breath in the elevator. My mind is brimming with chaos. Guilt. There's so much guilt.

I feel like I'm about to claw my skin off. Hands shaking, I call Darrel before I drive myself insane.

He answers on the first ring. "Alistair."

"You're right. I do feel something for Miss Jones."

He's quiet. I imagine him staring intently into the distance, his brows tightening and his lips going flat.

"I know it's wrong."

"Why is it wrong?" Darrel shoots back. "You're not married anymore."

"Claire is dead." I flinch.

"Exactly. My sister is gone, Alistair. It wasn't your fault."

Everyone keeps telling me that like they know Claire better than I do.

"Tell me how to stop thinking about her."

"Claire?"

"Kenya."

Darrel sighs. "I can't do that."

Frustration boils in me. I stalk off the elevator. "You're a therapist. Hypnotize me. Induce amnesia. Do something."

"That's not how the brain works, Alistair. And you know it. Stop grasping at straws to hide from what you really want."

It's a cool night. Stars are beginning to shine through the cloudless sky. The car is in the parking lot.

I slow my steps. "I don't deserve to move on."

"If you could let go of Miss Jones, you would have done it by now. Instead, you're just falling deeper." His voice drops to a low, thoughtful hum. "Don't you notice that whenever you're around her, your guilt goes away?"

I pull my lips in. "It's not that my guilt goes away. It's that it changes into a different kind."

"Guilt for feeling happy when Claire is gone?"

"Yes."

"That guilt is holding you back from love, Alistair. If you really love her, the minute you hand your heart over to her, you gotta let the guilt go. You can't maintain both love and guilt at the same time or it'll chew you up."

I release a shuddering breath.

"Once you give your love to Kenya, you'll sever the tie that has you tethered to your wife."

"I can't."

"Then can you forget Kenya?"

I clamp my lips shut. Bernard is out of the car now, looking expectantly at me.

"Not wanting to let go of Claire is why you keep having those dreams. The minute you let go of that, your nightmares will slowly go away. Your heart wants to heal, Alistair. Your brain is letting you know. It's up to you if you'll let it."

Gritting my teeth, I end the call abruptly.

"Mr. Alistair?" Bernard asks, giving me a concerned glance.

"Let's go."

The night is weighing heavily on me. The last thing I want to do is socialize, but I don't make a habit of breaking my promises.

Bernard remains quiet on the drive. I see him slanting worried glances through the rearview mirror. I must look horrible if he's so obviously apprehensive.

Thankfully, he doesn't ask questions.

Bernard pulls the truck in front of the restaurant.

I glance at him. "Would you like to come inside?"

"No need. My wife is at home with dinner." He chuckles and ducks his head. "No offense, but it'll probably be nicer than anything in there."

A small smile leaks through.

"I'll be here the moment you call though. Shouldn't take me more than fifteen minutes in traffic."

"Don't worry about me, Bernard. Spend the night with your wife. I'll get back home on my own."

"Mr. Alistair…"

"It's fine." I wave him away, feeling weary. "You never know how long you have with her. You should treasure the time you can spend together."

His eyes widen. The worry is practically skittering off his skin.

I know I sound sentimental, but it's that kind of night. And hell, if I can't feel a little out of sorts on the day my baby asks me to get her a new mommy, then I don't know when the right time will come.

He swallows hard. "You can call me if you need anything. I'll have my phone on standby."

"I won't call." I shoo him away. "Go."

He lingers.

"Goodnight, Bernard." Climbing up the steps of the building, I give him a backward wave.

My attention swerves to the restaurant. I let the Belle's Beauty team choose the place since it is, *technically*, their win. However, the Fine Industries team was invited as well. With my credit card open and submitted before them, I thought they'd pick somewhere a little… ritzier.

The main room of the steakhouse looks like it's stuck in another century. Nothing like the sleek, modern bars that seem to be on trend. Large orange lights hang from the ceiling, illuminating thick wooden tables and vinyl booths.

There's a dance floor to the left and a long bar to the right. People are already populating both—some dancing in the darkness while others hunker over the counter, nursing their sorrows in booze. Everyone else is packed in the main room, filling the booths.

Ezekiel finds me immediately. He looks haggard. Like me, he prefers to wade through towers of files than socialize.

"You're here. Finally." He sighs. "I can't keep up with these young bucks anymore."

"You're hardly old, Ezekiel."

"I feel it in my joints when the weather gets too cold. I'd say I'm at *that* age." He nods to a table. "Come sit over here."

I'm stunned when I see Kenya sitting around the booth. I thought Ezekiel would try to keep me as far away from her as possible.

The others fall silent as I slip in beside Kenya. She's wearing a little black dress that hugs her body like it was made for her curves. The hem sparkles with some kind of gemstone and the top cuts into a deep V.

Holy crap.

She's a vision. My desire surges, roaring up with a thirst so uncontrollable that I have no idea how I'll get through the night sitting so close to her.

"Alistair," the head of my PR team sends me a sloppy smile, "you're late."

"And it looks like you've already opened the good wine." I nod to the bottle.

He slants me a cheeky grin.

Another reason why I hate coming to these gatherings? My employees always end up making drunk, stupid mistakes when they're too comfortable with me. I hear all their secret assassination plans when their tongues are loose. Apparently, many of my employees want me dead. Always an ego boost.

I sigh and drum my fingers on my leg.

It's a festive mood around the table, but Miss Jones is the only one who's scowling.

I scowl in reply. *What's your problem?*

She rolls her eyes.

Great. I barely got here and I've already offended her.

"Have a drink, Mr. Alistair." A beer appears in front of me.

I lift a hand. "No thanks."

Groans break out from the table.

The PR director grins. "If you won't drink, at least give a toast. Baby Box was a huge win for Belle's Beauty." He glances around mischievously and pumps his hands. "Speech! Speech! Speech! Speech!"

The room catches on and the sentiment spreads like wildfire.

Ezekiel smirks at me.

He's enjoying this.

The traitor.

It's the only reason he attends these things. To see how extreme the teams will be when they find their liquid courage.

Kenya hops to her feet. "I'll get another drink."

My eyes follow her as she marches across the room. The black skirt flounces around her legs. Her curls are loose and free around her face.

It's unfair how stunning she is.

I already see several eyes swerving to take her in. She's not just the center of my vision. She's the hottest woman in the room. It'll be tough for any red-blooded male to ignore someone who looks as good as she does.

Just thinking about a drunk loser making a move on her makes me want to punch a hole through the table. What's the possibility I can drag her away from this place when I leave in half an hour?

I catch Ezekiel staring at me.

Shoot.

I'm not ogling Miss Jones's perfect backside.

He arches an eyebrow as if to say he doesn't believe me.

I lurch to my feet to shift his attention. Get him to focus on something new. "Fine. I'll say a few words."

A roar goes up.

A drink gets tossed into my hand.

I grip it tightly. The cup is cold against my palm. "Belle's Beauty has seen many changes through the years. Most of that is my fault."

A chuckle rises.

'Yeah, that's right' clamors across the room.

I slant a sharp look at the hecklers.

They fall silent.

"There were times when I considered if it would be better to close the doors because the person who started the vision is no longer here to see it through."

A thoughtful hush sweeps through every table. Some of them were working at Belle's Beauty when Claire was there. I can tell by their pinched faces and solemn expressions. She was a much nicer boss than me. I'm sure they have plenty of fond memories.

"It's because of you," I glance around the room, "that Belle's Beauty kept limping forward. It's because of your hard work, dedication, and persistence in the face of all the changes."

Kenya turns away from the bar and watches me.

My heart climbs to my throat. I let out a deep breath. "Recently, we got a deal with Baby Box…"

Cheers break out.

"… But the PR team can tell you that it was a deal that nearly fell through." Nervous chuckles meet my statement. I stare intently at Kenya. "If someone hadn't stepped up and taken a risk, we probably wouldn't have a cause to celebrate tonight."

As one, the entire crowd turns and looks at Kenya too. She freezes like a deer caught in headlights. Her eyes are big, revealing two deep pools of dark chocolate. Her brown skin glistens and she licks her lips nervously.

"Miss Jones," I lift my cup, "thank you."

Ezekiel puts his hands together. Slowly, applause sweeps over the room, flowing like a roaring waterfall that rushes straight toward Kenya.

She blinks rapidly, her mouth open.

With a deep breath, I tip the beer back and drain the contents. Ezekiel lurches forward as if he'll snatch the booze from me, but I slam it on the table. Empty. Then I turn to the PR director. "You guys enjoy tonight."

"You're leaving already?"

I don't bother answering.

The music starts playing again and the festive mood returns.

They'll enjoy themselves more without me there anyway. I don't see a reason to stay.

Ezekiel moves with me. "Alistair, should I call you a cab?"

"No, I'll walk it off first. I don't want to go home smelling like alcohol in case Belle wakes up."

He looks at me the way Bernard did. Like he's afraid I'm going to fling myself off the nearest cliff.

Damn.

When will the pitying end? They all act like I'm some broken thing that needs to be put back together. I'm not. I'm a man on penance. I've got to make up for my sins. And I can't do that in peace if they keep trying to save me.

The restaurant doors open while Ezekiel and I are locked in our staredown. Kenya Jones storms into my line of sight just as she does in my dream.

Her eyes are two hot coals and her lips are pressed into a firm line. I want to push her away and pull her as close to me as I possibly can. It's aggravating. Confusing.

My head feels like it's splitting apart.

"Alistair," she yells at me.

Breath heavy, I march away from her and Ezekiel. Kenya follows me, her heels clicking on the sidewalk.

"Go back inside, Miss Jones."

"What kind of screwed up bull was that?" She flings the words like arrows. "You think I wanted a show in front of everyone? What the hell are you trying to prove?"

"You got your thank you."

"I got a spectacle. I couldn't care less about being acknowledged in front of everyone."

"You're being picky after I gave you exactly what you wanted. Now who's being unreasonable?"

"You're the unreasonable one." She narrows her eyes to slits. "You provoke me and goad me and taunt me and then you turn around and sing my freaking praises in front of the whole team? What gives?"

"In case you forgot," I whirl around, my nostrils flaring, "you work for *me*. Alright?"

"In case *you* forgot," she stuffs a finger in my chest, "you don't own me. I don't care how much money you fling my way, I will not give up control to anyone. Especially not you."

Oh, it would be so sweet to show her she's wrong. I imagine peeling that dress off her skin and letting my fingers slide up her thighs until—

I bristle, stopping those thoughts before they run away with my good sense. "Miss Jones, I've allowed you to speak your mind because you do great work, but *do not* push it. Now I suggest you take yourself back inside and enjoy the rest of your night far away from me."

"Or what?"

I blow out a soft breath. "Or you can follow me, and we might end up doing something we'll both regret."

"Something like what?" She tilts her chin up in challenge.

I stare at her, my chest expanding. She's freaking irresistible. Her dress, her heat, her scent—it's all burning my restraint to a crisp. I can't *think* with her looking at me like that.

I offer her a tight, warning smile. "Come with me and find out."

The night is cool. The wind blows against my hot skin. Trees hunker close to the sidewalk, offering shade even though the sun is long gone.

For a second, it's only my steps on the sidewalk.

And then I hear Kenya's heels clicking behind me.

My lips arch up in a smile.

When life is as sickeningly complicated as mine is, grinning about my little fantasy following me into the dark is the last thing I should do.

But I can't help it.

Forbidden fruit tastes the sweetest in the dark, and I have a feeling I'll find out just how sweet it is tonight.

CHAPTER 15
STARRY WITNESS

KENYA

I FOLLOW him because I'm an idiot. Obviously. And because alcohol is an inhibition killer. Which means I'm moving on pure instinct right now.

That's dangerous.

My impulses have been swerving more and more towards a carnal desire for my boss. Bad enough when he's barking at me. Even more annoying when he's dark and brooding and wearing his grief on his sleeve.

He's obviously torn up about something and, as someone going through my own emotional rollercoaster, I can see it a mile away. The agitation. The pain flickering close to the surface. The blistering need to drown it with something. Anything.

Am I offering myself as a sacrifice?

I don't know.

I only know what this *can't* be. A relationship.

He's my boss and he has a kid and a dead wife he still obviously loves. And I have... student loans and a sister who wants to marry my boyfriend.

Oh, right. Ex boyfriend.

And ex... sister? Is that a thing?

I lift my face to the sky and watch the stars parading overhead. The world normally feels so big when I look up but, right now, it feels like I'm shrinking. Like I'll disappear if it doesn't stop.

I wrap my arms around myself, trying to stay grounded. Alistair misinterprets the move and shrugs out of his jacket.

"I'm fine," I bite out.

He pins it roughly on my shoulders, totally ignoring me. As usual.

The jerk.

I shove the jacket off me. He stops and pulls it back on. This time, he takes my arms and slides them into the sleeves. His face is set like stone, but his touch is... gentle. Just as gentle as it was when he hugged me outside Sunny's apartment that night.

What is going on right now?

He's not a man that looks like he knows the meaning of 'gentle'. Until that night, I didn't think he had a pulse. If anyone told me Alistair was a blood-sucking vampire, I would totally believe it.

"There," he says quietly. "Take it off again and I won't be so nice next time."

That's the Alistair I know. Bossy, rude, arrogant.

When he's tender, when he's something close to a decent human being, it's too crazy. It makes it hard to breathe.

I glare up at him. "Where are we going?"

"I don't know. I'm just walking."

"You? The *Must Have a Back-Up Plan* guy is on the move without a goal?"

He scowls.

I scowl back. "Why did you thank me in front of everyone?"

"I scolded you in front of everyone." He makes a sharp gesture with his hand. "It's fair to reward you publicly too."

"People will talk."

"About what? Nothing I said tonight was a lie." His eyes burn into me.

There's something wild in them. Something unpredictable. It scares me. Not because I'm afraid he'll hurt me. I'm afraid he'll find that wild, unpredictable side of me too and yank it out.

I can't afford for that to happen.

Lifting my chin, I stop near a bench under a lamppost. "You know how suspicious everyone is about my position at Belle's Beauty. And you also know how much I wanted acknowledgement. So you gave me what I wanted in a way that'll be sure to hurt me."

"I didn't know you subscribed to conspiracy theories, Miss Jones."

I step closer to him. "You're diabolical enough to think of something that malicious."

"I see." A shuttered look crosses his handsome face.

My breath hitches.

"If I'm such an evil person," he takes a step toward me, "then why," another step, "did you follow me all the way here?"

I scramble back, but my thighs hit the bench. Gravity decides it hates me and shoves me into the chair. Instead of helping me, Alistair bends over the bench and cages me in with both hands.

"You poke at a bear and then you yell when you get clawed. Tell me, Miss Jones," his eyes caress my body, "how is that fair?"

An ache starts in my stomach and travels straight between my thighs. I swear, it's like I have a second pulse.

"You dared me to follow you," I whisper, my voice heated. "And you know I like a challenge."

"Will you do anything I dare you to?" His breath is hot against my face. His fingers dig into the back of the bench, not touching me and yet touching me everywhere.

I'm a puddle of aching confusion and clashing emotions. We're not equals. He's not even trying to pretend that he regards me as one. I'm just the most convenient person to toy with because I was foolish enough to fall for his crap.

Annoyed with myself, I put away the goo-goo eyes and push him back. He eases up with a proud smirk as if he made some kind of point. What that point is? I have no idea because I'm already in motion.

Grabbing his tie, I pull him down. The move wouldn't normally work because he's twice my size and pure muscle, but I catch him off-guard.

Alistair plummets into the bench, his palms going flat. The wooden chair trembles, but it doesn't turn over. It's bolted properly into the ground.

His eyes widen in shock. Good. I'm not his bumbling second assistant. We're not at the office. And whatever *this* is, it needs to be on my terms too.

I slam my hands on either side of the bench, my words low and clipped. Because of the height difference, his head is in line with mine. I probably don't look as intimidating to him as he did to me.

Whatever. It gets the point across.

"Don't mess with me, Alistair." My voice is a threat. "If we're going to cross a line, we do it together. You don't drag me. You don't trick me. You don't boss me around." I let the tie drop and smooth it down his chest. "If it's truth or dare, you play too."

His eyes light up with a primal glint. What was meant to bring us on equal footing has only pulled me deeper into his clutches.

A shudder runs down my spine when his lips curl up. His fingers tease a line down my shoulder blade to my elbow. "You don't know how dangerous this is, do you?"

The vodka shots I took must be curdling my better judgement because I really want to see how dangerous this can get.

His eyes flit to my mouth.

I can hear my breath thickening.

It's painful to keep my distance, but I resist the urge to plant my lips on his and get him back for all the ways he made my life a living hell.

It's a nice impulse, but it won't feel like a punishment. At least, not for him.

"Did you mean it?" I whisper.

His hands slide around my waist. They're big. Warm. Teasing. "Mean what?"

My knees buckle. I lean a little more against the bench. Which causes me to lean more into him. My chest is practically dangling in his face but, to his credit, he's keeping his focus on my eyes.

"What you said tonight." I frown. My second pulse is turning into a roaring, throbbing inferno. *Why are there words?* It's screaming. *Why are there still clothes on?*

I dig my fingers into the wooden bench.

Alistair stares hard at me. I can see his sincerity when he says, "You saved the Baby Box deal. That's the truth. And... I shouldn't have yelled at you. Even if you *were* out of line."

He's doing that uber masculine thing where he's apologizing without really saying the word 'sorry'.

I press him. "Is that a real, live apology, Mr. Alistair?"

"I'm only half the bastard you think I am, Miss Jones."

"That's still too much bastard for me."

His thumb traces a circle on my hip. "You have no idea how much trouble that mouth will get you into."

"I guess you're going to enlighten me?"

Our eyes hold and linger.

His is scorching. Second-degree burns.

Need claws its way up my chest. There's too much fabric in the way. His coat. My dress. My underwear. Too many barriers from my skin to his.

He caresses my cheek. "Thank you."

"Finally," I breathe out, moving my hand from the bench to his shoulder. "Although, now that I've gotten to hear those words from you, I need to find something else to work towards—"

Before I can finish the sentence, his big hands tighten over my waist and tug me forward. It's a quick, decisive move. One minute, I'm bent over him, the next I'm folding into his body.

My palms land flat on the back of the bench as my mouth collides with his. I stiffen in shock. My brain struggles to make sense of the kiss.

Then Alistair tilts his head, adjusting the angle.

Suddenly, I don't care about making sense of anything.

Screw being rational.

Screw worrying about where this leaves us tomorrow.

I push into him, allowing my hands to skate over the back of his neck and into his soft hair. It feels like silk against my fingertips.

I'm not used to that.

Every boyfriend I've ever had has been black. Black hair is different. When I rake my fingers in, I meet coils like mine. Beautiful and coarse and rough. I'm used to the thickness and resistance.

Of all the things to trip me up, Alistair's hair is the last thing I expected. It slips between my fingers. It's long enough to clutch. To tug.

And I do, delighting when he groans in response.

Oh, you like that?

He rewards me by bending his head and deepening the kiss.

I'm not being savored.

I'm being devoured.

He tastes my mouth, exploring the inside of my lip and inhaling every airy breath that escapes from me.

It's the hottest kiss I've ever had as the starry sky is my witness. And I wonder if I'm going to die right here.

Oh, but what a way to go.

I shift my weight over him. Right over the heat that's straining against me.

It's agonizing.

Perfect torture.

And I know I'm going to be addicted to kissing him if it keeps on feeling like this.

His arms are rock-hard. Chiseled muscles.

I can't feel my legs.

A moan slides out of me, pressing hard against his body.

He grips the back of my neck tight and I sigh, forgetting

everything but how amazing he feels. When he hears me, his kiss changes. The motions, the intensity. Like a switch, it moves from angry to gentle. Full of promises. All kinds of vows he can't keep.

This man will destroy me and I'll go quietly to my end, smiling at the privilege.

He leans back slowly. My eyes fall shut because I don't want to see what's left of the fire that burned us both. There's rarely anything beautiful in the ashes. I don't care how many fortune cookies claim otherwise.

Alistair leans his forehead against mine. The heat from the kiss lingers, cascading against the sliver of space left between us.

His thumb flicks across my bottom lip.

My mouth opens and my eyes meet his. An energy whips around us when our gazes connect. It's all anticipation and yearning. A yearning so strong it takes my breath away.

This doesn't feel like an alcohol-fueled make out session. It's almost like… he's been thinking about this—about me—for a very long time.

But that makes no sense.

The kiss must have melted my brain.

We hate each other… while wanting to tear each other's clothes off.

But hate… is… it's better if we keep that part simple.

I struggle to catch my breath, panting in short spurts while my body is still liquid heat.

Crap.

"I—"

"Don't." He stares at me and touches one of my curls reverently. "You can lie to everyone else, but not to me. And I don't want to lie to you. Not anymore."

My eyelashes flutter. I can't say anything.

His fingers wrap around my hand. He lifts it to his mouth. "I don't know what this is, but I know it isn't a mistake. I'm not going to blame it on booze. I'm not going to throw our hormones under the bus. I'm not going to ask you to be friends with benefits or whatever crap the kids call it these days."

"W-what?"

"You said we'd cross this line together. Fine. The line is behind us now. It's too late to walk it back with stupid excuses neither of us will buy."

I shake my head. "We can't."

"We can't what."

I glare at him. "You know what."

"No, Kenya. Spell it out."

His voice is hard again. Demanding.

"This," I spit it out. "We can't do this."

"You weren't complaining a second ago."

"Hard to complain when your tongue is stuck down someone's throat."

He blinks. And then he laughs.

I scowl at him.

"You're cute."

"I'll bite your face."

"Please do." He tilts his head to me. He's a caveman in an Italian suit. All grunts and growls and firm hands.

"I'm not offering any more than…"

"Than?"

I glance away.

"Your intentions were to hook up with me and then bring me coffee tomorrow like nothing happened?"

"Tomorrow is Saturday."

"Where else would I be but work?" His lips quirk up. "And nice attempt at changing the subject."

"You're not supposed to bring logic into this." Annoyance inches across my back. The alcohol isn't strong enough. Or maybe it's that Alistair's charisma is too intense. Not even liquor can win against him.

"Then how would you like this to go?"

"We never speak of it again. We keep on working together like nothing happened."

He tilts his head, his hands never leaving my waist. "You kiss me like that and you want me to pretend it never happened?"

"I—"

"I have a daughter, Miss Jones." His voice is hard, but his eyes are… they're begging me to find the answers hidden within them. "I have two businesses to run. I have… I need to make up for some things in my past. To make matters worse, you are my employee. The ramifications extend far beyond sleeping with you for one night. Or even two. Unlike you," his hands slide down my waist and there's a hint of affection, "I don't act on pure impulse."

I'm confused. It sounds like he's… like this isn't just…

Heat sears my throat. "What are you saying?"

"I can't stop thinking about you."

My heart goes still.

No way.

Mr. Evil Incarnate—my gorgeous, torture specialist of a boss—is not confessing to me.

"I know clearly all the reasons I shouldn't say these words. And I also understand what will happen if this relationship goes downhill. I know it all and I still can't get you out of my head."

My gut clenches and my heart jumps straight to my throat.

His lips arch up in a wicked grin. "No witty comebacks, Miss Jones? Now would be the perfect time to slip one in."

The taunting is just what I need to slap some sense into my head.

I push off his shoulders, trying to get back on my feet because I'm still draped on top of him. And that's not exactly the best place to be. Not with him confessing his feelings and blowing my mind.

But Alistair drags me down into his lap and wraps his arms around me. I'm trapped.

"What are you doing?"

"Don't ignore my question. It's rude."

"You're the rude one." I try to pry his fingers off.

He holds firm. "I warned you that following me might end in something you regret." He sighs into my neck, still using that annoying teacher voice. "But you just *had* to be difficult, as usual. If you weren't so headstrong, Kenya, neither of us would be in this position."

"So you're blaming me because you feel some type of way?"

"*Some type of way.* I like that. But I'm afraid we've gone beyond mere feelings. I have different intentions, Miss Jones."

"You're talking nonsense."

"What part of this is nonsense? Come on now. I know you can come up with something better than that."

"You're despicable."

"Keep talking dirty to me. See if I don't take you right here on this bench."

My jaw drops.

He nuzzles his nose against my cheek. "Hate me. Go ahead. Loathe me if you have to. But I'm not letting you go until I'm ready." His hazel eyes go electric. "Just in case you missed it, I mean more than just letting you out of my arms."

None of this is making sense. I knew there was sexual tension. Sure. I was willing to explore that. I thought he'd drag me to a hotel room. Let us duke it out. Crash a few lamps. Tear a few curtains off their hinges. I'd rake my nails down his back the way I always imagined raking out his eyes.

And then we'd clean up and leave it behind with the kinks out of our system. I'd return to my dartboard with the Holland Alistair picture. He'd return to barking orders at me like the grump that he is.

This is not... *that*.

He twines his fingers in mine. "Now that I've jumped off *that* cliff, should we go tear up a hotel room now?"

I shove him. "You're not funny."

"It was my first attempt at a joke in four years. Have some mercy on me."

The specific year count reminds me of his wife. My expression shifts.

His sobers too.

I clear my throat.

He squeezes my leg. "You can ask me."

"I have no questions." If I start prying beneath King Grump's hard shell, I might start unearthing real, non-jump-his-bones related feelings. And wouldn't that be a disaster for everybody?

Alistair sighs and opens his mouth but, at that moment, a car turns down the lane. The headlights are bright. Heavy. Spotlights on top of me. I feel exposed here, sitting on my boss's lap in the middle of the night

The restaurant isn't that far away. Any of my coworkers can see me. I don't want to imagine the stink Heather will raise if she catches me straddling Holland Alistair with my chest in his face.

Planting my hands on his shoulders, I scramble off him and land two feet away. Alistair gives me a strange look, but his attention is captured by the fancy car that slows to a stop near us.

I blink rapidly when I see Ezekiel climbing out of the vehicle and trotting over.

"There you are," he says with a worried frown.

"What are you doing here?" Alistair scowls. "Is that Bernard?"

"I called him."

"Why? I gave him the night off."

"You drank alcohol when you haven't touched the stuff in years. Then you stormed away looking like you were going to fall apart and..." His eyes catch on me and he clamps his mouth shut. "Miss Jones."

"Ezekiel." I dip my chin and hope like crazy he can't tell where my lips have been.

Alistair rises arrogantly, completely unashamed. He draws his thumb across his bottom lip, pulling my attention there. My eyes bug when I see the red sheen over his mouth.

That's my lipstick.

I cringe.

And my foundation.

Another thing I didn't realize about making out with a man the color of a napkin. Makeup transfers. And since mine is a dark burgundy brown, Alistair's face is the perfect white canvas.

Ezekiel, to his credit, makes note of all the evidence and coaxes his face into an expressionless mask. "Since I've verified that you're okay, I'll send Bernard back."

"No need." Alistair takes my hand in his.

My eyes bug. I try to squeeze my fingers out.

He holds steady. "We'll drop Miss Jones home first."

He's insane. He's arrogance personified and now he's pointing all that explosive billionaire ego at me.

It's not like I'm against having Holland Alistair on the side.

I want to kiss him again.

I want to tear his clothes off.

I want to hear him groan when we collide. I want that heat to consume me.

But I don't want to get lost in this man. Besides, people will misunderstand. I can't have anyone questioning how I got my position. Respect is something I worked my butt off to earn. One little rumor will destroy everything.

"I can get my own ride," I hiss.

He gives me a dark look. "It's late. And this ride is free."

"Nothing in life is free."

He smirks. "You're right. I have some ideas about how I'll collect from you."

My eyes widen.

He smirks, clearly enjoying my horror.

This isn't funny. I accelerated to my position because Alistair plucked me out of my entry-level job and thrust me into the big leagues. Despite the challenges, I proved that I'm capable.

Me.

I did that on my own.

But he can tear it all away from me.

Not that Holland Alistair cares.

He tugs me to the vehicle and opens the door. "Get in."

"You're a real prick. Have I mentioned that?"

"You have." He leans into my space, his eyes narrowing. "And I'll allow it because it's really freaking hot when you snap at me." He frowns. "But don't do it too often in the office or I can't promise I'll be able to control myself."

I grit my teeth.

Ezekiel clears his throat and shuffles awkwardly. "Alistair?"

"Save your concern, Ezekiel." He gestures to me. "Miss Jones hasn't agreed to anything yet, but I'm working on it. When I succeed, I'll inform you."

His cheeks get red.

Mine turn purple.

I hope a hole opens up in the ground and swallows him whole.

"We won't be able to hide anything from Ezekiel anyway," Alistair explains. "This information won't leave this circle."

"I'm going to kill you."

"Okay. But let me take you home first." Alistair ushers me into the vehicle while I'm still beaming laser eyes at him. He climbs in after me.

Ezekiel falls into the front seat. He and Bernard exchange looks before Bernard starts driving.

My phone buzzes a second later.

Ezekiel: I left you alone with him for five minutes.

I hurl angry eyes at the executive assistant. Is he blaming me for this too? Tonight would have been a tidy little one-night stand if not for Alistair. But now it's complicated because my gorgeous boss is a jerk who takes what he wants without apology.

Kenya: It's not what it looks like.

Alistair closes his eyes and murmurs, "If you're going to text about me, you might as well talk out loud."

Ezekiel clears his throat.

Bernard tightens his fingers on the steering wheel.

Awkward silence falls on the car.

Alistair speaks in a low tone. "I don't owe either of you an explanation as this is between myself and Miss Jones." He scowls at Ezekiel. "But since I'd like to spare her the interrogation, the truth is that I want her and she's trying her best to resist me."

My jaw drops.

"That is the most you'll get." He narrows his eyes at Ezekiel. "Kindly refrain from commenting until Miss Jones is gone."

I stare at Alistair, trying to understand how his brain works. The passing lights dance over his sharp jaw and rugged profile. He looks like a mythical prince come to life. I want to slap the handsome right off his face.

Unfortunately, there are too many of his people in the car. Ezekiel is going to side with him, even if he doesn't agree. And Bernard basically pledged his life in servitude because of what Alistair did for his wife.

If I swing on him, they're going to haul me back.

Controlling my temper takes effort. I manage to keep my mouth shut until the car slows in front of Sunny's apartment.

Unfortunately, a clean getaway is not in the cards. Alistair hops out of the car and joins me on the sidewalk. He easily catches up with me and shoots his arm out to bar my escape.

I crane my neck to look at him. He's not smiling. Not really. But his eyes still hold that glow of affection. I have no idea where it's coming from or when it even got there.

"We're meeting with Baby Box tomorrow to finalize the products for the subscription box. I need you to be there bright and early."

"It's the weekend."

"Have I ever given you the weekend off, Miss Jones?"

I narrow my eyes at him. "You're not human, are you?"

"How about I take you somewhere private and you can find out?" he whispers, leaning close to my face.

I grit my teeth.

His lips curl up slightly. He goaded me and I fell for it, but he's just so… insufferable.

"Goodnight, Kenya." He drops his hands on my shoulders and pulls me in for a kiss on the forehead. "I'll pick you up tomorrow."

"No thanks."

"I wasn't asking."

"Seeing your face early in the morning sounds like torture."

"And yet, you were willing to risk it all for a taste of me tonight. Were you planning on having your way with me and then disappearing before I woke up?" He shakes his head. "I'm disappointed. You should at least buy me breakfast."

I roll my eyes. Hard.

He's still the same jerkface Alistair. Except… he's… flirting with me.

"Goodnight," Alistair calls.

I turn back and notice him smirking.

Oh, I'm going to punch his face. At least once.

When I get inside, Sunny is at the door waiting for me. She grabs my shoulders and hauls me into the living room.

"I need an update and I need it now." Her dark eyes glisten like ancient jewels. "I saw everything through the peephole. Why was your boss staring at you like that? And why did he kiss your forehead?" She gives me a once-over and then gasps. "Wait, is that why you borrowed my dress tonight? Because you were going to see him?"

"No." I push out my lips.

"Oh yes you did!" Sunny flings herself into the chair and laughs with her whole body. Smacking her hands together and stomping her foot, she howls. "You went and fell for your evil boss!"

"I didn't," I hiss.

"Then why did he drop you home like he's your date to junior prom?"

"Stop playing. He's dropped me home before."

"That still doesn't explain the dress," Sunny sings.

Okay, maybe I was *hoping* Alistair would see me in this outfit.

Those office clothes, while chic, don't really express my personal fashion style.

I wanted his attention.

I just didn't actually expect to get it.

"How far did you two go?" Sunny peers at me.

"Not as far as I wanted." I frown. "He told me he couldn't stop thinking about me."

"Whoa." She jumps to her feet and starts pacing. "Whoa, whoa, whoa."

"He must be messing with me, right? This is all part of his twisted plan to get me back for destroying his fern."

"No, I think there's more to it. If you look back, the signs were there all along."

"What signs?" I squeak.

"He didn't fire you after Baby Box."

"Hey, I *saved* that Baby Box deal. It was going up in flames until I threw water on it."

"You threw his kid under the bus!"

"*Not* intentionally."

"And after that, what did he do? He protected you from that Baby Box creep."

"Walsh."

"Right, Walsh." She nods. "He dropped you home after the promotion date mix-up, got you tea and even bought you a humidifier."

"He said he got that for free," I argue.

She slants me a *get real* look.

I huff.

"It's all connected." Her eyes are wide and all that's missing is a tin hat made of foil.

I shake my head. "You're making a big deal out of nothing. All we did was kiss and then he started talking nonsense—"

"You *kissed* him?"

I cringe.

She flies over to me. "And it was good?"

My eyelashes flutter.

Heat floods my chest.

Alistair kissed me like a hurricane.

He kissed me senseless.

Then he told me it was more.

More?

What *more*?

"Woman, you do not have to tell me a *thing*." Sunny shakes her head. "Ugh, I'm so jealous. It's been years since I've gone out on a date. I don't even need a millionaire. Just a regular guy with a nice smile and an easygoing personality."

"It's not like that."

"What's it like then? You're into him too, aren't you?"

"I…" I lick my lips.

She studies me. "You want to kiss him, but you won't accept that you have feelings for him?"

"It's not that. I *do* have feelings for him."

"Okay, then what's the—"

"But I was with Drake for *three years*." I cringe hard. "We moved in together. We talked about marriage all the time. I didn't imagine a future without him by my side. And look what happened."

"Your selfish sister stole him away."

I curl a pillow into my chest. "What I feel for Alistair is… passionate. You know? It's kind of hate and lust all mixed up. But that kind of fire burns hot and fast and then it putters out just as quickly."

"You don't know that," she croons, rubbing my back.

"He's rich."

"So?"

"And he has a daughter to think of."

Sunny pulls her lips in.

"If he comes after my heart, he'll have it. That man gets everything he wants. Even if he has to tear down the world to make it happen." Sunny keeps rubbing my back and nodding in understanding. "After this phase passes, it might be easy for him to walk away, but I've already been hurt once. I don't want to get crushed again."

"Oh, honey."

"Last time, with Drake, I got blindsided. This time, if I walk willingly into the storm, I'll deserve the pain."

"Then tell him that. Find out if all he wants is a fling and end it quickly."

I glance down.

"Unless you don't want to." She frowns. "Unless you secretly want him to break your heart if that's what it'll come to."

I stay quiet.

"What exactly do you want, Kenya?"

I have no idea.

All I know is that Alistair should be off limits but, with every single breath I take, I can still taste his kiss.

CHAPTER 16
RUNAWAY HEARTS

HOLLAND

K‍ENYA JOTS NOTES IN A SMALL, wired notebook. A studious wrinkle forms between her eyebrows.

On the scale of one to stunning, she's a perfect ten of a distraction. Especially when she's in work mode.

The presentation changes on the screen. I only know because the colors across Kenya's face shifts from red to blue. The way her brown skin absorbs the hue leaves my mouth dry.

She's gloriously put-together this morning. The shirt buttoned to her neck and the long black pencil skirt must be intentional. Her attempt to dress down is a giant failure. This woman is a natural beauty. Makeup. Fancy clothes. She doesn't need any of it.

In fact, I'd prefer if she didn't have any clothes on.

My fingers tingle. I want to free her curls from that tight bun and watch it expand and expand until it touches the sun. I want to bury my face in her chest and kiss my way down until she—

Ezekiel taps me on the elbow like a miserable prep school principal.

I shoot him an aggravated glance and he returns it with a scowl.

After dropping Kenya home last night, my executive assistant was moodily silent for the rest of the ride. I didn't mind. A lecture from Ezekiel would have spoiled an otherwise great night.

But I should have known silence would lead to action.

Ezekiel is attending a Belle's Beauty meeting even though his presence is not required. Given the scolding look he's flashing my way, he's here on a mission to keep me in check.

As if anyone can keep my raging desire for Miss Jones in line.

I tried and failed.

Ezekiel doesn't have a flying fig of a chance.

"Mr. Alistair?" The marketing director glances at me. "Do you agree with these choices?"

I slap my folder closed and stare at Kenya. "Yes. I like what I'm seeing."

Kenya shoots me a curious look.

The rest of the room shuffles.

The marketing director stammers, "I'm sorry, Mr. Alistair. Did you say you... actually... like it?"

"Yes." My tone drops. "I like it a lot."

Kenya finally catches my drift. Her eyes widen in realization. Just as quickly, they narrow in annoyance.

Damn. Will I ever tire of her fire?

She quickly glances away.

"We'll go with that." I rise to my feet. The chair skates back from the movement. Buttoning my suit with one hand, I gesture to Kenya with the other. "Let Baby Box know of our choice and get the production team started on the samples. We'll need to be ready for the New Year's issue."

She nods. "Understood."

"Meeting's over." I glance at each of the team members. "You all know what to do. No one goes home until this order is placed."

They grumble under their breath. Some of them try to smile. Others barely manage a grimace.

I have them working on a Saturday. To most of them, I'm public enemy number one. But the Baby Box deal is a necessary accelerant for Belle's Beauty. We have to fit in the project amidst our regular end-of-the-year promotions and product launches.

"Good work, everyone," I say.

Twelve pairs of frightened eyes swing to me.

No one moves.

Eyebrows tightening, I freeze too.

The marketing director quivers. "S-sir?"

"I said good work." Annoyance bristles the back of my spine. Why is everyone acting so surprised?

A big, gleaming smile unfolds on the director's face. "Thank you." He blinks rapidly. "Thank you."

I lean back, confused.

The team starts to perk up. Frustrated smiles turn genuine and everyone eagerly darts for the door. Kenya is at the front of the crowd.

"Not you, Miss Jones," I bark.

Her heels skid so fast on the carpet I see a plume of smoke.

"I need a word," I murmur.

She whirls around, her eyes sharpening. "Regarding?"

I motion for her to come closer.

Ezekiel clears his throat again. "Alistair, might I remind you that you have a conference call regarding the software licensing deal?"

"I'll be there, Ezekiel." I wave him out.

His eyes darken in disapproval.

I arch a brow.

Growling under his breath, he prowls away after giving Kenya a squeeze on the shoulder. I roll my eyes at his theatrics. He's so obvious about his new loyalties. I should cut his pay for that.

"You shouldn't tick off the man who makes the best coffee in the building," Kenya warns.

I lean against the desk. "He's being overprotective."

"Of you?"

"No." I jut my chin out at her.

She laughs. "Ezekiel knows I can handle myself."

"But he also knows," I take her hand and pull her toward me, "how persistent I can be. Especially when I meet resistance."

A smile flits across her gorgeous face. She tamps it down and replaces it with a frown. "You shouldn't be like this."

"Like what?" I murmur, dragging her to stand between my legs.

My body salutes her nearness. I let my nose hover against her smooth neck and inhale her wildly intoxicating scent. She's wearing that perfume again. I need to make a note of it and buy her a year's supply.

"Alistair," she breathes.

An electric tingle flares through me.

"That's not my name."

She blinks rapidly. "I have work to do."

"Say my name and I'll let you go."

She purses her lips.

To prove my point, I lock my hands around her waist and paste her body against mine. She's warm to the touch. Softer than any woman has a right to be.

I want to keep her right here against me for the rest of my life.

She squirms. "What if someone sees?"

"Ezekiel is probably guarding the door," I whisper.

She stops struggling and tilts her face up.

I touch her cheek reverently. "What are you doing tomorrow?"

"My dad called this morning. He wants to have lunch with me."

"You think he wants to talk about the wedding?"

"I don't know." Her shoulders slump. "He's been weirdly silent about the whole thing."

"Do you guys normally go weeks on end without talking?"

"Sometimes." A sigh slips from her plump lips. "I know he and Felice have discussed it. And Sasha's clearly in touch with them, so he's heard her side of the story. With all that's going on, I thought he would reach out and check on me. You know? Since I'm his biological daughter."

I frown. "You and the cheater are step-sisters?"

"I don't see her as a step-sister." Kenya is a little too quick to point out. "We're really close."

"Is that why she did what she did?"

Her lips disappear into her mouth.

I touch her chin until they reappear. "What are you going to tell your dad when you see him?"

This time, when she sighs, she looks weary.

"Your sister was wrong. Everyone in the family should be turning against her. Why are you afraid of what they'll say to you?"

"It's not about right or wrong. It's about her health." Kenya glances away. "Sasha was... sick when we were teenagers. There's always a chance the cancer could come back. Nobody wants to see that."

"So it's your job to swallow your hurt and pain for her sake? That's ridiculous!"

"Now you sound like Sunny." Her lips twitch.

"Tell me what you want. Any form of revenge you need, I'll get it done. Quietly."

"I'm not going to put out a hit on my sister, Alistair."

"Holland."

Her nose scrunches.

"You need to say my name if you want to be free."

"Ew."

I blink, astonished. "Did you just say 'ew'?"

"I'm not calling you *that*. It's weird."

"Why?"

"Because it's your first name."

"I'm going to ignore the fact that you expressed disgust at the name my parents painstakingly chose for me. And I'm also going to ignore the fact that you indirectly insulted all the people who live in Holland."

"That's another thing. It's the name of a country."

I chuckle. "Kenya is also the name of a country."

"True." She smiles and it's so disarming that I almost lose my breath. "You love being right, don't you?"

"It's not that I love it. I'm just rarely wrong."

"Humility is a virtue, Alistair."

My phone starts ringing.

"It's not bragging when it's true." I bury my nose in her neck and rock back and forth.

She pushes me. "That's probably Ezekiel."

"Ignore it."

"We have work to do." There's laughter in her tone. I relish that.

With a groan, I let my arms fall away from her. "You win. *This* time."

"Get used to accepting defeat." She winks.

I capture her hand before she can walk out. "Hey."

She stops. Glances over her shoulder.

"I appreciate you being honest about your family situation. Thank you for trusting me."

Her breath hitches.

I bring her fingers to my lips and kiss her palm. "Now get out of here before I change my mind about letting you go."

She doesn't waste a second. Kicking up her heels, Miss Jones flees the conference room.

I chuckle at her skittishness. That woman has no idea how much I like a challenge. She's fighting her feelings for me, and I don't have a problem teasing it out of her.

Smirking, I stride out of the conference room.

Ezekiel joins me, his face harried and his eyes narrowed. "Are you going to make that a habit?"

"What?"

"Sneaking away with Miss Jones?" He shuffles behind me.

"I plan to."

"Alistair."

"We might have to get blinds for my office. That frosted glass is not going to work anymore."

"Are you insane?" he hisses.

I pat his shoulder. "Didn't you say I had a conference call?"

My phone rings again.

It's Darrel.

I pick up. "I'm busy."

"Give me a slot of your precious schedule."

"Are you asking or telling?" I bark.

His tone softens. "Sorry. I was asking."

"You okay?" It's unlike him to be so tense. He's a man of few words and even fewer facial expressions. Although he has the mug of someone who couldn't be bothered, he rarely snaps at people.

"I've got a client who's not answering the phone. She was being treated at my clinic and she's got two kids…"

I frown. "You need me to send Bernard? He can help with whatever it is."

"No, I'll handle it. I'm just worried. I hope the kids are okay."

"Why? You think she'll hurt them?"

"I can't discuss that with you, Alistair." He sighs.

"But you brought it up."

"Maybe I'm overthinking it. She missed the last two sessions. Something doesn't feel right."

"I hope you figure it out, Darrel."

"Thanks." He clears his throat. "Get back to work. I'll come see you tomorrow when you're free."

"I'm working tomorrow too."

He sounds astonished. "When do you sleep?"

"When the work is done."

Ezekiel capers to me. We're running low on time.

"I'll be at Belle's Beauty tomorrow. Text me before you head out."

"I will."

Ezekiel wrings his hands. "Does your brother-in-law know about…" Eyes darting around, Ezekiel whispers, "you know who?"

"He does."

"And he approves?"

"Yes."

Ezekiel looks stunned.

"Darrel believes that falling for someone else will help me—"

"I meant, he approves of letting you loose on an innocent woman?"

I scowl at him. "If this is your way of turning in your resignation, I won't accept it. You're stuck with me."

"Darrel is usually more objective."

"Not when it comes to his brain-science-kumbaya theories."

"Hmph."

I open the door to my office. "Oh, Ezekiel, would you make a cup of coffee…"

"Of course."

"… And send it to Miss Jones? She loves your brew."

He slaps a hand to his forehead and groans. "Is that what I've become? An errand boy for your secret love affair?"

"Remember she likes it as sweet as me."

"Then she must like it bitter."

I frown. "You have something to say, Ezekiel?"

"Not at all." He shakes his head.

"Spit it out."

"You're not going to listen anyway."

"You're right. But you can at least play along. It's more fun that way."

"It seems Miss Jones has elevated taste in coffee." Ezekiel tuts at me. "And such disappointing taste in men."

I scowl at him.

He lifts a hand, his poise intact. "I'll bring the coffee over to her at once."

"You've been getting really snappy lately."

"Call me if you need anything, Alistair."

"Hey!"

He ignores me.

"Don't forget who…" the door slams shut, "signs your paychecks."

I'm alone.

I purse my lips and then chuckle.

There's still… I check my watch… a couple minutes until the call. I pull up my email and start typing.

To: *Kenya Jones*
From: Holland Alistair
Subject: Coffee Instruction

Dear Miss Jones,

Ezekiel will be stopping by with a coffee for you to observe and analyze. I'd like you to think of me when the flavor hits your tongue as I expect a similar experience when you supply my coffee going forward.

I'm sure you are aware of how pertinent caffeine is to running my business and, since you are now my main supplier of java, I would like to underline the importance of this task.

If you moan, I would like to hear about it.

If you lick your lips, I would like to see it.

Yes, this time I am requesting an in-person report because an experience like this cannot be read about, despite your exquisite story-telling skills.

This report is expected by midnight tonight where I will personally quiz you on all the ways your mouth can experience pleasure. I'm eager for your feedback.

Until then, regards.

Holland Alistair
Fine Industries CEO

. . .

I don't care if I get a response. Just thinking about her reaction fills me to the brim.

Sadly, I'll have to wait until my appointment is done before I can check my inbox.

* * *

Two hours later, I arch my back and push away from the desk. The licensing deal for Fine Industries is coming along well. I was averse to taking my hands off the steering wheel at first, but I'm feeling better about the license play.

Belle is growing up too fast. It burns me every time I have to deal with a business emergency over spending time with her.

As soon as Fine Industries starts sharing the load, I can start to take my foot off the gas. I'll finally have time to take her out on picnics and to the zoo. I'll even brave those massively cheesy indoor playgrounds with the germ-filled ball pits for her.

And maybe I'll invite Kenya along. Introduce her to Belle. See how they click.

And maybe...

A ping from my phone jerks me out of the fantasy.

It's an alert from my email.

To: *Holland Alistair*
From: *Kenya Jones*
Subject: *Be Careful Or You Might Choke*

Dear Mr. Alistair,

I received *the coffee from Ezekiel. As per your instruction, I reviewed it and made notes as to your taste and preference.*

Unfortunately, I realize that the coffee was extremely hot and, in the future, it may prove a hazard as I can imagine it splashing on a very sensitive part of you and burning it to a crisp.

Also, the sweetness of the brew might cause you to overindulge. You might find yourself choking or even knocked out on the floor from trying to move too fast too soon.

Please note that an in-person report is not required. I will be out of the office with the rest of the production team as we convince the factory to make room for us in their production schedule. This task is quite a challenge as they are not interested in accommodating our Baby Box launch.

Thank you for that, by the way. I could think of no greater use of my Saturday. I'm truly grateful to have such a machine of a boss.

REGARDS,

Kenya Jones
   Sales Manager for Baby Box

I LAUGH SO hard that Ezekiel bursts into the room.

When he sees that I'm just pointing at my email, he rolls his eyes and backs out.

I read the email again.

Kenya Jones is a freaking delight. She stirs me up in ways no one has before.

I don't want to click away from that message, but I force myself to get back to work. She's made herself clear, and I think I'll be pushing it if I keep going after her today.

A knock on the door breaks my concentration.

It's Ezekiel.

"Sutherburg from Baby Box just called. He wants to know when would be convenient."

"For our biggest client?" I check my watch. "He could come now if he wanted."

"Should I inform him?"

I nod. Baby Box is the stepping stone to greatness that Belle's Beauty has been looking for. We're already receiving a deluge of partnership offers. Starting off with a brand as prestigious as Baby Box was the right move.

I rub my eyes and massage my back. It's embarrassing to admit, but maybe I'll have to invest in one of those orthopedic office chairs. It's better to use gadgets for the elderly than to ruin my back and *look* like one before my time.

Three knocks sound at the door.

I glance up in surprise. "Come in."

"Mr. Alistair." Sutherburg charges into the room like we're long-lost cousins meeting up at the annual Christmas dinner. "How have you been?"

I frown at his exuberance. "Sutherburg."

My voice is cold, but that doesn't seem to tamp down his brilliant smile. He tugs a red scarf off his neck and perches himself in my sofa like it's a guesthouse.

Annoyance crawls over my spine, but I let it go with a deep breath. Customer service isn't reserved for our sales clerks and admin department. It's my job to keep Belle's Beauty allies happy too.

Smoothing a hand over my jacket, I coax my expression into a less severe scowl and take the chair across from him.

"I didn't expect you to arrive so quickly."

"Oh, I was in the area and thought I'd stop in." He smirks. "Is Miss Jones around?"

"Why would you need to know that?" My voice has an edge.

"No reason. No reason." He waves away the words like they're harmless mosquitos. "I'm checking up on our star player for the January subscription."

"We're preparing as quickly as we can."

"I'll say. I was stunned when your assistant told me you were in the office on a Saturday."

"You're also here on official business," I point out. "There's something in the way his eyes are darting all over that doesn't feel right. He's a jovial man, but he didn't climb to his position by playing nice. "What exactly is this visit about?"

"Straight to the point, huh?" He slaps his knee. "I like that about you, Alistair. You're all business."

I frown at him. Flattery isn't going to work on me.

He tugs at his tie and swallows so hard his Adam's apple almost slaps me in the face. "The thing is, Alistair, Baby Box is really impressed by Miss Jones's work and reputation. We heard about her quick thinking during the pre-order event and we're also aware of her background in sales."

"I'm well aware of Miss Jones's strong points. It's why I gave her the position."

"Right. Yes. Well, we'd like to keep the collaboration between Baby Box and Belle's Beauty going."

"And what does this have to do with Miss Jones?" I hiss. He's dancing around the topic and it's frustrating.

"We... I mean *I* think she would be an asset to Baby Box and her skills would be more duly served in our organization."

My lips hitch in a cruel smile. "You're trying to steal my employee from me, Mr. Sutherburg?"

"Oh, no. No. If stealing was our goal, we would have used a talent scout and gotten through to her that way."

Ezekiel enters the room then, a tray in his gnarled hands. He sets it on the table and shares out the coffee, giving me time to get my temper in check.

Sutherburg rubs his hands together. He slants Ezekiel a nervous nod when the cup appears in front of him. Reaching out, he wraps thick fingers around the handle and brings it to his lips.

I lean back in my seat and rest my elbow on the chair handle. "If you'd tried to sneak off with my employee, I would have come after you with guns blazing." My head tilts to the left. "But you knew that."

Ezekiel's eyes go wide.

I nod at him. *I've got this.*

He returns my look with a bob of his head and leaves quietly.

I bring the coffee to my lips and drink. Taking my time setting it back on the table, I bring one leg over the other. "Mr. Sutherburg, why do I get the feeling that poaching Miss Jones and being brazen about it wasn't your idea?"

"I-I don't know what you mean."

Calmly, I take another sip of my coffee. "Walsh must have sent you."

"He's quite impressed by Miss Jones's abilities." Sutherburg plucks his collar away from his neck. I notice a flush spreading beneath the fabric. "We're both in agreement that her skillset would be perfect for a better position at Baby Box."

"Mr. Sutherburg, you *must* see how insulting this entire conversation is."

"Insulting? Alistair, no. We're peers. Comrades fighting for the same goal. What's a little shift in employees? I'm sure you can find another sales manager like Miss Jones."

"Then why don't *you* find another sales manager like Miss Jones instead of trying to take my people?"

He swallows again. The flush is moving up to his cheeks now. "Mr. Alistair, I'm not here to ask your permission. This is simply a courtesy given our business relationship. Baby Box would like a long and prosperous collaboration with Belle's Beauty. We wouldn't want anything to endanger that."

"Are you threatening me, Mr. Sutherburg?" I unfold my legs and press my feet into the ground. Leaning my elbows on my thighs, I look up with a dark smirk. "You don't want to do that."

"No. No. Of course not. No threats here. We wouldn't dream of—"

"Miss Jones is mine." My gaze narrows. "You can go back and tell Walsh that. And if he insists on coming after my people, I will be forced to take extreme measures. Now *that* is a threat." I set the cup down. "But I'm sure it won't get to that because neither of us want any issues. As you said, Baby Box and Belle's Beauty should have a long and prosperous partnership."

Sutherburg gulps.

I jut my chin at the door. "If you don't mind, Mr. Sutherburg, I have a very packed day."

He clamors to his feet. "I'll relay your message accurately, Mr. Alistair."

"Thank you." I wave him out.

He disappears and, a few seconds later, Ezekiel trots in.

"Sutherburg looked like he crapped in his pants. What did you say to him?"

"What he needed to hear."

"You know Baby Box can yank their support at any time. And where will that leave us? We're already pouring money in and pressuring the production—"

"Walsh wants Kenya."

Ezekiel's eyes bug. "What?"

"He wants her…" My fingers stretch out and then curve into fists. "As a woman. I knew that. But now he also wants her as a business play."

"I knew he had a reputation, but I didn't think he was this seedy. What are you going to do?"

I rub my chin. "Tell Bernard to follow Kenya to the factory. Escort her wherever she needs to go this weekend."

"What about you? You can't drive."

I release a shuddering breath. "Hire a chauffeur service."

"I can do that for Miss Jones."

"I want someone I trust with Kenya at all times."

"You don't think Walsh would do anything extreme, do you?"

"No, he's not stupid. I just don't want him anywhere near Kenya in case she takes him up on his offer."

Ezekiel leans back. "Is it so bad if she goes to work for Baby Box?"

I slant him a blistering stare.

"I'm not talking about putting her in dark rooms with Walsh." He scowls. "But… if it's a legitimate offer, it's not a bad deal. It'll be easier for you two if she's no longer your employee."

"No."

"The risk of getting caught is gone. In fact, you can broadcast your relationship if you want."

"I can broadcast it now. I'm not ashamed to be caught up in that woman."

"Yes, but for her, it's a different story, Alistair. I've been working in offices all my life. Women get the shorter end of the stick in these kinds of scandals. And, for a woman as capable as Kenya Jones, it would be vastly detrimental. She's worked hard and people are just starting to acknowledge it."

"I won't let anything happen to her."

"You can't protect her from gossip. Especially the way you're moving."

I run a frustrated hand through my hair.

Ezekiel steps closer to me. "You can't have it all, Alistair. At some point, you're going to have to make a choice. The longer you drag it out, the more people will get hurt."

"I won't give her up."

"Then you better have a solid plan in case the Baby Box deal falls through. Because choosing Miss Jones might mean the end of the company."

* * *

When I head home, I try to put the heaviness away from me so Belle won't notice. She's coloring with Mrs. Hansley when I walk in.

I take over from the nanny and plunk myself next to my daughter. We color together until my hands cramp and I beg her for another activity.

She punishes me with two rounds of princess movies and I'm relieved when she falls asleep in my lap before the final musical.

I will never understand these plot points. Why do characters break out into song at random moments? It's the most unrealistic thing ever. Who feels like singing when they just got kidnapped by an evil troll?

After putting Belle to bed, I grab my cell phone and text Kenya.

Holland: Did you get home okay?

I look over the latest data pulls on my tablet, while shooting constant looks at my phone.

At last, I see a notification.

Kenya: Yes. Bernard brought coffee and sandwiches. Your idea?

Holland: Thought you might be hungry.

Kenya: Thanks.

I smile. She's got me wrapped around her little finger. It should be scary, but it's freaking exhilarating.

Holland: Have a good time with your dad tomorrow.

I set the cell phone away and continue with the data pull.

I'm not sure when I fall asleep, but a loud sound startles me awake. Groggily, I roll out of bed and stumble into the kitchen.

Belle is up, bright-eyed and beaming. Her long brown hair falls in limp strands to her shoulders and she bounces on the tips of her toes. "Daddy."

"Baby girl," I plod toward her, "what was that sound?"

She points to a book turned down on the ground. My heart stalls when I recognize our wedding album.

"Where did you find this?"

Her eyes get big and round. "Mrs. Hansley hid it under her clothes in the closet."

I swallow hard. The nanny must have been reminiscing about Claire, especially with Belle's constant questions about where her mother went.

"Here, sweetie." I pull her into my lap and settle the photo album on the floor in front of us.

"This is mommy?" Belle points a little finger.

I get choked up. "Yeah. That's your mommy."

In the picture, Claire is beaming. Her eyes are brighter than emerald gems and her lips are curved up. Full of life. Full of promise.

"And she's in heaven?"

I choke out a yes.

Belle pats the pages. "Can I see her?"

My eyes get teary, but I refuse to cry. "Not today, sweetheart."

"But I want to see her," Belle whines.

"You can't, baby." I think of the headstone where Claire's remains were buried.

"I want to! I want to!" She kicks her legs and flails her arms.

"Belle."

"I want to see her!" She shrieks. "I want to see her!"

"Stop it," I roar.

Belle goes quiet.

I realize I shouted a little too hard and my heart breaks into pieces. "Belle, I'm sorry. I didn't mean to yell."

Her little lips trembling, she scurries away from me and runs into her room.

"Belle…"

The front door opens and Mrs. Hansley's cheerful voice rings out. "Alistair?"

"In here." I wearily walk out to her.

Her eyes widen when she sees me. "What happened?"

"Belle's upset." I release a giant breath. "I have to go to the office now."

"Now? It's Sunday."

I run a hand over my face. "The faster I can get the licensing deal settled, the more time I'll have with Belle."

She sighs, clearly not liking my answer.

I turn away without a word and get ready. When I'm done, I pass by Belle's room. "Belle, sweetie?" I rap my fingers on the door. "Daddy's leaving, okay? But I'll be back and then maybe we can go for ice cream. Huh?"

Still no response.

Defeated, I slump to the living room. Mrs. Hansley is folding

Belle's clothes on the sofa.

"I'll take her for a little walk. Maybe she'll feel better after getting some fresh air."

I nod solemnly.

"She'll be fine, Alistair."

I take her word for it and meet Bernard downstairs.

On the way to the company, I let my mind run circles around Belle's tantrum. How do I explain what I did to her?

A ball lumps in my throat. The only way I can face my daughter is if I get Belle's Beauty off the ground. If I can present a healthy, flourishing company to our daughter, it'll honor Claire's legacy. It's my penance. My one shot at redemption.

The company is empty when I walk in.

I pass Kenya's office and, even with the strain of my day, a smile flits over my lips. She must be meeting with her father by now. I hope that conversation turns out better than she expects.

Being a father is tough. I can't imagine Belle growing up and feeling like she can't come to me with her problems.

My thoughts take a long time to settle, but I finally get focused on work.

What feels like minutes later, my phone rings.

It's Mrs. Hansley.

I pick up. "Hello?"

"Alistair!" A frantic thread rings through her voice. "I'm sorry. I'm so sorry."

My body instantly goes on high alert.

"I lost her."

"What?" I jump out of my chair.

"I'm so sorry, Alistair. I turned my back for one second and…"

"Where is she? Where's my daughter?" I growl.

"I don't know," Mrs. Hansley whimpers. "She disappeared."

My heart in my throat, I fly out of my office and tear a path down the stairs.

CHAPTER 17
PRINCESS HOURS

KENYA

"Hey, dad." My eyes skate to Felice. "I didn't know you were both coming."

"Why would your father have brunch without me?" Felice says breezily, sliding her sunglasses to the top of her hair.

I swear, it's my first time hearing that snobby tone from her. Felice has always been nothing but kind to me. No Cinderella stepmother here. I still remember the way she dolled me up for my first homecoming.

No one had asked me to the dance that year. I'd been crying because it felt like all my friends were getting roses, while no boy wanted to talk to me.

Felice found me crying in the bathroom and wrapped her arms around me.

"Is it because I'm too dark? Or because of my acne?"

"Absolutely not. Those boys are idiots. They just haven't seen how stunning you are yet."

That night, Felice whipped out her makeup kit and hired a black hairstylist to take care of my hair. She became my fairy godmother and sent me off to the ball.

She was always like that. Never pushing to replace my mother's memory in my life, but being a mother figure at all times. I hardly remember that she's not related to me by blood.

But today, I'm keenly aware of it.

Disapproval glints in her brown eyes and she holds herself stiffly when I hug my dad. I hesitate before wrapping my arms around her too.

She pats me on the back and then edges away. "Let's sit down. I haven't eaten since yesterday."

"I'm surprised you two are still in the city." I grab a menu and lift it.

"Yes, well, there's a lot to do with the wedding and Sasha can't handle it all alone."

I set the menu down roughly.

Dad pats her hand. "Felice, let's not discuss that yet."

"Why?" Felice's voice rises to an offended shriek. "Can't I mention Sasha's wedding now? One of the happiest moments of my daughter's life and I'm expected to brush it under the rug?"

I dig my fingers into the laminated page until it crackles.

Dad clears his throat. "Let's talk about that after we eat."

"Talk about what?" I snap. "What exactly are you here to talk about, dad?"

He glances down.

Felice leans forward. "Sasha doesn't have a lot of friends."

"Gee? I wonder why? Maybe she slept with their boyfriends too."

Felice's jaw drops. "What did you just say?"

"Felice." Dad tries to tug on her arm.

She wrenches her elbow back. "Why can't you just let that go, Kenya? It happened so long ago!"

"Let that go?" My eyes nearly pop out of my head. "How do you expect me to get over something like that?"

"Sasha cries herself to sleep every night. It's tearing her up the way you're treating her. She's supposed to be joyful and excited. Instead, she has to worry about you." Felice shakes her finger in my face. "How selfish can you be? Don't you feel anything for your sister?"

My insides rearrange.

Selfish?

I hate that Sasha is crying and upset. I'm her protector. I was the one who talked with her for hours when something distressed her. I'd jump into a fight to keep her sane. It didn't matter who or what I had to face if it made her smile.

That sister side of me, it's still alive and kicking.

But I just can't breeze over the fact that she betrayed me.

"It's not fair to me," I speak through clenched teeth, "to expect forgiveness so soon. I'm still working through my feelings. It's only been a few weeks."

"And her wedding is in four months."

My eyes flicker up to her. "Why is it so soon?"

Crimson flushes her cheeks. "The point is, Sasha really wants you to be a part of it. For the sake of your sister, you should get over whatever issues you have and be there for her." Her eyes gleam wildly. *"That's* what family does."

I want to toss out a dig. Something about the fact that she's not my family. That she's not my mother.

But my tongue is heavy.

I can't find the words.

Felice stepped into my life when I was feeling insecure and lonely. She and Sasha were my people. We formed a girl team against my dad, constantly ganging up on him so we could choose the girliest movies on family night or blast cheesy pop songs on family trips.

My eyes lower to the table. "Dad?"

He jumps as if he didn't expect this conversation to involve him.

"Is that what you think too? That I should just forget about Sasha betraying me, lying to me and hurting me? Do you think I'm selfish too?"

Dad remains silent.

I glance up and look into his face. Age formed deep wrinkles in his forehead. His cheeks are bigger now, pressing against his eyes. Dark skin, a shade like crushed blueberries, stretches over a stout body and a beer paunch.

He's my father. I got my eyes from him. My love of reading. My determination to work hard and succeed at whatever I do.

My voice cracks. "Do you, dad?"

"I think Sasha needs you right now," he says. "This isn't the time for our family to be divided."

My heart shatters into a million pieces. I can hear it breaking like glass crashing to the floor.

Felice gives him an approving look and I watch the regard I had for these two people burn to the ground.

I'm not Felice's little girl.

I get that.

I understand that, sometimes, blood is thicker than water.

But it doesn't seem to be true in dad's case.

He chose Sasha.

His baby girl.

I blink rapidly, feeling the tears forming but refusing to let them loose. Is there anything more pathetic than weeping because you've finally come face to face with the truth?

I plant my palms on the table and rise as regally as I can. "I'm not hungry anymore. But you two enjoy yourself."

"Kenya," dad calls my name.

I ignore him.

Felice yells out, "Will you be at the dress fitting?"

She's delusional.

I stomp out into the bright sunshine. It's Sunday afternoon, but the sidewalk is filled with people enjoying a stroll or heading into restaurants.

My heart aches so much it feels like it's brushing up against a thorny gate. I brush away the tear that falls down my cheek. It's followed by another and I smack that down too.

No crying.

There's no use bemoaning my fate when I can't change a thing.

My family is firmly on my sister's side and I'm the bully for not caving to whatever Sasha wants.

Fine.

I guess I'll just stay by myself then.

But the tears keep coming. I pump my arms and run down another street, trying to get away from the pain that's clinging to my heels.

When I slow down, I realize my legs are burning.

The sun beats the top of my head like it's trying to teach me a lesson.

I glance around for a bench to sit and catch my breath, when I notice a little girl seated alone. She's small and adorable with two pigtails tied at the end with yellow ribbon. The dress she's wearing is fluffy, almost like a tutu.

Tears roll down her cheeks that are bright red—either from sunburn or her weeping. I glance around. Where are her parents?

When no one seems to be paying the kid any attention, I inch closer to her. Dropping to my haunches, I speak in a gentle voice. "Hi, sweetie. Why are you crying? Where's your mommy?"

"I don't know," she bawls. Then her mouth opens again and she starts crying louder.

Someone walks by and gives me a funny look. I want to raise both hands and tell them I didn't make the kid cry, but I resist the impulse.

Leaning toward the baby again, I say, "It's alright, sweetie. We can find her."

"No we can't." The child sniffs. Her eyes are familiar.

I stare into them, trying to place where I've seen them before. "Why not?"

"Because my mommy is in heaven."

My heart rearranges. *Oh, you poor thing.*

I give her a comforting smile. "My mommy's in heaven too."

She blinks and finally stops crying. "Really?"

"Yes." I nod.

"You think our mommies are together in heaven?"

"Oh definitely. I think our mommies are best friends. They probably have coffee together every afternoon. And read books. And play games."

She looks intrigued. Though her eyes are still glistening with tears, they no longer fall down her face.

"I'm Kenya." I offer my hand to her.

She stares at it and pulls her pudgy hand to her stomach. "My daddy says I shouldn't talk to strangers."

"Your daddy?"

She bobs her head.

I smile. So she has a parent. I just have to find a way to contact them. Or maybe I should call the police so they can locate the dad sooner.

"Sweetie, do you know your dad's number by chance?"

She opens her cupid's bow lips and starts to sing a jingle. I realize she's reciting a phone number. Her dad must have taught her how to memorize it in a song. *Smart man. If only he were more responsible. How did he lose track of his kid?*

"Hold on, baby." Excitedly, I rush to open my phone and touch the call button. "Go ahead?"

She sings it again.

I type in the first five numbers and my eyebrows start to hike.

Why is my phone telling me I know this number?

With trembling fingers, I continue to type in the number and my jaw drops.

Evil Boss

My head whips up.

It's Alistair's number.

I stare at the precious little girl with new eyes.

So this must be... Alistair's daughter, Belle.

* * *

"Belle, you scared me so much." Alistair whips his daughter into his arms and crushes her to his chest. For the first time ever, he looks frantic. Like he's coming apart at the seams.

He kisses Belle's cheek and hugs her even tighter. "Why would you let go of Mrs. Hansley's hand? Huh?"

"I was looking for mommy," she says, all innocence and big brown eyes. No wonder she looked so familiar. Her face is a carbon copy of Alistair's. I'm sure Belle has her mom's features too. I just can't see it yet.

"And I found her," Belle says excitedly.

Alistair's eyes lurch up and fall on me.

I stiffen in shock.

"She's with Miss Kenya's mommy." Belle gives her father a brilliant smile. "They're having coffee."

Alistair blinks and blinks.

I feel heat rush through my cheeks.

A thin, elderly woman with greying hair and tearful eyes pounces on Belle before anyone can move.

She starts bawling. "You sweet girl. You almost gave me a heart attack. Never do that again, you hear me? Never."

"I'm sorry." Belle pats the older woman's back as if *she's* the grown up.

"Thank you for finding my daughter," Alistair says to me, his eyes glistening like the sunset.

"Of course."

Another car careens next to Alistair's. A tall, handsome man stumbles out. He's wearing a plain T-shirt and pressed slacks, but he might as well be wearing military gear.

His steps are sharp and determined. His back ramrod straight.

He rushes to Belle and the older woman. "Thank God. Are you alright, Belle?"

"Uncle Darrel."

"Is she okay?" Uncle Darrel asks Alistair.

He nods. "Kenya found her."

At his words, all three adults turn and look at me.

Pure relief spreads across Uncle Darrel's face.

The elderly woman looks at me as if she wants to dress me in gold. Her bottom lip quivers and she tightens her grip on Belle like the little girl is the only thing stopping her from grabbing me and kissing my cheeks.

I squirm. They're making it a bigger deal than it was. All I did was run crying in this direction. I'm not a hero.

"Thank you," Uncle Darrel says.

"Uh, it was mostly a coincidence."

"My mom and Miss Kenya's mom are reading books in heaven," Belle announces. "Miss Kenya told me."

I wince. She's adorable. But I don't normally go around broadcasting that I lost my mother.

Alistair scoops his daughter in his arms and walks over to me. Belle tucks her head into her father's shoulder. It's clear Alistair adores her, but it obviously goes both ways.

"I don't know how I'll make it up to you, but I promise I will."

"Alistair really," I shake my head, "it wasn't anything worth talking about. You could even say that *she* found me. She's an extremely smart girl." I smile at Belle who offers me a shy grin in return. "She remembered her daddy's number and gave it all to me without forgetting a beat. She's the hero."

Alistair's smile is soft. Softer than I've ever seen on his gorgeous face.

He's not buying my deflection.

"Daddy," Belle pushes out her bottom lip, "I have to pee."

"Okay, princess. When we get home—"

"No, now," she hisses.

He shares a helpless look with the older woman.

"I can take her," she says.

"I'll go with you." He tightens his hold on his daughter. It must have torn his heart out of his chest to hear she was missing. He still looks rattled. Turning his hazel eyes on me, Alistair says, "I'll find a bathroom around here. We'll be right back."

"Sure."

"You'll stay, right?"

My jaw drops. I don't think I've heard Holland Alistair *ask* me for anything since I've known him.

Growl at me? Yes.

Demand his way? Definitely.

But ask in that *I won't be able to breathe if you don't say yes* way?

Never.

While he and the older woman walk off, I notice Uncle Darrel... well, *Darrel*—he's too young and too hot to be *my* uncle—staring at me.

Although I've seen him in passing, I don't think we've formally met. I decide to introduce myself. "Hi, I'm—"

"Kenya Jones." His expression gives nothing away and yet, I can tell that he's pleased. "I've heard a lot about you."

"Oh? From... Alistair?"

His smile is cryptic. I get the feeling that no one can pry any information from this man, even if they tortured him for days.

I tap my fingers against my arm. "You, uh, you're Alistair's brother?"

"Brother-in-law." His green eyes peruse my face as if he's taking note of every one of my micro-expressions. "Claire's brother."

I blink in shock.

He nods to the chair. "Would you like to sit?"

"Uh..."

He gestures to the bench and I follow him. Not because I want to talk but because my legs are about to give out. The excitement of meeting Belle distracted me from my exhaustion, but I'm starting to feel the strain again.

We fall into the bench together. Darrel glances out at the buildings around us, his back straighter than an arrow.

"Were you military?" I ask, unable to stop my curiosity.

"No. My dad was. It rubbed off on me and Claire."

"I see." I lean down and punch my fists against my thigh to

beat out the knots. "No wonder she built a successful company from scratch. It takes discipline."

"She was amazing."

I glance away. "Alistair never talks about her."

"He blames himself." Darrel squints in the sunlight. "He was in the car the night she passed. He was driving, actually. After that day, he's never gotten behind the wheel of a car again."

My eyes widen. It feels like I'm getting an inside look into the man behind the Godzilla boss suit.

"So he never drives? Ever?"

Darrel shakes his head. "After Claire, he locked himself up completely. Didn't talk much. Didn't laugh. Barely ate and drank. We had to convince him to keep holding on to life so he could be there for Belle. It was only then that he showered, shaved, and started eating again. Belle saved him."

"She adores him."

"It's mutual." He dips his chin. "She's the air that he breathes. Everything he's doing, beating himself into the ground for Belle's Beauty and trying to raise profits, it's so he can give it to her."

"That's why he's hell-bent on being personally involved in Belle's Beauty," I mumble.

"It wasn't his vision at first. He had a hard time thinking about that company after Claire passed but, at the same time, he couldn't let it go." Darrel's green eyes fall on me. "He only recently decided to be more hands-on and that's when he found you."

I shift under his probing stare. "I don't know what you've heard, but you have it wrong. I'm not that important in the company."

"No?"

"I'm a freshly promoted second-assistant."

"Come on, Miss Jones." His face breaks into a sliver of a smile. He's absolutely stunning and, if my heart wasn't already caught up on my beast of a boss with a surprising soft side, I'd probably fawn over him. "We both know that's not true."

My eyes dart away from his.

Darrel shifts toward me. "Alistair's been on a long, hard path. If I'll be honest, I thought he'd never find a new direction. But he found it in you. You're his light at the end of the tunnel, Miss Jones."

My heart skips a beat.

Just then, I notice Belle, Alistair and the older woman returning. Belle is all smiles as she drapes an arm around her daddy's neck.

When she sees me, her head whips up. "Miss Kenya!"

I smile and hop to my feet. "Yes, sweetie?"

"Can we have coffee like our mommies?"

"I think you're a little young for coffee, Belle," Darrel says, giving her a fond look.

Belle pushes out her bottom lip.

She's too adorable.

My heart melts. "I mean... we can have tea."

"I thought you hated tea?" Alistair says.

I slant him a sharp look. "I'll put sugar in mine. It can't be that bad with artificial sweeteners added."

He looks amused.

"Daddy, daddy, can Miss Jones have tea with me?"

"I don't know." He strokes his chin. "That depends on whether you can promise me that you'll never run off by yourself again."

"I promise," she says exuberantly.

The older woman clutches her hands to her chest and sighs. "How precious."

Same, lady. Same.

Alistair pretends to think about it and then nods. "It's alright with me." He arches an eyebrow in my direction and gives me a hot look. "Miss Jones, would you like to have lunch with us?"

I can't catch my breath. With the sunshine bouncing over his thick hair and his arms wrapped so protectively around his daughter, he looks like he could be the father of *my* children.

Which is ridiculous.

I gulp. "Are you sure?"

"I'll make a feast," the older woman says. "Something deserving of today's hero."

"Please don't call me a hero. Really. I didn't do anything."

Alistair strides over and slides an arm around my waist. "Then what should I call you?"

"Call her Miss Kenya," Belle says.

I laugh, absolutely charmed. "She's so cute."

"She's my daughter. Of course she's cute," he says. "All the people who belong to me are perfect in every way."

I blink rapidly.

Alistair steps back and grabs my hand. "Bernard is waiting. Mrs. Hansley, let's get back home." He glances over his shoulder. "Darrel, are you coming?"

"I'll skip this one. I was on a mission before you called about Belle."

Alistair stops and gives him a surveying look. "The client with the kids?"

He nods slowly.

"Has their mom been found?"

Darrel shakes his head, his lips tight.

A story's there, but I don't get to ask because Alistair ushers me into his fancy car and whisks me away to his castle.

* * *

AFTER PLAYING with Belle all day, Mrs. Hansley—Belle's nanny—invites me to stay for dinner. Since Mrs. Hansley sent me straight to food heaven during lunch, I'm quick to jump on that offer.

Turns out, what she did this afternoon was only a taste of her skills. This woman put her soul in tonight's meal. I've never had an experience like that.

Growing up, nobody in my house liked to cook. It was a chore we all approached with a lot of grumbling. But, with Mrs. Hansley, I finally understand how a meal can reveal someone's heart. She could have found a less fattening way to say thank you. My thighs will never forgive me. I flop back in my chair and undo the button on my jeans.

A loud yawn drags my attention to the little girl across the table. Belle's head is rolling around like her neck lost a few muscles. She jerks up, her eyes at half-mast. It's clear she's trying to stay awake and failing spectacularly.

I chuckle. "Looks like someone needs to get ready for bedtime."

"Come on, Belle." Alistair pushes away from the table.

"No." She shakes her head. "I want to stay with Miss Kenya."

My eyes widen in surprise.

Alistair smirks. "I do too." He leans toward his daughter. "What do you say we don't let her go home tonight?"

My mouth hangs open.

Mrs. Hansley chuckles under her breath.

I feel like melting into the ground. Especially when Alistair gives me a wicked smirk full of bad intentions. What on earth is he talking about in front of his *daughter?*

Mrs. Hansley pushes to her feet. "Come on, Belle. Let's brush your teeth."

"No." She squirms. "I want Miss Kenya."

I rise slowly, not sure if I'm infringing. "I don't mind helping out."

"Are you sure?" Mrs. Hansley looks dubious.

Alistair rests his chin on his palm and gives me another hot look. "If you stay and put Belle to bed, I'll return the favor."

I narrow my eyes at him.

Mrs. Hansley pushes his shoulder. "Alistair."

"It's a good deal." He nods at his daughter. "Right, Belle?"

"Yeah!"

"Continue, Alistair, and I'll put *you* in time out," I spit.

He gives me a playful grin.

My heart almost stops beating. This man is six feet of solid rock and sculpted muscle. He's the monster that stomps down the halls and sends employees skittering for cover. But, when he's here with his daughter, he's soft. Casual. His hair is mussed and his shoulders are relaxed. It's like seeing a different side of him. A privilege. And one that's still so confusing. Why is it being offered to me?

I shake my head because Alistair is *not* going to see how much he's affecting me.

Offering my hand to Belle, I lead her from the kitchen and take her into her room. It's a little girl wonderland full of plush toys, a child-sized kitchen and even a mini-mart.

Belle leads me to her walk-in closet—which is about the size of Sunny's entire apartment—and shows me the pajamas she wants to wear. I help her change and then let her lead me to her attached bathroom.

This little girl is living better than eighty percent of the adults in the world.

"All done!" I hoist her so she can spit out her toothpaste into the sink.

When she's finished, Belle clasps her arms around my neck. Her tiny fingers are soft and warm. I feel my heart lurch even more in her direction. She smells like baby powder and mint. I hold her a little closer as I walk her back to her princess bedroom.

Alistair is there, turning down the duvet covers. He looks tall and extremely manly next to the bright pink princess blanket.

"There are my girls."

I arch an eyebrow at him.

He winks and takes Belle from me. "Ready to go to sleep, sweetheart?"

"Miss Kenya."

"Mm?" I lean over her bed.

"Do you think our mommies have sleepovers?"

I exchange a look with Alistair.

He gives me a tender smile.

"Uh, yeah. I do. My mom loved slumber parties."

"Daddy?"

"Yes, Belle?"

"Did my mommy like slumber parties?"

His face gets tight for a second. And then he nods. "She sure did."

"Daddy?"

"Belle," Alistair says with just a hint of a demand in his tone, "you need to stop asking questions and go to sleep."

"One more."

He sighs, but I can tell that if she'd asked for a hundred more, he still would have said yes. "What is it?"

"Can I see Miss Kenya again?"

Alistair glances at me. "If I have my way, you'll see Miss Kenya at breakfast tomorrow."

Flames light up in my veins.

I swallow hard and glance away from him. "Goodnight, Belle."

"Goodnight." She raises her arms to me. I lean down and hug her. With that last embrace, what's left of my heart tumbles right into her pocket.

Alistair smooths the blanket over her when I step back. He caresses her hair, his eyes dark in the shadows. His touch is gentle, almost like he's handling a priceless vase.

He's sexy when he's barking orders at the office. Annoying, but no one can deny the charisma that shoots out of him like sunbeams. Yet, I prefer this contained, tender Alistair.

It's authentic. It's raw.

I can practically feel the love for his daughter flooding out of him. And it does something to me.

He takes my hand, leads me out of Belle's room and closes the door, leaving it slightly ajar. Mrs. Hansley is finishing the dishes when we walk into the kitchen.

I frown. "I wanted to help you clean up."

"Oh, you're such a sweet girl. But there's no need."

"I have to do something to repay you for that meal," I insist. "My soul left my body at least twice during dinner."

She laughs, her cheeks flushing. "You're a sweet talker. No wonder Alistair adores you."

I stiffen.

Alistair comes up behind me and wraps his arms around my waist. "You've got it wrong, Mrs. Hansley. It was her dirty mouth that got me."

I smack him.

He laughs and kisses my cheek.

She looks pleased. "I can't tell you how glad I am to see Alistair dating again. At one point, I thought he'd become a monk."

"He's no monk."

"Because I'm too sexy?"

"Because monks are all about peace and harmony. And you give everyone in the office an aneurysm."

He narrows his eyes at me. "You see what I mean? Even when I'm nice, she still gives me sass." He pulls me tighter. "I already told you that mouth would get you in trouble, Miss Jones."

A thrill travels down my spine. How much trouble are we talking?

Mrs. Hansley chuckles. "Good for you, Kenya. He needs someone to cut him down a size."

He frowns. "Belle is already on her side, Mrs. Hansley. You can't jump ship too."

I laugh loudly. This Alistair is… wow. He's so loose and at ease. I'm absolutely intrigued.

"I'll leave you two alone now."

"Let me walk you out."

"No need." She waves a hand.

He insists and follows her to the door.

While he's gone, I stroll around the living room. There are no pictures of his wife and I wonder if it's too painful to look at them.

According to Darrel, Alistair blames himself for the accident. It's hard to imagine my untouchable boss withdrawing into himself. He seems like someone who'll go down kicking rather than let himself be dragged into the darkness.

His footsteps patter back to me.

I gesture to the mantle full of Belle's baby pictures. "She's even more adorable now than she was then."

"Yeah." He picks up a frame. "She used to bawl her head off all the time. We couldn't figure out what she was crying for. We read every online article and countless books to figure it out."

"What was the answer?"

"Some babies are just fussier than others. Belle had the loudest pair of pipes and she wanted to use them."

I chuckle.

He stares at me like I'm some mystical creature who's about to grant all his wishes.

Shyness steals over me. I glance away. "Does she look a lot like Claire?"

I expect him to stiffen again or change the subject. His voice remains even. "Yes. She's a blend of both of us."

"Do you still miss her?" I ask casually, walking down the line of pictures.

Alistair remains quiet.

I glance behind me, wondering why he's suddenly got nothing to say.

Without warning, my crazy boss marches forward, sweeps me right off my feet and hauls me to the couch. Before I can protest, we're sitting on the expensive white sofa.

He curls me into his lap. "If we're going to do this, I need to touch you."

My heart patters. He's staring at me like he wants to suck the soul out of my body.

"What kind of touching?"

"This much." His voice darkens. "For now."

I swallow hard.

He grazes his fingers over my forehead. "I haven't told anyone except Darrel this. Not Mrs. Hansley. Not Claire's parents. No one."

Expectation builds in the air. Like a balloon flooded with water, stretched to it's limits. Like something about to explode. That'll coat me in something new. Something I can never come back from.

I wrap my fingers around his neck. The big, growly Alistair

with the penchant for driving me crazy is not the one sitting in front of me. This man is a father. A husband who lost his entire world and had to learn how to keep going.

"I'm listening."

"That night," his fingers tangle up in mine, "Claire and I were out-of-state attending a conference. I had a meeting early the next morning and I wanted to be there in time." He stalls as if the words are clogged in his throat. "Claire begged me not to drive that night."

His eyes shake.

His fingers tighten around me.

I brace myself even though I know what's coming.

"I insisted. Told her that I had it handled. She warned me that I hadn't slept. That it was dangerous. I told her it would be fine." His Adam's apple bobs.

I curl into him, trying to give him my warmth. My strength.

"I regret that choice every day. If I'd just listened to her. If I'd taken the early flight like she wanted, she'd still be here."

Watching this strong, capable man fall apart shakes me to my core. I want to fuse myself to him and put him back together in any way I can.

Alistair inhales a shuddering breath and holds me as if I'm the only thing keeping him sane. "Claire would still be alive if it wasn't for me. And I can't help thinking that I should have died instead of her."

"Alistair."

"She was a better person than I could ever be. Giving. Loving. Always willing to help. They took the wrong one."

I feel tears pricking the back of my eyes.

He clears his throat and pastes on a smile that barely hides his pain. "I had nightmares about it. Consistently. I'd keep reliving the moment she told me to stay. Then uh…" He rubs the back of his neck.

"What?"

"One night, you showed up."

"Me?"

He nods. Looks at me intently. "In my dreams."

I blink in shock. I don't know how to respond to that.

"I thought it was a one-time thing, but it wasn't. You kept barging in and you snapped at me." He chuckles and brings my fingers to his lips. "In your own, Kenya-way, you remind me that I'm not stuck in that hotel room."

I hold my breath.

"At first, it terrified me." His voice rises. "And it angered me. I wanted you out. I wanted to stay in the darkness because it's what murderers deserve."

"Alistair."

He shakes his head. "But you didn't care about what I wanted. You kept showing up with your sass and your smiles and your crazy ideas that somehow work out. That night, when I said I couldn't get you out of my head, that wasn't some line to get into your pants. I meant it. You're in my head, Kenya. You're freaking embedded in my skull."

My mouth forms an o.

"I don't show weakness. And I don't let anyone near my daughter."

"Trust me, I know."

He chuckles. "But if I'm going to open myself up and show this mess to anyone, it's going to be you. Only you."

Moved beyond comprehension, I turn in his lap and cradle his chin. "Holland."

His eyelashes flutter.

Surprise creeps over his chiseled face.

My heart beats so hard it's about to fly out of my chest. I hold onto him and say his name again. "Holland."

He sucks in a breath.

I lower my voice and whisper, "Even if it hurts, I want you to know that I'm glad you survived."

CHAPTER 18
HARD AND FAST RULES

HOLLAND

She says my name and I know I'm going to blow her mind all night long. I know I'm going to drag her straight to heaven and back. I know I'm going to hold on to her for the rest of my life.

"You're harder on yourself than you are on everyone else. And that's saying something." Her voice is soft. Her hands are even softer. "Because you are a *menace* to everyone else."

"I get results," I say. "You can't deny that."

"Can you *not* be arrogant right now? We're having a moment."

"This is a moment?" I'm past the moment. I've exposed everything I am. All the broken pieces.

I let it go.

That was me releasing my grip on the past.

Darrel was right. I can't hold on to the guilt and hold on to love. One of them has to give. And losing Kenya Jones is not going to happen.

I loved Claire. She was my wife and the mother of my child. I will forever regret what I did to her, and I'm going to pave the way for Belle because I know that's what she would have wanted. That's what she started Belle's Beauty for.

But this grip Kenya Jones has on me won't go away any time soon. I'm a prisoner to her and she has no freaking idea.

Is it sudden?

Hell no.

People think change is dramatic, but it's really not. It's coming to a new revelation. It's stumbling on a different way of thinking. Everything clicks into place when the time is right.

And the time is now.

Now I'm ready to tear her clothes off.

She gives me a stern look. "I wanted to give you compliments, but it seems your ego doesn't need any help from me."

"I have other things that need help from you," I murmur.

She narrows her eyes. "Alistair."

"Say my name, Kenya."

Her mouth twists into a frown. She's pure attitude and perfection. She's my biggest temptation squeezed into tight blue jeans. Jeans I'm absolutely rolling down to her ankles the minute she stops giving me those angry eyes.

"Where do you get that confidence from? It's boundless. I'm astonished."

"I came clean. There's nothing left to lose now. You know everything. You can destroy me if you want."

Her eyes soften. "I'm not interested in destroying you, Alistair."

"It's too much work?" I tease.

"I'm not afraid of work."

I know. I've seen the way she handles herself at the office. With integrity. With pride.

This woman can rule an empire given enough time.

"I wanted to take things slow. Tease it out." My eyes drop to her lips. My voice gets ragged. "But today changed things for me. You already met Belle. She already adores you."

Her lips tilt up. It's instinctual. I can see that she loves my daughter too.

I graze my hand slowly over her back.

She eases away. "It's not that I don't... feel something."

Feel something? Is she that afraid to label it?

"You know what I've been through." Her gaze darts away from mine. "My ex—"

"Was a bastard and I'm nothing like him. I wouldn't have brought you home and introduced you to my daughter if I wasn't serious."

Her breath hitches. She searches for another excuse. "The office. What if people find out?"

"Let them."

"I don't want people like Heather to misunderstand. I worked hard as a clerk. I worked hard when I was running around at Belle's Beauty HQ. And I damn sure worked hard when I started working for you. I don't want to lose that."

"Okay." I spit the word out. I hate hiding, but if it's what she wants... "We won't tell anyone else at the office." My fingers slide over her cheek. "And who knows? Ducking into storage closets to kiss you might be hot."

She rolls her eyes. "I want to avoid the rumors for as long as I can."

"Fine. I'll only ravish you in my office with the door locked."

"Alistair."

"Anything else? That first demand sounds easy enough."

She narrows her eyes. "You can't be staring at me in meetings. Or sending me coffee."

"Impossible. You're all I can see when you walk into the room. And you love Ezekiel's coffee."

"Alistair."

"Say my name, Kenya," I growl.

Her eyes sharpen in response. "You keep staring at me like you want to eat me alive and people are going to notice."

I hold her stare.

She doesn't blink.

I give in. "Fine. Any other requests?"

"You'll agree to anything?"

"Within reason."

Her fingers touch my chin, obliterating the space between us. "Then let's give this a shot."

My heart slams through my ribs, barrels into her hands and starts beating like a maniac. I kiss her fingers savagely.

Her sigh falls out of her like buried treasures I want to unearth one by one.

If I had to pick someone to parade through my nightmares and drag me out of my darkness, I don't think my heart could have stumbled on a better choice.

I tug Kenya close. She trembles in my grasp and I love that she can't hide how much I affect her.

"I need to tell you one more thing."

"Okay," she whispers.

"Sutherburg might come looking for you."

Her eyes get big. "What? Why?"

"Just stay away from him, alright? If he has any business with Baby Box, it goes through me. No exceptions."

"But—"

I place a finger on her soft lips. "No exceptions."

She looks into my eyes and nods.

Satisfied, I scoop her knees and shift her around so I have better access to her mouth. Framing her cheeks with my hands, I ease my head down and settle my lips on top of hers.

She sighs again, longer and lower this time. Her body inclines toward mine, pressing against me in all the right places and teasing the heat already flickering in my veins until it burns hotter than ever.

The desire in my body drives me up a wall.

Groaning, I attack her mouth until she opens and I deepen the kiss, holding her close enough that her body fuses into mine. No doubts. No guilt. No distractions.

Her hands skate over the back of my neck and into my hair where she tugs, like she did the night of our first kiss. And again, my body responds with a blazing shot of adrenaline that turns me into an animal.

Closer.

I need her closer still.

And she obliges.

Her fingers scrape my scalp and remind me that love can hurt as much as it heals.

I don't mind.

She's the only one I'd trust to hurt me.

My pulse hammers and I fold her legs around me, needing her body as much as I need oxygen. She understands the way I'm guiding her and rises to her knees, straddling me.

Through our clothes, the heat of the kiss blazes and teases me with the promise of more.

Kenya arches her back and digs her fingernails into my shoulder when I drive her down on top of my lap.

A tornado falling from the sky isn't going to keep my hands off her tonight.

I pull away from her even though it kills me and grumble, "Bedroom. Now."

She nods rather than argue, and I know her brain is still scrambled from our caresses.

Hauling her up, I wrap her legs around me and almost explode when she thrusts her hips. I know I should be moving, but I don't have the patience.

My lips fuse to her chocolate mouth again and I enjoy a taste that's more decadent than any coffee I've ever had. Her fingers dig into the back of my neck, matching my passion, begging to be claimed whole.

I'm so freaking happy to indulge.

With a rough groan, I pop away from her lips, trailing my hot breath and little nips of kisses over her neck. I taste every bit of her skin, exploring my way up to her ear.

"Kenya," I growl.

"Y-yes."

"You're going to be saying 'yes' a lot tonight." I press my lips against her jaw, where her neck meets her bone, and she trembles, grinding against the raging need inside me. "You're going to be screaming my name."

She's already on the edge. I can tell. Curls spilling down her shoulders, eyes glowing like twin torches.

My body almost convulses at that look.

I force myself to focus. "But when you call out my name, I want you groaning the right one."

"The country?"

My mind is delirious with desire, but that earns a chuckle.

I run my hands down her spine. My voice is rough. A warning. Vocal chords striking against sandpaper. "Do you understand?"

"You bark orders in the day and the night, huh?" Her voice is heavy. As heavy as her chest that pushes against me.

My lips attack her again, this time with raw hunger, with a bite, with a promise of all the wicked things I plan to do to her tonight.

Then, I whisk her into the bedroom and I tease her until she learns her lesson.

"Holland." She purrs. With need. With desperation.

Then, and only then, do I give her what she wants.

* * *

I KISS HER.

I torment her.

I worship her.

And then I hold her like she's the most precious person in my world.

Her leg wraps around mine, her breathing even.

I never thought I had it in me to give all of myself to another woman. I was so sure, after Claire, that I wouldn't lose my heart again.

Then Kenya Jones barged in and took it.

And she wasn't satisfied. This woman. After gunning for my heart, she took my mind. My soul. My body.

So I punished her for it.

I shattered her.

And then I put her back together so I could shatter her again.

She was a sticky mess when I took her into the shower to clean her off. And now her body is languid. Liquid heat. She's draped over me like we're one piece. Like something that can't separate. Not without breaking.

Her hair is a wild mess. She mumbled something about a bonnet before I pulled her into my chest and muffled the rest of her words with a slow, winding kiss.

Now, she's almost out.

Poor thing.

I didn't really give her a chance to catch her breath tonight. Too much pent-up want. Too many days watching her prance around the office in those tight skirts and those heels. Too many nights wishing she was in my arms when I woke up.

I wind hypnotic circles over her hip, needing her close even though I spent all night finding new and creatives ways to hear my name fall out of her mouth.

Her breath skitters over me. Her eyes are sliding shut, but I can still see a sliver of midnight black. Onyx jewels. So dark they consume the night.

Our lips brush because I need to feel her again, even if I know she's too tired for another round.

She glances up now, more awake than she was before.

My gaze doesn't soften. It intensifies. My finger strokes her hip more firmly. "Kenya."

"Mm?" Her voice is soft. Trusting.

It resonates in me. That tone. Those eyes.

"I meant to ask." I skim my lips over her forehead. "How did it go at brunch today?"

She stiffens and I wonder if I should have saved that question for another time. Maybe when we weren't naked. When I hadn't just pounded the life out of her like I'm barely freaking human.

With a deep breath, she rolls on her back and stares at the ceiling. The blanket goes with her, wrapping around her stunning body the way my fingers ache to.

I decide jealousy doesn't look good on me. Gripping the sheet, I tug her until she rolls my way again. I press my lips to her cheek, inhaling the breath that spills out of her.

"If you don't want to talk, you don't have to say anything," I rasp. "But you belong here." My tone hardens. "You belong next to me. Don't hide your pain… because I want it. I made room for it. Okay?"

The sorrow in her eyes drives a knife through my gut. She bites down on her lip. I want to tug it back where I can see it. Preferably with my mouth, but I let her have her space.

Finally, she glances down. "Felice was there."

"Did your dad give you a heads-up?"

"No." Her eyebrows pinch in the middle of her forehead. Whatever happened ate her up inside.

"You don't have to talk about it."

"You made room, didn't you?" She gazes up at me, her big brown eyes spitting more light than the moon. "You offered, so you can have it."

I caress her back and nod.

Her lips press together in a slight grimace. "They told me I was being selfish."

My body tightens with frustration. It's crazy to me that anyone would say that about Kenya. She's hardheaded and stubborn. Sure. And I'm obsessed with her because of that. It's sexy to see her take control of her work. She knows when to be firm. When to get to business. When to cut someone off and knife through excuses.

She's amazing. But she's not cold. Never harsh. And always willing to throw herself into the trenches to achieve something. If this woman is selfish, the world has no hope.

Kenya blinks rapidly as if trying to hold back tears. "Dad thinks I should get over myself and start being a part of the wedding prep."

"You're kidding. Are they that lost without you?"

"I think Felice is annoyed that she has to do it all on her own. Sasha was never good at party planning. I was the one always fussing about the details and putting things together."

I can see that easily. From day one, Kenya was making my life at the office easier. And she did it out of spite. I can't imagine how productive she is when she's working out of love for her family.

There's a fierce glow in her eyes when she says, "Felice jumping on me doesn't hurt as much. I mean, it does. But I also get it. Sasha's her flesh and blood. Of course she's going to side with her."

"That's no excuse," I growl. "You don't hurt the people you love and excuse the behavior by claiming you're related. Family isn't about flesh and blood. Hell, Darrel is more of a family to me than anyone I'm related to."

"Still, it's *understandable*."

I allow that because I can see that she doesn't appreciate the interruptions.

"But my dad... he's... I always thought he'd have my back. I thought, if anyone would say..." A fat tear rolls down her cheek. "If anyone would say, just once, that Sasha was wrong. That she hurt me. That it wasn't cool—maybe I'd be able to move on. Maybe I could shut my mouth and try to be there."

Stricken, I curve my finger under her eye and chase the tear away. "Kenya."

"But I guess that was wishful thinking." She sniffs.

My gaze drops to her trembling lips. I sooth her as best as I can, struggling to hold back my harsh thoughts about her family. Women are tricky. They're allowed to critique their relatives, but no one else can point out the flaws.

I decide to keep my mouth shut and just listen.

"When Sasha first got sick, my dad was the one who asked me

to drop out of all the after-school clubs I was in. He's the one who asked me to help out more around the house since Felice was gone so often with Sasha at the hospital. I never said no. I never told them I was tired. That I was lonely. That I wanted someone to hold me and tell me it was going to be okay. I knew I had to be strong because Sasha was going through something terrible. And they didn't have time for the both of us."

Damn. I want to punch something. She was a kid. How could they expect her to fend for herself when they should have been there?

"I took on more hours and I almost didn't graduate. I spent all my free time at the hospital. I gave everything without expecting any acknowledgement. Because that's family. That's what you do when you love someone."

"They drained you and they didn't pour anything back," I whisper. "And you still found more to give. Of course it hurts when they accuse you of being selfish. The family should have gone up in flames when they found out your sister cheated with that punk. There should have been such an uproar that a wedding wouldn't even happen."

She sniffs. Her tears spill against my chest like acid rain and fall into the pillow.

I rub her shoulder, kiss her hair and search for something, anything to fix it. When wracking my brain gets me nowhere, I ask outright. "What do you want me to do?"

She glances up.

"Where does your ex work? What does he do? I can ruin it. I know everyone. And anyone I don't know will know someone. Tell me how you want me to destroy them. I'll touch only the ones you want. I'll leave the rest. Just say the word."

She chuckles.

I blink down at her, shocked. Did heartbreak send her into temporary insanity?

Kenya covers her face and laughs harder.

"What?"

"You said that so seriously."

"Because I am serious."

"Alistair," she drops her hands, "this is between me and my family. Whatever I decide to do, whether I cut them off or suck it up and attend the wedding, they're still my people."

"Not to me. You treat me like crap, I'll treat you like crap. You don't have to be in my life if you're only making a mess of it."

"Maybe I'm different."

"Maybe taking care of your sister for so long made excusing her behavior a habit."

Her lips tug down.

I know I shouldn't go there, yet I can't stop myself. I've tiptoed around it for as long as I can, but I don't take well to seeing the people I care about getting hurt. Especially when the cut goes this deep.

"I'm not going to tell you what to do. Like you said. They're your family. But I do think that your sister needs to give you a proper apology. Something tells me she hasn't done that yet."

"She said sorry." Kenya's eyes fall away.

"And then she asked you to be a part of her wedding, threw a tantrum and sent your parents after you when you didn't jump for joy." I give her a dry look.

She returns it with a scowl.

I rest my forehead against hers and her harsh eyes soften. "Kenya, you decide what you allow and *who* you allow into your life. No one can force you to accept their bad behavior. If they care for you, if they love you, they're going to show it. It's not going to be a one-way street. And if it is, that's not family. That's a manipulator."

She sighs. "You're a therapist now?"

"I don't need a degree to diagnose this one. I'm a businessman. I see BS a mile away."

She cuddles into me. Her eyes go heavy again. "Who knew Holland Alistair could care about someone other than himself?"

"I'm not that bad," I mumble, nuzzling her hair with my cheek.

"You're pretty awful."

"And yet you were begging me for…"

"Sh." She places a finger on my lips. "I'm tired."

I kiss her temple. "Then go to sleep, Kenya."

She lays her head against my chest and I wrap my arms around her.

Time stops.

My body thrums with contentment and I pull her closer to me.

She fits perfectly in my arms. Where she belongs.

* * *

"M<small>ISS</small> J<small>ONES SENT LUNCH</small>," Ezekiel says, huffing into my office and plunking a container on the desk.

I stop drafting my email to the Fine Industries licensing attorney and smile at the lunch bags. The smell of savory sauce fills my nostrils.

"Is she still at the factory?" I ask, grabbing one of the bags. It unzips with a loud metallic sound.

"Yes. Bernard brought it over." Ezekiel gives me a stink eye.

"You have something to say, Ezekiel?"

"You've turned us both into your cupid service."

"Kenya wants to keep it a secret." I notice a text from her and pick up my phone, muttering distractedly, "You'll have to put up with it until she stops wanting me to meet her in dark stairwells."

"Humph."

Kenya: Eat something. Or you'll be even grumpier than usual.

Holland: How did you know I was thinking about you?

Kenya: Don't assume I was doing the same.

Holland: Admit it. You're obsessed with me.

Kenya: I'm helping you out because you're Belle's dad. There's no other reason.

I grin and set my phone down. She's great at dancing around what she feels for me but, in the past few weeks, her lips have been doing a whole lot of confessing. Mostly in the shadows with my hands down her skirt and my tongue...

"Alistair," Ezekiel taps my desk, "is there anything else?"

"Why are you in such a rush to leave?"

A pleased smile flits across his weathered face. "Miss Jones also prepared food for me."

I instantly scowl. "What? Why?"

"Maybe because she feels sorry for me?" He gives me a pointed stare. "And what I'm forced to endure everyday."

My eyes narrow.

His narrow in return. Damn. Kenya really has rubbed off on him.

I wave him away. "Go enjoy your lunch."

"You know," Ezekiel says, backing out of the room, "I truly enjoy the changes Miss Jones is bringing out in you. I've never had a real lunch break before."

"Should I rectify that? I have many tasks that need your immediate attention."

His face remains blank, but his lips fall slightly. "I'll be outside if you need me."

I laugh when he walks out. It's so like Kenya to prepare lunch for Ezekiel too. It wouldn't surprise me if Bernard got lunch as well.

What part of her is selfish? Her folks are crazy. There is not a selfish bone in that woman's body. She'd rather cook for three just to get lunch to me. She'd take it personally if others felt left out. That is the mark of a woman who needs to be cherished, not torn down.

I eat the food she prepared, savoring every grain of burnt rice and rubbery chicken. Kenya wasn't kidding when she said she doesn't cook often, but I'm honored that she's cooking for me. It means something, even if it tastes like recycled plastic.

After lunch, I get back to work and only emerge when Ezekiel informs me that Kenya is back.

I shoot out of my chair like a rocket and stomp outside. She's getting sneakier. I told her to report to me the moment she stepped foot in the building. Why wasn't she in my office, in my lap, on my desk, the second she returned from the factory?

I want to storm to her office and teach her a lesson. The kind that will have her toes curling as she pants out my name. But Kenya is determined to keep us under wraps, and it'll be suspicious if employees hear low, guttural moans two seconds after I storm over to her room.

Holland: Stairwell. Now.

I hit send and get on the move.

Greetings rise up like dust as I stalk my way down the corridor. As usual, I barely spare anyone a glance and nod in what I hope is a semblance of acknowledgement.

I crash through the door of the emergency stairwell and glance around. Kenya's not there yet. My eyes slide up to the winding staircase above. No movement or sound.

The door to the stairwell below opens. Kenya has a habit of taking the elevator and then walking up the stairs to 'avoid suspicion'. She truly put thought into this. Which I appreciate because my mind goes blank whenever I see her.

Slowly, her body comes into focus and my fingers tighten around the railings. From the maroon pantsuit that drapes her curvy body, to her tight curls, to her brown skin and those mysterious dark eyes, she's gorgeous.

Mind, body and soul.

I'd have to stab my eyes with knives to tear them away from her.

Kenya's gaze slams into mine. Both of us start smiling like idiots.

"What's so funny?" She stops a few steps down.

"Nothing." I shake my head.

"You're smiling for no reason?"

"I have a reason."

She tilts her head, waiting.

I just keep staring at her.

"Do I have something on my face?" She scrunches her nose.

"No, you're just absolutely breathtaking."

The confused expression melts into a smile. A happy exhale flees her lips. "Thanks for the compliment. Now what do you want?"

I descend the stairs until I'm beside her. Setting my hands around her waist, I pull her into me and inhale deeply. She slips her arms around my neck and hugs me back.

There's no denying that this woman was made to fit in my arms. She's soft. Pliant. At ease. She hasn't lost her strength. She simply doesn't need her shields up with me.

I love that she withdraws her little porcupine quills when I touch her. Her trust falls on me like silk. Smooth and precious.

I slide a kiss over her hair, inhaling her amazing scent.

She glances up slowly. Midnight-black eyes fall into mine.

"Are you expecting something?" I tease, noting the way she tilts her chin up and puckers her lips.

Her expression pinches with annoyance. She pushes away from me. "You're right. We both have a lot to do. We shouldn't be sneaking away for—"

I snap my fingers around her wrist and haul her back to me. My tongue slides across her bottom lip, coaxing her mouth open. She sighs into my kiss and it turns my body to liquid warmth.

I swear, I could hold this woman forever.

I'm that hooked on her.

Easing back, I caress her cheek and slide my other hand across her neck, loving how the light plays on her face.

"The Yazmite location sent their report. They were grateful for the extra set of hands from HQ. The promotion almost caused a stampede. Thankfully, no one was hurt, but it could have been wild."

"Mm." I fuse her hips to mine. My arms wrap around her like fleshy ropes and I run my lips down her neck.

"I'll talk to them about follow-up sales." She breathes out shakily. "If I can even catch a break with the Baby Box production. We're running all over the place trying to make the deadline."

"I'll assign more people from the admin team to help. If you have more hands, it'll be..." my lips brush over hers, "easier, right?"

She looks dazed. "More hands? If you put any more hands on me, Alistair, I might die."

My body hardens. It's crazy how fast she gets my engines revving. It doesn't matter what she's doing or where I am. If I even sniff a hint of her perfume, I'm already there.

Our lips meet again. The soft, slick heat of her tongue skating over mine turns my desire into a roaring inferno. Need presses against me, harder, longer, more desperate for release.

I've wanted her all freaking day.

She smiles against my lips, causing my puckered mouth to hit against her teeth. Her arms close around my back, kneading her fingers into taut muscles.

Shifting her hips against mine like she knows exactly how much I need her, she sighs. "I've decided to talk to Sasha."

My breath moves over her face. I study her carefully. "You need back-up?"

"Aren't you curious about what I'll talk to her about?"

"I know that whatever decision you make, it'll be the right one," I whisper, letting out my own rough sigh when she scrapes her nails across my scalp. "And," I bite out, "I know that I'll be there for you. Wherever the chips fall."

"Hmm."

I dig my fingers into her generous backside. "You want to explain that look?"

"Only if you promise to take me home tonight."

"Baby, I'll take you home, take you to heaven, take you wherever you want to go."

She giggles against my lips. "So I can see Belle."

I pull her plump bottom lip into my mouth. "Tease."

She laughs softly.

I stare at her in awe, my tongue too heavy to move. She's turned me into the kind of man who melts at the touch of the hand, who comes running whenever she's near, who thinks about forever and forgiveness and moving on.

I don't know what's wrong with me, but Kenya Jones has a way of making insanity feel like bliss.

"I'll take you home," I growl, "and then when Belle's asleep, I'm going to…" I whisper the warning, the wicked threat, in her ear.

Her knees buckle and I don't catch her. Instead, I pin her body to the railing and kiss her like we're in the middle of an apocalypse. She makes these breathy, shuddering noises that drive me wild, so it takes me a second to register the sound of a door slamming shut.

When I realize that I didn't imagine the thump, I jump back.

Kenya stiffens too.

We both look up in the direction of the door. Then our eyes slowly return to each other and a slow realization passes through her expression.

Someone was in the stairwell.

We were caught.

CHAPTER 19
KISS OF DEATH

KENYA

I HOPED it was the wind that closed the door. Or maybe a broken hinge. Or hell, I'd even accept a ghost sneaking around and playing tricks on us.

But my hopes are dashed the moment I step into work the next morning.

Whispers rage like wildfire. Curious eyes. Angry eyes. Jealous eyes. They're all aimed at me.

My fingers dig and twist into my purse.

Just be normal.

Easier said than done when my co-workers are staring me down like the town leper. How much longer to my office?

Sweat beads on my forehead when I notice how much farther I have to go. More and more people gather in the hallway. There's no relief from the heat of their whispers and hushed judgement.

Can I apply for a sick day? Or maybe work from home?

No, I can't run away like a coward.

I didn't do anything wrong.

Heather stomps down the hallway, her posse trailing behind her. And I know my awkward entrance is about to get a lot worse.

She stops in front of me and gives me a cruel smile. "Someone dressed up today."

I glance at my outfit. One of the first things I bought with my paycheck was appropriate office attire. However, I wasn't about to sacrifice my femininity to conform to black suits and ties.

Today, I'm wearing an A-line dress with a flirty skirt. I know I look good and, if the compliment had come from anyone other than Regina George's less charismatic sister, I would have responded with a smile and a thank you.

But since it *is* Heather in front of me, I don't bother responding. Lifting my chin, I stalk past her.

"The skirt really shows off your legs," Heather continues.

I stop, hearing the taunting in her tone.

"Makes sense… since you need those thighs to find job opportunities. A skirt gives a man easier access, right?"

I whirl around. "What did you just say?"

"Nothing." She sings.

My jaw works, and I struggle with the urge to slap her.

Heather slants me a victorious grin and sashays down the hallway.

When she leaves, the whispers start up again, louder than before. Everyone is watching me like they're waiting for me to break out in a song and dance.

I want to duck my head, but I force myself not to cower. The situation is bleak. Acting like I'm guilty will only make the vitriol worse.

When I get into my office, I find Alistair there already.

My eyes bug and I slam the door shut. "What are you doing here?" Frantically, I glance at the hallway where folks are poking their heads around the corner to see through the blinds. "People are staring."

"Ezekiel informed me of the rumors." He rises to his full height, all delicious muscles and manly concern. "Are you okay?"

I step back. "You shouldn't be in here, Alistair."

"Where else would I be in a situation like this?"

"Far away from me!" I hiss.

"They'll talk either way."

"And you're just feeding the gossip mills."

"Since the issue is like this already," he tilts his head, looking intently at me, "we should make an official announcement."

"No."

His eyebrows hunker down.

I run a hand over my face. "We're at work. Let's not talk about this right now."

His eyes turn stormy. "I disagree."

"Of course you do." I throw up my hands. It would be raining cats and dogs before he ever made things easy for me.

"Miss Jones," his tone is frosty, reminding me of when I first started to work for him, "I'll do what you want this time, but I need you to be open to changing that plan. I can take people saying what they want about me, but I cannot abide by anyone badmouthing you." His voice lowers. "If I hear that you're being harassed, I will not stay still."

"I'm fine. Really. I'm okay. I just want this to blow over." Nodding to him, I add, "And you being in here will keep that from happening."

He squints at me. "Are you sure?"

"Yes. I'm very sure." I walk closer to him. "We'll talk later, okay?"

He nods, still looking at me like he wants to cart me over his shoulder and steal me away from the building.

I hold his stare, silently begging him not to do so.

There's something on the tip of his tongue, but he keeps it to himself. A rarity. "Okay."

When Alistair's gone, I place my hand on the desk and wilt against it. It would be a mistake to check the office group chat, so I don't bother. I'm not going to bathe myself in negativity today.

Just breathe, Kenya. The hatred flocking to me is new. I've been a good girl all my life, quietly working, taking care of my family, and trying to help Sasha in any way I could.

There was no time for parties, wild underage drinking, or reckless abandon. When someone in the family is sick, *everyone* is sick. Not physically maybe, but in all the ways that count, I was living at the hospital too.

After Sasha got better, I was finally ready to venture into the world and make my own mark. To be seen for my own talents and capabilities.

I've been building myself into the kind of woman who can face the world proudly. I'm not afraid of being noticed, but I want to be noticed for the right reasons. For my talent. My skill. My persistence.

I don't want mud.

I don't want a sullied reputation.

After a few deep breaths, I collect myself enough to lean off the desk and open my door. If people want to talk about me, they're going to have to do it to my face.

There.

Open and transparent.

Ezekiel hustles in a few minutes later with a cup of coffee. He sets it on my desk and I'm too distressed to pick it up.

With a worried frown, he leans closer. "Alistair is trying to find the source of the rumors, but it's taking a bit of time."

"Why bother? This thing is already a wildfire. It doesn't matter who started it. As long as we don't feed the flames, it'll putter out eventually."

"I don't know, Miss Jones. This isn't some groundless rumor. There was a picture taken…"

"What?" My eyes widen. "Show me."

He turns his phone around to reveal a picture of me and Alistair. My fingers are twisted in his hair and his body is practically bending me over the stairway railing. We look like we're seconds away from tearing each other's clothes off.

My breath leaves my body. "I can't believe this."

"That's why we're scrambling to find the source. We want to scrub it. Keep it contained to this building."

I sink into my chair and press a hand to my forehead. "Oh my gosh."

"Don't worry, Miss Jones. Alistair will stop at nothing to get this handled."

"It's too late for that." My eyes dart back and forth.

Ezekiel worriedly slides the coffee over to me. "First, you need to drink this."

My fingers tremble when they slip through the handle of the mug. I can't bring it to my lips. My mind is tripping on that picture. Everyone knows. There's no way to out this fire now.

"There's another thing." Ezekiel's eyes dart away. "Alistair wants you out of the office today."

"What? No! I have too much to do."

"There's another Belle's Beauty location that needs overhauling. He wants you to work on it the same way you worked on the Yazmite project."

"He's kicking me out?"

"He wants you away from the heat." Ezekiel frowns. "I think he also wants to keep himself from firing employees without proper cause. He has a temper, but it's nothing compared to the ruthlessness that emerges when his people are targeted."

"Let me talk to him."

"I wouldn't advise that, Miss Jones." He steps in my way. "Alistair mentioned that you didn't want to be seen with him at the office. That's one of the reasons he made these arrangements."

"I can take care of myself. I don't need him ordering me out."

"Miss Jones." He holds his ground. "Bernard will take you."

It seems like I'll either leave or be escorted out, so I gather my things and flee beneath the watchful stare of my co-workers.

Ezekiel escorts me the entire way and it wouldn't surprise me to learn that was an instruction from Alistair.

When I'm in the car, Bernard slants me a reassuring smile. "Miss Jones."

"Hey."

"Are you okay?"

"You know about the pictures?"

"I do." He shakes his head. "I hope you don't let those comments get to you. People are making up wild stories."

"I can imagine."

"We know the truth. I believe everyone will see it too."

"Thanks, Bernard."

He drives the rest of the way in silence.

When I arrive at the new location, I stuff my worries deep inside. Work is work. Though I don't like Alistair's pushy methods, I'm grateful for a change of scenery. The office was getting claustrophobic and this is the perfect excuse to 'run away' without it actually looking like a retreat.

I step confidently into the elegant store and introduce myself to everyone.

Their eyes regard me with distaste.

Unease crawls through my stomach. I force my tone to remain upbeat. "Let's have a meeting with the managers in five minutes. Uh, where's the bathroom?"

"That way," one of the managers says snootily.

I shuffle past them. Inside the bathroom, I reapply my makeup and do a few breathing exercises. The managers at the Yazmite location were rude when we first met too. I won them over. I can do the same here.

A few minutes later, I walk toward the meeting room. The managers' voices carry over to me.

"Is she the one in the pictures?"

"Yes. You can tell by the crazy hair."

"She thinks she has the right to boss us around because she's the CEO's slut?"

"I can't believe some people get away with all kinds of things while the rest of us have to suffer."

"I'm not listening to a word she says. What does she know except how to seduce a rich man?"

"I can't believe they sent her here."

"What'll happen to the company now?"

"What do you mean?"

"If women find out the CEO of Belle's Beauty is a creep, they're going to cancel him. If they cancel him, they're going to boycott the products. You think the company will go bankrupt?"

My eyelashes flutter. Bankrupt?

Claire's legacy. Belle's birthright. What if it all goes up in flames because of me?

Panic grabs me by the throat, but I don't have time to fall apart. Alistair is at the office, fighting to make sense of the chaos. If I fall apart, I don't deserve to stand beside him.

Although it kills me to drag a smile from the depths of my pain, I slap it on my face and walk in.

Brightly, I greet the managers. "Thanks for waiting."

They regard me in stony silence.

My confidence wanes. I think about their bleak predictions. *What if the company goes bankrupt?*

A lump forms in my throat.

Maybe… this scandal will be a bigger problem than I thought.

* * *

BERNARD IS outside when I leave the location. I'm surprised to see him, but he just offers me a smile and a coffee. When he opens the door, he gestures inside.

I remain in place. "Alistair shouldn't be this worried. I'm fine."

"I'm here on Mr. Alistair's request, but the coffee is from me. You look like you could use it."

I didn't drink Ezekiel's coffee this morning and I don't touch Bernard's offering either. My hands are already jittery. I don't want caffeine in this state. Not when the buzz of my discomfort is already so strong.

"Where are we going?" My eyes slide over the landmarks that lead to the factory. "Not back to the office?"

"No, Mr. Alistair's instructions were clear."

I blow out an annoyed breath.

Pulling up my phone, I text Alistair.

Kenya: Do you plan to keep me out of the office for the rest of the year?

Holland: If that's what it takes.

Kenya: I appreciate your concern, but I'll have to face it sooner or later.

Holland: Then choose later. Let me sort out what I can first.

I rub my temples as a headache brews. The comments from the managers stuck to my skin and dug deep. I should have been more careful. If I wasn't so eager to spend time with Alistair, we wouldn't have been caught.

My eyes sweep closed and I try to find a solution. What if I come out and tell everyone that's not me in the picture?

It'll save you, but Alistair will still look like a woman-grabbing jerk.

I frown. What if I tell everyone we're dating?

And then all the work you've done will get dismissed as girlfriend privilege and no one will respect you again.

My fingers ball into fists. I have to *do* something. Belle's Beauty cannot, under any circumstances, be affected by this.

I'm just as invested in Belle's future as Alistair. His daughter is a sweet girl and we have a lot in common. Losing my mother at such a tender age blew a hole through my heart. To this day, I treasure everything my mother left behind. Her jewelry. Her pictures. Even her high school yearbook.

Belle deserves to have what her mother left behind. The company. An untarnished gift.

Just then, my phone chirps with an email notification. I expect Alistair's name in the 'from' line, but it's not him.

To: Kenya Jones
From: Stephen Sutherburg
Subject: Baby Box Job Offer

. . .

GREETINGS MISS JONES,

As we prepare for the first Baby Box launch featuring Belle's Beauty products, we'd like to reiterate how delighted we are to work with you.

Your creativity, determination and experience in the sales field has turned you into the ace of Belle's Beauty.

It just so happens that our subscription brand is about to expand overseas, and we are in need of a manager to oversee it. We would be delighted to offer you the position, starting as soon as possible.

We are prepared to offer you a sizable annual salary (open to negotiation as we want to make this offer as tantalizing as possible) along with a host of benefits including paid housing, transportation, and entertainment packages.

Please find attached your detailed offer letter. If you're interested, I would love to discuss this venture in more detail with you.

REGARDS,
Stephen Sutherburg
Baby Box Marketing Director

I SLAP my hand over my mouth to contain a gasp. Baby Box wants to poach me from Belle's Beauty. Which isn't an option I would entertain at any other time.

But right now...

I set an appointment with Mr. Sutherburg's secretary. It's irresponsible to meet about another job while I'm currently on Belle's Beauty business. We agree to discuss it after work.

A few hours later, when I'm at the production factory, I remember Alistair's heated warning to avoid Sutherburg at all costs. It seemed completely random, especially given the circumstances. Now, it makes sense. Did he know about Sutherburg's interest in hiring me?

My gut is telling me yes. Not only did he know, but he didn't want to give me the opportunity to accept or deny the position myself.

I curl my fingers into fists. How many times do I have to tell him? Holland Alistair doesn't own me.

We *both* got caught, so it's both our responsibility to find a solution. I have a choice, and I'll make the decision. Because this *is* my life and I'm the only one who can save me.

From now on, I'll do everything I can to protect the company, to protect Belle, and to protect myself.

* * *

Sutherburg meets me at a trendy coffee shop with futuristic artwork on the walls and the world's most uncomfortable chairs. I squirm in my seat, trying to find the best position.

"I appreciate you making the time for me, Miss Jones."

"Thank you too. I've been busy with the Baby Box promotions, so I'm glad you were willing to accommodate my schedule."

"We're the ones trying to convince you to abandon your loyalties. We'll be on our best behavior." He chuckles.

I don't. The betrayal of it… I'm not relishing that. Alistair is working extremely hard to quell the rumors. He's honoring my request to keep a distance in the office. He sends Ezekiel with coffee every day, and Bernard is always there to take me home.

I can *feel* Alistair taking care of me, even though we don't see each other outside of work. And it only makes me more determined to do my part.

"Let's get to the point." I tilt my head. "Why is Baby Box suddenly interested in hiring me?"

"You're a marketing genius. You're also the woman who turned a promo date error into an explosive PR success. Whatever you touch seems to turn to gold."

I narrow my eyes. "Is that all?"

"What else could it be?"

"Mr. Walsh seemed to have a personal interest in me on the day we met at Fine Industries. Is this a ploy to—"

"No. No." He shakes his head. "Walsh has... his proclivities, but I don't subscribe to them and I don't encourage them either."

My suspicious look doesn't waver.

"I'll admit, he was the one who brought up the topic of hiring you. He seems to want to prove something to Alistair—"

I scoff. "Thanks for being honest, but I'm no pawn in the game of powerful men."

"Miss Jones, please let me finish. Normally, I would never be so transparent in a pitch. It's counterproductive. But I told you that information for a reason. You don't trust Walsh. Fine. Then trust *me*."

I stare at the portly man.

He gestures with his hands. "I knew you were a gem the moment you opened up in the Belle's Beauty pitch. You see things from a different, fresh perspective and you have the discipline and maturity to carry it through to the end. It's tough to find someone like you. Someone with all those qualities. I'm here myself, instead of hiring a talent scout, because I know that you would flourish at Baby Box."

His words are convincing, but I still shake my head. "I only came today to hear you out, not to make any decisions."

"Fine. That's fair. So how about you allow me to be blunt with you?"

I gesture for him to go ahead.

"As we speak, Holland Alistair is desperately trying to suppress a photo of you two together in a romantic moment."

I curl my fingers inward.

"Yes, we know. News leaks fast in this business, and it's only a matter of time before the press catches wind of it." He sticks up two pudgy fingers. "There are many problems with that, but here are the main two. First, the image of Belle's Beauty as a pure and trusted brand will be destroyed. Second, Baby Box will have the authority to break the contract."

"What?" I lurch forward.

"There's a clause in our agreement that states, should Belle's Beauty lose its standing or do anything to jeopardize the reputation of Baby Box, we have the right to cancel the contract." He taps the table. "As you're probably aware, we have enough evidence to not only break the contract but sue for damages."

I blink rapidly. "It's one picture."

"It's a sullied reputation. Aren't you aware of our current political and social climate? Stories of men abusing their power can end an empire nowadays."

"Alistair isn't like that. We're dating. By choice. I was not manipulated into anything."

"The press isn't going to run a beautiful love story, Miss Jones. A heartwarming romance doesn't make for a sizzling headline."

I glare at him.

He releases a breath. "The world isn't fair. Nothing happens the way it's supposed to. The good guys don't always win. The evil ones don't get their just desserts. The little people, like me and you, we have to do our best with what we've been given."

"And if I don't 'do my best', which means doing what you want, Belle's Beauty will suffer?"

"It doesn't matter how you look at it, Miss Jones, the damage has been done. Even if Alistair marries you tomorrow, you're already tainted. His relationship with you is a black mark on his permanent record. He might be able to recover. The men in these cases always do, but can you?"

I blink rapidly. Doubts wind through me, but I put up a strong front. "You have no idea what you're talking about."

"I see that you care for Alistair. I won't judge either. Whether you're having an affair or not," he waves a hand, "that's none of my business. But this isn't a romantic movie, Miss Jones. This is real life. And in real life, you either make the hard choices or someone makes it for you." He pauses dramatically. "Can you trust him, Miss Jones, to clean up this mess without hurting you, himself or the company?"

I swallow hard.

"Shouldn't you think about yourself? What you want? If Belle's Beauty is *truly* it for you or if it's just a stepping stone into something you truly love?" He lowers his voice. "Perhaps something that employs that Lit degree?"

My eyebrows jump.

"I think, if you truly look inside yourself, you'll see that this offer isn't a bad one and that all the doors are opening right here, right now, so you can walk through them."

"I should go." Hurrying to my feet, I back away from the table.

"I'll be in touch, Miss Jones."

I stumble into the night, battling the tightness in my throat. No matter how much I try, I can't deny that Sutherburg has a point. Choosing my own path might mean letting go of Belle's Beauty.

* * *

THE NEXT DAY, Bernard picks me up from home.

He doesn't have to say a word. I just get into the car and let him drive me to the factory. It seems like Alistair still hasn't found a way to stop the gossip.

And he probably won't.

With every second that passes, Sutherburg's offer looks like the best way out of this. My reputation at the company is ruined. If the rumors crawl into the public eye, I won't have a chance to fix it.

But how do I tell my boss?

When my phone buzzes with a call from Alistair later that evening, I almost reject it. My thoughts are spiraling in a direction that leads me away from him. How do I tell him the truth?

Nervously, I answer his call.

"Hey." His voice is subdued. I can *feel* his exhaustion. With all the chaos going on at Belle's Beauty and his licensing play at Fine Industries, this headache is the last thing he needs.

"Where are you?" I ask.

"At the office."

"We need to talk."

He goes extremely quiet.

"Can you make time?"

"I've got a meeting later, but I can try to wrap it up quickly."

"Okay. I'll wait for you."

The hours crawl by until I see Alistair again.

He crashes into the diner, a tiger on the prowl. Sharp eyes cut through the crowd before they land on me. I can see electric currents bristling under his skin as he strides my way.

Heads turn to follow his journey down the aisle. Not surprising. Alistair is mind-blowingly gorgeous. Everything about him—from the thick hair to the square shoulders to the long, long legs commands attention. It's like a magnetic field that doesn't ask permission. It just grabs everything in its orbit.

He slides into the booth across from me. His jaw is clenched tight.

"You look tired," I say softly. It's true. His eyes are bloodshot, and his hair is falling messily over his forehead. Usually, his hair is styled back, every lock in place.

"There's a lot going on." He reaches out and takes my hand.

I glance around anxiously before sliding it out of his grip.

His eyes narrow. "Kenya."

"I met Sutherburg."

His shoulders get stiff, muscles coiling beneath rippling tan skin. "When?"

"A few days ago."

"And you're just telling me?"

His tone makes me bristle. "I don't need to report my daily activities to you, Alistair."

"I told you not to."

I snarl at him. "And?"

"And you went ahead and did it anyway."

"Because I am my own *person*. You don't pay me for the privilege of controlling my thoughts and actions. There's not enough money in the world to buy that privilege."

"Don't try to play this like I'm a controlling jerk."

"You kind of are."

He scowls. "You know I don't trust that guy as far as I can throw him. Walsh is into you. It's clear as day."

"Walsh wasn't the one who—"

"Sutherburg is his puppy. Walsh is for sure pulling the strings."

"It's a legit offer."

He slams his fist against the table and cups start shaking. "I found out who leaked those pictures. It wasn't someone in the company."

My jaw drops.

"Someone was tailing us. Me, specifically."

"Walsh?" My voice rises in pitch.

"He's denying it hard now, but if I investigate more, I know I can tie it to him."

Confusion makes my head spin.

"That's why I told you not to get in contact. They're playing games you don't want to be a part of."

"Walsh is seedy. I knew that from the start, but it's not like he made up those pictures. All he did was expose the truth."

"To what end? Have you ever thought of that?"

"He offered me a job, but the decision was approved by the board at Baby Box. They must see the benefit of having me."

Alistair's nostrils flare. He raises a hand and gets a waiter's attention. When the young boy hustles close, Alistair grumbles out an order and the boy flees the scene like he's running from a bear.

I fold my arms over my chest. "I haven't completely made up my mind, but I'm thinking of saying yes."

"Dammit, Kenya. Didn't you just hear me?"

"I did. Walsh is a creep, but the job isn't to be his mistress. It's to work for his company."

"But he—"

"Belle's Beauty is at stake, Alistair. And so is my reputation."

"I'm handling it."

"You can't stop a monster as powerful as gossip. It's going to take root and it's going to ruin you. Me. Even Belle."

His eyes narrow at the mention of his daughter.

"Do you want her to look up your name one day and find seedy articles about inappropriate workplace conduct?"

"We didn't do anything wrong."

"No one knows that."

"I know that. And so does Ezekiel. When Belle's old enough, we can explain everything. She'll understand."

"It's too dangerous. The rumors are already out of control. They're saying I…" My eyes slide away. "I seduced you to get that office. That I was with you when you were with Claire. That I called you the night of the accident and that's why…"

"Nonsense."

I pull my lips in.

"Kenya, you know I didn't hire you so I could sleep with you. You're a damn good worker."

"That's true." My lips curve up.

His remain flat.

"If I leave, it takes the heat off Belle's Beauty, preserves the Baby Box deal and it allows us both to quell the rumors in a big way. No one can accuse you of being a predatory boss if you're no longer signing my paychecks."

"What do you mean 'leave?' Leave the company?"

I glance away. "The country."

"Hell no." His cheeks turn a mottled red. "I'm not letting you go anywhere."

I bristle. "You don't *dictate* where I go, Alistair."

"You know sure as hell that they're poaching you just to get to me."

"So now I can't be acknowledged for my skills?"

"Stop twisting my words," he spits. "Why are you moving so fast? If you give me a bit more time, I can get the nonsense stories to disappear and I'll make sure that no one touches Belle's Beauty."

"It's a good opportunity. The kind of opportunity that I might never be offered again."

He leans forward. "Admit it, Kenya. This isn't just about Belle's Beauty or your reputation. You're running."

"From what?"

"From me."

I scoff. "This is not about us."

"You started opening up to me, but there was always a little doubt in your eyes. A little part of yourself that you were holding back from me. I didn't want to push you. I got that your ex-boyfriend and your sister did a number on you, but this is ridiculous."

"What about you?" I snap back. "I haven't heard a word from you in four days. All I get is Ezekiel's coffee and Bernard giving me pitying looks from the rearview mirror."

"Damn, woman. I've been killing myself trying to fix this!"

"Exactly! You do everything on your own, the way *you* like it. You take full control of a crisis that involves my life without coming to me so we could fix it together. You bark orders at me and tell me where I can go and when I can come into the office. Once again, it's either Alistair's way or the highway."

A vein pops out in his neck. "Kenya."

"You don't listen to anyone. You insist on treating people like they're your employees. Like they all rise and fall on your word. Well, let me make one thing clear Alistair, I don't work for you when I'm off the clock. You don't get to treat me like your employee and call it a relationship."

His eyes flash cruelly. "I won't let you go."

My chest rises and falls. The sound of my own heartbeat racing in my ears echoes back to me.

"Try and stop me."

"Don't think I won't." He snarls. "Don't think I won't follow you to the ends of the earth and drag you back to my side. I already lost someone. I'm not losing anyone else again."

High on my emotions and frustration, I whirl around. "I'm not Claire."

A shuttered look enters his eyes.

Pain pours out of him like frantic waves.

I drive the knife in deeper, unable to stop myself. "She listened to everything you said and where did that get her?"

Alistair's fingers curl into fists.

Regret starts building in my stomach and flowing to each of my fingers and toes.

"Fine," he growls. "Go."

"Alistair…"

"If that's what you want, there's the door, Kenya. Don't bother looking back when you walk through it."

My heart shatters into a million pieces. I didn't want the conversation to end like this. I didn't want to dig him where it hurts.

But I also refuse to give up my independence. I am not his property. And the one thing Holland Alistair needs to acknowledge is that he doesn't own *me*.

CHAPTER 20
THE AFTERMATH

ALISTAIR

My whole brain is on fire. No amount of headache reliever pills or booze can fix it.

I'm straddling a tightrope and, right beneath me, is an ocean of shark-infested waters. It feels like I'm going to topple to my death at any moment.

I stare at the email that just crawled into my inbox and tighten my fists.

To: Holland Alistair
cc. Human Resources Director
From: Kenya Jones
Subject: *Official Resignation*

To whom it may concern, *due to an unexpected opportunity, I regret to inform you that I will be resigning from my position as Belle's Beauty Sales manager. I would like to use my vacation days—all of them—as per the company policy regarding emergency leave.*

Thank you for the lessons the company has provided me. I've learned so much in these few months and will never forget what I endured.

Respectfully,
Kenya Jones

It feels like a slap to the damn face.

She didn't even bother to write my name.

I'm 'to whom it may concern' now?

Gritting my teeth, I shoot out of my chair and stumble to the window. I pound my fists against the glass. It does nothing to ease the chaos in my chest.

She's really leaving the company.

Damn.

After our disastrous conversation in the diner, I went home and fumed. Throwing Claire in my face was low and she knew it. I should have been furious, but the anger didn't even last long.

I can't get through a day without thinking of her. Taking care of her. Being around her.

The fact that I walk past her empty office every day is freaking unacceptable.

Belle's Beauty is in an uproar. A scandal like this won't die down soon. Especially now that Kenya hasn't shown up to work in days.

It's almost ridiculous to hear what they've come up with. The explanations swing from 'she's pregnant' to 'Alistair kidnapped her and stashed her body in the trunk'.

Gossip is for empty-headed people with nothing better to do. I don't give a damn what the employees are saying about me. They've been whispering about my prickly personality since before I started Fine Industries.

What I care about is Kenya. That woman punched a hole

through my chest, and even if I miss her like crazy, I'm not going to chase her. I'm not going to force her to be with me.

She doesn't want to be controlled? Fine?

Then I won't crawl on my hands and knees like a freaking punk and beg her.

She can go.

Whatever.

Ezekiel knocks on the door. "Alistair?"

"Did you see the email?"

He swallows nervously. "What would you like me to do? The HR director is asking. This isn't how we normally process resignations."

My eyes lift to his. "Give her the vacation days."

His face goes ashen. He barrels close to my desk, moving faster than I've ever seen him. "Alistair."

Stubbornness winds across my chest, burrowing deep into the pain that hid away when Claire left me behind. It's a different kind of anguish. Different because Kenya's still alive but she's *choosing* not to be with me. She's choosing to leave.

It's like getting clawed in the face over and over again.

"Let her go."

"Have you lost your damn mind?"

My eyes whip up.

I'm getting yelled at by my cool and composed executive assistant.

Everyone has officially gone insane.

"Who do you think you're talking to?" I snarl.

"I'm talking to the man who needs a good old-fashion pop in the face to knock some sense into him. And since Miss Jones isn't around to do the honors, I might as well give it a go in her place."

I fold my arms over my chest. "You've really decided this is your last day, haven't you?"

"You can try and threaten me, Alistair, but I see right through you. You growl to keep people at bay just so they don't brush close and get a glimpse of what a coward you really are."

I slam my hand on the table. "She asked to leave!"

"And you didn't fight for her to stay."

"I told her to—"

"You don't fight by ordering." He glares at me. "You don't fight by assuming you can control someone else. If love was about control, then everyone would be miserable. The only way to prove it's true love is if there's choice."

I growl at him. "Miss Jones had a choice. She didn't choose me." I lift a hand. "Let her go. I don't need her anyway."

"Bull." Ezekiel shakes his head. "She is an asset to this company. She worked harder than ten men. She was always here early and the last of us to leave. She challenged you in the right moments and listened to every instruction you gave in others. Now she's jumping ship because of a little rumor that we're working hard to clear up? I don't buy it."

"She wants to go."

Ezekiel blinks. "Didn't you hear me? Did you give her a reason to stay?"

I swallow hard.

Fine. I'm the massive bastard who treated her like an employee even when we were dating. I'm the one who took our problems on my shoulders and drove her away, made her run right into Walsh's arms. It's on me.

But acknowledging that won't change anything. I know Kenya. Once she's made up her mind, it's over.

"Have you talked to her?"

"No." I grab my chair and fold myself into it. "And I won't either."

"Alistair."

"If you're done with your rant, Ezekiel, you can leave."

He doesn't move.

I glance away. Anything I say to Kenya at this point will make this raging dumpster fire worse. Kenya doesn't want to hear from me. And I wouldn't know what to say to change her mind.

You don't own me.

No. If I did, I'd never let anything harm her. I'd never let a single harsh word enter her world. I'd roll her in bubble wrap and keep her far away from the dangers in life.

But I can't do that.

Not with her.

Not with Belle.

And I sure as hell didn't with Claire.

The night I lost my wife was the most helpless moment of my life. I was the one who told her to get in the car. I insisted we head out on the road, and it resulted in my wife dying on impact.

I watched the blood drip down her face.

I cried her name and shook her.

She didn't so much as blink.

When control is ripped from your fingers like that, you either give in to it and admit that you're nothing compared to the storm or you fight back. And that's what I did. I worked myself into the ground so that control would always be in my grip. So I'd never feel that helpless again.

"Is the opportunity she's referring to the one at Baby Box?" Ezekiel grinds out.

I scrape my hands over my face, suddenly weary. "I don't know. Probably."

"Is she really leaving the country?"

I keep my mouth shut.

Ezekiel releases a breath. His eyes bore into me like twin skewers. "She won't go if you ask her. For some crazy reason that I'll never figure out, she loves you, Alistair. She's not the type of woman who'll run around shooting out flowery words, but she does. She stayed right by your side, even when you were pushing her to the limits. At first, she had something to prove to herself. To you. And then it was about being close to you."

Kenya loves me? Then why is she running in the opposite direction? Why is she forcing me to confront the charred pieces of myself? Weaknesses I don't want to touch with a ten-foot pole.

"Fine. Stay there. Hold on to control if that'll keep you warm at night. I'll let HR know that Miss Jones will receive all her vacation days."

"Ezekiel."

He glances over his shoulder, his eyes calling me 'idiot' in about three different languages.

I glance away. "Give her a generous severance package. She put up with a lot at this company."

"People will misunderstand. It'll come off like hush money."

"I don't care what people think. She worked like mad for Belle's Beauty. And she put up with me..." I swallow. "She deserves to be compensated. This has nothing to do with our relationship. I'd do the same with anyone else." I pause. "I'll need a new list of management companies as soon as possible."

"You're really doing this?"

"What the hell do you expect me to do, Ezekiel? Cry? Listen to sad music? Wear sweats and lie in bed eating ice cream? I have a company to run."

His whole face caves in, like he's sucking on a tart lemon slice. "You can find someone to replace Miss Jones. It'll be tough to match her work ethic and brilliance, but it can happen. You have enough money in the bank to search the world for it. But the chances of you finding someone willing to call you out on your crap and love you through it, that's once in a lifetime." He gestures to the door. "I won't overstep my bounds again, but I thought you should know, as the man who works the closest with you, that I think you're making a mistake."

"Don't go too far, Ezekiel. Or I'll be processing your resignation along with Miss Jones's."

His eyes sharpen.

That one hit him in the center of his chest.

Ezekiel turns swiftly and slams the door behind him, leaving me filled with regret and a startling realization. Now that she's officially gone, I miss Kenya even more than before.

* * *

BELLE CHASES a butterfly around an oak tree, her hair streaming behind her and her eyes lighting up with glee. I watch her and the ache in my chest gets a little better. Not by much. But it's tolerable.

Darrel hands me a bottle of water. "You haven't asked for the sleeping pills in a long time. Has it gotten bad? Are there nightmares again?"

No. There haven't been nightmares. Just beautiful dreams. In my dreams, Kenya is still with me, smiling so warmly that it lights me up inside. She's there, brown skin soft and supple. Fingers dancing over my arms. Lips pressing to mine in a sweet kiss.

When I wake up, that's the nightmare. Life is a giant, yawning chasm of emptiness. Ever since Kenya stormed out of that diner and sent in her resignation letter, I feel like the world is happening around me, but it's completely removed.

Darrel gives me a worried glance. "You don't look so good, Alistair."

"I'm fine. I'm just busy. We haven't found a management company yet and all the assistants we hired have been a complete waste of time."

They're nothing like Kenya.

Or maybe it's that they *aren't* Kenya.

Sure, they can sort spreadsheets, get me coffee and write reports, but they don't mouth off when I'm particularly brutal with my tasks. They don't send passive aggressive emails that are one giant middle finger wrapped in a bow. They don't find ingenious ways to work smarter instead of harder.

Darrel purses his lips. "You've been drinking."

Only a few and just to take the edge off. But I know it's tampering with my work, which is why I'm asking for the pills. I don't want to turn into a drunk. Belle deserves better than that.

Darrel takes his eyes off me and studies a bird fluttering around a tree branch. "Have you heard anything about her and Baby Box?"

"Ezekiel attends those meetings for me. The PR team is completely in charge of the project."

"You're running."

"I'm choosing to guard my peace. She's the one who walked away."

"And you're the one who didn't chase her down." He rests his elbow on the back of the bench. "Why aren't you getting your woman back?"

Sunlight slashes across my eyes. I think of the dream I had this morning. Kenya was draped in sunshine. *Nothing* but sunshine. We were wrapped together, our limbs tangled so tightly it would take a crowbar to pry us off.

Her eyelashes fluttered against my chest and the heat of her hand seared all the way to my heart. A brand. A tattoo. A lock that could only be undone by her fingerprints.

"I was already thinking of what the rest of our lives would look like." My eyes narrow. "She made me into that kind of idiot."

Darrel watches me quietly.

"I've never met anyone like her. I never trusted anyone as quickly as I trusted her. She's intelligent, beautiful, capable—"

"You're not helping your case here. Why don't you know where she is? Why aren't you burning her phone up? Why aren't you making a move?"

I clamp my mouth shut.

"Because that would require taking a risk," Darrel says, as if he's got a brain scanner out and he's picking my thoughts up with a shovel. "Because that would mean throwing those walls down and begging someone to stay for the first time in your life. It would mean giving up control and showing that you have to depend on someone. Depend on them so much that you can't breathe."

Belle giggles and waves a flower around. "Look at this, daddy!"

I nod and wave back. Then I turn to Darrel. "It was a whirlwind relationship."

"Bull. You introduced her to Belle."

"She found Belle—"

"Don't lie to me, Alistair. It makes you look pathetic."

I grit my teeth.

Darrel folds his hands together. "My sister was the kind of person who saw the good in everybody. She liked bustling around family. She despised drama. She didn't challenge you. She wasn't the type who liked conflict. It's why we had to get a nanny. Mom and dad were gone all the time. Claire was always frail, sad and lonely. She needed to rely on someone. She needed someone to tell her it would be okay. That they'd take care of it all and she wouldn't have to think. And she loved that about you. That you would take charge. Take control. It made her the happiest when you asked her to jump because she could prove her love by jumping as high as possible."

I bowl over, my shoulder slumping and my hands flat on my knees.

"Kenya is different. You ask her to jump and she'll tell you to jump first. She doesn't need you to take charge because she takes pride in the scars she's earned from surviving all life has thrown at her. I spent only a couple minutes in her company, but I observed a lot. She's confident in the silence. In her own skin. She didn't feel the need to make dull conversation. She didn't shy away from your past or any of the deep topics we discussed. She was comfortable, cool, didn't give a damn of my opinion of her."

"That's not true. She hated that people were talking about us. She cares about their opinions."

"Was that it?" He arches an eyebrow.

I clear my throat.

"You think she was that shallow, Alistair?"

"No." I bite out. "It was more than that. She hated that her reputation was going down the drain."

"Why?"

I narrow my eyes at him. "Are you quizzing me?"

"I'm getting you to wake up and smell the coffee. Now, why did it bother her that her reputation was being tanked?"

"Because she's worked hard to make her own way. She's had the things she liked stripped away from her before." I think of her confession that she had to drop out of after-school clubs for her sister. "And she doesn't want to lose anything of hers again. She wants to fight to protect herself even if I promise I'll fight for her."

"What do you think she needed from you, Alistair?"

I frown.

He stares, unblinking, at me.

It feels like my insides are being scrambled, and Darrel's not letting up until he has everything in my heart stretched out and clarified.

"Partnership," he says sternly. "She's not Claire. She doesn't want you to smother her. She wants you to propel her up so she can fly. So you fly together."

She's not Claire. He's echoing the words Kenya hurled at me. The ones that tore my heart out of my chest and sent it careening into space.

"Daddy!" Belle dances over to me. She's wearing a frilly dress with tiny petals on the hem. She has a bouquet of wildflowers in her hands. Her lips curve up in a brilliant smile.

"That's beautiful, Belle," Darrel says.

"Is that for me?" I ask.

"No." She giggles. "It's for Miss Kenya."

My eyes widen.

Darrel gives me a knowing look. "Is it, Belle? Do you want to see Miss Kenya again?"

"Yes. But daddy says she's busy. So I want to send this to her. And invite her for tea."

"I wonder who should send that invitation?" Darrel croons, arching an eyebrow in my direction.

Belle looks expectantly up at me, and I realize there's a similar yearning in my heart. Kenya already left her mark on our lives. There's no way I can go back to the way things were before. No way I can keep living in this misery.

Taking the flowers gently from Belle, I lift her into my arms and press a kiss to her cheek. "Don't worry, Belle. Daddy will make sure Miss Kenya gets these flowers."

"And tea?"

"I don't know, but I'll try my best so we can see her again."

* * *

STANDING outside Kenya's apartment with nothing but my heart in my hands is a position I'm still not used to.

I have never begged a woman for anything. Ever.

But then Kenya is new to me in so many ways. She's sharp and soft all at the same time. She can be loud or quieter than a whisper. Her mouth can cut me, or it can heal everything that's broken inside.

I'm in love with her.

And I can't go another day without letting her know.

I knock on the door and wait a beat more, wondering if no one is home.

But that's not right.

I see lights under the door. And I see shadows.

I'm staying here until she acknowledges me. It's the only thing I can do since she's not answering the phone, replying to my emails or reading my private messages.

Knocking on this door and being ignored is humiliating, but I won't dwell on how foolish I look. I'm throwing my pride aside in a desperate effort to save my heart.

"Kenya." I knock again.

Again.

Again.

She can hide if she wants. I've got all day. It's not like I've been getting any work done. I'm coming apart at the seams and the frayed edges are starting to show. Even Ezekiel ditched his scowls and subtle cold shoulder to berate me about not getting enough sleep.

Kenya Jones ruined me.

And she needs to take responsibility before she goes traipsing off to another country to meet some guy who probably isn't as broken as me.

I knock on the door again. "Hello?"

The door swings open and a tall, slender woman with dark skin and striking eyes scowls at me.

I clear my throat. "Hi, Sunny."

"Why are you here again?"

"Because you ignored me the other times." I glance past her. "Is Kenya here."

"No." She slams her hand against the doorway, barring my entrance.

I lean back. "I brought coffee."

Her eyes flit to the paper cups.

"Ezekiel's secret coffee. I know she likes his brew more than any of the coffee shops'."

Her eyes narrow. "What exactly do you want, Mr. Alistair?"

"I want to see her." My voice is level. "Is she home this time?"

"No, she's not home." Sunny folds her arms over her chest. I see that both friends have attitude for days. "And even if she was, she wouldn't drink your coffee. She's finally opened her eyes and realized how bad it is for her. It's overbearing and detrimental to her health."

From the stink eye she's giving me, I'm starting to wonder if she's referring to me instead of the java.

"I find it hard to believe that Kenya would give up coffee."

"What you believe is none of my concern. Are we done here?"

"Are you sure Kenya isn't home?"

"Are you calling me a liar?"

This woman looks like a slight breeze would blow her over. I could push her aside and storm in like a menace, but my instincts warn me to reel that side of myself in.

She slides in front of me when I try to peer into the room. "Move back before I break your nose with the door."

"Kenya told me you were her best friend. If she's not home now, you must know where she is."

"You're correct. I *am* Kenya's best friend. And because I'm her best friend, I would never sell her out to the outrageous boss who made her life a living hell." She bats her eyes at me. "Does that answer your question?" She starts to close the door.

I slide my foot into the crack. "Wait."

"You're just begging for a beatdown, aren't you?" She huffs.

I thought Kenya was as blunt and stubborn as they came, but her friend is giving her a run for her money.

"I really need to speak with Kenya."

"And I need a contract with HGTV, but neither of those things are happening. So move along."

"Look," I growl because my reserve of calm is wearing thin, "tell her that I'm sorry, and that I just want to talk to her." My mouth trembles over the word, but I push it out. "Please."

I'm pleading.

Kenya Jones has me pleading just to hear her voice.

Sunny frowns. "You're too late. She's not here."

My heart wallops my ribs. "What?"

"She's already left for her assignment with that other company." Her hands whipping through the air, she waves me back. "Last I checked, she was swimming with nurse sharks and flirting with the locals. She's enjoying her freedom. I doubt she remembers your name."

Horror fills my chest. I lose all patience and ground out, "You're lying."

"Contrary to what you think Mr. Big and Bad Billionaire, the world doesn't revolve around you and neither does Kenya. She's living her best life without your involvement and she'd like to continue, so see yourself out and don't come back." Sunny prods at my foot with her flip-flops.

"Wait." I hold out Belle's flowers to her.

She gives it the stink eye. "What is this? Some kind of voodoo doll?"

"No. It's from my daughter."

Surprise flickers in her eyes before she hides it.

"I'm hoping you can pass it on to Kenya."

For a second, it looks like Sunny will shove the flowers into my mouth, hog-style, but she swipes them from me. "Fine. Goodbye."

The door slams shut in my face.

I plod aimlessly down the hallway. What if Kenya meets someone else overseas? A rush of jealousy singes my veins as I imagine some other guy adoring those gorgeous curves and taming that sharp mouth.

There's no way she'll find someone else that quickly. No way…

But what if she does?

Determination fuels my fire. This isn't over. Not by a long shot.

I hurry to the car. Bernard gives me a hopeful look, but it drops the moment he sees my face.

"She didn't see you this time either, sir?"

"Take me to the Baby Box headquarters."

"Baby Box? Why all of a sudden?"

I crack my fists. "Kenya's left the country and I'm going to get her whereabouts from Walsh one way or the other."

CHAPTER 21
RED INK

KENYA

Sunny prances into my bedroom and creaks the door open. "Girl, you did not tell me your boss was *hot*-hot!" She fans her face. "His pictures do *not* do him justice. And he's so intense. I thought he'd storm into the house and stomp around trying to find you."

"I'm surprised he didn't," I mumble, my voice shaking.

Sunny has no idea how hot Alistair's temper can get. All he cares about is results, and the journey to getting them? Well, he'll treat you like a workhorse if it gets the job done.

"It was kind of sad though," she admits. "He must have run up the stairs because he was dripping in sweat."

My eyelashes flutter. "He was?"

She nods.

It's hard for me to imagine it. But then… there's more to Holland Alistair than his legendary jerk-ish ways.

He's the kind of man who'll pay off the medical bills for his driver's sick wife.

He's the kind of man who honors someone's efforts whether they come from a good school, have a fancy degree or not.

He's the kind of man who'll work himself into the ground to provide a legacy for his daughter.

He doesn't show that side to everyone, but I've seen it. I've seen his grumpy expression soften into tenderness. I've felt his harsh mouth brushing softly against mine, making my heart flutter and seize. I've heard his voice get low and rough when he talks about his wife and his regrets about that night.

"You're upset," Sunny mumbles. Falling into the bed, she rolls on her stomach and props her pointed chin in her palm. "Should I have told him you were still here in the city? Should I not have told him you were making mad, passionate love with a half-naked scuba diver in the Caribbean?"

I roll to a sitting position. "You what?"

Earlier, I heard Alistair's voice and I almost started crying. With every word he spoke, my heart stirred, and I wanted to reveal myself. I knew I had to get away, so I locked my door and put on loud music to drown him out.

I had no idea Sunny would go off the deep end in her attempt to drive him off my scent.

Sunny slants me a giant grin. "All I did was insinuate that you were dating again. I didn't say anything about a scuba-diver, but I should have! It would have served him right."

I shake my head.

She leans back. "I have to admit, he surprised me. Given the way the articles talk about him being all about business, I thought he'd be a little more… deadpan. But when I mentioned that you might be with someone else, I thought he'd bust a spleen." She covers her mouth to muffle the laughter. I have no idea how she can find any of this funny. "He looked like he was about to fly to wherever you were and send that guy into a coma."

"That non-existent guy."

"Hey, if you don't like it, I can call him up and correct the story. He won't mind."

"No." I pounce on her hand. If I go back to Alistair, nothing will change. He'll still tackle problems on his own. He'll still treat me like I'm his employee, someone he orders around, instead of someone in the war with him."

Her eyebrows draw together. "Oh, he also brought the weirdest bouquet of flowers I've ever seen."

"Flowers?"

"He said it was from his daughter." She huffs. "He's using the kid to get to you. That's some next level manipulation right there."

"Alistair would *never* use Belle to get what he wants." I think about the first huge blow-out we had after the Baby Box pitch.

Sunny looks taken aback. "Are you sure?"

"Where are the flowers?"

"Wait here. I'll get them." She tumbles out of bed and returns a second later with a cluster of dry flowers that looked like they were plucked by a mischievous four-year-old let loose in the park.

I stare at the flowers and tears prick my eyes.

Sunny studies me worriedly. "Geez, am I missing something? He's a billionaire, but this thing looks like he picked it up off the street."

"It was Belle," I whisper hoarsely. Alistair can afford to buy me a flower shop, but it wouldn't be worth as much as these flowers right here.

A harsh longing scrapes the center of my heart. I'm unable to breathe, unable to take one more second of the pain.

"Was he... did he seem okay?" I croak.

Sunny's eyes bug. "What?"

"You said he was sweating." It's hard to imagine Alistair looking that sad. He's usually GQ model ready in Italian suits and perfect hair.

Unless he's with Belle. At those moments, he trades three-piece suits for a Henley and jeans. His hair falls however it wants to. His hazel eyes sparkle with contentment. My brain conjures the image like it was orbiting around, jumping at the bit for a chance to spring free.

"He looked," Sunny taps a long, delicate finger on the blanket, "tortured. Like someone beat his heart to within an inch of his life. Miserable." She scrubs her chin. "As miserable as you are."

I rake a hand over my mouth and let out a shuddering breath. Alistair looking tortured? Miserable? It's hard to imagine.

He doesn't need anyone. At least, he'd never admit it. Never let anyone know. It felt to me that all he needed was a toy soldier. Someone he could move up and down without a fight.

I swallow hard.

It doesn't matter if I'm wrong about that. Doesn't matter if he's suffering.

We're done. Over.

But Belle…

I stare at the bright flowers. Suddenly, I scoop them up and head out of the bedroom.

"Where are you going?" Sunny asks, scrambling behind me.

I glance back and forth until I find a vase. Carting it to the sink, I fill it with water.

"Kenya, you're scaring me." She frowns. "I know Lord Hotness keeps showing up on our doorstep, begging you to talk to him, but you can't make it that easy."

I storm past her with the vase that's heavier because it's filled with water.

She steps back. "You can't let him get to you."

"Belle sent this."

She narrows her eyes. "How can you be so sure?"

"Because I am." I tenderly take the flowers and place them, one by one, in the vase.

"Fine. Say it *is* his daughter's. Given the tender look in your eyes, he probably sent them on purpose. He knows you have a weakness for his little girl."

I arrange the flowers with care.

"Kenya, are you listening to me?"

"Not really."

She grabs my wrist and lowers her voice. "You said you didn't want to play damsel in distress while some rich jerk decided your life for you. You're the one who said he was a major alpha prick who hadn't learned to control his caveman instincts. You said that. Not me."

Yeah.

But turning my back on Alistair doesn't mean I have to turn my back on Belle.

* * *

"Thanks for meeting with me." I slide my fingers around the mug. It releases a plume of smoke in the air. The scent of strong coffee gives me courage.

Darrel sits straight and tall in the chair across from me. His shoulders strain against a thin white T-shirt. Thick fingers stay flat on the table.

"Honestly, I'm surprised that you reached out."

"I wanted to call Ezekiel, but his loyalty belongs to Alistair. He wouldn't be able to keep this a secret."

"What exactly is the secret? That you're meeting with me or that you're back in the city?"

"Both." My gaze darts away. "I haven't actually left the city."

His green eyes widen to the size of emerald pools.

I offer a strained smile. "Surprise."

"Alistair was so sure you were gone. He almost stormed the Baby Box offices, looking to pick a fight with Walsh. Bernard had to drive him to my practice so I could calm him down or he'd be spending the next few months in jail."

Stricken, I tighten my fingers on the cup.

Darrel lets the quiet linger and I realize that, with him, there's no awkwardness in the silence. It's different with Alistair. His silences are thick. Pulsing. Full of crackling, raw energy. Even his quiet moments are loud.

Darrel is a different kind of powerful. The kind that sneaks up on you when you feel that you're most invincible. It isn't loud or aggressive, but it's just as potent.

"What are you doing now?" He takes a sip of his coffee. "I'm guessing you're not at Baby Box. If you were, someone from Belle's Beauty would have seen you and reported it to Alistair."

"No, I decided not to take that deal."

"Not enough money?"

"It wasn't the money. Or the position. Or even Walsh." I blink rapidly. "It was me. Thanks to the hefty paychecks I got from working with Alistair, I finally had a chance to stop running around frantically trying to pay the bills and really think about what I want to do with my life."

"And what did you discover?" His words are patient. His eyes are fully focused on me. He's probing and yet I feel completely at ease.

"My first love is Literature. Even when I was writing those reports for Alistair, it leaked out. He scolded me for it once." My lips curl up unconsciously. "He called my report 'flowery'. I was so offended at first, but I realized it was a kind of compliment." I drum my fingers on the table. "I didn't have the right references before, but with the power of Belle's Beauty on my application, I got called back for interviews at some of the biggest publishing houses in the city. I received an acceptance letter yesterday. I start next week. As an assistant editor."

"Good for you, Miss Jones. I'm glad you get to realize your dreams."

"Yeah." My fingers slide over the rim of the cup.

He continues studying me. "Miss Jones."

"Mm?"

"Why did you call me out to speak today?"

"It's about Belle." I glance down. "Is she okay?"

"You should ask Alistair more than me."

"I know, but…"

His hard expression softens a smidge. Folding his hands together, he leans forward. "Belle asks about you often. It's getting to the point that Alistair is running out of excuses she'll buy."

My heart lurches and I feel like I'm free-falling. "Really?"

He nods. "They both miss you very much."

"You said both."

"I meant it."

My phone buzzes.

Glumly, I lift it and scroll to the new text.

Holland: Belle is refusing to eat until she talks to you. I know you have every right to ignore me, but please, Kenya, can you spare some time to talk to her?

I blink in shock.

Darrel hikes both eyebrows. "What's wrong?"

"Alistair is…"

"He's what?"

"He's *begging* me." I turn the phone and show the message to him. "He said please."

Darrel's jaw clenches. I can see the fight in him. The split between being an uncle and being an objective party.

"It's your choice, but if I can speak for Belle, I think she'd appreciate a simple video call."

"I'll call." How can I not when Alistair is pleading with me for the first time in his life?

"He's changing, you know," Darrel says quietly. "You forced him to confront the parts of himself that need fixing. Maturing. He's come to a few realizations because of it."

"This isn't about getting back with Alistair. I just want to make sure Belle is okay."

"Alright. I respect that. I won't get involved in your relationship, but I thought you should know." He nods to the phone. "That he's willing to beg for the people he loves. And you're counted in that number."

I crush my napkin into a ball. "Thank you for seeing me today, Darrel."

"Of course." He rises to his full height and grabs the bill. "I'll take care of this."

"Wait."

He turns and glances expectantly at me.

"Can you... not tell anyone about this? About us meeting?"

"No one will find out your whereabouts from me." His smile is grim. "Trust me. I'm good at keeping secrets."

I nod because I believe him. His shoulders are that broad. His face is apathetic. He looks like nothing gets to him, and it makes me wonder what would shake that stony personality.

When Darrel's gone, I respond to Alistair.

Kenya: I'm free today. When you get home, let me know and I'll call her.

His response is instant.

Holland: I'm home now.

My eyes almost pop out of my face. He is? Since when does Holland Alistair take Saturdays off? He doesn't understand the concept of a weekend. He's always at work making people's lives miserable.

My phone lights up with an incoming video call.

In a panic, I scramble around to find a part of the cafe that won't give my location away. I'm moving so jaggedly that my thumb swipes against the screen and I accept the call.

Mortified, I lurch to my feet and walk backward, searching for the nearest blank wall. My smile is nervous and my voice shakes when I say, "Hey, Belle."

"Miss Kenya!" Her pretty face fills the screen. A slight flush coats her cheeks and I wonder if she'd been crying.

"I'm so happy to see you." I settle into a chair by the wall and hope it's not too noisy in the room. The cafe is relatively empty, but the whirr of coffee machines makes it sound like a factory.

"Did you get my flowers?"

"Mmhm." A genuine smile spreads on my face. "They were so pretty."

"Daddy says you're far away."

"Uh..."

"But it's not like mommy. Mommy's in heaven. I can't see her, but I can see you."

My heart turns over like a long-jumper knocking down all the hurdles. Can this child be any more precious?

"Yes." I bob my head. "Yes, you can see me whenever you like."

"Yay!" Belle does a cute dance.

The phone shifts and rattles.

Alistair's deep voice rings out, "Be careful, Belle. Mind you fall off the bed."

I stiffen.

"Daddy," Belle yells cheerfully, "come and see Miss Kenya." Her little fingers reach for the phone and the scene gets chaotic again. A moment later, Alistair's handsome face appears on screen.

I didn't think I had enough of a heart left to shatter, but I find that what's left of it explodes out of me. At the sight of him, my hands shake. If I don't get myself together, I'll have to call Darrel to schedule a session.

"Hi, Kenya." He says my name lightly. Reverently. Like it's too special to be pronounced above a certain decibel.

It just about undoes me. "Alistair."

I try not to let my longing show. If we were together, if we didn't end the way we did, he would growl at me to say his name. And I would pretend to ignore the request until he least expected it.

But we aren't together.

And I'm determined not to fall for that strong, hypnotizing hazel gaze.

Belle turns the phone away from her dad. "Miss Kenya, when are you coming back?"

"I'm not sure," I say as cheerfully as I can. "But don't worry. You can call me whenever you miss me."

"Really?"

"I'll always answer."

"You promise?"

An ache claws at my stomach. "Promise."

Belle just about vibrates with excitement. Her smile blossoms and her chubby cheeks press against her eyes.

"Alright, Belle. Miss Jones has things to do. Say bye."

"Bye." Belle gives me a gleeful wave.

I return it. "Bye, Belle."

"I'll call you again, Miss Kenya! We can have tea!"

"That sounds lovely," I croak.

Alistair turns the phone on himself. With darkening eyes, he mouths, *"Thank you."*

I nod and sign off.

My head is heavy, and I feel like my entire world is spinning out of control. I was doing so well staying away from them. From him. But now that I've gotten a little taste, I'm like an alcoholic falling off the bandwagon.

I know this high is just a fantasy. And maybe it's all going to crash and burn. But if I can keep Belle and Alistair in my life, in this tiny way, maybe it won't hurt so much when I finally have the strength to leave them behind.

* * *

That phone call is one in a line of many.

Turns out, if you tell a four-year-old you'll answer every call, she'll call… a lot. And since I made a promise, I always try to answer.

Sometimes, I'm caught up at work and I can't get to her.

Being a professional editor at a publishing house is not the romantic experience I imagined. I thought I'd be curled up with a best-seller-in-the-making, sipping hot coffee and marking words with red ink.

Turns out, I'm married to the printer again. And there are no manuscripts except the ones that are tossed into the slosh pile.

In a publishing house, the deadlines are fast-paced, the pressure to create a best-selling package is fierce, and it's almost like my stressful job at Belle's Beauty.

Except my boss isn't a crazy gorgeous man with eyes that spear you in the gut. She's an older woman with very high expectations and a passive aggressive personality that makes life difficult.

Because of my managing editor's snide remarks, I've come to appreciate Alistair's gruff and upfront personality. He doesn't mind hurting your feelings to your face, which sucks. But it's better than being insulted behind your back and undermined in quiet ways. I can't believe I miss Alistair's leadership style, but it's the truth.

Right now, everyone is even more anxious because of the upcoming merger. Ownership is changing hands, and no one at the publishing house is sure if they'll still have a job when the dust settles.

My managing editor is taking it out on me and, because of her, I finally understand the difference between a boss who's hard on you to get the best results and a boss who's hard on you because she has raging insecurities and a vindictive spirit.

Since it's been crazy at work for the past few days, I've started to call Belle during her bedtime.

Sometimes, she's asleep and it's Alistair who answers me. Although I know I should probably hang up the phone, I ask him about Belle, he asks me about my day, and it usually turns into a conversation that lasts all night.

It's been happening more and more often lately.

I'll call to ask about Belle.

He'll answer.

And then the conversation will spiral from there.

I know I'm playing with fire. And it wouldn't surprise me to find out that Alistair is leaning on my love for his daughter to keep my heart hooked on him.

But I can't deny that it feels *good* to bounce my thoughts off him. Especially when I'm stressed out and have my back against the wall at work.

It's not that I don't have other support. Sunny jumps on my side because she's the most amazing best friend a girl can ask for. But agreeing with me all the time isn't helpful.

Alistair doesn't suffer from that issue. He's brusque and rough. Every problem I hand over to him is met with a cold but tactical solution.

Sometimes I want to apply his advice. Sometimes I don't.

But I've come to find out that his insights are invaluable and always offer a different perspective.

He's an asset in my life.

And he still makes my heart race.

Thankfully, there's a built-in boundary between us. The fact that he thinks I'm overseas is a wall that he can't climb.

I'm safe.

For now.

* * *

A FEW DAYS LATER, I arrive home and notice Sasha's vehicle in the parking lot.

My entire body floods with anxiety. Her wedding is right around the corner. What is she doing here?

I keep my head down and try to shuffle past her without notice, but I fail terribly. Sasha's car door flies open, and she leaps to the sidewalk.

Moonlight spills over her wavy brown hair and brown eyes glistening with tears. She grips the top of her door, her manicured fingernails exquisite against the green paint of the car.

"Kenya, can we talk, please? Just hear me out this once."

My feet slow to a stop on the sidewalk.

She's still your sister, I tell myself.

Hesitantly, I turn and face her again. She stays by the car, a tear dripping down her cheek and her eyes searching mine in desperation.

After breaking up with Alistair, I wasn't in the right frame of mind to talk to Sasha, so I blocked her number, ignored all the messages from Felice and basically stuck my head in the sand.

But no one can outrun the lessons they're meant to learn.

I stalk over to her car.

She slams the door shut and steps toward me. "Let's go upstairs—"

"No way. Sunny will kill you if she sees you." I gesture to her car. "We do this in there."

She looks like she wants to argue.

"Take it or leave it, Sasha." I tap my fingers on the windshield. "What do you want to do?"

She unlocks the door, slides in and pops the passenger door open for me.

I get into the car and stare straight ahead. "What's wrong?"

She shakes her head, wiping at her eyes. "Nothing."

My scoff is less than gentle. It's not hard to understand why I'm short on patience. In a few days, my backstabbing sister will marry my backstabbing ex. I can't seem to find my compassion.

"I'm not an idiot, Sasha, so don't treat me like one. What's wrong?"

She rakes her fingers through her hair. "Nothing."

"Really?" I hiss. "I guess random crying is totally normal. Since you're fine, I don't need to be here."

"Wait. I… it's not random…"

"I know. There must be a reason for—"

"… It's hormones."

Her words sink in.

I whip my head around. "Hormones?"

She nods. Swallows. "I'm pregnant. Drake and I."

The pieces click into place.

Felice was so frightened about Sasha's health. It wasn't just about the cancer returning. It was about the baby.

And no wonder Drake married her right away. He's always felt a strong sense of responsibility to family. He wanted to be nothing like his dad who walked away from his mother.

It also explains why the wedding is happening so quickly.

I press into my chair, my mind whirling with thoughts.

"I know what I did was messed up, but I cared about Drake.

And he loves me. We're going to have a family. Why can't you be a part of it?"

This can't be happening. My sister isn't here berating me. Again.

She betrayed me. Stomped on me.

And it doesn't matter.

I'm expected to suck it up and be her lady-in-waiting like I've always been. Like I did gladly.

"Sasha, you better stop now."

Her eyes glint with determination. "I heard you were messing around with that billionaire boss of yours. You've obviously moved on."

My patience drops into an abyss of frustration.

She leans forward. "See? You were with him even though you knew the stakes of being found out. You loved him so much you couldn't stay away. Don't you understand me now?"

"I'm not dating my boss," I spit.

"But you were."

"It's over."

"So you played the game and you couldn't handle it. You got screwed over. See? You can't control your heart, Kenya. None of us can. Love has a way of making even the craziest things feel right. You see where I'm coming from now?"

"It's not the same thing," I spit. "Don't you dare try to compare what you did with Drake to me dating my boss."

"Are you still angry, Kenya?" Her lips purse on my name. "Do we really have to drag it out for this long?"

I stare straight ahead. The night is still. Nothing moves except for the trees bending with the wind.

"Family isn't about flesh and blood." I hear Alistair in my head.

"You know," I whisper, "I've always regarded you as my sister, even though we weren't related by blood. I was willing to give up everything to be there for you because *that* is what family does. But if I'm the only one giving up everything and you're the only one taking, that's not family." My eyes swerve to hers. "That's ownership. You keep expecting me to cave to you because that's the way it's always been. And you can't accept that you're not getting your way again."

She slings an arm over her stomach. "Kenya, I'm pregnant. I'm going to have a family. You'd seriously turn your back on me and my child?"

My heart pounds. I resist the guilt that wants to creep into my resolve and take a bite out of it. I've always given into Sasha. Always. It's one of the reasons she thought sleeping with my boyfriend wouldn't affect us.

I lift my chin. "I love you, Sasha. You are my sister and we will always have our memories together. We'll always have our history. But I will no longer allow you to use me and mistreat me. I will no longer allow you to walk all over me and tell me I should accept it because of love. This isn't what love is. And this isn't what family is."

"Kenya, please." She reaches out and grabs my hand.

I shake her off. "I will not be anywhere near your wedding, so don't look for me and don't expect me to change my mind."

Big tears roll down her face. One after the other.

I stay motionless in the passenger seat. "Now, I'm going to call a taxi for you and you're going to let them take you home because you're not driving in this state. That'll be my last act as your sister."

"Why are you doing this to me?" Her voice flays through the air with venom. "Why are you being such a b—"

I smile and cut her off by grabbing my phone to call a taxi.

She trembles like a hurricane, her chest rising and falling.

I shove my door open. "The driver will be here in ten minutes. I recommend you take care of yourself. For you and the baby." My eyes drop to her stomach. "Have a nice life, Sasha."

When I step out of the car, I hear the horn honking in short bursts. Sasha is slamming her hands against the steering wheel and crying. Through the tinted windshield, I see her wedding ring glint.

Heart heavy, I drag myself up the stairs even though a part of me still wants to run down to my sister and make all her problems go away.

Sunny scrambles to her feet when I walk into her apartment. "I saw Sasha. Say the word and I'll go down there with my bat."

"She's pregnant," I say wearily.

"What?" Her jaw drops.

I lift a hand. "I don't really want to talk about it."

Sunny watches me worriedly as I plod to the bathroom and sink against the wall. Tears well in my eyes and fall down my cheeks.

I'm a horrible person.

I'm awful.

She's pregnant. She needs me. I should be there for her no matter what.

Doubts creep out of the shadows and attack me like little bugs. They crawl all over my skin and dig into my hurts until they're burning.

At that moment, my phone rings.

It's Belle.

I quickly dry my cheeks and beam at her. "Belle, hi baby!"

"Hi, Miss Kenya."

"What's up?" My voice is stuffy.

Thankfully, I don't have to say too much. She starts chatting about her day and takes over the conversation.

I manage to smile and nod at the appropriate points. She seems satisfied.

After a while, Alistair gently pries the phone from his daughter and tells her to go and help Mrs. Hansley with dinner.

"Okay." She pops up cheerfully, her two ponytails swinging. "Bye, Miss Kenya."

"Bye, sweetie."

I expect Alistair to end the call, but he studies me with a sober frown. "Were you crying?"

"No."

"Kenya." The way he says my name, all tender and sweet like that, almost starts the waterworks again.

I rub my forehead, unable to hide my emotions. "Sasha told me she's pregnant." One tear pops out of my eye. "She asked me to be a part of the baby's life and I told her…" A sob cuts my words short. "I told her no."

"Kenya." His voice is a rumble. "Damn, I wish I could hold you."

Call me an idiot, but I wish he could too.

"Tell me I made the right choice. Tell me I'm not an awful human being."

"You're not an awful human being, Kenya, but you are human." He sighs. "How you feel right now tells me if you've moved on. And if you're still hurt by her, then you're not fully healed. You have the right to demand distance until those wounds are healed. No one should have the authority to force your healing."

I sniff, lifting my head. "You're saying no one should be forced? You?"

He laughs. "I'm learning."

I smile.

"When you're finally healed, you'll move on. You might even let her back into your life again and forgive what she did."

"I don't see that happening any time soon."

"Well," his lips inch up slowly, "if you have somebody else that you love, someone who loves you even more in return, it might be easier to deal with the hurt. My suggestion is to let go and focus your love and attention on that person."

I laugh. Who said this man wasn't good at sales?

"Alistair, are you trying to pitch yourself to me?"

His smile flashes across his face and almost takes my breath away. "Kenya, it just so happens that I have a trip out of the country soon. I'll be in your area next week." He leans closer to the camera. "If you're willing, I want to see you."

CHAPTER 22
FERNS OF LOVE

HOLLAND

THE MOMENT I ask about meeting up, Kenya's tears disappear, her eyes dart back and forth, and she makes a lame excuse about needing to go back to work.

As if I buy a single line of that.

I smile in satisfaction. She might be panicking, but I got her mind off the conversation with her sister.

Score.

"You finished talking to Kenya?" Ezekiel asks.

"Yeah."

"She good?"

I'm one hundred percent sure that she's more focused on what she'll do to protect her lie than on Sasha's shotgun wedding. That should keep her busy for a while.

"She could be better, but I gave her something else to think about."

"Hm."

"Ezekiel, can you set these plates?" Mrs. Hansley croons, handing him a stack of dishes.

"Sure thing." He plods away.

Mrs. Hansley sends him heart-eyes that he completely ignores.

I chuckle. Since the Fine Industries licensing deal went through, I've decided to move my office home. Reasonably, my executive assistant has to make the move with me.

Mrs. Hansley seems to be *very* happy about that.

Frankly, so am I. I'm still involved in the company, but I'm determined to spend more time with Belle. No matter the cost.

"Daddy, look." Belle storms out of the kitchen, holding a giant bowl of leaves. "I made salad."

"Good job, Belle."

The doorbell rings.

Belle's eyes light up. "Uncle Darrel!" She takes off like a shot and I hustle behind her.

Belle jumps up and down when Darrel walks into the room. He softens his stiff expression to offer her a smile.

"Hi, Belle." He scoops her into his arms and gives her a hug. Then his green eyes shift to me. "Thanks for the dinner invite."

"Mrs. Hansley's idea. She wanted a certain someone to stick around and a random dinner party was the best excuse."

His eyes twinkle. "I see."

Belle points to the table. "Let's eat!"

Darrel sets her in a chair and I fold a napkin over her lap.

"Daddy," Belle says.

"Yes, sweetheart?"

"I wish Miss Kenya were here to eat with us."

"Me too, darling."

There's not a day that goes by where Belle doesn't mention Kenya. I had no idea my little daughter adored her so much. Not until she couldn't see Miss Jones at all.

The day Belle threw her biggest tantrum was the day I told her that Kenya wasn't coming back.

Big mistake.

My daughter burst into tears and refused to eat another bite until she could speak to Miss Kenya.

If Miss Kenya isn't in heaven, then why can't I see her?

I couldn't argue against logic like that. And it pulled my heart out of my chest to see my baby in tears. Since I missed Kenya just as much as she did, I decided to swallow my pride and beg for just a bit of Kenya's time.

Best decision I ever made.

We've talked almost every day. Sometimes it's just about Belle. Other times it's about her work, my progress with Fine Industries, or my complaints about the new management company.

"We're gonna kidnap her someday." Belle munches on her food.

My eyes widen.

Ezekiel snorts.

Mrs. Hansley shakes her head. "Belle, we don't go around kidnapping people. That's not a nice thing to say."

A wrinkle forms between her brows. "But daddy said that about Miss Kenya. He said he missed her so much that he wanted to kidnap her."

My cheeks flush with heat. "Uh... why don't we talk about something else?"

"What's wrong with kidnapping?" Belle asks innocently.

"Miss Kenya isn't in the country, remember, Belle?" I clear my throat. "So even if you wanted to, it would be hard to kidnap her."

"Oh man." Belle pushes out her bottom lip and hunkers in her seat.

I notice Darrel glancing guiltily away. It makes me curious so, after dinner, I corner him on the balcony.

The city sprawls in front of us, skyscrapers with lights more dazzling than the stars. The dark sky stretches over the horizon, falling into a thin line at the edge of the world.

I press a hand on Darrel's shoulder and squeeze. "You know something."

"I don't know what you're talking about."

"How long were you aware that Kenya hadn't left the city?"

His eyes narrow on me.

"I found out from the first call. Weeks ago." Kenya tried her best to disguise her surroundings, but I caught a glimpse of the coffee shop before she pointed the camera at a wall.

I recognized the room and my suspicions blossomed. After that, I harassed Sutherburg until he finally admitted that Kenya had turned down the Baby Box offer.

The rejection came along with a threat about what would happen if they broke the contract with Belle's Beauty. Turns out, Kenya isn't just a lioness with me. She's not afraid of anyone.

And I love her for that.

Even if it means I have to work twice as hard to get her back.

"You should have told me." I scowl at him. "I looked like a fool."

"I don't disclose confidential information, and you don't need my help to look like a fool."

"Do people actually come to you for comfort? I can't see why."

His lips relax. It's not a full smile, but it's his version of it. "If you've known for this long, why didn't you go to her?" He arches an eyebrow. "Still scared?"

"No." I lean against the balcony.

He does the same, looking out over the night sky.

"After Claire died, it took me a long time to accept that I deserved to keep on breathing. I had so many thoughts of ending it, but I couldn't leave Belle. I couldn't let Claire down a second time."

He nods.

I fix my eyes on the moon. "So I got stronger. Harder. I decided someone would pay. They'd regret keeping me alive. I didn't care about anything but my own goals. I got used to taking what I wanted because Fate didn't ask for permission to take Claire so why should I? Life was simple that way."

He rubs his hands together, still listening.

"But with Kenya, I knew that wouldn't fly. I knew that barging in and demanding she admit her lies and come back to me would result in me getting slapped in the face."

"Or karate-chopped in the neck," Darrel says.

I give him a weird glance.

"That woman is not above violence."

I chuckle. "The best way to win her back wasn't to use my usual tactics. I needed to earn her trust. Slowly. Over time. I need to prove that I can go at her pace without dragging her to the speed of mine."

"Wow. You almost sound like an empathetic human being, Alistair."

"Screw you."

He chuckles. "How is it going?"

"We act like she's really long distance. We talk on the phone for hours. We discuss everything from politics to popcorn toppings. I feel like I know her better now. And I'm more in love with her than I was before."

That's a two-edged sword. The more I learn about Kenya, the harder it is to keep my desire in check.

I go to sleep every night aching for her. It's driving me up a damn wall and nothing I do helps to take away the yearning.

I miss her little moans, the ones she makes over coffee. And I miss the way her breath catches when I touch her. I miss the way she melts into my arms when I wrap them around her waist. And the way she groans my name like it's the last word she'll ever say.

My world turned upside down when she sassed her way into it. And now my fern isn't the only thing she's destroyed. My heart is there in pieces right beside it.

"What are you going to do?"

I wrap my fingers around the safety railing. I had them installed so Belle never accidentally climbed on the ledge and fell.

"I asked her to meet me in person."

His eyes widen.

"She doesn't know I know."

"What if she flies all the way to a foreign country just to keep on lying to you?"

"She's not going to do that."

"How are you so sure?"

"Because I know her." My jaw softens. "She doesn't run when she's cornered. She faces things head-on. She fights. That's the way she's wired." A grin spreads on my face. "She'll stay here and she'll come at me."

"And what will you do?"

"Me?" I massage my wrist with a smirk. "I'll be ready for her."

* * *

Kenya arranges for us to meet at a park, claiming that she's 'back for the holidays'. I buy that about as much as I believe that Santa Claus is real.

But I'm not complaining.

It feels good to see her again.

I slide Belle over to my other side and try not to drool over the woman standing in the park.

Kenya looks like a dream. Her hair's in a shapely afro. Her dress is long and silky. A tropical print. Her brown skin is sun-kissed, almost like she really spent the last few months in paradise.

My arms immediately twitch, wanting to close around her and kill the distance between us. Instead, I set Belle gently on the ground and watch her stream into Kenya's arms.

Kenya absorbs her, pulling Belle in and closing her eyes like she was waiting for this moment for ages. When they separate, it's only by an inch. They're both holding on tight.

"Miss Kenya, you look so pretty."

"You too, sweetie."

"Can I touch your hair?"

"Thank you for asking and you sure can." Kenya inclines her head toward my little girl.

Belle feels her hair and makes an astonished sound. "It's so soft."

I'm surprised when I see Kenya fighting tears. My jaw tightens. I don't ever want her to cry. I only want her to smile and laugh from now on. To be the happiest she's ever been.

"I missed you." Belle hugs her again. "Daddy did too."

"Did he?" Kenya's brown eyes jump to mine.

I pretend to frown. "Belle."

"But you said to tell her that." My daughter stares at me with wide, innocent eyes. "Remember?"

I blink in shock. That's the last time I ask Belle to play a part for me. She has no problems throwing me under the bus.

Kenya rises to her feet, looking amused. "What else were you supposed to say to me, Belle?"

"Um," she taps her chin, "that daddy loves you. And um… he'd do anything for you. And can you please come back?"

Kenya kisses Belle's cheek. "Wow. How hard did you have to work to memorize that?"

I interrupt them. "Belle, why don't you tell Miss Jones about your teacup?"

"Oh yeah!" Belle starts chatting about the new set Darrel bought her. While my daughter talks herself blue in the face, Kenya settles her on her lap and holds her close.

I watch them both and this feeling of… completion hits my chest. Like our family is finally healing. Like I've found what I've been missing for so long.

At that moment, Kenya looks up at me and smiles.

My heart dances and I can't even catch my breath. She is the most beautiful woman in the world. It's unfair the way she squeezes my soul at her leisure. Without even lifting a pretty finger.

"Belle," I say when my daughter's finished her spiel, "why don't you and Mrs. Hansley go play for a bit while I talk to Kenya?" I motion to the nanny who was hanging back in the car while Kenya and Belle had their reunion.

"And what exactly do we have to talk about?" Kenya asks, arching an eyebrow as Belle trots into Mrs. Hansley's arms.

Still spunky as ever, I see.

"Walk with me."

She remains in place.

I sigh, close my eyes and fire out the word I know she's waiting for. "Please."

Kenya jerks her chin down as if to say *that's better*. She follows me as we stroll through the park.

Sunshine flits between the trees. The branches on either side are so long that they intertwine in the middle, forming a sort of leafy canopy.

"Did you fly in for your sister's wedding?" I ask, pulling my hands behind me.

She crosses her arms over her chest, studiously avoiding my eyes. "I didn't go."

"Did your parents scold you?"

"They didn't say anything." Something fascinating must be on the ground because her eyes are glued there. "They cut me off."

My heart aches for her.

"I'm sorry." I stop and trace a line under her chin with the tip of my finger. "Are you okay, Kenya? You look… tired."

For a second, her eyes flicker with longing. I sense how much she wants to melt into me, to shift from stony to languid heat. She can't hide how much she wants me, but she's trying hard to fight it. Full of contradictions, as always.

"I'm working hard. Baby Box has me on a strict schedule." Her words are slow as if she doesn't buy her own story. "I'm surviving just fine without a tyrannical overlord boss telling me what to do."

"But is that boss as handsome as me?"

I expect some kind of sharp response, but she just side-steps me—and the question—and turns to walk back to Belle.

My lips inch up. "I have something for you, but you're going the wrong way."

"What do you mean?"

I gesture to the path we were on.

She squints up at me. "Alistair."

Damn. I missed hearing her say my name in person. Her voice is soft and fluttery. That perfume I love floats in the air, merging with the scent of sunshine and dried leaves.

I decide to shift the order of things a little. Pulling an envelope out of my jacket, I hand it over to her.

She frowns. "What's this?"

"Take a look."

"If this is some kind of lawsuit threatening me to come back to Belle's Beauty..."

I smirk. Her mind works in mysterious ways and I love every inch of it. Even if it drives me crazy.

"As much as I would love for you to come back to Belle's Beauty, I understand why you won't. And I want whatever makes you happy."

The suspicious look flees her eyes, leaving only curiosity in its place. "So you wouldn't order me to come back and work under you."

"Oh, I definitely want you under me." Preferably wet with sweat and bawling my name like she's going down with the ship.

Her eyes widen.

Mine narrow in teasing. "But I don't have any thoughts of ordering you to do anything. Right now." When I get her alone in bed however...

"You're so sure that whatever's in here is going to change my mind about you? About us?" Dark brown eyes hold mine hostage.

I nod to the envelope. "Open it."

This time, she doesn't scold me for not adding 'please'. Her head tilted to the side, she tears the envelope apart and shakes out the contents.

It's the contract I signed a few days ago. The paperwork outlines the takeover of her publishing house. By me.

"You bought the publishing house?" Her jaw drops.

"Not just me. Us." I tap her name that's written out in black and white.

She stumbles and I quickly wrap my arms around her to keep her up. Kenya remains in my embrace, too shocked to push me away or say anything.

I don't mind the proximity. I love that I can hold her like this. It's been so long.

Leaning down, I inhale her scent.

She smells amazing.

"Why is my name there?"

"Turns out, if you're a medium-sized publishing company, you're always hurting for cash. The publishing house had a good name and empty coffers. It wasn't hard to get them to sign the deal."

Her eyelashes flutter. "Alistair."

I set my hand into the dip of her hip. "I'm the main backer, but I gave you controlling shares. That means you can do what you want with the company. I'll follow your lead. When it comes to that business, I'll do everything you say."

She looks up from the paperwork. "You're insane."

"You don't like it?" I arch an eyebrow.

She pushes out of my arms and takes a step away from me. Her eyes flash. "You're overwhelming."

"In a good way, right?" I tilt my head confidently.

"You can't just…" She waves the paperwork around. "Buy me a company! Especially not the place where I—" Then she goes still. "Did you know all along where I was?"

"I did."

Her eyes narrow.

I step toward her. "Kenya, I went along with your lie because I knew you weren't comfortable meeting me. I want to make an effort to respect your space. To respect your independence. But I also want you to know that I will burn the world down if it'll keep you warm. And whenever you're tired of fighting alone, and proving whatever you need to prove, I'll be there to run with you. Fight with you. Hold you if it ever falls apart. I won't tie you to my side as long as you promise you'll keep coming back to me. As long as we can always be a team."

Her eyes lock onto mine.

I stop when I'm right in front of her. "Living without you was one of the hardest things I've ever had to do. I realized that I don't have control. Not really. But what I have is family. You're mine, Kenya. And I want to be yours."

She folds the paper into two and shoves it in my chest. "I never asked for anything this big, Alistair."

I frown. "What about a field of ferns that spell out 'I love you'?"

She goes still.

"I had them arranged over there." I point behind her shoulder.

Her head tilts back and she sighs at the sky like I'm the bane of her existence.

I wait for her to look at me again.

"Do they really spell out 'I love you'?"

"You have to watch it from a certain angle…"

Her nose scrunches and then she bursts out laughing. Not exactly the response I was hoping for after spending thousands of dollars arranging the sign.

"Ferns… it's the plant I kicked down the day we met. It's…" She holds her stomach. "Alistair, I don't know what to do with you."

"If you love me a quarter as much as I love you, I'll be happy," I growl. Then I pull her to me. "My heart is in your hands, woman. This is no laughing matter."

She wraps her arms around my neck, melting into me. All my dreams culminate in this one moment. Kenya looking into my eyes as I hold her close. Of course, my dreams are usually of her in my bed, but we'll get to that when she's ready.

Her fingers slip into my hair. "I'll accept the ferns on a few conditions."

"Name it."

"You lend me your office to use after hours. I'm thinking of writing a book about all that's gone on in the past few weeks, but my apartment is too noisy. I worked the best when I was in the Fine Building, and I want to see if my muse finds me again."

Kenya Jones? Back in my office? In my sight again? After hours?

"Done."

She laughs. "I don't want to sneak around the office anymore. Whenever I come in, you keep the door open."

"No way."

"Alistair."

"You want all my employees to see me ravishing you?"

Her fingers tighten on my neck. Her body shudders.

I trace my fingers down the curve of her spine. "What else?"

"You let your employees go home on Saturdays."

"I'll think about it."

"Alistair."

"How about half-days on Saturday and Sunday?"

"Holland."

Hell.

"Alright. No Saturdays." This woman can run off with all my wealth and I'd still grin like a lunatic.

She smiles up at me.

I let out a breath. "I love you, Kenya. Living without you was a waking nightmare, far worse than anything I endured in my dreams. I won't do anything to jeopardize this again."

"I'll give you one more chance." She lifts a finger and leans her head closer. "Don't screw this up, Alistair."

Heat envelops me.

I lean down, ready to brush my lips against her perfect mouth.

"Daddy!" Belle gasps.

I jump back, still holding Kenya's waist.

Belle skips up to us, stars in her eyes. "Is Miss Kenya going to be my new mommy?"

Kenya chuckles sheepishly.

Mrs. Hansley blushes and ushers Belle back. "Sweetie, I told you not to come this way yet."

"What do you say?" I ask Kenya. "You want to make a sweet little girl's dream come true?"

"Kiss me first and then I'll think about it."

I'm happy to oblige.

My lips graze hers and I'm no longer reeling in darkness. She's pure, electric light and I'm holding on to her for all I'm worth.

Slowly, gently, I kiss her until she understands that she belongs to me. But I belong, just as equally, to her. With a sigh, she kisses me back like she understands. A frantic, desperate kiss that sends my head spinning.

"Easier ways to say you missed me too, but I like it," I tell her.

"That obvious?"

"You don't have to say anything. Your eyes tell me all I need to know."

"I'll say it anyway because words are important too." She snuggles against me. "I love you."

I struggle for breath.

This woman has all the power to end me. It's freaking terrifying and exhilarating at the same time.

Belle squirms on the sidelines. "Yay!" My daughter takes off and flings herself at my legs.

Kenya laughs and scoops Belle into her arms.

"My girls." I glance at each of them. Wrapping my arms around Kenya, I kiss her temple and whisper, "Let's go home."

CHAPTER 23
SHOWER CRASHERS

KENYA

Sunny points to a curtain. "Is yellow a good color for writers? I don't know. Doesn't feel inspiring enough." She scratches her chin. "Maybe something calmer? Ocean waves. Blue? Turquoise or navy?"

"Babe, I have no idea. This is your territory," I mumble, slightly bored.

"I'm finally getting to makeover another office at Fine Industries. The *boss's* office. And Alistair told me he wanted the room to look welcoming in case you end up writing in there with him."

As if I can ever get any writing done when Alistair's in the room. He's so gorgeous he turns my brain to mush. And don't get me started on what his hands do to me.

"This is huge for my portfolio. I put Fine Industries on my resume and people went nuts. I'm overbooked, honey." She tosses her shiny hair over her shoulder. "You're lucky I squeezed you in."

"Hey, I have best friend privilege."

She chuckles.

In the distance, I spot a familiar face. The department store has a children's section filled with a cute showroom and lots of character-themed furniture.

"Darrel?" I notice the giant man nosing around, looking totally out of depth.

Sunny pushes the cart behind me as I hustle over.

Darrel startles. Green eyes slam into mine and then swerve to Sunny. They widen just a bit before he quickly glances away.

"What are you doing here?" I ask.

"Looking around," he says in a low, agitated voice.

"For Belle?" I glance around. Belle's in her princess stage. None of these boy-themed gifts will work.

"Uh no. Two guests are moving into my place. Just for a while. While their grandmother recovers." He slants a look at Sunny again.

I catch him watching her and realize I haven't introduced them. "Oh, this is Sunny, my best friend. Sunny, this is Darrel, Belle's uncle."

"Nice to meet you." She holds out her hand.

He stares at it and turns away. "If you'll excuse me."

Sunny's jaw drops.

My eyebrows hike.

I watch in shock as Darrel storms away like we just set his house on fire.

Sunny's mouth sinks into a frown. "What is wrong with him?"

"I have no idea. He's not usually like that."

"Like what? Rude as hell?"

My shocked gaze returns to Darrel's back. "Seriously, he's never done anything like that before."

Sunny huffs and smacks her hand against the cart.

"Have you two met?"

"I've never seen him before in my life," she spits. "Even if I did, does that give him any right to be a jerk?" She scoffs. "No wonder he's related to Alistair."

"Hey, Alistair wouldn't just ignore your hand. He'd smack it away. Darrel is still calm compared to him."

"And you sound so proud," she says sarcastically.

"He's not like that anymore."

"Hmph."

"It's true. He's working on being kinder. Especially now that he's cutting back on those ridiculous hours. He has less time to bark at people."

"You can take the jerk out of the office but you can't take the jerk out of the man."

"That's not how the saying goes."

She scrunches her nose and glances in Darrel's direction. "Remind me to avoid any party that Darrel guy attends. Unless it's your wedding."

"Whoa. We're already at a wedding?"

"You think Alistair will keep playing along with you? He's ready to put a ring on it, girl."

I loop my hand through hers and laugh. The thought of being Alistair's wife is sweet, but I do enjoy dating him. A lot. And I'm not in a hurry to get married.

"Let's keep shopping."

Sunny smiles again. Nothing like the promise of interior designing to get her in a good mood.

We complete our purchases and then she drags me to a fancy coffee shop.

"Isn't this place a little... rich?" I ask, glancing nervously around.

"Girl, your boyfriend paid me hella well." She smirks. "I need to reward the woman who allowed me to have a billionaire for a client."

I smirk.

We order coffees.

It's good, but definitely not as good as Ezekiel's.

Sunny stirs her coffee. "How does it feel to work in a publishing house that you own?"

I laugh softly. After Alistair presented me with a publishing company—like the crazy over-doer that he is—I decided not to tell anyone about it. I'm still working for my tyrannical managing editor.

It's funny. Every time she mistreats me, I think about the fact that I can have her job in an instant. There's a power in it that no amount of money can buy and I absolutely love Alistair for agreeing to keep my controlling shares a secret.

"It's a little like an undercover boss, noh?" Sunny tilts her fork, slipping into her Belizean accent. "You've got all the power but you're *letting* the employees tell you what to do."

"I've just started learning the ropes. I barely know how to edit manuscripts, proof books and deal with copyrights. It would be foolish of me to take control of a ship I don't know how to steer. I love Lit. I love books. I love words. I want to do them justice. That means starting from the bottom and earning my way to the top."

She sips her coffee. "Girl, you're better than me. I'd bust that company open and hang my picture everywhere. All the people who bullied me? I'd put them to clean my office."

"You so would."

"You know it."

We finish chatting and then leave the coffee shop.

Just then, I notice a black car parked next to the cafe. Alistair emerges from the backseat.

I'm slowly working on convincing him to give driving a try. I'm not trying to put Bernard out of a job, but I hate the thought that Alistair is held prisoner by his trauma in that way. He deserves to be free. And I want to be the one to help him.

Alistair steps toward us, confidence personified. He's wearing a simple white button-down and black slacks. His hazel eyes pin me down and his steps are slow and languid.

I feel like I'm watching a movie star.

Excitement bubbles in my chest.

"Hello, beautiful." Alistair's firm baritone voice sends a thrill through my body.

I take a deep breath and set my face in an irritated frown. "Were you spying on me the entire time?"

"I was driving by and saw my girlfriend in the window. I figured you'd be moaning over good coffee without me."

Sunny rolls her eyes. "Can you two *not* be obnoxiously cute right now? Geez."

I laugh.

Sunny stands in front of Alistair and plants her hands on her hips. "By the way, Hot Shot, what's up with your brother?"

"Brother?"

"Darrel," I supply.

"Oh, my brother-in-law."

"He was a total jerkwad to me today."

"I thought you were over that?"

"Seeing *his*—" she points at Alistair—"cocky mug reminded me of it, and now I'm annoyed all over again."

Alistair turns sober. "Darrel's taking on temporary guardianship of his client's children. Their grandmother got sick and the mother can't be found. It's stressing him out."

"Really?" I slant him a concerned look.

Sunny loses a little of her steel. "Oh, but it... I don't know. It felt like it was more than that. Like he had a problem with *me*."

"I'm sure you're overthinking it." I massage her shoulder.

She shakes her head. "Whatever. Alistair, are you taking your woman now?"

"We can drop you home," I say, gesturing to the car.

"And force my pure, innocent eyes to watch while you two are all over each other in the backseat? Thanks but no thanks. I have no idea how Bernard doesn't demand a raise the way you keep assaulting his eyes with your PDA."

Alistair catches my eye and winks.

Heat flushes my cheeks. We have gotten... carried away in the car before, but it was always with the shade up.

Alistair juts his chin at her. "Does she know where we're going?"

I nod.

Sunny rolls her eyes before I can speak. "I know and I totally disagree with it. Which is why I'm pretending it's not a thing."

Laughter pours out of me.

Alistair smirks.

"I'm leaving now, lovebirds."

"We'll wait until you catch a cab then."

"I'll flag one for you," Alistair says.

"It'll be tough. It's rush hour. No one will stop…" Sunny's words trail when Alistair simply walks to the edge of the sidewalk, raises a hand and flags a car down. Turning around with a cocky smirk, he gestures. "There you go."

"He's irritating," Sunny whispers.

"I know. But I love it."

Sunny leaves and Alistair comes up behind me. His arms slide over my waist and I close my eyes, melting into his embrace.

He takes a big breath of me, as if trying to commit my scent to memory. I really don't understand why he's so obsessed with my perfume. All I know is, the factory that makes my scent is now property of Fine Industries and I've been inundated with a lifetime supply.

It's my favorite fragrance but, again, Alistair just has to go overboard.

"You want to slow down, buster?" I tease him when he drops a trail of kisses down the column of my throat.

"Not unless you say please."

I laugh.

He kisses my neck in broad daylight because he's a jerktastic billionaire who does whatever he wants. But he's my jerktastic billionaire and I secretly love being the center of his affections.

His wicked hazel eyes hold mine. "Did you have a nice time?"

"I did. Sunny's going to go crazy with your office."

"Good. I want you to feel comfortable and she knows you the best." He cocks his head. "Aside from me."

"Oh?"

He grabs my hand and brings my fingers to his lips. "Ready to go?"

I follow him to the car.

Bernard is in the driver's seat. He looks over his shoulder and gives me a large grin.

"Miss Jones."

"Hi, Bernard."

"Your clothes are in the back. I'll be playing very loud music." He winks.

"I appreciate that." My lips tremble from how hard I'm smiling.

The window goes up and Alistair hands the dress bags to me.

"Need my help?" he whispers in my ear.

I start unzipping my skirt.

There's no distance between us because he destroys it all. And the hot beat of my pulse rides with the rhythm of my heart.

I am so in love with this man.

There's no doubt. Not a speck of unease in me.

The car moves off.

And Alistair makes use of the privacy.

It takes twice as long to get changed but, by the time we slow down in front of the hotel, I'm dressed in an expensive red gown and high heels.

I have to do my makeup again and Alistair has to wipe his face clear of my foundation. When we're presentable, he opens the door and rounds the car to my side.

I take his hand and step out. The wind lifts my curly hair and it dances in the breeze. My lips, coated in red lipstick, stretch into a grin.

"Wait." Alistair stops me before we walk inside. "There's one more thing."

"What?"

He produces a jewelry box from his pocket.

I gasp when he opens it for me. "It's beautiful."

"It takes years to produce this stone, but it's stronger than diamond. Just like you."

My eyes water. "You're going to make me ruin my makeup. And it was so hard doing my face in the car."

"You're beautiful even with mascara running down your face." He kisses me sweetly. "Even when you're snapping at me." His fingers curve over my side. "And especially when you're kicking down my ferns."

I laugh.

He clasps the necklace around me and then holds out his elbow.

I take his arm as we stride into the hotel and walk straight into the banquet room. There are blue balloons everywhere and a giant cake with a pacifier. Diapers holding chocolate pudding (whoever came up with that idea needs to be thrown out immediately) are lined up on the table.

A hush envelops the room when we walk in.

Alistair leans over and whispers, "There's still time to back out."

I lift my chin. "No freaking way."

A proud glint shines in his eyes.

I stalk over to where Sasha, Drake, Felice and dad are seated around a table. Sasha is wearing a tight blue dress. Her stomach is so swollen, she looks like she'll burst at any moment.

Her eyes widen. "Kenya."

"Surprise." I wiggle my fingers. "I missed your wedding, but I thought I'd attend the baby shower." I nod at her stomach. "My nephew didn't do me anything wrong. It was his lying, cheating parents."

Felice's jaw drops.

Dad squirms.

Alistair chuckles. "This is a gift from us." He sets an envelope on the table that contains a very generous check. Enough to make me feel less guilty for being rude at Sasha's baby shower.

I'm learning a little from Alistair too.

"Oh!" I point to the side. "Holland, there's champagne."

Alistair wraps his arm around my waist, tilts my chin back and plants such a hot kiss on my lips that the room starts spinning.

He pulls back while I'm dazed and growls, "How many times have I warned you about calling me that in public? I can't control myself when you do."

I blink rapidly and try to regain my composure, but my knees are about to give out.

Alistair knows me well and wraps his arms more firmly around my waist. Then he turns to my dad. "Sir, if you don't mind, I'd like to talk to you later. There's a personal matter I need to discuss with you."

Dad just blinks.

Alistair grabs my hand and hauls me away from their table. As we go, he tucks me under his arm and asks in a concerned voice, "You okay?"

"I can't think. You just kissed me deaf and blind."

He chuckles. "I probably shouldn't have done that in front of your father. Now how do I ask his blessing for your hand in marriage?"

I shove him.

Alistair just grabs my hand and whirls me onto the dance floor. As we dance, he keeps asking if I'm okay, if I need to leave, if I'm uncomfortable.

He's sweet and attentive, even if he's barking out his questions. And I smile because I know that his tone and his intensity is how he protects the people that he loves.

I keep assuring him that I'm okay.

And I am.

Alistair was right. I kept running, crying, and complaining about Sasha's betrayal because I was hurt. They're my family. Of course they'd have the power to hurt me.

But over the past few months, Alistair has patiently and steadily showered me in his love. He and Belle are my focus. And their presence in my life made me want to *thank* Sasha for showing me what a douchebag Drake was.

If they didn't send me into a tizzy that day, I never would have found a backbone and argued with Alistair. And he probably wouldn't have been impressed enough with my courage to hire me for a job at Belle's Beauty.

I wouldn't trade him and Belle for a thing.

We keep dancing. And then we eat. And we win all the games because Alistair's a show off and I'm super competitive in my own right.

At the end of the night, we drink Sasha's champagne and dance together in the middle of the floor. After a while, we give up on trying to make it seem like we're dancing and just rope our arms around each other, kissing like we need each other's oxygen to survive.

Sasha keeps a wide berth. Whether she thinks I'm crazy, whether Felice told her to stay away or whether she just doesn't care about me, I don't know. I don't care. I'm having a great time because I'm here with Alistair. And I want to celebrate my nephew's life even though I don't celebrate the way he was conceived.

When we stumble off the dance floor, Sasha finally confronts me.

Alistair squeezes my hand, looking down at me with a question. *You want me to stay?*

I squeeze back. *I'm good.*

He walks off, probably in search of my father.

Sasha waddles toward me. "Thank you for coming, Kenya. Even with all the…" She gestures to Alistair's retreating back, "shenanigans. I'm glad that you finally understand the meaning of family."

"Oh no, Sasha. I'm not here for you." I motion to her stomach. "I came for this little one because, after meeting Alistair's daughter, I realize that the kids are totally innocent in the adult drama. And I want my nephew to know that his aunt was there for him. I'll keep being there for him even though his mom is a selfish brat."

Her jaw drops. No one's ever talked to her this way.

I never have.

Again, Alistair is a really bad influence.

"How can you say that at my baby shower?"

"Because I won't say it behind your back if I can't say it to your face."

She frowns.

"I don't want to be friends, Sasha. You broke my trust and you're still unapologetic. But I do want you to know that if you need help for the little one, you can still come to me. We don't have to be friendly, but we can still be family."

Tears flood her eyes. She lets out a breath. "I'll take it."

I leave her behind and find Alistair.

He glances at me. "Ready to go?"

I nod.

He takes me outside to wait for Bernard and I cuddle into his chest. The stars are bright. The trees tower overhead.

He strokes my forehead and presses a kiss to my temple. "I'm proud of you."

"What else?" I tease.

"I love you."

My smile grows.

His eyes caress me. "I love you, Kenya. I love you a little more with every breath that passes. And I'll make sure you never regret being a part of my family." He cradles my face. "I promise to always support you, lift you up, fight for you—"

"And with me?"

His eyes fall over my lips. "Only if you push me."

"I love you," I whisper. "Thank you. I wouldn't have had the guts to face my family tonight."

"I cherish you." He strokes my chin. "And so does your dad. Believe it or not. When we talked, he told me to take care of you. He seemed torn up. Said he'd like to meet with you. Without Felice."

I sigh. "Him sneaking around to talk to me will mess up his

marriage. Felice looked like she wanted to stab me in the face when she saw me."

"It's your call."

"I'll think about it." I look up at his gorgeous face. "Just so you know, all my family members will probably be calling you trying to ask for favors."

"I'll put you in charge of that. I'll help whoever you want me to."

"What if I wipe your bank account dry?"

"You can do whatever the hell you want with my money, as long as you're mine."

I smile and rise on the tips of my toes to meet his lips. "That was the right answer."

"I'm always right," he murmurs.

I shake my head because he is still one cocky bastard.

But he's my cocky bastard.

And then I kiss him until the world disappears.

* * *

Enjoyed *Grumpy Romance*? Then you'll also enjoy Kayla's story. Grab **BE MY ALWAYS** at **niaarthurs.com/books**.

Want to spend more time with Alistair, Kenya and Belle? Get an exclusive epilogue by signing up to my mailing list at **niaarthurs.com/subscribe**.

BE MY ALWAYS
EXCERPT

BE MY ALWAYS
CHAPTER ONE
KAYLA

THE LIFESTYLE REPORTER has a thing for smirking.

Or maybe he's just trying hard to hold back a laugh.

He clutches a thick tablet in his pudgy grip like it's an extension of his very self and slouches in his chair.

As if he doesn't care.

As if we're not mid-interview.

I tap my nails against the back of my phone.

Try and fail to tamp down my rising irritation.

To hell with this journalist-exposé-wannabe who thinks my life's work is beneath him.

If I hear one more condescending question…

The smile remains on my face despite my rising irritation.

Media interviews are a part of my job whether I like it or not.

Whether this journalist is a prick or not.

I keep my voice level. "Matchmaking is *still* relevant."

"In this age of online dating?" He smirks again. *Yeah right.*

"I help people make real connections." My gaze slides over his overtly skeptical expression. "Even jerks who'd be better off staying single."

The insult flies way over his head.

Disappointing. I was hoping to piss him off and cut this boorish interview short.

I'm so done with this guy's B.S.

"Love can't be manipulated by strangers."

Shows how much he knows.

Manipulation is the name of the game. My mission is to cut through the screen-savers, the lies, and the catfishing and get to the meaty stuff. "Feelings can't be controlled, but intimacy between like-minded people can lead to love. Our strategies have proven that."

"Strategies? Care to share?"

I look at him with a frown and toss my hair over my shoulder. "If I told you trade secrets, it wouldn't be good for business, now would it?"

"I guess so." He laughs. A high-pitched, yapping sound.

Damn, he's annoying. It's difficult to stay seated and professional.

My fingers clutch the handles of my chair. I start to push up. "Is that all?"

"One more question." He tilts his head to the side. Drops his eyes to my ring finger.

I know what's coming.

Why do they always go for the jugular in these stupid interviews?

"What about you?"

"What about me?" I play dumb.

"Have you found love?"

"I don't plan to."

His face wrinkles in confusion. A matchmaker uninterested in her own romance? I understand. I'm not exactly fitting the stereotypes here.

But at least I got him to drop that stupid smirk.

I feel a pair of eyes barreling into me. From the corner of the room, Venus crosses her arms. *Don't mess this up.*

Though my fellow matchmaker and friend isn't actually saying anything, I can hear her loud and clear.

A wave of annoyance washes over me. Venus is much better at these inane conversations than I am. And she actually enjoys them too.

Too bad I'm the one suffering.

Interviews are supposed to be a reward for good performance. Something I'm guilty of. Highest number of matches three years running. Whispers around the office claim I'm Cupid.

It's dumb.

And untrue.

I don't fly around in diapers trying to impale my clients with arrows.

As much as I'd want to do that sometimes.

Impale my clients, not wear diapers.

If I don't watch myself, Venus will catch up to my record soon enough and then *she'll* be the one in this chair.

I'm sure she's looking forward to it.

I used to at one point.

When I'd first started the job, young and starry-eyed.

Before Drew…

Well, I definitely won't discuss that here with this ignoramus.

I shoot the reporter an innocent look. "Everyone is different, but my personal beliefs have nothing to do with our results. We have enough satisfied clients to prove we're on the right path."

Venus flashes me a thumbs-up from the sidelines.

I barely restrain the eye-roll.

When will the torture end?

The guy leans forward, intrigued.

Not now, obviously.

He slants me a smile. The first genuine one since I sat down beneath the blaring lights and introduced myself as a matchmaker. "How does it feel, giving women their happily ever after without getting your own?"

"Who said marriage is the only happy ending a woman can have?"

"If it wasn't, your company would've gone bankrupt long ago."

"Maybe people are just tired of hook-up culture."

"Casual sex is on the rise."

"Getting naked with a man for one night does not translate to a lasting, solid relationship."

He arches an eyebrow.

I quirk my lips. "You want to talk statistics, let's talk."

"It sounds like you're getting defensive."

"You're missing the point."

"And that is?" He leans forward.

My eyes narrow. Last I checked, this was an interview, not a therapy session. I've been through enough *so how do you feel about that* moments to recognize when someone's prying.

Damn him.

And damn his silly little magazine that's clinging to relevance too.

But I can't say any of that. I'm getting paid to promote my company and I won't jeopardize my position because of this twat. "The point is… Make It Marriage isn't a hook up service. We don't use algorithms to sort through a million dating profiles. We help real people make real connections. My happy ending is wrapped up in theirs."

He stares me down. Searches for signs of a crack he can exploit.

I hold steady.

Meet his gaze.

He backs off. Surrenders with a nod. "How noble."

I shrug.

"Thank you for the interview, Ms. Montgomery. It's been a pleasure." *Liar.*

"I had a lot of fun."

Okay. So maybe that's the pot calling the kettle black.

He extends a hand.

I shake it firmly.

He holds on when I try to pull back. Barely-there lips curl into an oily smile. "If you're free after this—"

"I'm not." I yank my hand back. Subtly wipe it against the side of my red pencil skirt.

It won't be the first or the last time a male interviewer asks me out after learning I'm a single matchmaker. It's like a primal side of men awakens when they hear those words. Grunts of *conquer, conquer* echo in their head.

Lord, I hate it.

I hate all of it.

"Kindly see yourself out from here." I rise from the chair and move to the door.

It's bad manners to leave before the journalist, but I don't have the patience to endure another moment.

A quick, staccato rhythm—stilettos bashing hardwood—tells me that Venus is following. The rhythm quickens. She's behind me. Then in front of me, shooting me a dark look with equally dark eyes.

I try to lengthen my stride.

Doesn't work.

Wavy reddish-brown hair slaps her back with each quickening step. "Did you have to shut him down like that? Now the last thing he'll remember is your attitude."

"I don't owe him a date."

Venus glances over her shoulder at the door I just vacated. We have an interview room here at the agency. It's small and cramped and not very welcoming, but it's not used for anything else.

Her gaze returns to me. "I'm not saying you had to accept. Just… cut him some slack. He shot his shot."

"A severe miscalculation on his part."

"Men like to fix things."

"That's assuming I'm broken."

"And?"

"I'm not. I like being single. It's ten times better than being in a relationship."

"Says the woman who sets people up for a living."

"I never said I was uncomplicated."

Venus huffs. "You're such a Scrooge. How the hell are you so successful?"

"Luck?"

"Maybe you really are Cupid."

I groan. "Don't you start too."

Venus chuckles. "He might be on to something. When was the last time you've gone on a date?"

A date?

An ache springs to life in my head.

A hammer against my skull.

It's immediate.

Painful.

I flinch. "No."

"No?"

"I'm done with dating."

I don't even deserve to think about it.

Not after everything.

"How 'bout a tryst then?"

I stop. *A tryst?* What are we? In the nineteenth century. "Would I summon the guy via carrier pigeon?"

"If you're into that." Venus smirks.

She doesn't give a damn about my sarcasm.

Sometimes, I hate her too.

"There's another bachelorette party tonight…" She wiggles perfectly groomed eyebrows.

Around here we have enough bachelorette party and wedding invites to fill the building.

"I'm not going."

"I knew you'd say that."

"Then why bother asking?"

"Because," she slides in front of me, barring me from getting into my office, "you need to loosen up."

"And letting a strange man of questionable sexual health screw me will help?"

"Exactly." She winks.

"I'll pass." I try to move past her.

Venus slaps her palm on the door. "I'll pick you up at eight. Wear something tight and slutty."

"Sure I will." I gesture to the office. *Out of the way.*

Her playful expression sobers. "I'm worried about you, K."

The words are sincere.

And she has a reason to be.

A reason I haven't admitted to anyone.

Not even my close friends.

A reason that's taken over my life.

When did I become so unrecognizable?

I pause in the doorway.

Another wave of hopelessness attacks me.

I didn't start out being this much of a downer.

I was always on the quiet side but this…

It feels like I'm living life in a cage. A prison with no escape.

Work became my sunshine.

And sleep became my only way to cope.

I don't even count the days anymore. They all kind of blur together in one big mush.

I'm not really living.

Maybe something *does* need to change.

Venus is already turning away when I push out a sigh. "I'll meet you there."

She whirls around, big smile on her pretty face and hope in her eyes. "In something slutty?"

"Goodbye, Venus." I grab my door. Push it forward.

"Keep it low-cut," she presses her face into the sliver of space left and gestures to her chest. "You've got a nice—"

I slam the door.

My headache worsens.

I'm already starting to regret this.

***

Ready to enjoy the rest of Kayla and Brendon's romance? Visit **niaarthurs.com/books**

ALSO BY NIA ARTHURS
VISIT NIAARTHURS.COM/BOOKS

Doc Exclusives
Respect Me: Part I
Respect Me: Part II
Cover Me

Fragile Vows
Value Me Part I
Value Me Part II

Caribbean Crush Series
His Exception
Her Deception
The Complication

Grudging Hearts Series
Forever Loving You
Forever Craving You
Forever Claiming You

Make It Marriage Series
Be My Always
Be My Forever
Be My Darling
Be My Lady (A Make It Marriage Short)
Be My Light
Be My Spark
Be My Wife

Be My Hope

Be My Bride

Be My Compass

Be My Reason

Be My Baby

Be My Revenge

The Love Repair Series

Earn Me

Deserve Me

Choose Me

Trust Me

Show Me

Promise Me

The Parallel Love Series

Trapped In You

Caught In You

Bound In You

Sign up for the Nia Arthurs mailing list at **niaarthurs.com/subscribe**

Printed in Great Britain
by Amazon